Emily Hourican is an Irish journalist and author. She has written features for the *Sunday Independent* for fifteen years, as well as *Image* magazine, *Conde Nast Traveler* and *Woman and Home*.

She lives in Dublin with her family. *The Other Guinness Girl* is her seventh novel.

Previously by Emily Hourican

The Glorious Guinness Girls
The Guinness Girls: A Hint of Scandal

The Outsider
The Blamed
White Villa
The Privileged

How To (Really) Be A Mother (non-fiction)

EMILY HOURICAN

The OTHER GUINNESS GIRL

A QUESTION OF HONOR

A Novel

HACHETTE
BOOKS
IRELAND

First published in Ireland in 2022 by
HACHETTE BOOKS IRELAND

First published in paperback in 2023

1

Cataloguing in Publication Data is available from the British Library

ISBN 9781399707992

Typeset in Sabon LT Std by Palimpsest Book Production Limited, Falkirk,
Stirlingshire

Printed and bound in Great Britain by
Clays Ltd, Elcograf S.p.A.

Hachette Books Ireland policy is to use papers that are natural,
renewable and recyclable products and made from wood grown in sustainable
forests. The logging and manufacturing processes are expected to conform to
the environmental regulations of the country of origin.

Hachette Books Ireland
8 Castlecourt Centre
Castleknock
Dublin 15, Ireland

A division of Hachette UK Ltd
Carmelite House, 50 Victoria Embankment, London EC4Y 0DZ

www.hachettebooksireland.ie

For David, again

Cast of Characters

Lady Honor Guinness
Rupert Guinness, 2nd Earl of Iveagh – Honor's father
Gwendolen Guinness, Lady Iveagh – Honor's mother
Arthur Guinness, Viscount Elveden – Honor's brother
   (nicknamed 'Lump' by his family)
Lady Patricia Guinness, 'Patsy', and Lady Brigid
   Guinness – Honor's sisters

Doris Coates
Esther Coates – Doris' mother
Harold Coates – Doris' father
Isabel, Marianne and Maxim – Doris' siblings
Mabel Suggs – Doris' friend, fellow resident at Curzon
   Street

Aileen Plunket (née Guinness) – Honor's cousin, wife of
   Brinsley Sheridan Bushe Plunket, 'Brinny'
Maureen Guinness – Honor's cousin, soon to be wife of
   Basil Blackwood, 'Duff', 4th Marquess of Dufferin
   and Ava
Oonagh Kindersley (née Guinness) – Honor's cousin,
   soon to be divorced from Philip Kindersley

Cloé Guinness – Honor's aunt, mother of Aileen, Oonagh and Maureen
Diana Mitford – ex-wife of Honor's cousin Bryan Guinness, mistress of Sir Oswald Mosley

Lord Bertram Lewis, 'Bertie' – friend of Doris Coates
Lady Lewis – Bertie's mother
Bright Young People: Teresa 'Baby' Jungman, Zita Jungman, Elizabeth Ponsonby, Sebastian Wright

Henry Channon, 'Chips' – American diarist and politician
Lady Maud Cunard, 'Emerald' – London hostess, married to Lord Cunard
Alfred Duff Cooper – 1st Viscount Norwich and British Conservative politician
Lady Diana Cooper – Viscountess Norwich, wife of Duff
Perry Brownlow – 6th Baron Brownlow, close friend of the Prince of Wales, later Edward VIII
Lady Kitty Brownlow – wife of Perry
Prince of Wales, later Edward VIII
Mrs Wallis Simpson – American socialite, wife of Ernest Simpson, mistress of the Prince of Wales

Sir Oswald Mosley – British politician and founder of the British Union of Fascists (BUF)
David Envers – associate of Sir Oswald Mosley

A note from the author

A great deal of this book is based on real events and the interactions of real people, but they are placed within a story created by me and linked by imaginary connections, with some imaginary characters.

Honor Guinness is of course based on a real person – she was cousin to Aileen, Maureen and Oonagh, the three Glorious Guinness Girls I wrote about in the first two books in this series – but she is my imagined version of this real person. Whereas Doris Coates, a young Jewish woman living in London and Honor's close friend, is an entirely invented character.

A word about the social and political landscape of the book. The 1930s in Britain was a troubled time. Unemployment figures were rampant throughout most of the decade, and many of those in employ weren't earning a living wage.

So bad was the outlook that the usual run of politicking was suspended and a National Government was formed in 1931.

Meanwhile, at grassroots level, ordinary people were looking for their own outlets. And they were finding these in political extremes – Socialism on one side, Fascism on the other. With both came plenty of public disorder.

And, rumbling in the background was the rise of Hitler and the Nazis in German – watched, certainly at first, with admiration by many in the UK.

Prologue

Elveden, Suffolk, December 1936

The chalky green mound of Elveden's copper-domed roof rose high above bare branches that scraped fretfully at a white sky. There were many houses – 'town' was Grosvenor Place in London, Pyrford was the house where her mother had grown up – but 'home' for Honor was still Elveden. The broad three-storey front, built of honey-coloured stone, that undulated out from either side of the round copper roof comforted her as she had hoped it would. Here, in this solid expression of her parents' way of life, it would be possible to escape the anxious turmoil of the king's abdication, and her husband's obsession with it.

She leaned back against the upholstered seat and pulled the thick fur of her turned-up collar tight around her neck.

It was cold. Frost nibbled at the close-cropped stubble that showed pale winter gold above the hard brown earth of the bare fields. In the places where sun didn't reach at that time of year, the frost deepened its dusty cover so that the land was unevenly divided into warmer straw-coloured heights and chill white hollows.

Beside her on the seat, Bundi lay asleep, head sunk on his paws. On the far side of the dog, Chips sat and stared out his own window. He was silent, one hand buried in Bundi's thick fur, moving rhythmically, scratching the dog's neck. He had been already awake when she got up that morning, wrapped in a maroon silk dressing gown, drinking coffee and re-reading the newspapers from the day before as he waited for that day's to be delivered. Hunched over his desk, worrying over what the papers would say, whether his name would be mentioned and in what context, he had reminded her of nothing so much as a large sad child with a small broken toy.

Half of her had hoped he would say he wouldn't come to Elveden. How much she longed to be alone with her parents, and darling Paul of course. To feel herself once more contained within the careful structure of their lives, the life she had grown up with – there, in that house, at school in Bath, the regular summer visits to her cousins in Ireland. That was a life that had neat edges, boundaried by the causes to which her parents gave their time – politics, science, charity. Those were solid things, where the effort one made received the outcome one expected; so unlike the shifting sands on which Chips built his existence, the treacherous bog of society where he had set up his tent. How nice it would be to have a few days off from that – from his embarrassing ambition and petty disappointments, and now this, the thing he described as 'the dashing of all my hopes'. It was the dashing of his hopes, but it was also the unpicking of a monarchy, and a national crisis. But those things held little reality for him.

Had he always been like that? she wondered. The truth was, she knew he had. Only she had not always understood it. At first, she had believed in his talk of a passion for politics, for change. Over the years of their marriage she had learned that really, what he meant was politics where he was at the centre, change that brought something glittering to him. How long it had taken her to understand.

'We are arrived,' she said as the motorcar drew to a halt before the vast double doors of Elveden. Chips sighed and stayed where he was. 'My parents will be eager to see you. And Paul.' He smiled briefly at her mention of their son. Then lapsed into silence again.

'We came so close,' he said. 'I did it for Paul. For you.'

But he hadn't. He had done it for himself. She wondered when, exactly, she had learned not to be bewitched by what he said. To see, instead, what he meant.

Part One

1930–1934

Chapter One

London, summer 1930

'I heard you come in.' Lady Iveagh crossed to the windows and twitched apart the heavy green silk curtains. The sharp sunlight of the June morning flooded the room and Honor struggled upwards in bed to meet it. She propped herself against a stack of pillows as her mother tugged impatiently at a high-backed armchair, dragging it closer to Honor's bed, and sank down into it. 'After four, wasn't it?'

'Yes. About that.' Honor rubbed her eyes, which felt dry and heavy. She looked at the tiny gold and white marble clock by her bedside. It wanted two minutes to eight o'clock. No wonder she felt tired. But her mother had been up, no doubt, for several hours already, and eager to wake Honor for at least the latter half of that.

'Amusing evening?'

'Not very.'

Lady Iveagh laughed, a sharp bark. 'No. I imagine not. Lady Meredith doesn't much go for amusing. Well, worthwhile, then?'

'Not that either.' Honor stretched, or tried to. The raising of her arms above her head was cut short by the bunching of her heavy cotton nightgown under her.

'You stuck it out a jolly long time.'

'What is one to do?' Honor shrugged. 'One must make some kind of effort.'

'Certainly one must,' her mother said energetically. 'Who was there?'

'The usual crowd.'

'Your cousins?'

'Yes.' Honor gave a gurgle of laughter and sat up straighter against the pillows. 'Mamma, I must tell you, Maureen wore the most outlandish costume. She said it was because she was going on – some costume party or other, you know how she likes to go about – so she was dressed as a *circus* performer. One of those that wears tights, and not much else.' She laughed again, and began describing the costume.

'Certainly there doesn't seem to have been very much of it,' Lady Iveagh agreed when she had finished. 'Oonagh?'

'Also there. And going on to the same party, but dressed meanwhile in a perfectly charming but simple evening dress. Marriage has steadied her, I think.'

'And perhaps will steady Maureen too,' Lady Iveagh said. 'Although I wouldn't bet the Elveden silver on it.

Duff himself, I sometimes think, for all that he is brilliant, is not exactly dependable.'

'I can't see much steadying Maureen,' Honor agreed.

'Who brought you home?'

'Freddie Birkenhead.'

'Any good?' Her mother looked at her, round, bright eyes quizzical for a moment.

'None.'

'No. I imagine not.' They both laughed at that and Honor thought what a relief it was to have a mother who understood that one couldn't make oneself like Freddie Birkenhead, simply because his father was an earl and he would one day inherit, and who didn't care at all that one didn't. 'Here's tea now,' Lady Iveagh said, as a housemaid came in with a tray. Then, 'Will you come with me to the Women's Institute? They meet at half past nine.' She poured out two cups, handing one to Honor.

'Of course. What is it today?'

'Relief for those left destitute by the crash.'

'Still?'

'Yes. If anything, the poverty is getting worse. What began with large fortunes disappearing on the stock market has run off so that there is now hardly a household in the country that does not feel the pinch. Those who were rich are poor, and those who were poor are starving,' she said briskly. 'We cannot expect Ramsay MacDonald's national government to do so very much. And so, where they are ineffectual, we aim to be efficient. I'll order the motor for nine. Better get on.'

She left, closing the door gently behind her, and Honor sank back onto her pillows and finished her tea. She yawned. These first moments were the worst, she knew. Once she was up, and about, busy with her mother and her mother's many plans, the tiredness would abate.

How many years now had she done the London season? Four? Five? Too many, anyway. But she had learned how to manage it so that it was far less of an inconvenience than it might have been. She had friends – not many, not in the way her cousins had; crowds of people to call them 'darling' and insist they were 'too funny' – but enough. She didn't go to the 'unnecessary parties', as she thought of them, by which she meant the parties that happened with only young people, no chaperones, where jazz was played and shoes kicked off so that beautiful girls, and boys, might dance until dawn and beyond. Where cocktails were drunk in abundance and, if the whispers were to be believed, other things, too, fuelled the energy and abundance.

Honor's name rarely appeared in print, for all that she was the daughter of the Earl of Iveagh and heiress to a fortune so large she had no real idea of it. 'Do not be thinking about that,' her mother said, the only time Honor had ever asked how much money there was. 'Better to learn to live as the wife of a poor man.' Her mother disapproved of spending that was indulgent: 'You will have jewels fit for a queen, and the habit of never taking taxis when you can walk,' she would say. And so she had brought Honor up as she had been brought up – to save a penny whenever possible.

But things were different that year, Honor thought, lying against the feathery bulk of her pillows, staring out at the treetops of Buckingham Palace Gardens, which lay opposite number 5 Grosvenor Place. She was 21 now. And even though her mother would never look for a different answer to the question of whether young men like Freddie Birkenhead were 'any good', Honor was conscious that her marriage – the when and the whether of it – was something her parents had begun to discuss quietly together after dinner. Lady Iveagh, who always had plans for every possibility, had begun to make plans for Honor in the event that she did not become a wife and mother.

For herself, she didn't care, Honor thought. Or not very much. Somewhere, the not caring worried her a little. She knew that the girls of her acquaintance – daughters of men like her father, born to the life Honor lived – did care. Very much. They talked of the husbands they wanted, the houses they hoped for, their plans for futures that included children, servants, other domestic responsibilities. Honor never talked of those things. Nor did she think of them. In everything she did, she was diligent and conscientious, but nearly always without any very great investment of herself. Secretly, that bothered her. What was the point of her? she sometimes wondered.

In any case, she hadn't met any young men that she liked, she thought. Although, maybe there was more truth in the thought that she hadn't met any young men who liked her.

Young men took her too seriously. She was too serious for them. And too serious a prospect – her money, her position, her eccentric father and brilliant mother. Her own thoughtfulness. Sometimes she wished she was more like her cousins – those glittering Guinness girls, Aileen, Oonagh, and especially Maureen. She knew well that when London society talked of the 'Glorious Guinness Girls', as they so often did, they did not number her among them. She was, if she was anything, the Other Guinness Girl.

But she never wished it for very long. An hour in their company – increasingly, less – was enough to remind her of all the ways she didn't wish to be like them. But all the same, she longed for a joke, a quip, some piece of dashing irreverence to bring forth, the way Maureen would, when yet another fair, dull young man asked did she enjoy hunting and had she been to the Royal Academy show yet.

But nothing ever came to mind, and so she would respond as politely, as desperately as they had asked, and then that topic would be used up and they would have to find another. Except that more often, the young man would find an excuse to leave her side, and go and flock around Maureen or Oonagh or their friends. And then, Honor would see that in their company, his dullness would fall away and he would become witty and daring, so that she knew it was she who had made him dull.

They didn't find her attractive, these young men. Honor wasn't slight and boyish and straight. She was large, with a face that she knew was inclined to be heavy. Her figure was womanly, her mother said. She said it approvingly. Lady Iveagh was far too much her own person to mind that her daughter was too. Then there was 'the eye'. A slight cast in her left eye that her parents had worked hard to correct. She remembered the black patch she had been forced to wear over the other eye, the 'good' one, in an effort to force the lazy one to correct itself. As though, she always thought, she were a horse with only one blinker. The efforts had been partly successful, thanks to a nanny who had followed her about the house like a gun dog, discovering her in whatever corner she had hidden with a book, and forcing her to put the patch back on. But there was still the slightest something off about that eye. 'It makes one wonder what, exactly, you mean sometimes,' her friend Doris said. 'Or rather, who you mean it *to*,' adding stoutly, 'and that's a jolly good thing!'

Sometimes, Honor wondered what it might be like to be vivid and outrageous and quick-witted, full of daring; willowy and shimmering in something silvery and brief, her face painted to look like a surprised doll, the way all the popular girls were now. The way Doris and her cousins were.

And then she would catch sight of herself, in a looking glass or window, and she would find herself laughing at the idea that the figure before her, so solemn and stately, like, she sometimes thought, a well-stuffed feather bed, could ever be transformed into someone gay and slender and quick.

Anyway, she thought now, pleating the embroidered white cotton counterpane, 21 wasn't so very old. Except that behind her were two little sisters, Patricia (Patsy) and Brigid, still in the schoolroom but growing up fast, as well as her brother Arthur – Lump, as they called him. And there was Oonagh, married at 19 and with a baby; Aileen also, and now Maureen, with a wedding just a month away at St Margaret's.

They may have the looks, but we have the title. Wasn't that what her mother had said, firmly, on a day when Honor, then maybe 15, had come back from a dancing party held at her cousins' house down the road at number 17 Grosvenor Place, and run up to the school room to cry. It had been a party at which no one had danced with her, or not without being coldly required to by Aunt Cloé, who gave the impression that she expected to find Honor's hand dirty when she had taken it and led her over to a young man with a sniffly nose, who was the only other person not dancing.

'Would you be so good?' Aunt Cloé had asked, handing Honor over as though she were a string bag of something uninteresting.

The young man had sniffed hard and surreptitiously wiped his nose on his sleeve before taking Honor's hand, so that for the entire dance – a polka – she had been achingly conscious of where his sleeve brushed her bare wrist above the white cotton gloves she wore like all the girls.

Later, while tea was served, she had seen Maureen – a deadly mimic, and never more so than when Honor was her target – imitate the way she danced, making her as clumsy as a bear. 'They may have the title, but we have the looks,' Maureen had said in what pretended to be a whisper. Cloé, Honor noticed, had permitted herself a small, chilly smile.

But that evening, when she'd told her mother – as she told her everything – even though she had hidden her face in mortification while she'd said it, Lady Iveagh had given a shout of laughter.

'Oh, that's very good,' she had said, after laughing heartily. 'Very good indeed. Almost, one admires Maureen.' And then, at Honor's baffled face, 'Don't you see? It's exactly the other way around. They have the looks – I agree that seems clear enough – but *we* have the title. Oh yes,' nodding her head decisively, 'we have the title.'

Not that titles seemed to be much use after all when doing the season, Honor thought then. Not the way they used to be. Titles no longer attracted men. Or not the way girls like Maureen, Oonagh and Aileen attracted men.

For just the briefest of moments, Honor allowed herself to think what it would be like to be loved by a man like Basil Blackwood. Duff, as Maureen called him with smug familiarity. To be watched the way she had seen Duff watching Maureen. To be touched the way he touched her – a hand on her arm, an arm about her shoulders, always as though his whole self was in that point of contact. She remembered the dark inward look he had when he watched Maureen, and the way Maureen, always, was conscious of him looking, no matter what she pretended. Honor shivered a little.

'Honor!' She heard her mother's voice, which carried effortlessly across the many rooms of Grosvenor Place. 'Don't dawdle. We must get on.'

Chapter Two

'What you need is a love affair,' Doris said, scratching the top of Mimi's head so that the little dachshund stretched out on her lap, writhing and twisting this way and that like a piece of shiny black liquorice.

'Why do I need a love affair?' Honor asked, amused.

'To take your mind off things. All that good work is really becoming too dreary.'

'So I need a love affair to distract me from charity work?'

'Precisely.'

'Isn't it usually the exact opposite?'

'Only for those lacking in imagination,' Doris said, taking a cigarette from her crocodile skin bag and fitting it into a long ivory holder. She rummaged in the bag again, found a heavy gold lighter, and lit the cigarette with a snap loud enough to make Mimi twitch.

Honor got up to open a window. Lady Iveagh disapproved of smoking. She said it made the house 'smell simply filthy, no matter what the servants do'. She disapproved of Doris too, Honor knew. But that, she felt, was because her mother didn't know Doris the way she did. At least, hadn't known Doris for as long as Honor had.

'Shut that window,' Doris said, placing her cigarette in the heavy crystal ashtray that sat on the table beside her and catching up the glossy fur coat she had thrown onto the chair next to her. She draped it over her shoulders and shivered, exaggeratedly.

'But the smell . . .'

'Never mind the smell. Now come and tell me what you've been doing with yourself. And I don't mean visiting slums. Any fun parties? You cannot imagine how long it felt, to be away.'

'You were gone for less than a month,' Honor said with a laugh.

'Yes, but to *Dorset* . . .' Doris shuddered again, blowing twin streams of smoke through her nose, and widened her enormous black eyes in a show of horror. 'They tried to make me go on a visit to Germany. To my mother's people. They are even richer than Father's lot. Factory owners. Intellectuals. Peculiar altogether.' It was the sort of thing she always said about that side of her family. As though to put distance between herself and them. 'I said I would love to, of course, but that it simply couldn't be, because' – she lifted the little dog high off her lap – 'Mimi would find it too terribly hard. Wouldn't you, darling?' And she laid her cheek against the sleek curve of the dog's head. 'But it is only a matter of time before they simple *force* one . . .'

Honor, stifling a laugh, thought back to the first time they'd met, at a boarding school in Eastbourne, run by Miss Jane Potts, who had once been governess to Queen Victoria's granddaughter, Princess Alice, and who began almost every sentence with a reference to 'dear, *dear* Princess Alice . . .'

Doris had arrived the same day as Honor, both of them new into a classroom of 14-year-olds who had all had a year together already. As the two 'new girls', they had stuck together, at first out of necessity but soon from affection. Doris had a wan, pale, clever face, with those enormous dark eyes, beneath which were permanent char-coal smudges that gave her a weary, sophisticated air. She was slender and elegant even at 14, even in the lumpy skirt and cardigan they all had to wear, and generally exuded, Honor thought, a kind of drooping hothouse flower fragility. In those first days, Honor had worried that Doris would not survive the spartan regime of the boarding school. Feeling protective, she had given Doris one of her two blankets, and even half of her bread and jam supper. These, Doris had accepted with a remote grat-itude, as though doing Honor a favour.

In fact, Honor soon learned, Doris was strong, energetic, almost hearty. She loved hockey, lacrosse, hunting and the outdoors. It was Honor who felt the cold, Honor who crept into Doris' bed after lights out and pressed close against her. Because Doris, thin as she was, radiated heat with an intensity that was, Honor said, like the iron bar of the heater in the nursery at Elveden: 'straight and hard and not terribly cosy, but glowing red hot'.

Doris came from a family of Dorset merchants: 'Quarries,' she explained, 'Portland stone and marble. Now factories too.' She pulled a face.

'You could say your father built this country,' Honor said kindly, because she could see Doris was embarrassed. Even more so than by her mother.

'You could.' Doris smiled. 'Although really, he built his fortune, and a large, quite ugly house.' She had been sent to school 'to get me out of the way', she cheerfully said, because her parents found her to be 'too much' now that there was a baby brother as well as two little sisters.

'Just like me,' Honor had replied, 'two sisters and a brother. But you can jolly well give me back my blanket. I don't believe you feel the cold at all.'

'Hardly ever,' Doris had agreed in a husky voice, handing back the blanket.

Doris, from the start, was determined to 'do better' than her parents, as she put it. 'Say it again,' she would implore Honor, of certain particularly tricky words, such as 'cup' and 'supper', and she would practise and practise, imitating Honor until no trace of Dorset – or the funny lilt that Honor assumed must come from the German side, her mother's people – remained. By the time they finished school, and

Doris came to London with Honor, she had refined herself into someone impossibly weary and *ennuyé* so that Honor, laughing, had said, 'Anyone would swear that the exhausted blood of generations of decadent European royals ran through your veins . . .'

'Rather than that of sturdy Dorset merchants and a lot of German *burghers*,' Doris agreed, adding complacently, 'I'm a better match for father's money than he or Mother could ever be.' In fact, she did her job so well that Lady Iveagh, on meeting her for the first time, later told Honor abruptly, 'I don't like that girl. She's empty-headed and indolent.' And when Honor tried to explain that, no, Doris just pretended to be, her mother had looked more astonished than Honor had ever seen her, and said, 'But that's worse. Much worse!' She did not forbid Honor to see her, because that was not her way, but Honor soon realised that any time Doris called, her mother was quick to find a reason to leave them. And quicker then to return with a reason why Honor must leave too.

'So, that love affair . . .' Doris said now, putting Mimi down and snapping her fingers so that the dog danced lightly on its hind legs. 'You must choose carefully. Ideally, he must be married already, because you don't want to find yourself married in a hurry just to pay for a little fun.' She raised her eyebrows at the look on Honor's face. 'Shocked?'

'No.'

'Well, you should be.' Doris laughed at her.

'I'm just not sure why I need this love affair.'

'It's to give you an element of tragedy. That's what you lack, you know. It's why you don't *take*. So much money, and the title. This beautiful house,' – she gestured around the first-floor drawing room that glowed with the careful certainty of its own perfection – 'Elveden. Your societies and causes and distressed mothers. It's all much too . . . well, healthy and happy. There's nothing interesting there. Nothing to capture the imagination. And men are creatures of imagination.'

'What do you know of men? You barely have more experience of the world than I do, for all that you carry on as though you had knocked about forever. Less, even,' Honor said smartly, 'for I have several seasons more than you.'

'Ah, but I had a year in Paris.'

'To learn French. Staying with a family of merchants so respectable they never let you out without some *mademoiselle* in tow. I know, because I visited you.'

'And yet I know plenty,' Doris said. 'More than you ever will, I suspect. It's from being on the make. No, don't—' She put a hand up to silence Honor. 'We both know I am. And that's perfectly alright. But it means I must spend longer thinking about what people really want and mean and puzzling out the little tricks of their personalities. Men are so much simpler than women, but women somehow never see that.'

'I do not at all know what you mean. But you think a hopeless love affair would help me to be less happy, and therefore I will *take* better?' Honor laughed, but she hoped

Lady Iveagh wouldn't choose that moment to come back into the drawing room.

'Oh yes.' Doris opened her black eyes so wide they almost swallowed her entire face. 'It would show that you are human, after all. And that you have . . . you know, *that* side to you, as well as the capable, managing side. Plus,' she looked sly for a moment, 'it would get you away from your mother.'

'But I don't want to be away from her.'

'I know that, but must the whole world? What man falls in love with a girl who is always attached to her mother, and in such perfect harmony that there is no room for anyone else between them? No, it's simply not *appealing* . . . But a love affair, especially one that can never be – that will take the hearty sheen off you. Now, I wonder . . .' She looked at Honor for a long moment, then, 'Yes. I have it. Duff.'

'Duff?'

'Your cousin Maureen's Duff. Nothing could be more perfect. So impossible. So tragic. So perfect in every way. And he is so very . . .'

'Don't be ridiculous,' Honor snapped, face flushing brick red. 'That's the silliest idea I've heard. Anyway, why don't you organise your own love affair?'

'Oh it's not the same for me,' Doris said.

'Why isn't it?'

'Well, first of all, I don't need to add hints of tragedy.' She smiled. 'My cheekbones do that for me.'

'You do look positively ghastly,' Honor said enviously.

'Yes, isn't it lucky? Now, second, I'm not the daughter

of an earl. Not to mention the hint of something *foreign* . . . It wouldn't have the same effect at all if I did it. What would be interesting in you would be simply *déclassé* in me. No, I must remain perfectly virtuous and without even a whiff of scandal, and then I may marry well. And then, well, then I can have as many love affairs as I like.'

'Absurd,' Honor said vigorously. 'I won't listen to another word of it.'

'So, Duff . . .?'

'Stop, Doris. Anyway, shouldn't you be getting back to poor Mrs Benton?' Mrs Benton was a respectable widow with a house on Curzon Street where Doris lived. It was an arrangement that meant her own mother, who hated London, didn't have to accompany Doris through the season. 'Thank God she hates London,' Doris liked to say, 'because certainly London would hate her.' Honor disliked it when she talked like that.

'Oh very well.' Doris pouted. 'Only don't blame me if we are still here a year from now, and you still have had no offers. Now, are you going to the Chadwicks' this evening? I have a new way of doing my hair . . .'

Honor tuned her out and, when Lady Iveagh put her head around the door some minutes later and said they must be off, she rose obediently and submitted to being kissed goodbye by Doris. She found the kissing exaggerated, given that they were to meet again in a few hours, but to say so would only have made Doris wrinkle up her nose and smirk at her. Doris knew very well Honor disliked such demonstrations. That didn't stop her.

Chapter Three

'Curzon Street, please,' Doris said, tapping the glass twice with a gloved hand to show the cabbie she was ready to go.

As the taxi drove away from Grosvenor Place, she turned to look out the back window at Honor and Lady Iveagh getting into a long silver motorcar that waited at the bottom of the front steps. The street was empty and she watched them until her taxi turned onto Hyde Park Corner. Then she turned to the front again and ignored the cabbie, who showed signs of wanting to chat. She stroked Mimi's smooth head and let the dog worry the seams of her leather gloves. Mimi seemed to think they were living creatures still, to be fought and subdued.

It was obvious to anyone who looked that Honor had a

crush on Duff, Doris thought. But then, she doubted anyone except herself much looked. Lady Iveagh, for all her bounty, thought mostly about herself and her own projects. It would simply never occur to her that Honor might fall in love where she shouldn't. And no one else cared enough.

But it was also obvious that it wasn't Duff himself who she was in love with, so much as the idea of being in love. It was the idea of romance that drew Honor. Ideally romance for someone she couldn't possibly marry. How unfair, she thought, that someone who looked so unromantic – solid, sensible, rather plain – should be the type to yearn secretly, while she, Doris, apparently perfectly made up for romantic yearning, should be so very matter-of-fact. Or maybe not unfair. Maybe very fair. If she wasn't matter-of-fact about her prospects, if she allowed herself to be dazzled by romance, she would never be able to arrange her life the way she needed to.

Anyway, Duff was an entirely safe crush. A luxury, Doris thought, permissible only to girls like Honor who had everything stacked in favour of their marriages so that it was only a matter of time, for all that Honor seemed chagrined by her lack of popularity.

'It doesn't matter,' Doris had tried to tell her, 'you are not the kind to be flavour of the season. It's all long term with you.' But Honor didn't understand. She took terribly to heart the balls where she wasn't asked to dance as often as other girls. She had withdrawn into herself since school, finding the larger stage of London society harder to manage than the easy routine of Miss Potts'.

Honor was much too nice to be jealous, but she clearly couldn't help comparing the way Doris was greeted with her own reception – 'I am as invisible as though made of a pane of glass; something to look through, not at,' she would say.

'You're wrong,' Doris tried to say. But all Honor could see were the throngs of young men who sought Doris everywhere she went, who vied to fetch her champagne, cocktails, her fur; who bought gifts for Mimi because they couldn't properly buy for Doris herself, so that the dog had an absurd selection of jewelled collars and trinkets to wear around its neck.

'If it wasn't for you, I wouldn't have a soul to talk to at these things.'

'You would have your cousins . . .'

'Who despise me.'

'. . . and anyone else lucky enough to discover how nice you are.'

Honor had said she was grateful, but the truth was that Doris needed Honor far more than Honor needed her, although she couldn't see that. So assured was her position, she was barely aware of it; saw not the advantages of money and name, only the drawbacks of a lack of beauty and whatever it was that made girls like Doris so popular.

The taxi drew to a halt outside Mrs Benton's and Doris let herself in with her key. The hall was quiet and dim, spotlessly clean but somehow withdrawn, with that feeling places get when they are forever used by different people – as though hesitant to be any more than impersonal.

I'm not for you, it seemed to say in the steady beat of the grandfather clock that stood under the stairs and in the fuzzy thump of a bluebottle that beat at the half-moon-shaped pane of glass above the front door. *You are not ours.*

She went to her set of rooms on the first floor – a bedroom, bathroom, dressing room and sitting room – where she had lived for the last year. She poured water from a jug into Mimi's enamel bowl, and began to look out her clothes for the evening. Her father had offered to send her maid with her but Doris had refused. The idea of being responsible for someone else, alone and new in London, was too much. As long as she had a generous allowance for clothes and regular visits to the hairdresser, she said, she could manage. She had learned to do her hair in Paris, and had practised enough in the time she had lived at home in Dorset, where there had been little else to do.

The rooms were lavish and comfortable, and Mrs Benton was respectable and rather jolly, but even so, Doris' arrangements meant she was considered odd. The fact that no one 'knew' her family made her odder again. Perhaps, she thought, she should let her mother come to London after all? They could take a house and her mother could come about with her. But that would be worse. Because then her background would no longer be mysterious. It would be known.

Her mother's accent would invite speculation. Her English was perfect, but it was too perfect. Her manners, though faultless, were not English manners. Esther spoke too directly. She refused to stay within the parameters drawn by polite society, asking abrupt questions because she wanted to know the answers, and not because she was playing an endless elaborate game of verbal hide-and-seek. There would be conjecture, questions, and finally some approximation of the truth. And the truth was sadly banal. Esther was a factory-owner's daughter from outside Berlin. She was German, Jewish; kind, thoughtful, intelligent. Since coming to England, she had tried conscientiously to be English. She went to church on Sundays and on feast days. Her four children had generous christenings and confirmations, just like the children of the surrounding villages. There were no oddly shaped candlesticks, no sign at all of the faith of her childhood. In fact, Doris thought, it was her very ordinariness that would deaden Doris' charm so completely.

No, much better to allow silence and emptiness to breed feverish mysteries, she thought: that Doris was the ill-gotten daughter of a duke; an orphan with no family but plenty of money; she had been married at 16 to a French count who then died, leaving her to reinvent herself – all these lurid explanations she had heard whispered, and more. And each time she only smiled and remained silent.

It wasn't that the truth of her background was hard to find, she thought, checking the time on the tiny travelling clock that had been a present from her father. A few questions in the right places and anyone who cared to could have known all about her: her father had gone to Germany as a young man, to learn more about his business – the quarrying and shipping of Portland stone. He had gone to study the ways of a successful factory owner, and chance brought him to Esther's father. Once there, he liked to say, he had got more – 'a great deal more' – than he'd bargained for. This he would say while reaching for one of Esther's hands, or, if he was holding that hand already, squeezing it even more tightly. 'It's a pity you look nothing like her,' he would say affectionately to Doris – who had her English grandmother's black hair and pale, pale skin rather than her mother's dark-blonde hair, brown eyes and skin that grew warm and brown in the summer.

'I think I am well enough,' Doris would answer with a laugh.

But no one looked, because everyone in society was as fond of the possibilities of deception as she herself was. It didn't suit the young men who fell in love with her, or the girls who wanted to be her friends, nor the hostesses who needed her for their parties, to know much more.

Only Honor knew the reality – and even then only what Doris had told of it. She had never been to the large, comfortable, ugly house outside Weymouth in Dorset, although they had talked of it. Easier, Doris had always thought, for *her* to visit Grosvenor Place or Elveden, wherever Honor spent the school holidays.

Honor believed Esther to be an invalid, or at least 'often unwell' because that was simpler for Doris than trying to explain that she was ashamed of her. Honor – so devoted to Lady Iveagh, so proud of that abrupt and forthright woman – would not have been able to imagine such a thing, and would have thought less of Doris. And Doris could not have explained that the shame she felt was confused – belonging as much with her friends and this giddy life she had chosen that she did not want her mother to see, as it did with her mother. She knew what her mother would say – the look that would cross her face – if she was to observe the way Doris spent her days and nights. And how she herself would feel at this proof of her mother's quiet disapproval. And so she made sure that didn't happen. She kept the two sides of her life far from one another.

As a child she had been all too aware of the way her mother hovered ever outside the circle. There had been a time that Doris had balled her fists tightly and choked down angry, cutting words, when she'd seen the subtle way her mother was first given a place, and then kept in it. The raised eyebrows and sly smiles as her mother unpacked a sponge cake layered with gooseberry jam at the village fair.

'Why don't you keep that delicious-looking cake and bring it home for your own tea?' one of the ladies had asked.

'But I made it for this and we don't need it at home.'

'I'm sure it's perfectly marvellous, but perhaps not for today.' The lady was firm. Doris, ever quick, had understood immediately: *They didn't want her mother's cake.* But she had also understood – known instinctively – that a sponge could not possibly be spread with gooseberry jam. She had felt a cold feeling inside, a kind of icy knot, as if she had swallowed snow, and realised that these women were discreetly mocking her mother. That they refused to allow her to stop being an outsider, even after ten years of marriage to an Englishman and the complete adoption of an English life.

'Why do you put up with it?' she had asked her mother as they'd walked home afterwards, the cake boxed up between them.

'Put up with what?'

'Do you really not see?'

'I see that they have funny ideas about jam.' Her mother had sounded amused. 'And terrible ideas about cake, but more than that, no. What else is there to see?' And Doris had said nothing, but ever after, she had hated charitable organisations, organisations of any kind, really, that brought women together and gave them tiny scraps of authority to fight over – the best marmalade, the biggest marrow, the most money raised for the poor of the village.

She swore then that one day she herself would be the point around which such circles turned. That she would be so densely meshed within it that to look sideways at her would be to look sideways at themselves. It was why she'd stayed at Miss Potts', even when she'd realised – as she quickly had – what a poor bit of a school it was really. Because she had realised that learning things such as geography and simple arithmetic weren't the point – the point was to be surrounded by English girls, girls who had never for one second thought of being anything else, nor wondered what exactly it meant, this being English.

They knew it as deeply as they knew when they were hungry, when tired. And Doris knew she could learn it from them, learn it better than even they knew it. And then luck had brought her Honor, and she had immediately understood that here, in this large, kind, untroubled girl with her kind, unworldly parents, was her chance. Later again she had understood it wasn't luck, but fate; because Honor was the dearest person to her.

Doris heard quick footsteps coming up the front stairs – Mabel. They came along the corridor, muffled by the thin rug that ran the length of the wooden floor. Mabel went to secretarial school. Her people were from somewhere in Hampshire and she lived in just two rooms, small ones, at the far end of the house. She was quiet and kept very different hours to Doris but she was friendly when they met and Doris was impressed by her diligence, even a little envious of her narrow sense of purpose. Sometimes they took tea together. Doris liked to invite her along to her sitting room, knowing it was warmer, with a bigger fireplace, than Mabel's bedroom.

Doris went to her room now and tapped briskly at the door. 'Come and have a cigarette with me. It'll be warmer than downstairs,' she said, standing in the doorway. 'And anyway, Mrs Benton isn't home, so you'd be all alone. You can tell me everything that happened last night.'

Mabel took her dinner at Mrs Benton's every evening, unlike Doris who was almost always out, and therefore could be relied on to know the latest in the discreet war waged between Mrs Benton and the retired teacher, Miss Wilkes, who lived on the ground floor. With much gentle sighing and protestations of concern for one another, these two ladies battled over everything – the merits of *The Times* as opposed to the *Daily Telegraph*, of ginger tea over peppermint tea, Brighton or Scarborough – always shored up by a host of relatives no one knew, always male, or at least deriving ultimate authority from men: 'My nephew takes *The Times* and he is a bank manager'; 'My sister swears by peppermint tea and says nothing is so good for indigestion, and she is married these 30 years to a doctor.'

Doris, on the few occasions she was present, found herself silently cheering on first one, then the other, depending on who brought more ingenuity to their soft duplicity. 'Well,' she said, when she and Mabel were both sitting, feet up on a large, over-stuffed ottoman, 'what was last night?'

'Bicarbonate of soda or cornflour for the leavening of scones. Miss Wilkes has a cousin who swears by cornflour, and won several times at the parish fair.'

'Victory?'

'Oh no,' Mabel laughed, 'for Mrs Benton's mother always used bicarbonate of soda, and *she* had the recipe from the pastry chef at Claridge's himself.' They laughed and Mabel described the dictation she had taken that day, the mistakes she had made at typing and a new way she had learned for filing. She spoke quickly, eagerly, as though she wanted to get her day straight in her head, the better to understand it.

'I am to go forward for a post,' she said then, trying – failing, Doris thought – to sound casual.

'What sort of post? A job?'

'Not exactly. A sort of apprenticeship, but where I will be trained in, and then, if I am satisfactory, I will be offered a job at the end of the training. It's how they do it these days.' She sounded proud to know how things were done.

'And will you be satisfactory?' Doris asked, teasing.

'I should think so,' Mabel said. 'I am the quickest at typing and dictation in my group.' She answered seriously, as though Doris had asked an important question, so that Doris felt bad for the teasing.

'You will be more than satisfactory, I'm certain of it.'

'What about you?' Mabel asked then, taking a last deep drag of her cigarette. She smoked without a cigarette holder, and always as far down to the end of the cigarette as she could, so that her fingers were faintly yellow at the tips and her thin brown hair smelt of smoke. It was, Doris knew, because she didn't have much money and must make every penny she had go its furthest. 'What have you been getting up to?' She liked listening to Doris' stories of parties and nightclubs, but always, Doris thought, a little as though she was humouring a child. She couldn't seem to understand that there was as much reality to Doris' stories as there was to her own.

Doris didn't want to talk to her about Dorset. She liked Mabel, but they were not, she thought, exactly friends. Instead she described a fancy dress party where the theme had been to recreate one's own christening photo, and where even the men therefore had appeared in long frilly white gowns and bonnets so that they all tripped over their dresses all evening, falling in and out of one another's arms. Mabel laughed politely. It did sound a bit silly. 'Never mind that,' Doris said, 'tell me what's been in the newspapers?' Part of Mabel's training was to read *The Times* every day and learn to summarise it. She began to recite now: more bad news. Men unemployed, families without homes, children with TB.

Doris leaned back and blew smoke. She watched a run in one of Mabel's stockings climb gradually up her leg towards the hem of her hairy tweed skirt. It was so different to her talks with Honor, to the grandeur of Grosvenor Place and the intensity of the parties and balls she attended, but it was restful too, and after her weeks in Dorset, she needed that before the return to society tonight.

Chapter Four

As she and Lady Iveagh motored back from Earl's Court, Honor wondered what Doris had been about to say about Duff, before she had interrupted. *'And he is so very . . .'* So very what? And did it have to do with the way Honor felt when Duff looked at her – which was the same way she felt when she got into her bath after a hard day's riding; a sort of luxurious slump? A letting go of everything, so that you tumbled gratefully down. Almost, she wished she had allowed Doris to continue, to see what would have come next. But only almost. Maureen's wedding was a month past, and the couple long departed for India and Burma on honeymoon. For one moment, Honor allowed herself to think about what it would be like, to be leaving the country with a series of beautifully packed trunks, going away, alone, with the man who was her new husband. She thought of the intimacy of steamer cabins, the warmth of lamplight in small spaces, the way the fringes of a shade might tremble and dance as the ship juddered and tossed, and how small a bunk must be when two were in it. She thought of the way Duff looked at Maureen, and what such a look might be like when it was so close to you that you were touching. She blushed, and turned her face away to stare out at the darkening streets.

It had been a poor summer and the sun, defeated by a day of on-and-off rain, had given up and was sinking behind the grey stone buildings ranged on either side of the slow-moving motorcar.

Lady Iveagh liked a stately pace. Almost, Honor thought with a sudden laugh, as though the motorcar must be considered the way a horse would be, were they travelling by carriage as they sometimes still did at Elveden. Something to be nursed along, saved from too much exertion. Like the pennies that must be saved wherever possible, regardless of the vast fortune that lay so heavy behind everything, that Honor fancied she could almost hear it breathing whenever the house in Grosvenor Place was quiet.

'We must see what can be done about rehousing the Heckfield Place families.' Lady Iveagh interrupted her thoughts. 'Those children will not survive another winter in there. The walls are running wet with damp and when they are all packed into one room together, it is impossible to prevent the spread of infection. I will see what can be done.'

And she would, Honor knew. Would telephone men she knew, men who were as much in awe of her energy and determination as her daughter and husband were. These men would do what they could – never very much, but they would try – because to refuse Lady Iveagh anything was simply to invite repeated conversations and new approaches to the same subject until they gave in. The Earl's Court slums weren't even her constituency. There was, really, no reason why she should concern herself. And yet she did. And because she did, others must.

'How can you bear it?' Doris had asked, the one time Honor had persuaded her to accompany them.

'What do you mean?'

'Those children with their great staring eyes and thin little chests. The mothers, filthy and empty and exhausted by bitterness.'

'But they must be helped.'

'Not by me. I never want to see them again, and to forget their very existence as quickly as I can.' Doris, who usually drawled everything in her husky voice, spoke quick and sharp, her words landing like the hooves of a trotting pony on cobblestones. 'Honestly, Honor, how can you? Already, I know I shall find it almost impossible to get them out of my mind. To forget those dreadful faces. Do they not haunt you?' She had watched Honor out of the corner of one eye, fidgeting with the buttons of her gloves to distract from how closely she observed.

No, Honor had to admit. They didn't.

'I wondered . . .' was all Doris said.

'After all, what is the good of being haunted?' Honor had asked calmly. 'They need practical assistance, not sympathy, is what Mamma says. And so that is what we give.'

'Of course,' Doris murmured, squinting close at a frayed thread on the sewing of a button.

'You sound . . . disapproving?'

'No. Not at all. Only . . .'

'Only what?'

'We are very different, you and I.'

'Are you about to be rude and tell me again how dowdy I am?' Honor had asked cheerfully.

'No. I mean, you are.' Doris smiled. 'But you have an energy . . . It makes you rather . . .'

'Hard?'

'Yes, but effective too. I almost envy you.'

'You do?'

'Only for that.' And Doris smiled again. Not the small, vague smile she gave in society – the one that said she was hardly listening and couldn't be expected to show any real interest – but the broad grin that she kept for a very few.

'I thought we would go to Italy for November,' Lady Iveagh said then, interrupting Honor's thoughts. She had, of course, moved from thinking about the slums to thinking about something entirely different. 'And then Elveden for Christmas. I wonder who we might ask to join us . . .' Her mother's restlessness meant that, as well as moving around often – from London, to Elveden, to Pyrford Manor, abroad to Italy – there was always talking and planning for moving to be done. It was, Honor sometimes thought, like being caught inside a snow globe such as the one that sat in the nursery at Elveden; caught up and vigorously shaken by an unseen hand. She looked again out of the motor window, watching the sun slip without protest into the pale flat grey of the evening sky, swallowed up as surely as a fly falling into milk.

Chapter Five

It was a party like so many other parties, Honor thought, watching the flow of people up the front steps of the house on Cadogan Square, through the marble-floored hall and on into the ballroom. She stood at the top of the stairs looking down. Behind her, the powder room was full of girls stowing wraps and furs, peering into the speckled mirror and twitching at their hair.

Honor could hear snatches of conversation: '. . . better like this?'; '. . . Mother got it in Paris for herself but it wasn't her style so lucky me . . .'; 'He said he would be sure to be here, but I don't care a bit whether he comes or not.' This was said by a girl with tight blonde curls arranged about her face like frills and a small disappointed mouth. She tossed her head as she spoke so the frills wobbled,

and the dark girl with her looked admiringly on. The blonde
girl threw her fur coat carelessly down on an armchair then
so that it slipped and would have fallen to the floor had
the dark girl not caught it and set it to rights upon the
mound of other coats. The blonde girl bumped Honor as
she went past, and didn't apologise. Honor watched her
walk down the broad stairs with their river of red carpet
down the centre; like a tongue, she thought. The girl moved
awkwardly, something with her hip, Honor thought. She
wondered was it that that made the girl spiteful, and if so,
was that sufficient reason.

'You look glum.' Cousin Oonagh appeared beside her,
face powdered so pale that her eyes stood out like the
headlamps of a car on a foggy night. She wore a silvery
dress that was stretched a little tight across the middle and
under the powder there were violet shadows under her
eyes. Honor wore white – Lady Iveagh thought it fitting,
even though they both knew it didn't much suit her.

'So do you,' Honor said, truthfully.

'Not glum. Rather fagged, though.' Oonagh leaned
heavily on the banister beside her.

'Baby Gay?'

'Yes. Such a darling. But you know babies . . .' Then
she looked guilty suddenly. 'I mean . . . you will know
babies.' She squeezed Honor's arm. 'They are no end of
trouble. Why, I swear I do nothing these days that isn't
taking care of him. For I am determined to do it myself,
with only Nanny to help me.' Oonagh looked at her in
triumph then, as though challenging Honor not to be

amazed. Honor thought of the women in the Heckfield Place slums, the weary way they managed two and three babies, helped only by an older child, a child never as old as their face would have them.

'Have you heard from Maureen?' she asked, to change the subject.

'Only a postcard from Port Said that said she missed no one.' Oonagh laughed. 'I don't know why she bothered to send that. As if we didn't know.' Then, 'Coming down?'

'In a moment.' Honor watched Oonagh descend, saw the way she straightened her shoulders and tilted her chin in the air as she went. Saw too how those people still gathered at the bottom of the stairs turned to watch her walk down, and stayed watching. In her silver dress with her silver-blonde hair, and despite the violet shadows and tightness around the middle, she was, Honor thought, like something glorious and mechanical – one of Uncle Ernest's clever toys – made flesh. As she reached the bottom, a footman moved forward with a tray of glasses and Oonagh caught one up. A man offered her a cigarette and another his arm so that she entered the ballroom as part of a procession, hailed and heralded on all sides.

Honor followed her down then, treading the same stairs, reaching the same marble floor at the bottom, her heels making the same clicking sound as she crossed it, though heavier. But the footman with the tray of glasses wasn't looking her way and didn't spring forward. No man offered her a cigarette, an arm, and she entered the ballroom alone.

Inside was a roar of noise as though, she thought, she

stood in the mouth of a waterfall. Mrs Chadwick, whose party it was, smiled over at her and made a gesture of apology. The man beside her was saying something in her ear that appeared urgent, and Mrs Chadwick let him carry on talking, signalling regret to Honor with her eyebrows even as she nodded at the man's words.

Honor smiled. She squared her shoulders and went to look for someone to talk to. If she found someone now, quickly, she thought, she would be okay. It was the times she didn't – times she sank too far into not talking – that were the problem. The more she thought about it, the harder it would be. She looked around, a bright smile fixed to her face, trying to catch a sympathetic eye. No one returned her gaze.

The room was cold. As though the process of heating it had begun too late. Lady Iveagh, when they entertained on that scale, began early, lighting fires and oil heaters in the big rooms days in advance. 'Nothing worse than people who are cold,' she would say. 'Being cold makes everyone spiteful and cynical. Useful in politicians, perhaps, but not at all good for a party.'

Maybe, Honor thought, it was the room's fault, not hers. She looked up. Above her, a dusty chandelier cast a reluctant light. The walls, where they met the ceiling, were bare of the pale green wallpaper and painted panels that covered the lower half. In one corner she saw a blooming stain, probably damp, she decided. There were thick cobwebs, and places where the paint was flaking. She dropped her eyes. So many rooms looked like that now, since the crash a year before that had snatched so much money from the country that what was left had to work hard, too hard, to spread around.

All about her, busy groups stood at an angle to each other, that they might lean forward to enter a conversation, then back so as to keep an eye on who came and went. A woman in a deep purple dress close to Honor was complaining that it had been a 'dreadful season', and Honor listened, wondering what kind of season she meant. If it was agricultural, Honor thought, why, then she could contribute. Thanks to her father and his endless schemes for the drainage of farmland at Elveden, she knew plenty on that topic. But a man beside the purple lady, who had a face so white it looked powdered – surely it couldn't be? – and a cigarette in an absurdly long ivory holder, interjected, 'All anyone ever talks about any more is money. Who has it. Mostly, who doesn't.' He shuddered. 'And how quick everyone is to say they haven't a penny.' He sounded peevish. 'Even when one knows well they don't mean it and only hope to avoid notice.'

'Yes,' the woman in purple agreed. 'Why, I was at dinner with the Bessboroughs the other night. Only five courses, when one knows very well they could feed *armies* and never even notice.'

Honor stifled a laugh, trying to imagine the looks on their faces had she interjected something about the dairy herd at Elveden.

Beyond the pale man and purple woman, Oonagh was talking animatedly to Aileen, who must be on a visit from Dublin. She leaned against a small table, looking slender and elegant in buttercup yellow silk so that, with Oonagh beside her, they were like the sun and the moon. Honor wondered had they done it deliberately. It was, she thought, entirely possible. They must be taking advantage of Maureen's absence, she thought with an inner giggle. Maureen would never allow them to be sun and moon; she would need to eclipse them both.

She wondered for a moment what it must be like to have a sister close in age. Patsy and Brigid, only two years apart, would have one another, but both were too young to be companions to Honor. And Lump, darling Lump, was soon to go up to Cambridge, and anyway a boy, and anyway not given to conversation. Or not with her.

She sighed.

Conversation.

So much came down to that. She remembered the agonised silences of her childhood, when to speak had seemed an effort too great to make. It wasn't that she was shy, so much as slow. Her tongue had felt thick and clumsy, unable to form words fast enough to keep those around her interested. The weight of these unspoken words lay upon her, like the nights she woke, twisted into the heavy feather bolster so that she couldn't untangle herself, panic rising up inside her as she fought to free herself from the clogging knot of covers. Speech seemed to be something that had to happen quickly, like a light rain falling swiftly, or the person in front of one would simply move on, bored, and tell others that you were 'frightfully quiet'. Nothing, her mother warned her, alarmed a young man more than a girl who was 'frightfully quiet'.

She had learned to have conversations in company; pleasant enough, but still she preferred those that happened between two or three people, seated, dedicated to talk, whether that was about politics, literature, even fashion. Parties, where there were so many competing conversations that one's own must sparkle and bid for attention, still unnerved her. Because if one's efforts failed – fell flat – they would be allowed no time to recover, but hastened to a stuttering finish by the bored, flickering eyes of the person in front of one.

She sighed and threw back her shoulders, dipping behind the group with the purple woman and joined Aileen and Oonagh at the same time as their friend Baby Jungman, whom Honor found as silly and incomprehensible as though she spoke a different language.

'Darlings!' Baby kissed them all extravagantly. 'Too delightful!' she exclaimed as though the meeting were entirely unexpected. 'Why do we come to these simply frightful parties?' She said it loudly, looking around, hoping, Honor was sure, that she would be overheard. An older man close by gave her an appalled look and turned his back. Baby smirked. 'Did you ever see such a collection of old stiffs?' she asked.

Oonagh laughed. 'Better be careful what you say. Aileen has come all the way from Dublin and will be frightfully cross if she thinks she's at the wrong party.'

'They're all the wrong parties these days, aren't they?' Baby said, twinkling reassuringly at Aileen.

'What would be the right party?' Honor asked.

'Honor!' Baby said, surprised. 'I didn't know you were here.'

'But you just said hullo to me,' Honor said, then wished she hadn't.

'No,' Baby insisted. 'Wasn't me. Someone else perhaps, not me. I couldn't be more astonished to see you.'

'But . . .'

'I wouldn't bother,' Aileen murmured kindly.

'I think it's a jolly nice party,' Honor persisted. She didn't, but the need to correct Baby's flow of foolishness was too strong for her to ignore.

'Of course you do.' Baby beamed at her so that Honor didn't know was she being commended or insulted.

Mrs Chadwick swooped on her then: 'Honor, I've been looking everywhere for you. Come – I have a divine chap I want you to meet.' And then, in an undertone as she led Honor away, 'I promised your mother . . .'

Behind them, Baby's voice, piping like a child, followed. 'You must be so pleased, Oonagh, and Aileen, to be married,' she said. 'Such a relief not to have to meet any more "divine chaps". Who always turn out to be frightful.'

Honor turned to look at her but Baby was busy lighting a cigarette and didn't look up. Oonagh and Aileen carefully studied a painting on the wall behind them.

In any case, Baby was right, Honor thought, half an hour later. The 'divine chap' was, not frightful, she thought conscientiously, but very dull. Or maybe he caught dullness from her. In any case, they were dull together and soon he said he would go and get her a drink, that she must be parched.

Honor didn't expect him to come back – they never did – but thought she'd better at least give him a chance and so she waited, then went to look for him, and found him, talking to Baby. As she was about to force herself forward, to say something gay that would show how little she minded about the drink, she heard him saying in a complaining tone, '. . . like wallpaper, she fades into the background.'

'More like blotting paper, with that complexion,' Baby responded. Of course, they could have been talking about anyone, she told herself as she slipped quietly back to the small room off the main ballroom. It was foolish and self-centred to assume they were talking about her. But still, she couldn't go out. Not yet.

She sat on a window seat, half-hidden by a heavy pale blue satin curtain, and, taking off her glove, pressed her bare hand against the cool window panes and then to her face, to try to transport some of the chill to her hot cheeks. The sound of the party had retreated, no more now than the steady roar of a waterfall or crash of a sea wave. After a while she looked out, through the chink in the curtains. The room was a place the men – one of them Mr Churchill, whom she knew well; he had, as a child, shared a nanny with her father – had claimed for their own, she saw. A group of them had drawn high-backed chairs up before the fire, and passed a decanter around between them, so that all she saw were hands emerging from the deep wings of the chairs to take the decanter, pour, then pass it on. The hands were old, sometimes gnarled, but capable and strong. Inside the decanter, cradled by the cut glass and kindled by light from the fire, was port that glowed a thick blood red.

The men talked in low voices that rose and fell with the flicker of the fire. She soon realised they were talking about the economic crash, its consequences, and what must happen now. She had heard enough, from her father and mother, to follow. They talked of 'demand management' and something called 'deflation', which she didn't understand. She caught names – Keynes and someone called Friedrich Hayek – and there seemed to be disagreement over what needed to be done, but disagreement that was not the sharp kind of personal disagreement she was used to, when her mother wanted to do something that her father didn't wish for, or when her sisters quarrelled over a doll or book. This was disagreement that moved slowly and measured itself constantly.

Honor wished that she, too, could be part of such discussions. That she could know and understand and have opinions that would be listened to and consulted. She imagined Mr Churchill staring at her with those goggly eyes and saying '. . . do go on, Lady Honor . . . What you say interests me.' She giggled at that, at the very idea of it. And gave herself away.

'There you are!' Mrs Chadwick twitched violently at the blue satin curtains so that she released a small cloud of dust. Honor watched her be distracted for a moment by a worn and tattered edge of the curtain, before her focus snapped back: 'I've been looking for you.' She gave Honor an accusing look. 'I have a delightful fellow who is simply dying to meet you.'

Over her shoulder, Honor saw a young man whose ears stuck out from the side of his head, blushing and casting longing glances back inside the ballroom, now busy and roaring like one of the cattle sales her father took her to. The men around the fire had stopped talking and looked, all of them, in her direction. Waiting for her to go. She got down from the window seat, conscious that she did so without grace, and prepared to follow Mrs Chadwick.

'How do you do?' she asked, extending her hand to the young man. The fingers of her white satin gloves were, she saw, grubby. The window seat. She wondered was the back of her dress grubby too. 'I say,' she said to the young man, who was still blushing. 'Help me to find someone, will you?'

They moved through the crowd, which divided smoothly to allow them pass, and Honor thought how different it was to be with a young man – even one whose ears stuck out – than to be alone. She saw Doris at last, seated on a long, low divan upholstered in dull yellow, surrounded by men. She wore a dress of heavy caramel-coloured silk that flowed around her like a swirl of coffee through cream, and lay back as though too exhausted to sit upright. The men around her leaned forward eagerly to catch whatever it was she said.

'Darling,' Doris said, stretching out a languid hand. 'Do sit. Who's this?' And she looked up at the blushing young man through her thick lashes. Immediately he began to blush more.

'I say, you're Doris Coates, aren't you? I've seen your picture. In the papers.' He blushed furiously then, but instead of looking agonised, as he had whenever Honor had addressed anything to him, he was smiling eagerly.

'Sweet,' Doris murmured.

'Pup!' muttered one of the men beside her, shifting his shoulders to block the boy from view.

'Am I all over dust?' Honor asked, turning slightly to indicate the back of her dress, so skimpy beside the lavish folds of Doris' silk.

'A little,' Doris said. 'Have you been sweeping chimneys?'

'No, sitting on a window seat. Rather filthy, I should think.'

'Hiding!' Doris said. 'I should have known. Baby told me you'd gone home, but I knew that wasn't true. I knew you'd stay, oh so dutifully, to a respectable hour, and all the while talk to no one at all. Do sit down, you will upset us all.' As though the divan was a boat that might be overturned, Honor thought with a laugh.

'What do you think a parliamentary sub-committee is?' she asked, sitting down in the space reluctantly vacated by one of the men, at Doris' insistence.

'Something too boring for words that you need not concern yourself with.'

That evening when she got home, Lady Iveagh was still awake. 'Couldn't sleep,' she said, coming into Honor's room and taking the hairbrush from Molly, the maid. 'Go to bed, Molly. I'll do this.' She sat down behind Honor and began to brush her thick shoulder-length hair, which was neither blonde nor brown but somewhere in between. 'Mrs Chadwick?' she asked.

'Frantic and anxious and so terribly eager to introduce me to all manner of "divine" young men.'

'Hmm. Yes?'

'No.'

'I see.'

'I say, Mother, I think I should like to do a course. Something that will help me to understand the world we live in. The reasons why countries can be rich, and then poor, and what to do about it for the people who live in them. Or at least, how to think about it.'

'There is always the London School of Economics,' Lady Iveagh mused. 'There are courses there one might do. Shall we look into it?'

'Let's,' Honor said. 'And I don't want to go to any more parties.'

That much at least she was certain of. She liked the idea of study – the neat structure of it – well enough, but mostly what she liked was the excuse it gave her to retreat from a skirmish she felt she had lost.

Chapter Six

After Mrs Chadwick's party, they went on to the Café de Paris where Doris' lot made great play of the relief they felt at no longer being 'stuck in that impossibly stuffy old mausoleum'. They shrieked and threw themselves about on the dance floor, pressing powdered faces to the shoulders of black-clad young men so that the young men came away with dustings of white on their evening clothes and the pleased look of those who consider themselves very dissolute.

They met people who would never be invited to Mrs Chadwick's – pretty shopgirls, untidy artists, a couple of suspiciously rich fellows who traded in motorcars or some such, and others considered too bohemian even for hostesses who hoped to add a modern frisson to their evenings.

Doris was about as 'modern' as the ambitious hostesses could take, she thought wryly.

Around the large oval-shaped room ran a long, curved balcony where a second, upper layer of tables were dressed in starched white cloths. These tables were full, so that each time Doris looked around, she saw eager faces leaning over, hands waving and hailing them.

'Goodness, don't look up,' Baby muttered to her. 'Elizabeth Ponsonby is up there. I saw her just now. We don't want her spotting us.' But it was too late. Even as she spoke, Doris saw Elizabeth wave and begin to push her way along the balcony and then down the staircase that divided into two, like arms outstretched to encircle the bandstand. She walked straight through the elegantly swaying figures on the dance floor, looking neither right nor left, so that one couple had to swerve sharply to avoid her.

'I thought it was you,' she said with satisfaction, reaching them. 'Doris, I like your hair. You've done something new.' Her heavy-lidded round eyes, like a surprised infant, travelled across Doris' face, then down the full length of her to her feet. She looked, Doris thought, exhausted. That was nothing new. But there was something dishevelled, even unravelled, about her that evening. Her short dark hair was dusty and needed to be set, and she wore lipstick that had been carelessly applied, a slash of red that didn't quite follow her mouth. She was thinner even than usual so that her collar bones, beneath the straps of a tired-looking dress, were sharp bars that held themselves up for notice.

'Elizabeth! We missed you at the Chadwicks',' Baby said, eyes wide with innocent wonder.

'Shh.' Oonagh nudged her sharply, then whispered, 'Elizabeth wasn't asked.'

'Why wasn't she asked?' Baby asked loudly, so that Doris had to pretend to be fishing a cigarette out of her bag to hide her laughter. Not that she cared if Baby saw her laughing, but it seemed cruel to Elizabeth. Aileen, perhaps untroubled by any thoughts of Elizabeth's feelings, laughed openly.

'I'm asked almost nowhere anymore,' Elizabeth said with satisfaction. 'Not to those types of parties, anyway. And I don't care.' She tossed her head, setting the dusty waves trembling. 'I'd rather not go. Too dull for words. You should all come to Sandy's white party next week. It's going to be divine. I'll go and tell Sandy now that he simply must invite you.' And she was off.

'Must she move about quite so much,' Oonagh complained. 'She was never restful, but Lord she's like a stiff breeze at sea now, constantly chivvying one.'

'She's involved in rather a revolting sort of triangle,' Baby said then, leaning in closer to them. 'With Denis the silent husband and a chap called Ludy Ford. Apparently he owns a *garage* or some such.' Baby squealed at the idea.

'How frightful,' Aileen said, and Doris didn't know was it the 'revolting sort of triangle' or owning a garage that was frightful.

'I say, let's order.' It was one of the young men – the undergraduate brother of a girl Doris knew – his face pink with excitement.

'Order what?'

'Some of the other chaps and I have a bet. Who can order the most disgusting combination of food, and eat it. I'm going to ask for oysters and devilled kidneys,' he said defiantly. His name was Fred, Doris remembered.

'How sick-making.' That was Aileen.

'Isn't it?' Fred agreed happily. Then, 'I say, would you dance with me?' he asked Doris, blushing furiously.

'Only if we dance now, and not after the devilled kidneys.'

He bounded forward and took her hand, leading her through the circling nests of round tables to the tiny dance floor.

He said little while they danced, and what he did say Doris suspected he had spent rather long rehearsing in his head, but she didn't mind. It was a chance, away from the constant barbs of Baby, away from Oonagh's demands and Aileen's airs, to look around and think a little. Teddy Brown's band were playing something melancholic and all around them couples were pressed tight together, swaying gently more than dancing. A woman beside them, in a dress cut very low at the back, stumbled and almost collided with them. Fred tightened his arms around Doris, drawing her closer and out of the woman's way. The lights were low and tinted a kind of pink, so that poor Fred looked as though he blushed more rosily than ever. It was, Doris thought, like floating inside a silk ballgown. The air felt very thick, as if it might hold them up should they lean forward, and swirled with the smoke from a thousand cigarettes.

'I say,' Fred said, lifting his head to look at her, 'you're frightfully pretty.' He stammered a little over 'pretty', and Doris understood how much it had cost him to say it.

'You are sweet,' she said. And then, quickly, 'Have you seen the couple at the table by the door? I think she's been asleep this past half hour.'

Immediately Fred stood straighter, relaxed his clasp of her, enough so that they were no longer pressed so tight together. How Doris wished she could have blushed and smiled and leaned even closer in to him, given all the shy encouragements that would make him feel he might have a chance. How she wished it were that simple. But it wouldn't do. He was too young, too much a younger son. He didn't have the heft she needed.

On the other side of the dance floor, visible now and then as the couples between them shifted and turned, Doris caught sight of Elizabeth, in the arms of a tall man with a prominent chin. Though she was tall herself, his greater height made her seem positively fragile. Her eyes were closed and she looked more peaceful than Doris had ever seen her. She wondered was the man Ludy Ford.

Back at their table, another young man had joined them and was trying to tell a joke, through many interruptions. He was beautiful, Doris thought, with a pale face and pale blond hair. He was also very drunk. 'A Jewish gentleman and an Oxford don—' he kept saying. 'Fred, you'll like this one,' he shouted when he saw Doris' companion. 'A Jewish gentleman and an Oxford don—'

'Oh let him finish,' Baby said wearily. 'Or we'll get no peace.'

'—were in an aeroplane that was about to crash. The Jewish gentleman blessed himself, and jumped out and landed in a pile of hay. The don did the same and joined him and as they climbed down off the hay, the don said, "I say, sir, I couldn't help but notice that you blessed yourself when you jumped out of the plane. You made the sign of the cross. I didn't think your sort did that."'

The young man leered over the words 'your sort'.

'"I wasn't blessing myself," the Jewish gentleman said. "I was checking the essentials."'

Doris noticed that the young man put on a sort of comic voice for the Jewish gentleman, a kind of rasping, guttural accent, as though, she thought, a ruminating animal – goat or sheep – had tried to talk.

'"The essentials?" the don asked.'

'"Yes."' Here, the young man raised a hand to his head: '"Spectacles,"' he said. Then lowered the hand to below his waist: '"Testicles."' Then raised it again, touching his left side: '"Wallet."' And finally across to his right side: '"Watch."' He roared laughing. 'D'you see? The essentials: spectacles, testicles, wallet and watch. Because he's Jewish, you know.' He looked around, keen to draw them all into his joke. 'His wallet and watch are so important.'

Aileen and Oonagh laughed politely. Baby ignored him, lighting another cigarette.

'I say, you aren't offended, are you?' Fred asked Doris anxiously.

'Why should I be offended?'

'Well, that word . . .'

'Testicles?' Doris asked. She pronounced the word crisply, making sure it was known that *that* was the offensive word.

Fred blushed again.

'Not in the slightest. I just never find jokes that begin with men leaping from aeroplanes terrible funny. One always knows one will have heard them before.'

She said it loudly enough that the young man who had told the joke flushed crimson and after a moment went away, saying angrily, 'Why can't these fool waiters bring more champagne when we need it?'

Doris wished it were always so easy. It wasn't even that the joke was so terribly offensive, she thought. It wasn't. But it seemed these days that all the jokes were about Jewish gentlemen.

'Sebastian Wright. He's a writer,' Baby said, by way of explanation. 'Or at least wishes to be. Another of Elizabeth's young men. Harmless, really. He's been wrestling with his "great novel" for years. Although mostly, he seems to drink and complain about a lack of inspiration. And tell dreadful jokes. You did think it dreadful, darling, didn't you?' She gazed at Doris, head tilted slightly in inquiry.

Behind her, Doris could see Sebastian try to break in on Elizabeth's dance with the tall man. He was rebuffed by both of them. 'Hardly dreadful,' she said firmly. 'Dull.'

The oysters arrived, and the devilled kidneys, and more young men flocked to their table so that soon they were the noisiest group there. The band played faster music and they went to dance, coming back to pour more champagne and drink it quickly.

Much later, Fred drove her home in a tiny white sportscar with an aggressively loud engine and walked her to the front door. He didn't try to kiss her – he didn't dare; Doris had made sure of that – but he begged to be allowed to ring her up the next day and she said, 'Why not? If I'm here, I may even come to the phone,' with a friendly smile. He was no good to her, but he had been pleasant and polite and eager.

He stood at the bottom of the steps and watched her go into the house. Behind him, the sun was coming up and the sky leached darkness like curds strained through a muslin. Doris waved to him in the doorway and shut the door. She took a deep breath and stood still for a moment, breathing in the quiet. There was a loneliness that waited for her in the dim hallway every night. It crouched behind the single lamp that Mrs Benton left on, then expanded into the silence that was the silence of a house where no one was awake. Where no one, other than her dog, watched for her return or checked a clock and thought, *How late she is!* before turning over to sleep more soundly in the knowledge that she was back. Doris was used to this – indeed, had chosen it – but even so it had the power, sometimes, to claw a little at her.

She moved quietly up the stairs. Mabel would be getting up soon. It would be unforgivable to wake her. In her rooms she turned on all the lights, disturbing Mimi, who left her basket and came to Doris. Doris picked her up and pressed the little dog tight into the side of her neck. She wished again that she had even a spirit lamp or single gas ring, where she might prepare cocoa. It wasn't that she was hungry; it was for the comfort of something warm and sweet.

She took off her toffee-coloured silk dress, wrinkling her nose at the cold breath of cigarette smoke that came up from the folds, and changed into black satin pyjamas. At her dressing table, she smeared a thick layer of cold cream onto her face and wiped it off, badly, with a tissue, then peered at herself in the tilted looking glass. She looked almost exactly as she had done when setting off to Mrs Chadwick's earlier. Indeed, she could have stayed out another few hours, but the evening had become dull as those around her drank too much and grew dishevelled. For all that Doris knew how to be exciting, she also understood the moment at which an evening shaded from dashing, to something darker. Usually, she thought, still staring at her reflection, it was by watching Baby and her sister Zita that she understood it best. There was a particular glazed look those girls took on, a looseness to their movements and an empty quality to their smiles that told her. Maureen Guinness was a good barometer too and increasingly, in her absence, Oonagh was beginning to drift through long evenings with them, smiling that vague smile, answering whatever questions were put to her in a childish voice.

Doris could see exactly how much Honor was humiliated by her lack of success. How much she squirmed at parties where, as she said, 'all conversation is like pushing something heavy up a hill, knowing that the very second one stops pushing, it will simply roll right down and crush one'.

And yet, when Doris saw the parade of eligible young men presented to her friend, she couldn't help but sigh. Mrs Chadwick had served them up all night, one after another, eyes gleaming with the thought that she might hit on a lucky choice, and become the hostess who made an important match. And at the very same time, Mrs Chadwick, and all those society matrons, ruthlessly dislodged these same eligible young men from Doris' side if they lingered too long or began to look too besotted. For all that they wanted Doris at their parties – needed her, Doris thought – they certainly didn't want to run the risk of an irate parent ringing and asking how, exactly, their son had become 'entangled' with a girl from who-knew-*where*.

All evening, even as Doris had behaved as though half-asleep, she was in fact watchful, careful of what she did and said – enough to be daring, not so much as to be shocking, charming but not overly flirtatious, pretending an indifference, even ignorance, of rules that she understood perfectly. What was it she had said to Honor: *I must spend longer thinking about what people really want* . . . And part of that thinking was to seem, always, as if she knew nothing.

She yawned a little, brushed her hair, a few quick strokes, then jumped into bed. It was almost dawn and she had promised to walk in the park with Honor in a few hours. At the far end of the house, she heard the sounds of Mabel getting up and drawing a bath.

Chapter Seven

London, spring 1931

'If you go to the lending library, will you take out Mrs
Christie's new mystery for me?' Lady Iveagh asked
Honor over breakfast. 'And I would be glad of your
company at a meeting this afternoon.'

'Soup kitchens?'

'TB. What else have you planned for the day?'

'I thought I might call to Maureen. She and Duff are
settled into Hans Crescent at last and she has asked
that I visit. The pregnancy has her too tired to go out
at the moment. I suppose she is dull and wants company,
poor dear.'

'Doesn't sound like Maureen. Will you take the car?'

'No need. I can walk.'

Her father, busy picking bits out of the marmalade he had spread thinly on a slice of toast, looked up. He had the newspaper folded and balanced on the silver toast rack in front of him, and Honor knew that later, when she took it to the library to read after the breakfast things had been cleared, it would still smell, faintly, of toast. 'Let me drop you,' he said. 'Then you can take a taxi to the House when you're finished and we can come home together. If you arrived early, you could sit in the peeresses' gallery. Parmoor is to speak on the Coal Mines Bill. You might find it interesting?'

He looked anxiously at Lady Iveagh as he spoke, and Honor wondered had they discussed what he would say, as they discussed everything. Often, she came home late at night to hear their voices – well, her mother's voice – still rising and falling behind the library door. Once, she would have stuck her head around the door to say goodnight, but these days, she did that less. It was the way they broke off talking when they saw her. The brightness in Lady Iveagh's voice as she asked how the evening had been. The extra furrow in her father's always furrowed brow.

'Very well,' she said, privately thinking she would make sure not to arrive in time for the Coal Mines Bill debate. 'I'll call for you at the House at around five o'clock.'

Five o'clock, she thought, a little while later, as she positioned her hat and pinned it in place. And now it was just after nine. How much, and how little, she had to do.

The course at the London School of Economics had been exactly as she had hoped – absorbing, difficult, with reading to be done and even essays to write. Honor had been diligent and interested, and so had her mother. It had almost been as though Lady Iveagh had done the course with her, so eager had she been to discuss every aspect of what Honor learned. Together they had read the books and pamphlets required by Honor's professors, and Lady Iveagh had also read the papers Honor wrote, adding observations and queries in her neat hand in the margins. With Lord Iveagh they had discussed the ideas and how these applied to the world of politics and even agriculture. They had been, the three of them, in perfect harmony.

And then the course finished, and Honor had to choose – study more, and deeper, or cease studying. And in the face of her mother's blunt questions – 'Why? What are you studying for? What do you intend from this?' – Honor had found she had no real answer. What indeed? She couldn't become a professor, didn't wish to write, or teach, or any of the obvious things. And so she gave up, and tried to ignore the sense of a dangling piece of her life – embroidery threads left unstitched and unsnipped that fluttered in mid-air.

That afternoon at Maureen's, she found Oonagh and her aunt Cloé as well as Maureen. Cloé was turning the pages of a book and looked up when Honor was announced.

'How is your mother?' she asked. And, when Honor had replied that Lady Iveagh was well, immediately countered with 'How is your father?' and then 'And your brother?', until Honor feared she would have to go through every member of her family. Except Cloé lost interest abruptly and turned back to her book. Oonagh caught Honor's eye, rolled her own slightly and grinned.

Sitting beside Oonagh was a man Maureen then introduced as 'Henry Channon. If you haven't already met him you jolly soon will. He's *everywhere*. Like rain in an Irish summer.'

'Gracious as ever, Maureen,' the man said with a smile, then, standing and coming forward to bend low over Honor's hand, 'Enchanted, Lady Honor.'

Honor almost snatched her hand back in fright. She wasn't used to such formality. No one in London now behaved like that except the old men, and he wasn't old, though a good ten years older than her, she guessed.

'He's American, you'll have to forgive him,' Maureen said, enjoying Honor's discomfort. But Channon smiled reassuringly at her and asked, 'What are you reading?' gesturing to the parcel of books she had placed on a table by the door.

'Aldous Huxley, J.B. Priestly, and the new Agatha Christie for my mother, who doesn't usually read mysteries but makes an exception for Mrs Christie.'

'Very wise,' Channon said, twinkling at her. 'And what do you think of Mr Huxley?' He asked her more questions, and offered reflections of his own, and all the while, she watched him. He was, she thought, so handsome as to be almost beautiful. A broad forehead – fully exposed by carefully brushed back dark blond hair – straight nose and firm mouth divided his face into perfectly equal sections within which his brown eyes were lively but steady. His skin was clear and golden, and his lips a delicate red. It wasn't just the lottery of nature that had handed him such a well-moulded face – it was also how deeply he appreciated his own good fortune. He kept his face still, she saw, the better that it might be appreciated. When he spoke, his lips moved but the rest of his face remained composed. Except for the eyes, which moved to rest on one for so long that one was obliged to look back, and listen to what he said. His voice held traces of American, but discreet ones, like the rumble of a train that passes somewhere out of sight but close enough to be felt.

She found herself comparing him, as she compared all men, with her father. He had the kind of confidence in himself that Lord Iveagh had – not in society, where he was awkward and often bored, but when discussing dairy herds and farm machinery.

When they had exhausted the topic of Mr Huxley and his novels, Honor prepared herself for the American to make a gracious excuse – fetching her a cup of tea, seeing if Cloé needed anything – and turn away from her, back towards the conversation Maureen and Oonagh were now having – something about Diana Mitford which sounded rather daring. But he didn't. Instead, so smoothly that she noticed only because it was so unusual, he led her slightly away from her cousins, to a seat beside the window, where he settled her, lit her cigarette and sat down beside her. The butler offered a tray of drinks, some kind of cocktail.

Channon waved him away, although Honor had seen a drink in his hand when she first arrived. Now, he poured himself a cup of tea. Maureen, she saw, shot him a furious look and took a drink from the tray. She already looked a little wild-eyed.

'You must tell me which of our American authors you enjoy,' Channon said, leaning a little towards Honor. 'Of course, they cannot hold a candle to your British writers – your D.H. Lawrence and E.M. Forster.'

'You think anything British is better,' Maureen said, getting up and coming to join them. She rolled a little as she walked. 'You're like a retriever who hears gunshot. You simply can't sit still but must be forever charging after the chance to put down your fellow countrymen. Why is that?' She looked at him with her cold blue gaze, like a sea bird eyeing something moving below the surface of the water. An empty glass was held loosely between her fingers and she twirled it a little. 'I daresay there must be some reason. Perhaps you just weren't very popular at home? I've noticed people are often particularly cruel where they never felt they got much notice.'

Honor bit back a laugh, waiting to see how Channon would respond. Would he be furious, the way some were with Maureen, whose rudeness was always calibrated, a careful accounting of every weakness she suspected in her victim. But those who knew her well knew that there were distinctions within the rudeness too – including a variety that almost bordered on affection, reserved for those few she considered worthy of her notice. Channon, Honor saw, was in this category. So, would he recognise that? Or simply be blinded by the affront?

He threw his head back and laughed. 'Oh very good, Maureen,' he said, the American in his voice suddenly stronger. 'How one admires your dexterity.' But he refused to be drawn by any more of her questions, answering with brevity, then turning straight back to Honor.

Maureen tried again. 'Carry on with what you were saying about the Prince of Wales,' she demanded.

But Channon said he couldn't remember what they had been discussing.

'Something about bathrooms, and *companions* . . .?' Maureen prompted. Behind her, Oonagh was laughing into her hand.

Channon waved his hand airily. 'I cannot for the life of me recall. But speaking of, Lady Honor, tell me, have you seen *The Good Companions*? Gielgud is terrific, I tell you, simply terrific.'

'I haven't. But I enjoyed his Hamlet very much at the Old Vic. It is clear he has studied his craft.'

'But I must get tickets in that case,' he cried. 'Would you do me the *honour*,' he smiled, 'of accompanying me? Lady Iveagh also, of course, and I believe there are some little sisters who might enjoy an excursion?'

Honor was flustered. Did he mean it, or was he being polite? Is that what Americans did? One heard so much about their excessive nature. Was this an example? And would she be made a fool of, if the plan never came to anything? In the end, it was Maureen's face that decided her.

She couldn't have looked so peeved if she hadn't believed Channon meant it.

'Very well,' Honor said, 'that would be delightful.'

Weeks later, at a party, she joined a group that included Doris and two men with what she thought of as 'Hollywood moustaches', that is to say thin, glossy pencil lines that lent cruelty to their mouths. They were talking about someone called Chips, with an eager pretence at restraint that meant they had the scent of blood.

'Who is it now?'

'Well, Viscount Gage, of course.'

'Still?'

'Oh yes. Apparently marriage to Mogs makes very little difference there. Also Isabelle Clow.'

'Chicago?'

'Yes.'

'Married already, so that's no good.'

'Diana Bridgeman?'

'Lady Abdy now,' the other corrected. 'He rather missed *that* boat.'

'Others?'

'Oh yes. Many. And terribly pally with the Prince of Wales and all that Fort William set.'

'Who is this Chips?' Honor asked, laughing at the restrained eagerness of their talk; the way they pretended their interest was inconsequential – they were like children who have hidden something and want you to find it but pretend they don't.

'Channon,' one of the men replied, casting a bored glance at her.

'Our new American,' the other said, leaning forward a little. 'You must meet him. Knows everyone and goes everywhere even though one has no real idea where he comes from. Tremendous fun. And quite the most *energetic* of fellows . . .' They both laughed at that, and even Doris, fidgeting with the clasp of her diamond bracelet, lifted her eyes and gave a vague smile.

'But I've met him,' Honor said in a rush. 'At Maureen's. He was . . .'

'Charming?' one of the men enquired. 'I'm *sure* he was,' with a look at the other man.

And he had been, Honor thought. Not just to her, but a few days later to Lady Iveagh and little Patsy too; collecting them for the theatre, escorting them with so much genial care that he barely watched the play at all. He talked Shakespeare and Gielgud's interpretation of Hamlet with Lady Iveagh, told Patsy a ghost story he swore was true and that managed to be chilling enough to thrill her 14-year-old love of the macabre, while not straying into territory Lady Iveagh would have considered unsuitable. He fetched drinks and proffered opera glasses and shepherded them in and out of His Majesty's Theatre swiftly and ably. And all through, he had smiled at Honor, whispered little snatches of observation and comment to her about other theatregoers – 'Do you see Emerald, Lady Cunard, greatest hostess of the age, for sure, but how can she stand upright with the weight of all those diamonds?'

Honor looked and saw a rather wizened lady of 60 with the bright, eager eyes of a child.

Then, 'Don't you think Kitty Brownlow must be able to see almost a full circle with those wide-apart eyes?' Henry continued, and Honor was impressed at the familiar way he spoke of these people. Kitty, as he so casually called her, was greatly admired for her extreme thinness and chic, appearing in the society pages with – and often without – her husband Perry, who was known to be close with the prince. Henry's observations were cosy and sharp, and made Honor feel a delightful complicity, quite as though she knew these people, who were all far more grown-up and exciting than her meagre circle of gauche debutants. He nodded and smiled all around him – indeed, it seemed he knew 'everyone', because the nods and smiles came back – but never for a second did he forget that he was their escort. No matter who called to or saluted him, he stayed by their sides.

And when he said goodbye, properly, at the door of number 5 Grosvenor Place once the evening was over, he had pressed her hand and said, 'May I call on you tomorrow?' And he had, and the days after. They had walked slowly through Hyde Park, and taken tea at the Ritz. They had talked about books – and only then had he admitted that he too was a writer, with two novels published and work begun on a third. She had admired the restraint that had allowed him to talk of other, more famous authors, without the need to untimely wrestle the conversation around to himself. She had felt time slow down in his company, so that instead of thinking about the next thing, as she so often did – either because there was an immediate next thing that must be done, or because there wasn't, so that she wondered how to fill her days – she thought only about the things they talked about. They had walked slowly and talked quickly, and whole afternoons had gone by – three of them now – in which he asked her questions about herself and listened closely to the answers, responding in the same thoughtful way to the questions she shyly asked him, so that she felt she knew him as she knew no one else other than her parents and Doris.

And now here she was, pretending to herself that she hadn't kept one eye on the door all evening, hoping he would arrive, and listening to these men cut him up as easily as though he were butter and they knives hot and sharp with scorn. She felt her face grow red, almost as though it swelled up, and that in turn made her feel conscious that she was broader than either of these slender men with their delicate wrists and carefully waxed moustaches. She took a step back, away from the little group.

'Well?' the shorter of the young men said, staring at her. 'What did you make of him?' and Honor didn't know how to answer.

She looked in desperation at Doris, who blinked at her, then yawned and said, 'I cannot stand here a second longer. I'm leaving this instant. Honor, will you come with me?'

'Thank you,' Honor said gratefully, when they were seated in a corner by an open window so that the cool night air came to them with that hint of the weedy damp that was London in an unpromising early summer.

'What was that about?' Doris demanded. 'Your face went on fire. I thought I should have to throw my champagne on you.'

'The man they spoke about . . .'

'Chips?'

'Yes.'

'Well . . .?' when Honor didn't say anything for a moment.

'I know him.'

'Yes, you met him at Maureen's. I heard you. He was charming. What of it?' Then, with a laugh, 'Oh, I see . . .'

'What?'

'He was charming.' And, when Honor said nothing, 'Have you seen him since?'

'Yes. He escorted us to the theatre.'

'Us?'

'My mother, Patsy, Brigid me.'

'Ah.'

'Ah what?'

'Well, isn't it obvious?'

'Yes, I suppose so.'

'Now what?'

'I don't know.'

'You wait,' Doris said with decision. 'You do nothing, and you say nothing. Because you know nothing – not really. Only the tattle-telling of idle gossips. So you wait.'

And because Doris knew about men, and love, far more than Honor, and because she barely understood what the men had been hinting at, only that there was unkindness in their voices, she said she would.

But she couldn't, not when confronted by Henry – must she now think of him as Chips? – and the eager energy he focused on her, quite unlike the drifting indifference of the other young men she met.

'I've been looking for you,' he said, coming upon her an hour or so later in a corner of the drawing room where she talked politely to a friend of Lady Iveagh's who wore a dress so lumpy that it seemed, Honor thought, to have been made of several dresses. 'Ever since I arrived I've been looking for you.' He smiled down at her and she wondered again at the regularity of his features, those four perfect quadrants. 'May I borrow her?' he asked the lady in the lumpy dress, who smiled vaguely at them both. He took Honor's arm. 'Come and sit with me and tell me how Lady Patricia is doing with her lessons. Has she learned those French verbs that were causing so much trouble?'

His brown eyes were hot and cool at once, with a warmth that seemed only for her, but that maybe seemed only for everyone, she thought.

'You are out of sorts,' he said after only a few moments, looking more closely at her. 'Are you unwell? Would you like me to bring you home?'

'No. I'm alright.'

'Well then, what is it? Because I can see it's something.'

'Some men were talking . . . About you.'

'I see. Were they? And what did they say?' He seemed so unruffled, humorous and light, just as he had been when

Maureen had tried to nettle him. Maybe, Honor thought, maybe it was alright after all.

'They said you have a great many *friends*,' she ventured.

'Indeed. And am I not lucky?'

'No . . . You know what I mean . . .'

'Do I?'

He looked angry then, so that she blurted out, 'You do. Please . . .'

'Well, maybe I do.' As though he took pity on her, would not force her to say what she meant. 'And who are these friends they assign me?'

'Viscount Gage?'

'A dear friend from Oxford.'

'Isabelle Clow?'

'An old friend from America. One of the few I have left. A respectable married lady.'

'Diana, Lady Abdy?'

'She illustrated the cover for my last book. We worked well together, we are creatively suited' – she was impressed by the way he said that, she had never thought about people being 'creatively suited' before – 'that is all. But you know, I could tell you almost exactly what those men said, even without hearing it.'

'How?'

'Because it is what the gossips say. Gossips, everywhere, are the same. They look around, they find someone who shines a little brighter' – he almost winked at her – 'and then they look around again, and they find names. Any name will do, so long as it is known, and unsuitable.

Anyone who is a friend, an acquaintance, a kindred spirit. And they couple the names together with a smirk and a wink, and their work is done. Our own imaginations do the rest. But' – he held up a hand to stop her speaking – 'only where those imaginations are not better occupied. I' – he threw back his shoulders and spoke a little louder – 'never listen to gossip. I have too much to think about.'

She felt shamed, as if the larger dimensions of his mind had exposed the shrunken nature of hers.

He looked at her for a long moment, then said, 'Shall I be direct and straight with you, Lady Honor, in the way I feel your intelligence deserves?'

'Please,' she said. How else to answer such a question.

'I think we would do well together, you and I. We have the same interests. Spend a little more time with me, and you'll see that it's so.'

'They made you sound so . . . frivolous.'

'Because that's all they see of me. It's all most of the world sees of me. But there's more. I'm not that, I swear to you. I wish to write, to think, to have time alone to do those things. The endless parties and lunches and dinners – that is all a distraction from what I really care for. Which are the same things that you care for, I believe.' He spoke then of politics, his interest in it, his desire to 'do something vital' with his life. 'And I will,' he said with magnificent conviction. 'I will do great things, I know it. And you will do them with me.'

Everything he said, she responded to as though it were a series of notes she recognised, a tune she wished to sing along with. She had been disturbed by the sly way those men had spoken of him, and sickened by the things they said, but, to her surprise, she had felt protective too. She had recognised something small and mean in their mockery, which came from the fact that their target was American, and not one of them. It was the instinct of bullies everywhere, she knew – to expose and jeer at difference. The same instinct that led some girls of her acquaintance to ignore her, Baby to say cutting things about her looks. And so she let Henry talk, and she listened, and she allowed herself to hope that what he said was true. That he was indeed what he claimed to be – serious, dedicated to noble aims and ambitions – and not what they claimed he was – a person without restraint, an opportunist, a sensualist.

'Don't listen to the gossips,' he said at last. 'If there is anything you need to know, I will tell you. Is that a deal?' He put a hand out for her to shake and she took it. His was warm and sturdy and enveloped hers in a way that was reassuring.

'There is something . . .'

'Ask it.'

'Where did you get the nickname?'

He looked at her a moment, considering, then smiled. 'I gave it to myself.'

'Why?'

'Your name is Guinness; it's not something you would understand.'

Chapter Eight

The first time she met Chips, Doris recognised in him the very same watchfulness she knew in herself. No matter where he was, or what he did, no matter how absorbed he seemed in a conversation, dinner, dancing, he was always – as she was – intensely aware of what went on around him. Who came and went, how they were greeted, what they wore and who they spoke to. And, she thought, he was easily as clever at it as she was. More. But even knowing this, she was no proof against his easy charm.

'So you are the dear friend?' he asked, taking her hand and shaking it vigorously the first time Honor introduced them. 'The society beauty everyone talks of.'

'And you are the new American everyone talks of.'

'What then must you and I talk of, if everyone else talks of us?' he asked, in a way that was flattering and gracious and seemed to draw the two of them together into a cosy and exclusive conspiracy.

'Why, we talk about Honor,' Doris said, smiling at her friend, who was looking anxiously from one to the other.

'In which case we will never be short of conversation,' Chips said. It was pompous and facile, Doris thought, but he said it so naturally, as though he meant it, that she forgave him.

And in fact, it was true, she soon realised. She wasn't important enough in the kind of society Chips had set his heart on – the Fort William set that clustered aggressively around the Prince of Wales, against which Chips was butting his head for entry; the world of political salons and influence in which he revelled – for him to pay her much heed, but Honor was a link between them, and because of her they were very often together, at the theatre, at lunches, over tea at the Ritz or Claridge's.

At first Doris watched Chips closely. She had to, she told herself. His sudden appearance and immediate laying-siege to Honor required it. Not for a second did she imagine that Honor with a name that wasn't Guinness, without a title or fortune, would have been irresistible to him. But that, she told herself, was perfectly fine. That, she was prepared to forgive him, if he was good to Honor. Good *for* Honor.

And he was. She saw that immediately. He was all the things Honor was not – easy in his manners, amusing and willing to be amused, eager to meet new people, quick to make friends of them. He had a confiding kind of charm that was, Doris thought, a little like a creature that considers nothing of how much it might be wanted, but only what it wants. He was never stuck for conversation, knowledgeable about books and the theatre, with a store of easy opinions that he seemed to stitch together from the scraps let fall by others, but always placing them carefully into a new and interesting order. Like a quilt made up of patchwork pieces of cloth that is more beautiful all together than any of the bits are individually.

And in his company, Honor stopped hiding behind her own stiff good manners. She relaxed and became easy and funny, the way she had been at Miss Potts'; even daring. Her observations about the people around them – her cousins, Baby Jungman, Elizabeth Ponsonby, all that group of bright, beautiful and cruel young people – now that Chips was by her side, were bold and witty. 'They are like moths,' she'd said, watching a group of them at a ball shortly after she and Chips met, 'blundering and sleep-walking towards the light that will burn them up. Except that instead of actual light, what they blunder towards is even more intangible – it is the idea of themselves as daring and scandalous that is so seductive.'

'Go on,' Chips said.

'Well, and it is no more to be had than the light those poor moths think they can fly into. It will burn them up even as they reach it.'

'Bravo!' Chips said.

'Aren't you inspired?' Doris had said later, when she

and Honor, having escaped the party for some air, stood together on a balcony off the main ballroom, overlooking the street below that was lit in uneven yellow pockets by the gas lamps. As they watched, a cat slipped out from the area railings of the house opposite and stood for a long time in the empty street.

'You cannot imagine how it feels,' Honor said, leaning forward over the wrought iron of the balcony.

'How what feels?'

'To set off out each evening, now, and know that I will enjoy it. That I will be amused, and included and will go home almost reluctantly. Before, I used to gird myself as though for battle—'

'Certainly, you looked as if you did,' Doris said with a laugh. 'That expression of yours . . . so grim, so determined . . .'

Honor nudged her arm with her shoulder. 'I wasn't that bad. But, then, every night was an ordeal, and now every night is marvellous.'

'I'm glad,' Doris said.

'But I do wonder . . .'

'What?'

'Well, what it is that attracts him.'

'It is you, silly. Your blue eyes and pink cheeks.'

'Oh I am well enough,' – Honor made an impatient movement with her hand – 'but no, it isn't that. And nor is it that he likes what I bring to marriage – or at least, not entirely.' She laughed. 'Rather, it's that he seems to *approve* of me. Of everything about me.' She sounded wondering.

'He is in favour of all the things I am – not just the things the rest of the world approves of, like my family and my fortune. But also of the way I speak, the time it takes me to be certain of an opinion, my dislike of going to too many parties . . . I mean, all the things that I began to think were terrible drawbacks—'

'Like damp in a basement, if one were buying a house?'

'Exactly! But no, he approves of the lot. And I can't understand why.'

'Must you understand? Is it enough that he does?'

'It is.'

'Well then.' And after Honor had gone, saying she must look for Chips because she wanted him to take her home, Doris stayed on the balcony, and watched the cat from the house opposite. It sat in the shadow beyond the pool of gaslight and stared at that golden space for a long time, as though it expected something to walk into the light, Doris thought; as though the lighted part of the street were a stage, and the cat part of an audience. But nothing happened. After a while the cat got up and walked into the warm lighted space and sat down, as if it had decided to be its own entertainment.

Happy as she was to see Honor so content, Doris soon found that she missed her company. She saw so much less of her, now that Honor was so often with Chips. He seemed to need her constantly by his side, whether he was shopping, paying calls or conferring with art dealers.

'She is perfectly silly about that chap,' Maureen said one morning as they walked about the park, slowed by

Maureen's fat pug, who waddled wheezily behind them so that they had to keep stopping to let it catch up. Mimi, dancing ahead on a slim leather lead, looked particularly fed up, Doris thought. Maureen was stouter after the baby – a girl, Caroline. And yet she had had the child the way a cat might, Doris thought. Or indeed, the way someone might set down a parcel, only to forget, first where it was, and later that they had ever had it.

'She's in love,' Doris said.

'Yes, who would have thought it.' Maureen giggled. 'Honor, so little built for romance, to fall so hard. And for . . . that.'

'You don't like him?'

'What has like to do with it?' Maureen looked baffled. At first, Doris knew, she had been put out by the match, but once she saw how much London society approved, she'd switched to telling everyone that it was of her making. 'I introduced them, you know,' she liked to say. 'I just had a *feeling* . . .'

'I see very clearly who and what he is, that's all,' she said now. 'And I hope Honor does too, otherwise it will not be an easy marriage.' And then, just as Doris was about to ask what exactly she meant, Maureen said, 'I say, did you hear about Elizabeth's latest scrape? A car she was in, driven by one of her young men, crashed and the fellow was killed.'

'That's hardly a scrape, Maureen. That's a tragedy.'

Maureen made an impatient twitching movement. 'They say the car was being chased by another of Elizabeth's *amours* . . . That girl really is the limit! Now, let me tell you the latest about Oonagh and Philip . . .' She launched into a story about her sister, her sister's husband, and the trouble in their marriage that, once she'd understood what it was that Maureen was really saying, left Doris feeling as though she had been given a soiled handkerchief to hold.

As Honor grew closer to Chips, and needed her less, Doris began to spend more time in her rooms at Curzon Street, with Mabel. They played cards in the afternoons – gin rummy and double patience – after Mabel came home from secretarial school. They smoked and talked of home and their hopes for the next parts of their lives. Doris even dined there some evenings, willing to be amused by the back-and-forth battles between Mrs Benton and Miss Wilkes.

'Did you notice,' she asked Mabel after dinner one evening when they sat in Doris' rooms, 'that Miss Wilkes has a new ace? Her sister-in-law has introduced her to a chaplain who once travelled with Lady Brentworth, and I swear she will soon make him an authority on all things.'

'Poor Mrs Benton. She'll have to do better than a nephew who is a bank manager.'

'Tell me, how is the apprenticeship coming along?'

'There will be an announcement soon, but I am certain it will be me.' Mabel glowed. 'In every test I am first, and I have practised and practised so that I cannot make a mistake. This will mean everything, Doris. Simply everything. With this, I am assured of work and a salary and maybe, one day, a little flat of my own.'

'I am happy for you, Mabel, you deserve this.'

A new position would, Doris realised, mean that Mabel was busier, with even less time to spend smoking and chattering. And then, perhaps, the flat she spoke of so hopefully. A flat where she would live alone. And a few weeks later, when her mother asked, again, would she go to Germany with her on a visit the following summer, Doris, instead of inventing excuses as to why she couldn't possibly, said, 'Very well.'

Chapter Nine

London, summer 1933

The day before her wedding, Lady Iveagh insisted
Honor come with her to deliver old clothing to a
place in the East End, where it would be distributed
to tenement families. 'There are more of them all the time,'
Lady Iveagh said, with what might have been despair in
a lesser person. 'So that it is almost impossible to know
how to assist them.'

'Must I?' Honor asked. The day was sultry, a heavy
airless heat that clogged the blood in her veins so that she
wanted only to sit still. There were thunderstorms forecast
for later, and the next day – the wedding – was to be
bright and crisp. For that, she was grateful, but not enough
to wish to move.

'I know you don't want to, but it will be for the best. Otherwise you will be driven to distraction by Patsy and Brigid.'

The girls were to be bridesmaids, and were so charmed with themselves that they couldn't leave Honor alone. They demanded to see her dress, stroke her veil, the satin on her white shoes, all the while asking questions: 'Will you have a tiara?' 'How will you do your hair?' Even 'How will you disguise The Eye?' That was Brigid, just turned 13, and by far the prettiest of the three sisters – something she was, Honor thought, all too aware of.

'Brigid,' Patsy had said, shocked, 'Honor is to be a bride. She will be beautiful.'

Honor had smiled at her, grateful for Patsy's sweet nature. But even so, she thought, it would be a relief to get away from their soft patting hands and insistent admiration for a time.

'Very well, I will come.'

Once in the motorcar, with the windows down to catch at any breeze there was – although Honor did wish her mother would allow the chauffeur to drive faster, that they might create some breeze of their own – Lady Iveagh drew closer to her.

'I wanted to have a little talk with you,' she began.

'I rather thought you might,' Honor said, amused.

'This has all been rather fast. Your father was not at all sure he approved.'

'I know. I am surprised myself. But once Chips explained that he couldn't see any reason to wait, well,

I knew that I couldn't either. Not once I knew the dress could be made in time.'

'He is very impatient,' Lady Iveagh said. But tolerantly.

Honor knew her parents liked Chips. He had made sure of it. He talked to her mother about politics and schemes for the clearing of slums. He talked to her father about farming and new ways to kill rabbits. He knew all the latest stories about their friends, but the right kinds of stories – not the ones he whispered to Honor when they went to the theatre or out to dine, that made her eyes grow round with surprise. To them, he talked of who had bought a new house, was about to publish a book or bring out a daughter. Most of all, she thought enviously, he made them laugh. Everyone treated her parents as though they were a specially delicate kind of glass or crystal, to be handled with care. But Chips did not. He told them things to amuse them, brought them silly gifts, and generally teased them. And they adored it. Adored him.

'He says he is anxious to begin,' Honor said, only vaguely clear on what exactly it was that Chips wished to begin.

But Lady Iveagh seemed to understand. 'I can see that,' she said seriously. 'I like him for it.' Then, 'It's not the life I had foreseen for you,' she said thoughtfully.

'No?'

'No. This way, you will be a hostess. A patroness. Your role will be in society. I had seen something different for you. But this is better.'

Which is how Honor understood that her mother had not expected her to marry; rather, had anticipated Honor the unmarried daughter, constantly on hand for charity and committee work. And that she was happier that, after all, marriage had wriggled itself into Honor's future. That for all her kind words about a husband being unnecessary to someone with Honor's title and fortune, still it was what she had wanted for her daughter.

'Is there anything you wish to talk about?' Lady Iveagh said then. She leaned forward briskly and closed the partition between them and the chauffeur, Banks.

Honor felt sorry for him. Her mother would not allow him to drive with his window open – 'Something common about it,' she'd said thoughtfully, 'though I am not sure what' – and Honor knew he would be more stifled than ever now.

'Well, I have thought . . . a little, about some parts of marriage . . .'

'I wondered would you ask,' her mother said thoughtfully. 'Well, I will do my best. What is it that you want to know?'

'Well . . .' Honor was silent a minute, trying to pick words that she could say, that could be brought to express what she wanted to know. 'It's that . . .' She thought back a few weeks, to the days after Chips had asked would she marry him.

After he had asked, she had said she needed to think, and she had gone away, but she had not thought. She had cried – mostly with relief – and then, after an hour or so, had dried her eyes, washed her face, and telephoned to him.

'I will,' she'd said in a rush, in answer to his 'Hullo?'

Two nights later, in the box he had taken at the theatre, while John Gielgud as Richard II declared his love for Anne of Bohemia, her face hidden in the comforting dark and knowing that Chips' attention was only half – less – on her, Honor had whispered, 'If we are to be married, should we not, you know, be *certain* of one another first?'

He would never know what it had cost her to say that. How much she'd wanted him to understand instantly, to put an arm around her and whisper yes and hold her tight and spare her from saying more. But he did not.

'What do you mean?' he'd asked, a shade too loud, so that a man in the box beside them frowned.

'Only . . .' Honor had tried again, 'if we should, perhaps, go to a hotel together. To see if *that side of things* . . . is alright. We could, you know. I could easily manage it.'

Chips had laughed. 'No need for that,' he had said, patting her hand with his. She had heard him repeat "*that side of things*" to himself in a whisper, and laugh again.

Honor had been mortified. How was it possible, after all she had been told in sly warnings about men and what they sought, that she had offered herself to this man, and he had said no?

But how to ask her mother what she really wanted: *How will I know if my husband desires me? How can I make him desire me?* As she turned over possible phrasings, her mother shifted. She still sat, knees planted firmly apart, hands flat and heavy, one on each knee, but closer to Honor now.

'I know. You wonder what all the fuss is about?' Lady Iveagh said. 'I have never really understood. All those people, leaving their husbands and wives and running off with one another, killing themselves for love or destroying themselves with drink because of it. I never could understand why.' She sounded almost wistful for a moment. Then, 'Better that way, I think. That sort of love seems to bring no end of trouble.'

It wasn't what she had been trying to ask, but Honor couldn't say that. Instead, she said, 'But you and Papa . . .'

'Lord Iveagh and I are entirely content together. From the very day we met, at Elveden, where my papa had brought me for a shooting party . . .'

'Love at first sight,' Honor said wryly.

'Certainly not,' her mother replied, just as Honor had known she would. 'That kind of love never lasts. It cannot. It burns like potassium, and then it is gone. Leaving nothing at all, only a faint residue.'

Her mother was nothing if not literal. Honor changed the topic. Clearly, Lady Iveagh could not tell her what she wanted to know. And small wonder, when she herself could not articulate it.

She leaned forward and opened the partition. 'Mamma, you must let Banks breathe or he will expire.'

Chapter Ten

Berlin, summer 1933

Those weeks in Berlin, as summer grew dusty and tired and the leaves of the linden trees curled tight and crisp above them, falling slowly to the ground in indifferent waves that chased each other through the days, Doris realised that she was longer in her mother's company than she had been in many years. And that she liked it.

They stayed with her mother's sister, Hannah, a serious woman with dark blonde hair and skin the colour of a buckskin pony just like Esther. She lived in a tall house with a great deal of white plasterwork on the outside and polished wood inside. A long staircase turned around itself up through the interior with rooms branching out from it and leading one into another, their panelled walls and high yellow-ish ceilings trapping sound so that there were only ever murmurs, never shouts, like swallows flying swift and high in the eaves of the barns at home.

Doris' cousins were all boys, and younger than her. They wished to be doctors and when not studying, practised music, or drawing, so that she saw them only at mealtimes. But it didn't matter, because there was so much to do. Her mother seemed determined to see every gallery, every play, every recital, but actually what Doris liked most were the days when they simply walked about the city, talking, looking, pointing out all the things that were different to Dorset and even London. The shop windows displaying different kinds of cakes; books bound and printed in a language Doris spoke well but read only haltingly; strange fashions and hats that told of all that was unfamiliar in the lives of German women.

Everything about Berlin was different, she found. The city was just as large as London, but lighter somehow. Maybe it was the colour of the buildings – instead of the soot-blackened façades and grimy red brick of London, she saw walls painted white and even pale pink, with plasterwork that was bleached to the colour of bone by the sun. The air was light and dry compared with the heavy damp of London, and the wide, wide streets meant there seemed to be time and space for everything, not the hurried crowding she was used to.

She had always imagined Berlin – Germany – as a silly sort of a place. Somewhere that didn't count, much, because it wasn't England. A country full of people who must wish themselves born elsewhere. Instead, she discovered a sophisticated city that seemed to have no idea at all that it was inferior; quite the opposite. When she and her mother spoke English together, the tram drivers and shopkeepers who overheard them smiled and nodded in a way that was almost sympathetic, and that became far more respectful when her mother switched to German.

It was on one of the idle mornings, when they had stopped at one of the city's coffee-houses, over a plate of lavish cakes, that Esther said, 'You know this is not worthy?'

'These cakes? I should think they are worthy of a prince,' Doris said, knowing well her mother didn't mean that.

Sure enough. 'I mean your life in London is not worthy.'

'It's not *unworthy* . . .' Doris tried to deflect. 'I don't do anything terribly shocking, you know.'

But her mother wasn't like her friends and did not allow the deflection. 'It is. You hang about London, doing nothing except attending parties, and all with the sole aim of being married. Which is not a good aim at such a time when there are many other things you could be doing.'

'But what else am I to do?' It was a relief to speak plainly, Doris thought. To say exactly what she meant, and to be told, in turn, exactly what her mother meant. 'I'm not educated for anything else.'

'You could go to university. There are many girls at Oxford now.'

'Impossible. Miss Potts', although very jolly, wasn't exactly top drawer.'

'There are other things.' Her mother signalled the waitress for more coffee, had a rapid conversation with her in German about a *kirschtorte*, a sweet tart that she liked. Doris admired this unfamiliar person before her. She loved to see her mother so confident and at ease, so completely certain of herself that her words and gestures were somehow harmonised, and mirrored by the waitress who smiled and responded eagerly. This was not how her mother was in England – there, she was stiff, a little withdrawn, uncertain still in simple things, like the correct way to serve asparagus, the quantity of orange peel pieces to be included in marmalade, where to seat people and when to move conversations along before they became too entangled. Too many years of being outside had left her reluctant to try to move further in. She remained at the edges. Like someone looking in the window of a lighted room, but knowing their path lies elsewhere.

'You mean like secretarial courses?' she asked, when her mother had finished with the waitress and sat back in her spindly wooden chair. She thought of Mabel and her typewriter, her words-per-minute and dictation. Of her pride in what she was able to put on paper – tangible proof of all that she knew and learned. What must it be like, Doris wondered, to see your achievements stacked up in that way. Counted and reckoned: the speed of your fingers on typewriter keys, certificates of attendance and distinction. A trail that could be followed, one certainty to the next. Evidence of yourself. A road, mile-marked, with a clear destination.

'That. Other possibilities,' her mother said, pouring coffee for them both.

Doris disliked coffee, but the tea in Berlin tasted strange. 'I don't see it,' she confessed frankly. 'I find little to interest me in the idea. It seems . . . dull. Every day the same. An office in Mayfair or such like. The typing pool. Lunches at Woolworths or a Lyons Corner House. No. I couldn't bear it. I wish to be free.'

'Free?' her mother said. 'What is that? You are hardly free now, staying in that boarding house in Curzon Street.'

'Married women in London have a freedom you couldn't imagine,' Doris said with a laugh. 'The rich ones anyway.' She thought of Honor, married already a month by then: *I'm sorry that you will not be here, but Chips sees no reason for a long engagement and nor do I, and so we are to be married almost immediately* . . . Honor had written at the beginning of July.

'But you are not married,' her mother continued.

'Not yet. But I will be.'

'To whom?'

'I don't know, but I will find the right person.'

'And who might the right person be?' Her mother sighed, loudly. Impatiently. And because of that, Doris, nettled, didn't give the charming, evasive answer she had ready.

'Someone who means that my children will live at the heart of the country, the way that Honor and her family do,' she said. 'I mean right close to the heart of it, so close that they cannot even see where they are; or see that there is any other way to be. And if I do it right, even Isabel and Marianne will find their lives easier.'

'Your sisters may have other plans.'

'They may. But if they intend on marriage, then they will find that a lot simpler because I have been before them, smoothing their path.' What, Doris wondered, did she want? Her mother's approval? Her to collude with Doris in the bringing about of her plans? Yes, but her mother would not, and she knew it. So why did she seek what could never be?

'You could come here, to Berlin, to your cousins,' her mother continued. 'You could improve your German. You could even study at the university – I'm sure they would not mind Miss Potts' as much.' She smiled.

Doris thought about that for a while. The visit had been, she admitted, delightful. Her aunt's house was the most restful place she had known, as though the house itself absorbed noise and small irritations, smoothing them all out and tidying them away. It might, after all, be a place to be. And a university course would be more than a secretarial course.

'I thought you said you didn't like the way the wind was blowing here. The fighting on the streets. Their lot.' Doris gestured out the window of the coffee shop, to the wide avenue that ran, straight to north and south, in front of them. A group of young men in camel-coloured shirts and trousers with the distinctive red-and-black armband stitched with an angrily twisted cross passed by, jostling one another and laughing loudly. They swaggered the way Doris had sometimes seen a bull swagger as it was brought into the ring of the cattle mart in Weymouth, so that the man driving it had, always, a readiness about him, to jump out of the way or run for the barrier.

'They are vulgar, and troublesome,' Esther said, looking with disdain at the men. 'But they won't be any trouble to you. You are English. And you would come to study, not to work. It is Jewish businesses that are shunned, and Tante Hannah says that will not be for much longer.'

'I'll think about it,' Doris promised.

She wouldn't, not really, but she didn't want to spoil the rest of their visit. It was so new and pleasant to be with her mother like this.

'Lady Iveagh must think me very peculiar, never to have called,' Esther said then.

'It doesn't matter,' Doris insisted. 'All that matters is Honor, and she doesn't care.'

'What kind of a friend doesn't want to meet someone's family?' her mother persisted.

'The best kind.'

The next day, they walked in the Tiergarten, the vast park that lay in the centre of Berlin, with Tante Hannah and her quiet, serious sons. They admired the thousand-year oak trees with their gnarled trunks and defiant leaves, the level stretches of grass turning dry and tufty as summer advanced, and the formal lakes. Everywhere Doris looked were statues in stone and bronze – men on horses or fighting savage beasts; a pair of magnificent lions, a deer with many-pronged antlers. Statues that spoke of conquering and vanquishing, the vivid, sometimes tortured celebrations of victory and glory at odds with the tranquillity of the day.

She carried the picnic basket they had packed, and when they had walked enough her aunt Hannah took a plaid rug from the youngest of the cousins and spread it on the ground beneath a tree.

'Let's sit at a picnic table,' Esther said. 'We will be more comfortable.'

'Better to stay here,' Hannah said.

'We'll be covered in ants. The picnic table is far better.' Esther reached for the basket.

'We can't sit there.' That was Doris' cousin, the eldest, a boy of 14. 'Jews can't sit there now.' He sounded defiant and his voice was loud. He looked around, although there was no one close enough to overhear them.

Doris saw that her aunt kept her head low, bent close over the rug that she was straightening, trying to get it to lie flat on ground that was lumpy.

Esther looked at her sister for a moment, now plucking at the edges with sharp little movements. 'Then we will sit here,' she said quietly. She unpacked the basket, laying out the bread and meat and cheese they had brought. When they were finished eating, they tidied away immediately, although the day was still warm and the spot where they sat was shaded. They talked little as they walked back to the tall, thin house. And after that, her mother no longer spoke of Doris moving to Berlin.

Chapter Eleven

London, autumn 1933

Doris came back to London, to a city that was half-empty. Even Curzon Street felt uninhabited. Miss Wilkes was away, taking the air at Eastbourne where she had a sister, and Mrs Benton was in Scotland. Without them, the food, Doris saw immediately, would be terrible – bread thinly spread with margarine and a stale scone were all that appeared for her afternoon tea – and the house lay as though under a heavy blanket, barely stirring.

She unpacked her suitcase, and reminders of Berlin drifted up from the silk tissue paper her aunt's maid had used to fold her things: the smell of lavender beeswax and the rather heavy amber scent her aunt used. But there was also the faintest hint of rose otto, which Doris associated with her mother, so that she felt lonely for a moment, in a way she hadn't since she had first moved to London. She wondered was Mabel back. She should be, but Doris hadn't heard her come in.

She went along to Mabel's room and tapped at the door. 'Come in.'

She opened the door and stuck her head around. 'I'm back. How are you? Come and chat to me. Don't think you'll get a decent tea – you won't. I had mine and it was dreadful, but I brought some sweets back from Berlin and you can have those.'

Mabel followed her through the silent hallway and Doris installed her in an armchair close to the fire. She arranged the sweet almond pastries Tante Hannah had insisted she bring home on a plate and handed it to Mabel. 'Here. So,' – she sat down and lit a cigarette – 'tell me everything.'

'Nothing to tell.'

'There must be. I've been gone weeks. What about Miss Wilkes and Mrs Benton?' Doris coaxed. 'Don't tell me they haven't advanced matters? Surely one of them has discovered a deacon or a surgeon or some other man of distinction to appeal to?'

'Hmmm.' Mabel stared out the window.

'What is it? Mabel, has something happened?'

'Something hasn't happened,' Mabel said gloomily. And, when Doris continued to look at her, 'I didn't get the post.'

'The post?'

'Remember, the apprenticeship I told you of.'

'But you said you were the fastest at typing and dictation.'

'And I am. But all the same they gave it to Flora Elmsworth, who can't type five lines without a mistake but who wears dresses from Harrods even if they are last season, and has a father who works in the bank.'

'Oh, Mabel.'

'Oh indeed. I can't believe I was such a fool as to think I'd get it.' Her voice was like tea that has stewed and thickened and gone bitter.

'I can lend you clothes, if it's only that.'

'But it isn't only that. It's everything else too,' Mabel said bitterly. 'The way she speaks. The way she does her hair. Even the way she holds her pen when correcting all those mistakes she's made. I can be clever as anything with my shorthand, and I'll never be chosen first.'

'You will.' Doris tried to reassure her. 'Of course you will. You mustn't be glum.' But would Mabel be chosen? she thought, even as she spoke. Or would it always be the Floras, the Honors of the world? In her mind, Doris suddenly saw the hours of parties and nightclubs, of treasure hunts and supper clubs, all those nights and after-noons and lunches, all laid out and joined like beads on a string or words typed on a page – a chain of them that led nowhere, only to hopeless young men like Fred and the sniggering sympathy of girls like Baby. She shook her head slightly, to clear the vision. 'You must simply keep trying and not give in,' she said, with new determination. 'And then they will choose you. They'll simply have to.'

Chapter Twelve

'**W**as it frightful?' Honor asked sympathetically. 'Berlin?'

'Oh, frightful,' Doris assured her. 'But also . . .'

'Also what?'

'I don't know. Interesting.' Doris had called for her at the new house, number 21 St James's Place – a house that Honor thought delightful, but Chips insisted, almost hysterically, was temporary – and now they walked through Hyde Park, Mimi prancing at their feet. They were due at a hair appointment. Autumn was cold that year. Even so, Honor, trained by Lady Iveagh, had decided not to order the motorcar, saying, 'A walk will do us good.'

'Interesting?' she asked.

'Yes. I'll tell you more another time. I haven't entirely worked it out myself . . . But I did improve my German.'

'Did it need improving? You always sounded terribly fluent at school.'

'According to my mother, it did. She says I spoke like a barrow boy.' She laughed. 'But it's better now. More elegant.'

'Well, I'm glad you're back,' Honor said.

'So much has happened.' Doris smiled at her. 'Here you are, married four months. And already, you look different.' She surveyed Honor critically, eyes narrowed, so that Honor blushed. 'Yes, I see it,' Doris continued, watching from under the furred brim of her hat, black eyes sparkling.

'See what?' They approached the fountain, silent beneath a thin layer of ice in which wisps of skeleton leaf were trapped. A small boy wearing a knitted bonnet leaned over the rim and poked the leaves with a stick so that the ice cracked.

'There is a difference. But I wonder what it is.' She gave a gurgle of laughter. 'Is it the difference of love, or the difference of relief?'

'Why relief?'

'Well, obviously relief. You are married. You're safe.'

'Safe from what?'

'Don't pretend to be a fool, Honor,' Doris pleaded, 'because you are not that. You know very well the letting-go, the exhalation that comes with marriage for women. We've seen it enough times now. Why, your cousin Aileen nearly broke into a victory run as she came down

St Margaret's as Mrs Brinsley Sheridan Plunket. I hope to feel it myself one day soon.'

'Anything?' Honor asked, wrinkling her nose sympathetically.

'There have been one or two, but you know the sort: a Polish count with holes in his pockets, a chap called Fred who is sweet but hopeless, one or two ambitious stockbrokers who can't tell the difference between me and the real thing.'

'You are the real thing.'

'I'm not and you know it.'

'Too German?'

'Mmm. That, yes. Too Jewish.'

'I see. But you cannot think that matters?'

'I cannot think it doesn't.' They were both silent. Then, 'In any case, there is nothing that fits. Not yet.'

'Doris Coates is a very good name.'

'It's not and you know it.'

'Well, now that I am married, you can stay with us.'

'You are kind, but stay with a honeymoon couple?' Doris laughed. 'No, thanks. I will give you a little longer *a deux*.'

'The bliss of one's very own house, Doris, you cannot imagine . . .'

'Oh yes I can! It's all I think about.' Then, 'So, you are happy?'

'We are. Chips was right.'

'About what?'

'He said we would be happy together.'

'Did he, now?'

'He did. On our wedding night. He said he would be a good husband to me.'

'I'm glad to hear it, for you deserve that.' Doris grabbed hold of Honor's hand and squeezed it. 'I was so sorry to miss it. Though if you will get married in such a tearing hurry . . .'

'Once it was decided, Chips couldn't see the point of waiting.'

'I'm sure he couldn't. But do tell – how was it?'

'The wedding?' Honor paused, wondering how to describe the day. 'I suppose the usual . . .'

'Meaning?'

'Rather dreadful, even alarming. All those people, looking at one . . .'

'So, not usual.' Doris grinned.

'Well, maybe not . . .' Honor pulled a face. She talked of how she had arrived with her father, on that July morning, to find the crowd outside the church already thick. Expectant faces peering into the motorcar, looking for her. Looking to assess her. What, she had wondered then, did they want from her, those crowds and crowds of people – women mostly – standing so respectful but insistent? She had felt crushed by their silent scrutiny.

'I'm sure Chips was delighted,' Doris said.

'He was, rather. All emotional about their loyalty: *The way they turn out to salute you, so faithfully!* No idea at all that what they really want is some dramatic turn – a horse to bolt, a guest to faint. It isn't admiration but expectation that animates them; the hope of something horrible. And so he waved, graciously.' Honor laughed. 'Nodding here and there to anyone he recognised.'

'And you didn't enlighten him?'

'Certainly not!'

'I saw the photos,' Doris said, and squeezed her arm.

'Of course you did,' Honor said. She sighed. All through the ceremony at St Margaret's she had dreaded walking back through that door and into the too-bright July day and meeting again that wall of considering curiosity. And her uneasiness showed. In all the photos of their wedding, Chips beamed, while, by his side, she looked wary and even surly.

She had immediately thought of her cousins, married in that same church: Aileen, gracious and elegant, with Brinny beside her; Oonagh, tiny and sparkling, a pantomime fairy on Philip's arm; Maureen with the intense glow of a newly polished diamond, Duff looming protectively over her.

'He didn't say he loved me,' she said, suddenly. 'Only that he would be a good husband.'

Now that they were out of the park, Doris had moved a little ahead, to make way for the people coming in the opposite direction, but she dropped back. 'A good husband is better than a loving one,' she said, after a pause which acknowledged the sting of Chips' words in a way neither of them ever would openly.

'But surely they are the same?'

'They are not the same.' Doris stooped to pick up Mimi, who was hopeless on a crowded street: too small to keep up, liable to twist her lead in and out of strangers' feet.

There were more things Honor wanted to ask – she felt sure Doris knew the answers, for all that Doris wasn't married. But she didn't know how to say what it was she wished to understand.

Chips wanted a baby. He made no secret of that. In fact he talked so openly of it, sometimes with her mother too – saying that he wanted six children, 'five boys and a girl with the looks to marry well' – that Honor was mortified. Why then, when he came to her room at night, did he seem more remote than at any other time they were together? Surely that should be a time of greatest intimacy, when he should be most fully hers? But no.

He was affectionate, charming, attentive in the mornings when he drank coffee sitting at the end of her bed. Over lunch, if it was the two of them, he would pull his chair close to hers at the round table he liked to be set in the window of the first floor drawing room of St James's Place. He would question her about her day, tease her gently – 'Have you and Lady Iveagh set the world to rights yet? We await our orders' – ask her opinion on whatever was in the newspapers, and persuade her to plot with him for whoever was dining that night. When they walked in the park of an afternoon, he took her hand and tucked it through his arm, pulling her close to his side. Then, he was relaxed and effortlessly intimate, his voice low as he confided something to her of the dreams and ambitions that churned within him. But at night, when he came to her while she was in bed, he was brisk and efficient.

He would take his dressing gown off and double it neatly before placing it across the end of the bed. He would fold back the bed covers and settle himself beside her, then, every time, turn out the bedside lamp, leaving the room entirely in darkness before he reached for her.

'I cannot see you,' she had said the first time, on the night of their wedding at a hotel in Brighton where they spent the first days, before travelling to Italy. He had quoted something about night and darkness that were the friends of lovers, but he hadn't turned the light back on.

There had been no fumbling that first time, no hesitant awkwardness as she had expected. Instead, his hands were smooth and efficient, moving her about this way and that. And she had been willing, interested in this – the great mystery about which she had been curious for so long. But she had not felt that she was really sure of what was happening. There had been very little pain, certainly less than she had expected. More, it was the sense she had of scrabbling to keep up, of not knowing what came next, and of being therefore at a disadvantage. Like meeting someone whose name one couldn't remember, she had thought with a hidden laugh, even though they knew all about one.

Afterwards, when he put back on his dressing gown and tied it firmly at the waist, bending to kiss her briskly and saying, 'Well, I'll say goodnight,' she had wanted to call after him: 'Wait! Stop, and tell me, what was that? Was that it? Was that as it is supposed to be? What should I do that I have not done?' Except that she had no words, no precise ones, only 'that' and 'it', and they were hopeless.

Also, there had been nothing in his demeanour that let her believe he wanted to be questioned by her. He hadn't wanted to tarry, or explore. He had wanted to be done and then be gone. She knew the signs of that. It was the same as she felt when in the grip of the dressmaker, the coiffeur, some other duty that she cared nothing for but knew she must submit to: outward obedience, inward impatience. And so she had let him go, thinking it would be easier the next time to understand, to ask. But it hadn't been easier the next time. If anything it had been harder; as though not saying anything the first time was now the established way for both of them.

And so he came to her room night after night. But he never stayed. Often, afterwards, she heard him go from her bedroom to his study, and knew that he must be writing his diary, setting down all that had occurred during the day. He had once told her that he did this religiously every night before sleep. 'I must keep track,' he had said when she'd asked him why. 'I must have it all in front of me.'

Did he write about her? she wondered. Did he write about the two of them, together in her bed? What might she learn from reading what he had written? Some nights, she thought, she could almost see what 'all the fuss' was about, as her mother put it; moments where she felt she began to understand why this love-making was something that seemed to madden people, cause them to destroy their lives and one another. Almost. And then it would be gone again and she would feel the frustration of something half understood. Perhaps his diaries would tell her what she needed to know.

But when she went looking, she couldn't find any of the leather-bound books he liked. His desk was bare except for a copy of *Debrett's*, a life of Ludwig of Bavaria, and an unfinished letter to his mother: 'Dear Madame . . .' it began.

'Shall you need more space for your diaries?' she asked him at lunch the next day. 'I can ask Andrews to clear some shelves.'

'No, for I no longer write my diary,' he said.

'Why not?'

'I have no need. For the first time since I was an adult, I feel that I am where I am meant to be. I am content, and I have found that being content has made me lazy.' He laughed and reached a hand out to take hers, squeezing it warmly before letting go.

'I'm happy that you're content, but I wouldn't wish to be the cause of your indolence.'

'No. Indolence is a sin in the eyes of your family, I know that. But it is not indolence exactly. I am biding my time, is all.'

'He says marriage has made him lazy,' she said to Doris suddenly then. They were nearly at Monsieur Raymond's salon.

'Well, that's good,' Doris said at last, 'a lazy husband is no bad thing.'

'That's not what Mamma thinks,' Honor said with a laugh. 'She was most concerned when I told her. She's worried about "where it will end". But now that Chips has decided he will stand as MP, for Mamma's seat in Southend, I suppose he will have to be less lazy. Although, she writes a great many of his speeches. As do I. He says there is no way he can lose, that it's a safe seat. She says the same to me, but to him she says that anything is possible in politics, and one must be prepared. But tell me about you now. How was Berlin? And your mother's people?'

'Frightfully serious. It's not at all like being in London. Fewer parties, and those there are terribly high-minded and concerned.'

'About what?'

'Everything. Concerned that this interpretation of Wagner is less stringent than another. That Thomas Mann's essay is weak. That the political life of the country is taking an evil direction, and what must be done to stop that.'

'You should talk to Chips, he loves anything German. He says the new Germany is an example to us all. He admires the way the National Socialists have provided work and housing for working men and their families. But then, he is liable to see the good in everything that is done there. I think because his mother is such a friend to the French, and he despises his mother.'

'My own mother has found new ways of making my life difficult,' Doris said gloomily. 'She talks of having my German relatives to stay.'

'A visit? How nice.'

'Not a visit. Or at any rate a very long one. She wants them to leave Germany, because she says it isn't safe for them.'

'Chips says the street violence is just teething problems,' Honor said. 'That not everyone can accept they have a strong leader for a change, when they are so used to weakness. But that soon the benefits of Hitler will be obvious to all and they will settle down.'

'Well, I hope so. Because a long visit would mean I would have to go to Dorset, and that I will not do. Berlin was bad enough. The theatre, Honor, you can't imagine . . . hours and hours of it, and absolutely no fun at all. The women in such plain dresses, not anything like here . . .'

They reached Monsieur Raymond's and Doris surrendered her fur to the girl at the front desk, then her hat and gloves. She settled Mimi into the crook of her arm and Honor watched her vanish into the scented steam at the back of the salon, before settling herself with a pile of magazines. Monsieur Raymond, the girl at reception had told her, would be out '*himself*' immediately to see her. Waiting, she flicked through a copy of the *Tatler*, pausing at a photograph of herself and Chips exiting the theatre some weeks earlier. How handsome he was, she thought. How *married* they looked.

How lucky that she had gone that day to call on Maureen. And that Chips had chosen the very same day to visit her. For all that Maureen pretended she had made the match, it wasn't her, Honor thought – they had made it themselves. And they would be happy together. He had said it. She would ensure it.

Chapter Thirteen

The following morning, Chips came to the room where Honor was writing letters after breakfast, and settled himself on the small sofa beside her, the puppy, a golden ball of fur whom he had called Bundi, in his arms. 'The chairs have arrived,' he said. 'Now we may plan our first proper dinner.'

'They have not been proper, up to now?' she asked, putting down her pen and turning to him with a smile. Briefly, she reflected that her moments of greatest married intimacy came, in fact, like this – when she and Chips planned how they would entertain. When they discussed the exact positioning of tables, what cocktails to serve, what food, music, even down to the placing of lamps. Then, he would ask Honor for her opinion on everything, and, laughing, she would give it, knowing well that it was his opinion that mattered.

He was strict about who they entertained. Everyone needed to compete on a scale that only he fully understood – a scale in which someone's beauty or good marriage would be set against his knowledge of their husband's career or prospects. He liked Maureen, who amused him, but had little time for Oonagh, whom he thought foolish, or Aileen, who he said was dull. Neither did he care for their friends – Baby, Zita, Elizabeth, whom he said were 'too silly to bother with'.

'You know they have not. Impossible to have a formal dinner party without the proper chairs. But they have arrived at last and they are perfection. The dining room is pokey but will seat 16.'

'Hardly pokey,' Honor protested.

'Pokey. But we will squeeze in. People will not mind, because they know it is temporary and that we will move just as soon as we find somewhere really suitable.'

By which, she knew, he meant somewhere really grand. So many of their days were spent visiting large houses in London, and their weekends exploring country estates that Chips had 'a mind for us to buy'. Sometimes, they looked at a place several times, but so far, always Chips wavered and fretted that whatever house they had looked at was not sufficient for them. Or, if the house suited his impression of himself, it was too much money, even for them.

'We must balance brilliance with beauty, culture and political heft,' he said then, thoughtfully stroking the dog's thick fur. 'Perhaps Ivor Churchill . . . No, not Ivor, he is ill and mean these days; the Cavendishes . . .' and off he went, throwing names around until he had settled on a series of perfectly matched pairs. 'We will use the gold plate. With the new chairs that will do wonderfully.'

Honor smiled and nodded, enjoying his self-congratulatory exuberance, only half-listening, until he rose and said, 'That's settled then. We will have your cousin Maureen and Ava tonight' – every night, something – 'supper and cards. I have already telephoned to Maureen. Oh, and I have commissioned Sexy Beaton to take your photograph.'

She looked up, startled. 'Whyever?'

'Because I wish him to record your loveliness,' he said, clearly pleased with himself for the graciousness of the gesture. And so she had smiled and thanked him and after he was gone cursed quietly under her breath. Beaton had photographed nearly all her friends, many of them twice or more, so it wasn't that. It was that Chips had paid him.

That evening, after supper, with the card table set up, Maureen began to tease Chips with the same merciless wit she inflicted upon them all.

'Why do you call Duff "Ava"?' she demanded.

'Habit,' Chips said smoothly. 'Picked up in Oxford.' He smiled at Duff, who ignored them all, concentrating heavily on his hand.

'But you weren't up at remotely the same time,' Maureen said. 'You were there years before Duff.'

'Hardly years,' Chips protested.

'Definitely years,' Maureen insisted. 'Although how many, exactly, is a bit of a mystery, isn't it? How old are you actually?'

'Why I'm 34, as you well know because you were at my birthday celebrations in March.'

'Doesn't make sense,' Maureen said.

'What doesn't?'

Chips was irritable now, Honor saw. 'Are you going to play that card or not, Maureen?' she asked.

'Your stories.' Maureen wasn't to be distracted. 'From Paris. You say you were there with the American Red Cross, after the war. Before Oxford.'

'I was.'

'But you had already taken courses at the University of Chicago? You told me that once. You said that's why it didn't matter that you took a third from Oxford.'

By now, Chips was thoroughly nettled. He hated any mention of his hopeless degree. He looked at Duff, an appeal – one man to another – but Duff had chosen to devote himself to drinking that night, as he sometimes did, and ignored Chips in favour of pouring himself another measure of crème de menthe. The liquid, sticky and dark green, glistened thick on the sides of the blunt-cut balloon glass. Beside Chips' golden beauty, he seemed uncouth, barely civilised.

'And what of it?' Chips snapped.

'You would have had to be about 16 going to Paris, but how could you have gone to the University of Chicago at that age?'

'Your sums are quite wrong, Maureen,' Honor interjected. They were wrong, even a cursory tallying in her head told her that. And she knew that Maureen knew they were wrong – she was too sharp at numbers not to. But she also knew, they all knew, that Chips' stories didn't add up, unless he had indeed been a prodigy of some kind. 'Anyway, what does it matter?' she said, and played an ace that she knew would annoy Maureen.

That night Chips was more than usually vicious in his dissection of the evening. 'What a morose fellow he can be. I see that his brilliance will go nowhere now, except into fighting with her. He is like someone with his finger in a leak – unable to move and get what's required to dam it, because he knows that the moment he does, it will pour through and drown them all. She has been a bad influence in his life, distracting him from his potential. I won that game for him, while he could hardly tear himself away from the bottle. And *she* does nothing to help, only distracts with her poisonous gossip. I wonder you are friends with her, Honor.'

'You invited them,' Honor said mildly.

'Well, they are family,' he said. 'And,' he began to cheer up, 'our equals in other regards. In fortune, for example. How much must we have had between us, in that room?' And he began to calculate the sum of their fortunes in a way that was, Honor thought, horribly eager.

'I'm going up.'

'I will look in,' he promised.

Honor almost sighed. How late it was. But she knew that

would not weigh with him. His eagerness to be a father – to have an heir – was more to him than anything. To her too, she told herself. Even if she did wish he could be a little less businesslike about it.

Beaton arrived some days later, with his assistants and complicated equipment. 'I will set up in here,' he announced when he had looked about him in a way that made Honor think that he shared Chips' view of the St James's Place house – that it was well enough for starters.

He looked at her for a long time then, walking around and around her as though she were something in a gallery. 'I will photograph you in profile,' he said at last, and Honor knew immediately that he would turn her so that her squinting eye would not be seen. Chips had insisted she wear the ruby and garnet matched set he had given her on their honeymoon, even though she thought the heavy, dark lustre of the necklace and earrings too much.

Beaton positioned her against an ornate glass screen, with a large vase of flowers by her feet, so that Honor thought the photograph would be so busy that she herself would be lost within it. Perhaps that was what Beaton wanted. 'Tuck your chin down,' he said, and then said it again, almost cross, so that Honor understood that he found her chin too large and prominent. He moved lights around, here and there and back again, dissatisfied always until, with the brightest of his lights directly behind her, he said, 'Aha, that's it! Now hold still. Chin *down*, darling,' in a final show of irritation.

Honor dropped her chin, tucking it demurely in, and tried to smile.

The finished photographs arrived on the morning of the dinner party. Honor, when she saw them, had to laugh. Beaton had arranged the light behind her so carefully that it shone brightest at the lower half of her face, blurring the line of her chin and softening it so that the viewer was drawn to look at her nose – handsome enough in profile – and forehead. 'Very clever,' she had said, squashing down the miserable feeling that even despite Beaton's best efforts, she was terribly plain.

It was something she felt more, now that they went about with Chips' friends so much. Before, doing things mostly with her mother, it hadn't mattered. Thinking too much about one's appearance – that is to say, thinking at all, other than to ensure one was tidy and properly dressed – was considered frivolous and pointless. Nothing could have indicated this more clearly than Lady Iveagh herself, who wore dresses from many seasons ago with her remarkable diamonds; hair that was styled to be neat rather than modish, and never make-up of any kind.

'Her diamonds are perfection,' Chips complained. 'If only she would dress them better.' But Lady Iveagh wouldn't, and even he had to concede, 'I suppose it doesn't matter what she wears; she is magnificent.'

But his friends were nothing like Lady Iveagh. They were the glittering, mobile creatures he had pointed out to her on their first night at the theatre, who now inhabited their lives to a degree that was, to Honor, odd. Excessive, even. Emerald Cunard, born Maud Burke and American like Chips, but somehow, through her marriage to Lord Cunard and her own intense personality, become London's greatest hostess; Duff Cooper, MP for Oldham, and his beautiful wife Diana. The Brownlows, Perry and Kitty. They were older than Honor, more worldly, with a way of speaking and listening and questioning that was entirely new to her. They were rapid in everything – in speech and in thought, impatient of slowness, interrupting each other constantly and often conducting several conversations at once, seemingly able to keep track of exactly what was being said at opposite ends of a table. Beside them, Honor felt thick-tongued and clumsy. She watched carefully to see if Chips saw it too – the ways in which she was gauche and awkward – and was relieved, and grateful, that it seemed he did not.

She placed the photograph in its ornate frame on a table in the corner where she hoped no one would see it. Perhaps she could hide it altogether once Chips had forgotten about it?

Chapter Fourteen

Honor dressed with more care than usual that evening, coming down in a new dress of grey satin that showed her arms and was cut low at the back. Tonight – their first 'proper' dinner party – was to be different, she was determined. A chance to be herself rather than the blushing inarticulate creature Chips' friends so often made her.

Chips was fussing with the drinks tray, ordering Andrews to make something called a sidecar 'with a twist of burned lemon peel. It must be burned, do you understand?' Andrews left, to fetch more lemons, and Honor watched, as Chips took a small paper package from his inner pocket and began to tip white powder into a jug of freshly squeezed juice.

'What are you doing?'

'Just something to make the party go with a bang,' he said, winking at her. 'Keep things lively?'

Honor went and sat on the sofa by the fireplace, resolving not to drink anything Chips offered her.

It was a cold night, with the damp that settles heavy over London in the winter, and that is clever at finding cracks and crevices through which to creep, so that only by banking the fire high and drawing closed every curtain, can it be kept at bay. Sometimes, Honor felt as though her very bones were porous, filling with the chill of London streets and the vague blur of London fogs. She edged closer to the fire that was heaped high with logs and that crackled energetically, throwing out light to bounce across the many shiny surfaces of the room. Chips loved mirrors. He said it was for the way they created 'light from light', though Honor suspected it was his own reflection he loved. And why not? He was more beautiful than ever. Honor did not like mirrors, or rather, she didn't like to catch herself unexpectedly in them. Bad enough when she deliberately looked at herself, to fix a hat or apply lipstick. Then, at least, she could ready herself. An unexpected glimpse showed her, always, someone she didn't recognise. Didn't wish to recognise. She looked again at her photograph, standing in its obscure corner. Beaton hadn't wanted anyone to recognise her either; wreathing her in light and careful shade. Even Chips had done his bit, smothering her with rubies and garnets and the bold patterns of her dress.

Andrews announced their guests, men in evening dress and women trailing furs over their bare arms and shoulders. Chips glided about the room pressing drinks, cigarettes, lighters on them, offering compliments and observations, warming them up with praise, gentle jokes and whatever was in the white powder. There was nothing for Honor to do except sit and watch.

'Are you expecting to get on a horse?' Lady Cunard asked, coming to sit beside her.

Honor was puzzled, then followed Lady Cunard's eyes, to her own knees, which were planted far apart. It was just as her mother sat, and Honor had unconsciously imitated it. She looked around the room then, at the other women. They were, she saw, pressed tightly into themselves, all sharp angles and elegant jutting bones. Diana Cooper was almost contorted, so many times had she wrapped one leg across and around the other. The result was a tiny, angular shape, like a pocket handkerchief tucked away, or paper folded the way the Japanese did, into something tricksy and exquisite. In comparison, there was something gross, Honor felt, about her own frank solidity. She drew her knees neatly together and sat up a little straighter.

'Better,' said Lady Cunard. She had large, bright eyes – eyes that had seen everything, considered everything, asked more of everything – a hooked nose and tiny pursed mouth like the questing beak of a bird. 'You'll have to work to keep up. But you won't mind that. I see that you are devoted to the dear boy, as we all are.'

Only later did Honor think it was curious that Lady Cunard should place her own claim on Chips, and that of his friends, as high – higher – than his wife's.

'It's good that you are so young,' Lady Cunard continued. 'You'll take to it all much more quickly that way. Now, you may call me Emerald.'

'Even though your name is Maud?' Honor said. It was time, she decided, to stand up for herself a little.

Lady Cunard laughed, throwing back her head, and Chips looked over approvingly from his seat by the window, drawn up close beside Duff Cooper.

'I think you and I are going to be friends,' Lady Cunard – Emerald – said, tapping one of Honor's neatly pressed knees with a bony finger. Then, 'I see you have been sitting for your portrait.' She nodded towards the photograph. Honor sighed. Nothing escaped this woman.

'How divine,' Diana Cooper said politely, coming to join them.

Honor thought of how Beaton had posed Diana as a medieval Madonna complete with stone cherub in her arms, and again in a high white satin headdress. Emerald, Lady Cunard – no beauty, in Honor's opinion – he declared 'an exquisite canary-like little blonde'. How he had begged to take Doris' photograph, then begged again, so enraptured had he been with the first set. She remembered how they had all laughed at Beaton and his gushing ways, and was painfully conscious of the difference between those who laughed knowing he had pursued them to be included in his *Book of Beauty*, and those who laughed knowing he had not thought to trouble them in that way.

Feeling shy and gauche among these vivid, flickering creatures, Honor wondered how she could possibly answer Diana. She looked up then, and caught Chips' eye, and he smiled broadly at her. She smiled back. 'Not divine at all,' she said brightly, 'quite the opposite. But Chips insisted,' and she shrugged and Diana shrugged with her. *Men*, the shrug said; *husbands*.

Andrews announced dinner and they went through. The dining room, Honor thought, wasn't pokey a bit, not even with the table let out to its full length. The curtains were drawn and fell in luxurious folds to the floor. There was far too much fabric in them really, but Chips had insisted. 'Nothing worse than meanness in small things,' he said. 'A skimpy curtain is an abomination. Why, Mrs Vanderbilt had yards and yards of cream velvet so that the curtains were like the sails of a yacht, billowing gently.'

Chips began to tell them all about the china plate. 'I bought it in New York, it had belonged to Mrs Rockefeller McCormick. I used to see it when I dined there.' It was important to him, Honor knew, that his friends understood that he had, indeed, been 'someone' at home in America before England. He picked up a delicate side dish, asking them to turn it over and admire the French imperial crown stamped on the back. 'It was made at the order of Napoleon, as a wedding present for his sister Pauline.'

'Fancy buying your own plate,' a sniffy-looking

woman who had been introduced as Lady Milbanke, said. 'How queer.'

'That's quite enough of that,' Emerald snapped at her. 'We are all long past the stage of pretending to be shocked at people buying their own furniture. There simply isn't *time*, any more, for such nonsense.' She tapped the flat of her hand on the table firmly, almost slapping it.

Honor wanted to cheer. It was exactly the sort of thing her mother would have said, only Lady Iveagh would have said it even more bluntly, so that the sniffy woman would have been offended and the others made awkward. Somehow, Emerald didn't have that effect. Instead there was general straightening of spines and throwing back of shoulders. As though they readied themselves for combat.

And indeed, Emerald was like the rough wind, come to shake them all, Honor thought, watching as she challenged, questioned, proposed, making them all, especially the men, work to say something that was original, informed and clever enough to win her approval. Like a storm tearing through a wood, any broken or rotted branches were dragged loose and flung to the earth. She quizzed Duff Cooper on government and when there would be a general election and what he really thought of prime minister Ramsay MacDonald.

They all talked about the world as though they owned it, Honor noticed, as though the conversations they had together around that table were decisive and would shape the future. They had the ear of politicians, princes, royal dukes, as well as composers, novelists, newspapermen and playwrights. They set fashions and made favourites, and they believed that within that dining room, and perhaps a half-dozen others concentrated within a square mile around the finest streets of London, real power resided. Power that wasn't answerable to a fickle thing like democracy. And Honor sat and watched, and marvelled at the turn life had taken, to bring her there and land her safely, so far from the dread world of Mrs Chadwick's balls.

Dinner was many courses: Russian blinis with caviar, served with ice-cold Swedish schnapps, followed by soup, then salmon, an elaborate chicken dish which Chips had spent many hours with the cook over, then pudding and savoury. Every detail of the meal had been planned and revised and tested by Chips, apparently in consultation with Honor but in reality, the decisions were his. In fact, the cook was more his confidant than Honor in these things. For the simple reason that the cook cared, and Honor did not.

'He is tiring of Thelma,' Emerald announced to the table suddenly. 'I see it. He has begun to talk of politics – socialism in particular alarms him – and that is a clear sign that the urgencies of his heart are waning.'

Who was tiring of Thelma? Honor wondered. Who, indeed, was Thelma?

'Perhaps that pinched face and uncouth accent have begun to pale on him,' Chips said. Then Honor understood. Thelma, Lady Furness. Mistress to the Prince of Wales. 'He' therefore must be the prince; 'our little prince

charming of Wales', as Emerald called him, with a familiarity that thrilled Chips.

'Not that he cares for her in any way as he cared for
that poisonous Freda Dudley Ward.' There was venom in
Chips' tone. Freda was rude to him – was rude to almost
everyone; it was her very rudeness that had enchanted the
prince for fifteen years, or so it was believed – and as a
result he couldn't bear her. 'Freda is still his only real *amour*.

'He should be married by now,' Chips continued, '– his
position demands it – and I had the perfect match. Princess
Marina. And indeed it would have taken,' he was starting
to sound aggrieved, 'had Freda not stopped it, selfishly and
short-sightedly. It was her duty to see the prince married
as much as it is any of ours.'

Honor had heard this so many times – how he had
engineered a perfect marriage, only for Freda to spoil it.

'She could have been Queen of England,' Chips continued,
peevish.

'It would not have suited her,' Diana Cooper said dreamily.

Honor wondered how she could sound so certain.

'You mustn't mind her,' Emerald said in a low voice,
as though she had read Honor's mind. 'She dabbled with
acting for a time, and played Queen Elizabeth in a dreadful
film some years ago. Since then, she isn't always certain
that she *isn't*, after all, royal.'

Honor giggled and looked again at Diana, who wore
a dress of rose-coloured silk, a band of the same-coloured
silk threaded through her short curls. The front of her
dress was low, and around her neck she wore a single

strand of pearls that reached to her waist. She ate, Honor saw, nothing. Nothing at all. Did not even touch her knife and fork, which remained neatly to the sides of her plate.

'She's very beautiful,' Honor said.

'She is. And very clever too. Which is good, because otherwise she'd be a frightful bore. Beautiful, stupid women are the worst.'

Honor looked then at the man opposite her, Diana's husband, Duff Cooper, with his baby head and too-big forehead.

'He looks better with a hat,' Emerald whispered, following her gaze.

Honor giggled. 'They seem an unlikely couple,' she said.

'Less unlikely than you might think. Though it is true that Diana married him out of loyalty and sorrow and regret.' Emerald lingered on the words, drawing them slowly out to burnish their full meaning. 'He was the last of the brilliant friends of her youth. The others were killed during the Great War. Only Duff was left. It wasn't he that she loved, but he was all there was. Loyalty is one of her many appealing qualities. Do you know what he wrote to her, before they married?'

'What?'

'"I hope everyone you like better than me will die very soon." She showed the letter to me.'

'Goodness. What did she say to that?'

'She said, "They already have." And then she married him, and has been devoted ever since, although everyone is in love with her. It is the fashion, to be in love with Diana, who loves no one but her brilliant, ugly husband.'

'And him?'

'Loves all women.' Emerald gave a sharp laugh. 'Makes the most frightful passes. Don't let yourself be alone in a taxi with him.'

Honor looked again at Duff Cooper. To her, he looked square and plain and unimaginative and old. Surely anyone who grew that boring, bristly little moustache was incapable of writing something so violent? Further down the table, Diana brimmed with mirth and absurdity. Her eyes sparkled merrily as expressions chased one another across her face as fast as shadows. She was eager, haughty, petulant, impish, all in rapid succession. Looking up, she saw Honor staring, and winked.

Emerald began talking about a seance she had attended, and once more the entire table turned to her and listened. She had, Honor thought, the kind of energy that replenished itself. Her father would know the type she meant. It wasn't a restless energy – such as Maureen had, or Chips, who was energetic and inert by turns – but rather a steady, reliable, repetitive kind of energy. She wondered could she ever learn it. And if Chips would want her to.

Watching Emerald, and Chips' obvious admiration for her, made Honor worry about all the ways in which she was not like her. She resolved to listen more closely when he laid forth his plans and dissected the bits of society that interested him. To try to be more informed of his causes.

After all, if their greatest closeness was to be in the drawing room, not the bedroom, then that is where she would concentrate her efforts.

Chapter Fifteen

Later, they went to the Embassy Club, although Honor was dropping with tiredness and astonished that anyone would want supper after that dinner. They sat in one of the square booths below the balcony, and Honor watched as Chips, conscious that theirs was the best seat in the house, settled back against the padded banquette and looked happily around him.

After a while, someone asked Honor to dance, and by the time she came back to their table, the prince himself had joined them. He had taken Honor's seat, a fact he ignored, just as he ignored her. She had met him several times at Elveden, where her father kept up the shooting only because the king had said he hoped he would. Each time, when they'd met, the prince had looked through her while lavishing his legendary charm on her mother and father. She was not, she well knew, his type. If the fashion was for slim women, the prince took that to extremes. Lady Furness was slender, Freda Dudley Ward almost boyish, with a neat, shuttered little face and tiny ears. They were clever at making jokes – rather funny ones at that – and passing them off as the prince's, even to him, almost as though they were ventriloquists, Honor thought.

The prince didn't even turn his head to acknowledge her presence, and Honor stood awkwardly until Duff Cooper rose politely and offered his chair. She thought of what she would say to her mother the next day when they spoke, as they did every day, either by telephone or in person. Often both. Because for all the charm the prince turned on Lady Iveagh, she remained resolutely unimpressed by him. 'Those strange, light eyes,' she'd mused, 'indifferent and knowing at once.'

It was one of the few points on which she and Chips diverged. Willing to bow to her in almost everything else – because he admired her, and hated conflict, and agreeing with Lady Iveagh was a sure way to a peaceful life – Chips was iron-clad in his devotion to royalty. All royalty, but chiefly the man who would one day be King of England. 'I've seen what a sad old deposed Hungarian princess can do to Chips,' Lady Iveagh had said indulgently. 'I won't ask him to give up his infatuation with the Prince of Wales.' Indeed, Honor had seen Chips, misty-eyed, at the Trooping of the Colour, and heard the husky quiver in his voice as he said 'God bless His Majesty' quietly as the old king passed by on his stocky black horse. He thrilled to princes and archdukes as though they were the sun and he a plant that could make something vital from their light.

The prince leaned back in the booth now, one arm resting lightly along the top of the banquette. With the other, he tapped his cigarette repeatedly against the massive black marble ashtray, as though any ash that might be left to gather at its tip would be interpreted as a sign of sloppiness. He was, she thought, unknowable, certainly unpredictable; wrapped so deeply within his own concerns – even though these often appeared trifling; questions of golf, or polo – as to be unaware of what went on around him. But then, the truth was that nothing went on around him except the furthering of his concerns, which became the concerns of those who orbited him.

He sat with one leg crossed carelessly over the other, and Honor admired the sharp crease that ran the length of his trousers, and the exactness of the point at which the hem met his highly polished shoes. She saw Chips look admiringly too. Beneath his own well-cut clothes – those rows and rows of Lesley & Roberts suits that gave him such joy – Chips was heavier in build. 'I suspect you of having been sporty as a child,' she had once said. He had been appalled. 'Do I look hearty?' he'd asked. 'Tell the truth. Do I?' And she'd had to protest repeatedly that she had been teasing and no, he didn't.

'. . . I hope and believe there will not be another war,' the prince was saying, in a voice that had learned to be petulant as well as pompous. 'But if there is' – he held up a finger, as though to say something startling – 'we must be on the winning side.' He looked around, waiting for them all to nod solemnly at what he said. 'And that will be German, not French.' He tapped extra hard at his cigarette.

Chips agreed enthusiastically. 'I find everything German to be superior, sir,' he assured the prince, who ignored him, carrying on to describe Germany as 'prosperous, industrious, agreeable', saying, 'I know it well. It echoes with work and song,' so that Honor wanted to laugh, so much did he sound like he was talking about a land in a fantastical story – an Elfland or Oz. But the prince was certain – he knew it in his blood, he said – that the English people were kindred souls to the German people and would find their common ground with them as long as they were not led wrong. Chips agreed enthusiastically. Beside them, Duff Cooper, who had squeezed into the booth – the prince reluctantly making room for him – stayed silent.

'That's a jolly pretty girl,' the prince said then, looking at a tiny elfin creature dancing nearby with a dark-haired man. She was light and graceful in his arms. 'Who is she?'

'Why don't I find out, sir,' Emerald said, getting to her feet.

Honor noticed that when the prince was actually present, Emerald was less intimate, not casual at all really.

Within minutes, the girl was brought over to meet him, blushing and smiling. Close up, Honor saw that her shoes were cheap and her dress bright but badly made. Perhaps the prince saw the same things, because after a few desultory questions – 'Do you golf?' 'Have you been to Bermuda?' – he grew bored and turned away, and the whole party turned with him as though they were a flock on the wing, so that the girl was quickly left standing alone, ignored, twisting her evening bag in her hands.

'Let me walk you back to your party,' Duff Cooper said, and Honor liked him for being the only one to notice the girl's discomfort.

She looked at Chips, hoping to signal that she was tired and could they go, but he didn't look back at her, and so she leaned in and whispered, 'I have a pain. Do you mind taking me home?'

'We have to wait for the prince to leave,' he whispered back.

'But he's not in our party,' she protested. 'He joined us.'

'He did.' And Chips leaned back luxuriously and cast another look around the club, to see who was watching them.

By the time they left, dawn was breaking over the city, and the pain Honor had claimed was real. She rested her head against the taxi seat and sighed. 'Now that we have our first "proper" dinner out of the way, I hope we can be quiet for a jolly long time.'

'I have invited the prince for two weeks' time. He didn't give me an answer, of course. But if I can plan something truly charming, I have hopes that he will come.' Chips spoke excitedly, as though he hadn't heard what Honor had just said, and his eyes glittered, with drink and perhaps the effect of his white powder. He took her hand and pressed it. 'There is nothing we cannot do,' he said. Then, 'Perhaps, when we have a son, we will consider David as a name? I feel it would be an elegant tribute.'

Honor wished he would not, so very often, talk about the children they would have. She wasn't, she told herself, superstitious – not a bit – but how was it right for him to talk so openly, with such lavishness, of the many he wanted, when as yet there were no signs of even one?

He put an arm about her shoulders then, and Honor, whose head had been resting quite comfortably, had to readjust herself, which wasn't easy with his arm now heavy on her. In the end she laid her cheek against his shoulder, where he patted her head absent-mindedly with his other hand.

Chapter Sixteen

'Why did you never tell me how wonderful Germany is?' Honor asked when Doris called to her the next day. 'The prince couldn't stop talking about it last night. When he speaks of it, it sounds like a cross between Oz and Wonderland – a place that "echoes with work and song".' She laughed. 'I wondered why your cousins would ever want to leave.'

'I imagine his Germany is quite a different place to theirs,' Doris said dryly. 'These days, it seems they are Jewish first, German very much second. At least in Germany. Here, they are just "bloody foreigners".'

Honor laughed, as though she had made a joke. Doris considered, as she often did these days, how much to tell Honor of what she knew – the picnic in the Tiergarten where they had sat on the ground, each one of them diminished though they would not say it; the tales sent back from Tante Hannah in Berlin, which were repeated to Doris in her mother's many letters. About the way the mood on the streets, and in the shops and schools, had changed. How ugly, now, were the words spoken, the looks given. The jostling and discourtesy that were everyday events, and how a deep kind of disgust had worked its way into the daily interactions they held with those around them, even into friendships of long standing.

They say it will blow over if they are patient, her mother had written in her most recent letter, *but I think they say it because they hope it. They are too close to what's happening and cannot see what I see – this is not a time of upheaval reaching its end. It is a beginning*. But would Honor understand if she were to explain? Not unless she explained so much more, things Doris barely understood herself.

They were, she suddenly thought, like Mrs Benton and Miss Wilkes – setting forth their claims, but always dictated by others: by Chips, by Doris' mother. No thought of their own: '*Chips says . . .*'; '*My mother writes . . .*'

'I suppose the prince's *everywhere* is different to ours,' she said instead.

'I should think so,' Honor said. 'For all that he says he hates ceremony and formality, what he really hates is when those things interrupt what he wants to do. He hates it even more if others forget what is due to him.' She giggled. Then sighed. 'Lord, how tired I am. Do you mind if we don't go out but just sit here quietly?'

'Not at all. Surely the point of you being married is you get to do what you wish.'

'If only,' Honor said with a yawn. They settled themselves in the drawing room with a dish of crumpets and Honor ordered that a jug of vinegar-and-honey water be made and brought up to them. 'It's disgusting, but Mamma swears by it, for the complexion, and so we will try to drink some. Not that your complexion needs any such help.'

'Sweet, but not at all true. Not today.' It was, Doris thought, the simple truth. For once, she looked tired, and she felt it. So many nights out, so many days. But it was not doing that tired her, it was waiting. Waiting for something to happen. For someone to happen. Her mother was right – it wasn't worthy. But what else was she to do?

They were still in the drawing room, having abandoned the vinegar-and-honey water for cocktails, when Chips came home, Bundi at his heels, with a blue enamel snuffbox he had bought, 'because it was too pretty to leave it'.

'But where will you put it?' Honor asked, having examined the snuffbox without much interest. 'There isn't any space.' She handed it back. 'Sometimes I think we will drown among Chips' *bibelots*,' she said to Doris.

'Yes, but we won't always live here,' Chips said smoothly. 'Soon we shall move to somewhere far larger, and then we will need more beautiful things.' He helped himself to a drink, then settled himself on the sofa beside Honor to recount the rest of the day. 'I walked with Hore-Belisha,' he said, satisfaction rising up within him the way yeast bread will rise in a warm, damp spot, Doris thought.

'Junior Minister. He is a demi-Jew, you know.' He looked around brightly at them. 'A brilliant speaker and an engaging fellow, but over-eager for publicity, and with the Semitic thrust for self-promotion.'

'He is all-Jewish,' Doris said, before she could stop herself.

'What's that?'

'Both his parents are Jewish. From Manchester.'

'A friend of yours?' Chips asked archly.

'I don't know him.'

'You know a lot about him, if indeed you don't know him.'

'I know only a very little. What anyone could know; certainly anyone who goes for walks with him.'

Chips looked at her, and might have been about to say something, only Honor interrupted. 'Ring for more tea, there's a dear.'

That evening, as she dressed to go out, Doris thought back to what Chips had said – more, the way he had said it. The casual contempt in his voice when he'd said 'Semitic thrust for self-promotion'. She put it in her mind alongside Elizabeth Ponsonby's friend, Sebastian Wright: '*Spectacles, testicles, wallet and watch*. . .' Was this the kind of thing her mother meant when she wrote about the disgust towards her family in Berlin? Was this where it began?

All over again, Doris wanted a new name, not Coates. Rather, she thought, she wanted an old name; a name that came with certainty and security so that no one would ever ask again, '. . . yes, but who *is* she?'

* * *

The party was large and hot and not terribly entertaining. It began to empty sooner than was usual for such things, and Doris thought she might slip away and go to bed. But her friends had others ideas. Beside the front door, she found a group gathering around Maureen. 'We're going on. The Embassy. You'll come?' Maureen said. It wasn't a question, more a command, and Doris, irritated, opened her mouth to say no. She was bored. She wanted to go back to Curzon Street and be alone with Mimi curled up on her lap. But after all, if she did that, there was nothing that could happen; who would she meet at Curzon Street, only Mabel or Mrs Benton or Miss Wilkes? And so she said, 'Of course,' and watched a young man with a too-short haircut leap forward to say he would get her fur.

They went in several cars, all of them packed tightly together so that there was much laughter as they went around corners and were flung this way and that in a hot mass of sequined dresses, feathers, small beaded evening bags and carefully brushed-out curls.

They tumbled out of the cars and towards the Embassy. A burly man moved to block their entrance, then said, 'Oh, good evening, didn't see you there, Miss Coates. On you go.'

'How is your wife, Albert?' Doris asked, hanging back a little to hear his answer.

'Much better, thank you.'

'I'm glad. Just a cold, then?'

'So it seems,' he said. 'She gave out to me for coming in noisily, night before last, so I reckon she's back to herself again.' He laughed at that and Doris laughed too.

Then, because she had held back, she found herself swept up in a new group arriving just behind her, all of them as loud and excitable as the people she had come with. She knew one of the girls vaguely – the younger sister of a girl she sometimes went about with – and nodded to her. Then to the young man beside her, who smiled and said, 'Please, let me' as they came to the heavy glass-paned doors with their long, curving wooden handles. He grasped one of these and heaved it open for Doris, saying cheerfully, 'You'd think they didn't want anyone in at all.'

'Perhaps it's only the very strong who are welcome,' Doris replied.

Beyond the outer doors was a dark corridor lit with small red lamps that glowed like hot coals mounted onto the walls at badly conceived intervals.

'The road to hell is paved with terrible lighting,' her new friend said cheerfully as they walked through the rosy gloom.

Doris laughed, and even in the dim light saw him blush.

'Doris!' one of her friends called her over as they entered. 'There you are! Come quick, for there is a man here who has brought a python and he swears it can squeeze itself up small enough to slither through a woman's necklace.'

'Well, it's not slithering through mine,' Doris said. Then, 'Who's that?' she asked, looking back at the young man.

'No idea. Ask one of the chaps.'

So Doris did.

'Lord Bertram Lewis,' came the answer. 'Bertie. Year behind me at Eton. Friendly sort of chap.'

He was a friendly sort of chap. Soon he came over and asked Doris to dance, and told her that she danced divinely, but not in a way that was excessive or embarrassing, rather as though he were congratulating her on something small and inconsequential – not missing a bus, say, or stepping over a muddy patch on the ground. And he danced well himself, but in the same sort of way – as if it mattered little to him, beyond the easy discharging of a duty. And when he stepped on her toe – they always stepped on your toes – he apologised without looking as though he wanted to die, or as if he were insultingly indifferent. What's more, he made her laugh again. Twice.

'I say, do you think the poor thing will be safe?' he said as he led her back to her friends, looking at Maureen, who had wrapped the python around her neck and was pretending to kiss it while its tongue flickered in and out, so that everyone around her screeched with disgust.

'Maureen is tough as old boots.'

'I meant the snake . . .' He watched her happily as she laughed at that, and when it was time to leave – because it was dawn and the burly doorman had come inside and begun firmly insisting that it was 'time to go, folks' – he said, 'I'd like to see you home.'

'I'd like that,' Doris said. 'Let me get my things.'

He didn't have a car and so he flagged a taxi and sat a polite distance from her, and when she told him about Curzon Street and Mrs Benton, he didn't say, 'How odd,' the way so many did, but rather, 'That seems a jolly good plan,' warmly.

He saw her to the door, and stood at the bottom of the steps until she was inside and the door closed – she knew because she slipped quietly to the dining room window and watched him. And Doris went up to her rooms feeling, not lonely, but sort of *pleased*, she thought. Warm and happy. As though someone had tucked a rug around her.

Chapter Seventeen

'Hold this for me, will you?'

Lady Iveagh handed Honor a pile of blankets. They were coarse-made and felt scratchy against her bare wrists so that Honor pulled the sleeves of her coat down and the tops of her gloves higher to protect them.

'Where are we taking them?'

They were in the drawing room at Grosvenor Place. Honor had called to see her mother, and been instantly asked to accompany her on a mission.

'To the Paddington Street tenements.' Lady Iveagh stood at the window, watching the street. They were waiting for the motorcar and it was one of her obsessions that the chauffeur not be kept waiting, in case he wasted petrol by idling the motor. So she would watch until she saw the silver hood of the Rolls-Royce rounding the corner, then go instantly down. 'Until the landlord can be made to fix the roof, it is the best that can be done. Tell me about your evening.'

So Honor told her: Lady Cunard's meddling cleverness, the way they all let her take the lead on everything; Diana Cooper and how she didn't eat a thing – 'Starvation cure,' Lady Iveagh said, nodding wisely. 'Nothing but water for days at a time. All the rage. But I don't advise it' – then the Embassy Club and the prince's arrival; how tired she had been, and Chips so unwilling to leave.

'You must have your own life,' Lady Iveagh said vigorously, taking back the blankets. 'Your own interests and amusements, and friends. Lord Iveagh and I have much that we do in common, and we each have interests that we keep apart. There is no need to be your husband's shadow.'

'But Chips seems to want it.'

Honor didn't say how hard she found it to discover her own 'interests and amusements'. How, outside of her husband and Doris, there was so little she found to occupy or engage her. So that it was easier, much, to simply drift along with his plans. Chips, she thought with a smile, always knew exactly what he wanted.

'It is because you are newly married. He will soon settle. Once you have a child . . .'

'He has been talking to you again, hasn't he?'

'He is concerned, that is all.'

'It has been less than a year.'

'Yes, but he is eager to begin. He is older than you, don't forget.'

Honor's mouth twitched and she thought of saying, *Yes, only we don't know exactly how much older*, but she didn't. Lady Iveagh – although herself the very opposite of deferential to her own husband – disliked anything she thought of as wifely impertinence in others. She was constantly critical of Maureen for being rude to Duff, and refused to see how much Duff enjoyed his wife's energetic barbs.

'What harm to see Doctor Gilliatt?' her mother continued.

'None, I suppose. But not yet,' Honor said. She hated the idea of being examined by a doctor, but even more she hated that her husband and her mother had discussed her in a way that was so intimate behind her back. The thought made her feel as though something had crawled in under her skin and wriggled there. She knew exactly how they would have done it – with an excess of matter-of-factness. Her mother prided herself on not being squeamish, and had been involved in the breeding of cattle for long enough that any overt delicacy was long gone, while Chips – already he had shocked Honor by his familiarity with things that she had thought were for her alone. The secrets of her monthly cycle, the times when she was indisposed and must rest – he knew them and anticipated them more even than she did.

If the passion of their married lives was less than she had hoped – and it was less – then that, too, had something to do with it. It was . . . indelicate, was the best she could come up with. His familiarity made her feel crude, almost bovine. As though she were not a creature of mood and air, but rather a very solid one of blood and bone; of fat and flesh and sweat. No woman, no matter how forthright, wished to feel that, she thought wryly.

'Very well. A few more months, perhaps . . .' Lady Iveagh said. 'A few weeks in Italy may be just what you need. Now, here comes Banks with the motorcar. Let us go down quickly.'

At Paddington Street, they got out, and Lady Iveagh sent Banks to park and told him he could wait in the car. Knowing how the street children would crowd around and pester him, Honor felt sorry for the chauffeur, but he simply said, 'Very good, m'lady.'

'You have the blankets?'

Honor did, their hairy weight draped over her arm. 'Yes.'

The street was busy with children, who ignored them – as Honor had expected, they ran straight for the silver motorcar and began touching the sides, the wheels, the winged lady on the hood. She could hardly blame them. In that tunnel of grey, where even the pigeons seemed covered in soot and cobwebs, beating their wings dully as though slowed by their dusty covering, the motorcar was the only thing that shone. The day had been cold and dark at Grosvenor Place; here, it was as though dawn hadn't bothered pushing back night at all but had allowed it to remain, only just diluting it slightly. She looked at the houses that reared up from the pavement on either side of her, shooting skywards at an angle so that they seemed to lean in towards one another, nodding in on either side of the narrow street to almost meet in the middle, denying the sky, the wind, any light that might have softened and freshened.

The house they went to was tall and stooped. The front door was open and so they walked straight into a hall with a high ceiling and battered wooden boards on the floor. A bucket of water with a stringy mop stuck into it stood in one corner and there was a smell of lye soap that caught at the back of Honor's throat. Their heels made little noise on the floor, so rotten and soft was the wood. The walls were splotched with damp in uneven spreading stains and from the ceiling a bare bulb hung. It flickered as they walked.

'Up we go,' Lady Iveagh said. She walked up the very centre of the scuffed wooden stairs that curved ahead of them into the darker upper floors, touching neither the banister on one side nor the wall on the other. Honor followed her but trailed a hand along the banister, before she realised how uncertainly it was fixed to the spindles and let it go. There was a smell of sodden newspaper and cold soot.

On the first floor Lady Iveagh rapped at a door on the street side of a dark hallway and, without waiting, pushed it and went in. An iron bedstead dominated the room like a ship in dock. On it, three children sat under a blanket playing some kind of game with empty cotton thread spools. A pile of clothes was heaped on a wooden table by the large window looking onto the street. Beside it, a woman sat stitching in the thin grey light that came in through the window, her hands moving quickly. At her feet was a battered cradle and in it a baby, who cried without much energy. The woman stood quickly when she saw them and ducked at the knees, a sort of odd little curtsey, then sat again. She ignored the children in the bed and the baby.

Lady Iveagh took the blankets from Honor and put them on the bed, whereupon one of the children, a girl, began pulling them about, trying to spread them evenly across all. She wore a blue gingham dress with sleeves that were too short so that her wrists stuck out, white and bony from beneath the frayed cuffs. With a start, Honor recognised the dress. It had once been hers. When she had owned it, it had a graceful ruffled neck, but that was gone now, torn off to leave a square-cut line that was harsh against the girl's white skin.

The woman parked her needle carefully in the jacket she was mending and pushed the heap of clothes to one side of the table. Into the space she had cleared, Lady Iveagh unpacked her basket – a loaf of bread, butter, jars of something that looked like oatmeal, a plate of sliced tongue. 'How are we today?' she asked. The children didn't answer but the woman stood again from her chair.

'The same,' she said. 'He's still in the fever hospital. Islington. I couldn't see him even if I wanted to.'

The baby began to cry harder. 'Pick up that child,' Lady Iveagh directed Honor, as she began cutting bread. The girl who had spread the blankets got down off the bed and came to the table. She began capably buttering the slices Lady Iveagh had cut, so that Honor felt more than usually useless. She reached down into the basket and picked up the baby. A boy, naked except for a yellow woollen blanket and a dirty white vest. Picking the child up only made him cry more, and she had no idea what to do with him. He smelt horrible – the acrid tang of old urine, overlaid with something sweetish that was worse, so that she didn't want to press him any closer into herself. Under the scant blond hair on his head his scalp was crusted in something scabby. She held him stiffly, at an angle to herself, and jiggled her arms a bit. The child cried harder, staring not at her but at his mother, who ignored him. Honor wished she could press him to her chest, wrap her arms tight around him so that he was warm and safe, and croon to him as she had seen other women do with babies. It was clearly what the child wanted. He strained in her stiff arms, trying to reach closer to her. But she couldn't. The truth was, he repulsed her. She kept her arms stiff, and a gap between her body and the child. She held her face away so as to breathe less of the rancid smell and longed to set him down.

'Give him to me.' The girl who had been buttering bread came and took the child out of Honor's arms.

Because the girl wore what had once been her dress, Honor found she could not but compare them – the girl's capable care with her own disgusted recoil. She couldn't have been more than eight, even allowing for what a scarcity of food had done to her size and height. She dragged the blanket more firmly around him, hoisted the child on her hip and put her finger in his mouth, to stop him crying. The finger was filthy and Honor started forward to say, 'Don't.' But she restrained herself. Everything was filthy. The child's face, his ragged yellow blanket, the room. What harm could that finger possibly do? The child sucked greedily for a moment, then almost immediately started to cry again, whipping his head around as Honor had seen calves do when the milking pail was taken away.

'What did you bring for him?' the girl asked her. She breathed heavily through her mouth, as though her nose was blocked.

'I'm not sure. My mother . . .' Honor gestured towards Lady Iveagh, who was putting slices of tongue on the buttered bread.

The girl gave her a withering look. 'He needs milk.'

'In the basket,' Lady Iveagh said without looking up.

Sure enough, there was a bottle of milk leaning upright against the wicker side. Honor fished it out and stood holding it. She was afraid if she handed the bottle to the girl, she would be given the baby in return. But the girl reached out, took the bottle from her, hoisted the child higher on her hip and went to a dresser in the far corner of the room where she took out a pewter mug and splashed the milk into it. By now the child was yelling and jerking against her, trying to grab at the bottle with his two hands. As soon as she put the mug close to him he took tight hold and began to drink noisily. The girl hoisted him up again where he had slipped in his agitation, and went back to the table.

'You,' she said to the children in the bed. 'Come over here.' She watched them critically as they got down off the bed and approached the table.

When the children were seated, and the baby back in his cradle, crying again but less than before, Lady Iveagh repacked her basket, took a few coins from her purse and gave them to the woman, who pushed them deep into the pocket of her drab dress. 'I'll call again,' Lady Iveagh said.

'How do you know who to visit?' Honor asked as they walked back down the stairs.

'You have to wait to be asked. Not everyone here needs our help. Some are managing quite nicely.'

Honor thought of the dark hallways, the wet smell of cabbage and soot, the crying children and ones who didn't bother. How could anyone there be managing 'nicely'?

'How do they ask? If they do want help?'

'It's Fr Blyth they speak to. He will tell the Women's Committee and that is how I will hear of it. Usually, as you know, I don't come myself. One can't do everything,' briskly. 'But the committee are short this month. So many have influenza. Half of London seems down with it.' She sounded disapproving; of weakness, no doubt.

Back home at St James's Place, Honor found Doris waiting for her and reading the *Tatler*. 'Come and listen to this description of your cousin Maureen's dress: "silver net laid over black tulle, sprinkled with seed pearls –"' Then 'Pooh!' Doris wrinkled her nose. 'You've been Ministering, haven't you? I can smell it.'

'I have.'

'Where?'

'Paddington Street.'

'The worst slums of all. How was it?'

'Alright, I suppose. We brought food, blankets. A family where the father is in the fever hospital and the mother must take in mending while he isn't earning. One must do what one can.' Honor tried to sound saintly, or at least matter-of-fact, the way Lady Iveagh would.

'Must one? I must not. And what you must now do is go and have your bath. You smell too awful. I shall ask them to keep tea.'

'Would you? That would be kind. It was rather . . .'

'I'm sure it was.' Doris went back to her magazine. '*Seed pearls* . . .' Honor heard her say as she shut the door behind her.

Later, Honor tried to tell Chips about the baby – how it had disgusted her, the revulsion she had felt at it in her arms, how obvious it was that the child wanted to be held closer. The way he had squirmed and tried to wriggle into her, and how violently she had wanted to put him down, get away from him. The relief when the girl took him and the strange sense of comparison she had felt.

'I didn't feel maternal at all, darling,' she said.

'Of course you didn't,' he agreed enthusiastically. 'How could you, with that sort of baby.'

'But surely any baby . . .'

'Not at all. You wait. When it's your very own baby, then you'll see.'

But Honor couldn't believe him. Surely, if one was to care

for babies, one would care for all babies? Perhaps especially a poor neglected baby like that one? She remembered again the corrugated scab on the child's scalp, and shuddered.

'But a *baby*, darling . . . It's not his fault he's hungry and poor and terribly dirty. Oh, if anything, I feel I should have been more inclined to love him, because he needed it so. His sister, only a child herself, seemed able.' She tried to explain.

But Chips couldn't see it her way. For him, there was nothing at all surprising in her inability to love a poor baby from a slum. In fact, he behaved as if her disgust did her credit. And so Honor, unable to explain what she meant, unable really to understand it fully, put it away, this small fear that she wasn't a suitable person to be a mother.

'I see you are writing your diary again?' Honor changed the subject. In fact, she suspected him of keeping score of the days she was indisposed.

'I am.'

'Does this mean you are no longer content?' It was a throw-away question, not the one she meant, but so much easier.

'Certainly not.' He bent and kissed the top of her head. 'I am the happiest man alive. But there is so much for me to record. It would be wrong to let all be forgotten. I tell you, my dearest, we are living through some mighty interesting times.'

She laughed at the solemn tone – who exactly did he think would be put out if he, Chips, didn't write what he saw and heard? – but was glad to see him so full of purpose. He had recently complained of not sleeping, of indigestion, saying that he wished to eat simple food, so she had spoken to the cook and asked for plain, nursery-style fare only to realise that they were out to dinner and lunch nearly every day.

'You would think that about any time you lived through,' she said fondly. 'It is your interest that makes these times interesting.'

'How lucky I am,' he said, taking her hand in his and pressing it. 'How happy. I have a wife who is so good to me, a dog I love, friends and companions to entertain. We want only one thing, and we shall have it. Of course we shall have it.'

And because of his eagerness, the completeness of his faith in their future, Honor agreed to see Doctor Gilliatt. It was only much later that she thought about the order and intensity of his affections.

Chapter Eighteen

It was like staring at the world through a glass of chartreuse, Doris thought sleepily, as the train from Paddington chugged solidly towards Bournemouth, where she must change. All that thick sooty London air diluted and diluted until it was made sparkling and fresh, the grey of London streets swapped for the benediction of fields that were the sturdy green-and-gold of late spring, and hills that sloped and tumbled gradually instead of the sharp heights of London walls and London warehouses. No wonder her mother disliked the city, she thought. Indifferent to the thrill of nightclubs and the bar at the Ritz, to the lure of shops and the Harrods shoe department, Esther liked only the theatre and opera, 'and even that not enough to tolerate the rest very often', as she said.

Looking out at all that fresh-wrung green, Doris understood; a little, anyway.

At Bournemouth she got out and waited for the smaller train that would bring her as far as Wareham, where her father's car would meet her and bring her to Weymouth. The journey was so long, no wonder she made it only rarely. But she had begun to hear a note of strain in her mother's voice when they spoke on the telephone. A very faint pause before she answered the question – 'How's father? – where there had never, before, been any pause. And so when her mother suggested she come home for a few weeks, saying, 'It is time you welcomed your cousins, now that they are here,' Doris had sighed and said, 'Very well. I will catch the morning train on Saturday.'

And here she was, she thought, missing a very grand party indeed, something that had caused her friends to wail, 'But you simply can't! How can we have any fun without you?' And, slyly, 'What about poor Bertie? He will be inconsolable!' Hardly inconsolable, Doris had protested. But she hoped he would be at least a little sorry. Since that night at the Embassy, he had taken her out several times – to lunch, the Royal Academy, a day's racing – and had tried to be the person who brought her home from parties. He had even bought a little car – 'More like a sardine can on wheels,' he said – the better to be able to drop her here and there. He was funny and kind and Doris felt easy in his company. It was not so much, yet, but not nothing either.

* * *

'Dotty!' Her sisters and brother came to meet the car at the bottom of the driveway, jumping down from the stone gateposts where they had been sitting – two little girls on one post, her little brother on the other – probably for half an hour, she knew, watching for the lights of the motorcar in the gathering obscurity of late afternoon that would tell them she had arrived. Doris opened the car door and they piled in, full of news.

'The kitten is grown so big! She caught her first mouse and Mamma says she will be a champion mouser and so we may keep her and not send her to the stables.' That was Marianne.

'I can do a standing trot on my pony, you must let me show you,' said Isabel.

'Did you bring us anything?' asked Maxim, her little brother, who knew very well that Doris never came without sweets and little presents for them.

'You spoil them,' her mother said an hour later as Doris, seated by the fire in the drawing room, handed out tins of butterscotch and Turkish delight to the little ones after they had come in from playing outside – a terrific game involving tennis racquets and a croquet ball that had been fast and occasionally painful. Doris had laughed so much her stomach hurt.

'I know, but it is so easy to make them happy.' She looked at the children, now busily dividing the sweets into three equal piles, with Marianne's kitten curled up beside her. She sighed luxuriously. Whatever she said – and even believed – while in London about the inconvenience of Dorset, home

– this house, where she had been a child and then a young woman – was forever a place that brought about a sigh, of relief and repose. The room was over-full of things – of flowers, books, paintings, plants that her mother had brought in from the garden to tend to – and was more comfortable than it was elegant. But it smelt as it ever had – beeswax, lavender, the binding of old books, faint traces of her father's cigars, the rose otto her mother rubbed into her face at night. 'So, what has been happening? Where are all the cousins?'

'They are in their own houses.'

'They have their own houses?'

'Your father has finished renovations on the rectory and two of the estate cottages. They are small, but they will do,' Esther shrugged a little, 'for now.'

'So what is the trouble? I know there is trouble, I hear it in your voice when we speak.'

'Work. Jobs.'

'Meaning?'

'It isn't enough that they have a place to live, they must have work too. And they know the business of the factories, as well as anyone.'

'But,' Doris asked, 'surely they will go back to Germany as soon as it's safe?'

'And when will that be?'

'Soon. Chips says these are only teething pains; a new political party asserting itself, and will soon settle.'

'Hmm,' her mother said. 'And in the meantime, they are here. But Harold says he has no jobs to give them. He says those jobs are promised.'

Doris understood – her mother did not. The jobs were promised. To the sons and brothers and cousins of the men who currently worked in them, to the people of the villages around Cranscourt Manor, who relied on Mr Coates to employ them and treat them well. There weren't spare jobs, like spare men at a dance, ready to be pressed forward into service, simply to ensure the German cousins had something to call their own.

But her mother wouldn't see it, and this, Doris saw immediately, was the source of the strain between her parents.

'She knows as much about the running of the factory as I do,' Doris' father said that evening when it was just the two of them after Esther had gone to bed. 'How can she think there are jobs just for the asking? Good jobs too; she won't accept that they should do anything that is beneath them. In any case, they don't need money, not while they live in my house.'

'I thought they didn't live in your house? Mother said you renovated the rectory and some cottages for them.'

'I did, and so we don't have to have discussion of the symphonies of César Franck or the books of Thomas Mann at every mealtime.' He smiled. 'But the tradesmen and victuallers bring their bills to me so that now I support three households, not one.' He looked worried.

'It won't be for very long,' Doris said, adding, as she had to her mother, 'Chips says it's teething pains.'

'I hope he's right. But I fear he is not. In any case, in the meantime, I am to support them, and employ them.

'They depend on you.'

'I see that. But so do the people round about here, many of whom have depended on the mine for generations, and now the factory. There aren't more jobs around here, no one to employ the men that I do not. I have responsibilities to them, too, and your mother will not see that.'

'I think it's more that she cannot allow herself to see that. The needs of her family are so desperate that she cannot allow others to have needs that interfere with that.'

'It'll make trouble,' her father said grimly. 'That's what she won't understand. Already she pays too much attention to what is written and said about Jewish people. She says she must "keep an eye", but I think it's unhealthy.' He scratched his chin where the work of the morning's razor was beginning to be undone. 'I wish she'd leave it alone.'

'It makes her feel safe, to understand the way the wind blows.'

'Well, it makes me feel uneasy. Things are said, and written, but what does that mean, any of it? It's only words, and outside of periodicals and newspapers, life goes on as ever.'

'It's not only words, not in Germany and Italy. Not now.'

She thought back to the Tiergarten, the hasty picnic on the hard ground. The way her cousin had said, 'Jews can't sit there now.' The newspaper reports of broken windows and beatings. It wouldn't last, but for now anyway, it was not only words.

'That's Germany, and Italy,' her father said, with feeling. 'Not England. Fascism is not English.'

Chapter Nineteen

London, summer 1934

'Say you are coming to the Wentfords' this evening,' Maureen demanded.

Doris had been back in London almost a week.

'Because I've got someone you simply must meet. And no, *not* Bertie Lewis, for all that he looks everywhere for you, as though you were the missing piece of a jigsaw or the answer to a riddle. No, someone else entirely.' She leaned closer over the tea table, hovering above the delicate bone-white-and-gold-rimmed Ritz china, but, being Maureen, she raised her voice so that Doris had to lean back, fighting the urge to rub her ear where Maureen's voice had fizzed. '*Quite* the most devastating man in London. Or was, until he disappeared to Italy for a few years. A rather awful divorce,' she continued, louder than ever. Two women at the table next to theirs looked over abruptly, as though their heads had been twitched simultaneously by an invisible thread. 'Not that anyone believed it,' Maureen said, with a quick sideways flicker of her eyes towards the listening women.

'Why awful?' Doris asked. Not that she cared, but it might keep Maureen from asking slyly, as she did so often these days, whether Doris had 'any news'. She knew very well that Doris had no 'news'.

'His wife wouldn't do the decent thing and allege adultery. She went for cruelty instead. Vindictive, you know. Couldn't bear to lose him, I expect. Can't say I blame her.' Maureen smirked, then took a tiny bite of a pastry. She made a face and placed the pastry back on the china cake stand. She picked a cigarette from the slim gold-and-enamel case in front of her and fitted it into a black holder. 'If I had met him before Duff, well, who knows . . .' She lit the cigarette and leaned back in her chair, blowing smoke over Doris. 'But here he is, back again, and all the interesting women in London already married.' She looked over at Doris for a moment. 'Except you.' She paused, so as to give a tiny flicker of doubt to the compliment. 'So you see, you must meet him. Although you'd better be careful. He has a frightful reputation.' She caught the eye of one of the women at the next table, still listening avidly, and almost winked at her.

Doris yawned and poured herself more tea. She had met these men before. These 'devastating' men with 'frightful reputations'. They always reminded her of some kind of laundry – stockings already worn, crumpled handkerchiefs.

They were always old about the eyes, brows pulled into sad wrinkles even as the mouths lifted in practised smiles. They were not for her, she paid them no attention and, after the occasional false start, they paid her none either. Those sorts of men, she saw, always understood where their chances lay, and wasted no time where there was no obvious opportunity. She had watched them, amused, from a distance, pull off easy flirtations, and wondered how any girl could be so foolish. This man, this David Envers, Maureen had said his name was, would be the same.

'I can't wait,' she said lazily.

In fact, she had forgotten all about him, and was looking for Bertie, by the time Maureen, plunging through a crowd of people, smoke and noise, found her that evening.

'Dreadful party,' Maureen said cheerfully. 'I imagine Envers is already wondering why he came back. Come and meet him.' And she took hold of Doris' wrist and pulled her along behind her so that Doris felt like a tugboat in the slipstream of a larger yacht.

They made their way to the other side of the over-crowded room, past the band playing something lively that had failed to get anyone dancing, past their hostess, who was looking quite desperate, Doris thought, and on to a small group, of whom she recognised only Duff. He was smoking furiously, pulling at his cigarette as though it contained air, not smoke.

'Darling, this is the girl I told you about,' Maureen said to a man with his back to them.

Doris sighed. These were the worst kinds of introductions. She wondered had Maureen done it deliberately. Probably. Now she would have to be a kind of pantomime version of herself. More aloof and wearily sophisticated even than usual, unimpressed with everything. Damn Maureen.

Envers turned around and Doris saw that he wasn't quite as she had imagined. Younger, larger, with wide shoulders and dark eyes under strong brows. He looked at her, silent.

'How d'you do?' she said at last, putting out her hand. She could feel Maureen, beside her, enjoying the faint awkwardness.

Envers continued to look at her and Doris felt, to her fury, that she was going to blush. 'You are prettier than your photographs,' he said.

That was more familiar landscape. The blush subsided and Doris was about to respond with an easy joke when he added, 'No, not prettier. Less pretty, in fact. But more . . . arresting?'

It was a question, but not a question for her. Rather, it was for him to decide, or so it seemed, because he continued to look at her, considering. Doris was irritated. But the blush came back. It wasn't even what he said, she thought – although part of her itched to ask, 'Arresting, how?' and despised herself for it – it was the way he looked at her. As if he saw her. Her, and just her. Not the person she was in company. Not the person she tried to be with Honor, with her little sisters and brother, either. Not the sleek hairstyle she had created, teasing individual curls so that they sat in shining waves. Not the creamy yellow satin evening dress and diamond-drop necklace she had put on. Just her.

She shifted uncomfortably. The thought shocked her, because it was only as it came to her that she realised she had never thought it before. Did that, then, mean that no one had ever seen her before? She pushed it away. That was silly. It was a trick. It must be. Men like him had tricks. So many of them. Tricks of being attentive, then indifferent, of seeming to admire, only to walk away. She had seen them played out so many times, and had pitied the girls who fell for them, were driven mad by them.

'So tiresome of me,' she said, trying for her usual indifference. 'I quite apologise.'

'Please, do not.' And he smiled down at her.

His eyes were dark grey, so dark as to be almost black, she saw, and she had the sudden curious thought that they were the exact same colour as her own eyes. She drew a breath and heard it catch somewhere in her throat.

'Maureen tells me we are going on, to the Embassy. Will you come with us?' he said then.

His voice came, without effort, from somewhere deep within his chest. It was low and somehow reassuring, and she found herself leaning a tiny bit forward, inclining in towards him, to catch what he said. She forced herself to straighten up. To lean back.

'Isn't that rather rude to our hostess? It's terribly early.' Doris remembered Mrs Wentford's anxious expression.

'And this party is terribly dull.'

Doris knew she should say no. Should stay and do her duty. Or go home and try to understand the thing that had just happened, in order to put it from her mind. But 'Why not?' was what she said.

'You must let me take you,' Envers said immediately.

And again Doris knew she should say no, knew that Bertie would be expecting to see her, to take her wherever they were going, but again she didn't do what she knew she should. She allowed this man to send someone for her fur – she noticed that he didn't go himself but stayed beside her, not talking to her but rather to others who came and hailed him and asked him things – how had Italy been? How long was he to be in London? – but always close enough so that she could feel the heat of him, and was quite unable to step away.

Someone arrived with her coat and he put it over her shoulders and took her hand, as though she was a child, and led her out of the house and down the front steps, saying, 'Parked just over here' as he walked briskly, her hand still in his, along the railings of Belgrave Square.

'You mustn't let me rush you, you know,' he said, amused, as he opened the door of a heavy black car and held it while she sat in. 'I'm very bad for that.'

'You have rushed me,' Doris said.

But she said it quietly and he was outside the car, crossing over to the driver's side, so he couldn't have heard her. She said nothing on the drive. It wasn't the nothing she usually favoured, part of her affected weariness – those long indifferent silences that had intrigued so many men. This time, she couldn't think of a single thing. And, much as she tried to pretend to herself that this was just as she normally behaved, that he couldn't possibly know that the origin of her silence was different, she had a feeling that he did know. That he knew very well what was happening within her. Twice he looked over, with a smile, and once he lit a cigarette and then handed it to her, and she knew he had seen her hand shake as she took it.

They reached the Embassy and he parked carelessly on a corner. The burly Albert was on the door again and hailed her cheerfully as she arrived.

'Miss Coates. You'll find Lady Dufferin and Lord Bertie already inside.'

'Known everywhere,' Envers murmured as he held the door for her.

'Stop it,' she said, but again quietly. Too quietly.

Inside, the first person Doris saw was Bertie, watching for her. He came forward. Envers, she noticed, left her side immediately. 'I heard you were going on, and I went to find you, but Maureen said you'd left already, so I came straight here.' He said it happily, without any sense that Doris had behaved badly, and Doris was grateful to be restored to herself by him.

'Aren't we frightful to leave so early,' she said, laughing. 'But really, people shouldn't have such dreary parties!'

And Bertie agreed and poured her a glass of champagne from the bottle he had waiting for her and started to tell her something he'd read that he thought she would be amused by. Later Baby and Oonagh and others arrived and he asked her to dance. So they danced, then again, and all the time Doris was aware of exactly where David Envers stood. How close to her, how far away. He didn't ask her to dance. Barely spoke to her for the rest of the evening, except once, as she came back from the powder room and found him in the dark hallway. They were alone and she knew it instantly, felt immediately the smallness of the place that contained only the two of them. He came from the opposite direction to her so that they had to pass in the narrow hall. Doris found that she didn't know which way to move – which side of the hallway to choose – and either he did not either, or he chose not to step aside, so that they met in the very middle. But again she couldn't think of anything to say – where were all her easy jokes and indifferent murmurs now, when she needed them? – and so it was he who said, 'Miss Coates,' in a tone of amusement.

'Don't call me that,' she snapped.

'Very well. Doris, then.'

That wasn't what she had meant, but she didn't know how to say that, so she pushed past him and went back to her table.

Later, Bertie dropped her home and asked could he take her walking in the park the next day and Doris said yes. But she fell asleep with Envers burning like a question in her mind, and woke with him in her head so that she knew he wasn't her first thought of the day, but rather that she had been thinking of him all night while she slept.

Perhaps dreaming of him, although she remembered nothing of that. She had brought him with her into sleep and he was with her awake. And when he telephoned in the middle of the morning, just before her walk with Bertie, and said he had got her number from Maureen and could he take her to dinner that night, she realised she had known he would. And she said yes, although she had hoped she would say no.

It was unusual for a man to ask her to dinner. That, too, should have made her say no. Bertie had never asked her – he asked her to tea, to the tennis, made sure they would be at the same parties, took her to nightclubs, walking, but always by day or in a group. This was the first time, at night, Doris realised, that she would be unaccompanied by half-a-dozen others. The thought gave her a guilty thrill.

Bertie called for her as he had promised, and they set out to walk through Hyde Park. He had brought a bright red ball for Mimi, which he threw as many times as the dog was willing to run for it, bending down again and again to scoop up the ball that was laid hopefully at his feet.

'You're jolly patient,' Doris said. 'I tire of that game much faster than Mimi does.'

'I've seen how much energy she has, alright,' Bertie said. 'I thought you might like a day off.'

'How sweet of you to notice.' Being with him was, Doris thought, like being with the little ones, Marianne, Isabel and Maxim – jolly and restful and somehow soothing.

'Maybe after this we can go and see the Royal Academy Show?' he said, 'and then, perhaps, tea?'

'Goodness, you have an entire afternoon planned out.'

'It's because I hope that if I have a jolly lot of things to propose, you'll spend longer with me,' he said.

His generous naivety was such that she burst out laughing. She wished she could say an instant yes to his plans. But the knowledge of seeing Envers later stopped her, as though that secret plan were somehow a physical barrier.

'Usually, I would adore to,' she said, 'but as it happens, I must be back at Curzon Street to see a friend, Mabel, who lives there too. I have promised . . .'

'Of course,' he said instantly. 'I know you have a great deal to do. Another time.'

'Another time,' she promised.

The lying made her feel curious. She had never, she realised, lied before. Because she had never cared enough to; had never before had anything that needed to be concealed. She hated it, and yet that day, she couldn't stop. 'I feel rather as though I have a cold coming on,' she said when Honor asked her to dine. 'I think I shall stay quietly here.' And when Honor tried to send around 'supplies: soup, a special kind of jelly Cook makes', Doris said no, she would go straight to bed and starve herself better. 'Just like Diana Cooper,' Honor said with a laugh. 'Only be careful, because sometimes I think Diana has done the starvation cure so very often that now she can hardly bring herself to eat at all.'

Doris promised she would be 'terribly careful', and spent the afternoon alone in her room, fidgeting in a way that was quite unlike her, and that made even Mimi agitated so that the dog barked and worried at the edge of the rug. She felt . . . sick, she decided, when she couldn't find another name for the lurching feeling within her. Sick. Perhaps she should cancel? But she had no way to reach Envers. No number for him. No idea where he lived or who he lived with. The nothing that surrounded him was part of the lurching feeling, she realised. The way she couldn't put anything into the sketch of him in her mind, no detail of place or person, except Maureen. And when Doris looked at Maureen as she appeared in that sketch, she was laughing in a sneering sort of way.

When Mabel came home, Doris was determined to make at least that part of her tale to Bertie true. Rather than wait for the girl to go to her room, then tap at the door, Doris wrenched her own door open and was waiting as she came past. 'I have cakes from Fortnum's,' she said. 'And I was just about to ring for tea. Come and join me?'

'Alright,' Mabel said, 'but I can't stay long.'

'Tell me what you've been up to,' Doris demanded when the cakes were arranged and the housemaid had brought the tea.

'The same,' Mabel said. She bit at a ragged corner of her thumbnail, worrying at it with her teeth so that Doris pushed the plate of cakes closer to her, to distract her.

'Any more apprenticeships?'

'No.'

'But there will be more?' Doris encouraged.

'Maybe.' Now that she looked at her, Mabel, Doris thought, looked scruffy. Scruffier than usual. Where before she had been scruffy in a rather charming way – someone too busy to bother with things like neat hair and perfectly straight stockings – now, she looked . . . careless, Doris thought. Her hair wasn't just untidy, it was dirty – as she leaned forward to take a cake, Doris caught a whiff of greasy, unwashed scalp that reminded her for a minute of Miss Potts', where they had only been allowed bathe once a week, so that all the girls – especially Honor, she recalled with a smile – had smelt too strongly. But with Mabel it was worse, because the not-washing was deliberate, of her own choosing.

'Mabel, you are not giving up, I hope?'

'Of course not,' Mabel said, but she didn't look Doris in the eye. Instead she stared at the cakes, shedding flakes of pastry onto the china plate now.

'Good.' Doris deliberately made her tone brisk. 'Because you simply can't. Something will come along, I know it will, and you must be ready to grab it.'

'I'm not so sure things do come along for girls like me,' Mabel said.

Which was much too close to what Doris feared, to the worst thoughts that went around in her own head, so that she snapped. 'Darling, don't be feeble.'

Later, when Mabel had gone to her own room, Doris tried to think about what else she could say or do to encourage her, but she found that her mind would not stay still, as though sent here and there by the lurching feeling in her stomach. She could neither settle nor concentrate, thinking about nothing except Envers and what she could possibly find to say to him that evening.

Chapter Twenty

Envers picked her up at eight, as he said he would. He rang the doorbell, then went back to lean against his car so that Doris, once she had opened the door, walked down the steps of Curzon Street alone, while he watched her. Bertie, she thought, had never done that.

'Where are we going?' she asked.

'Good evening to you too,' he said with a smile. They drove in near silence again, and Doris was conscious of the closeness of Envers' arm to hers as they went around corners – too fast, so that they were sometimes thrown against one another. It was, she thought, like wearing shoes that pinched. No matter what you did to ignore the fact, no matter how you put it from your mind, it was always, always there.

He took her to a small basement restaurant in Soho that had checked red-and-white tablecloths and candles stuck into empty wine bottles. It was unlike anywhere Doris had ever been, and she looked around, fascinated. Every other table was set for two, and those that were occupied were always a man and a girl, who leaned close in one to the other and spoke in low voices. She saw no one she knew, but Envers nodded briefly to a couple of the men. The maître d' behaved towards him with a discreet familiarity – as though he knew him but liked to pretend he did not.

Shown to a table in a dim corner, Envers took her fur, then held her chair as she sat down. When the waiter came with menus, he waved him away and ordered for both of them – 'There's really only one or two things worth choosing' – so that Doris, by the time the waiter left them, had been silent for so long she wondered would she manage to talk at all.

Envers lit a cigarette and handed it to her. Then lit another for himself. 'Now,' he said, exhaling slowly, 'we will have no interruptions.' And once his attention was upon her, not on driving, ordering, other people, she found there were a thousand things to say. He asked about Curzon Street, about Mabel, her home, the little sisters and brother, listening carefully to her answers, telling her things in return. At first, Doris sat upright, her back straight, as she had been taught, but bit by bit, as food was placed and eaten and plates removed, glasses filled and refilled, she found she leaned forward more and more so that soon she had her elbow on the table and her chin propped on one hand. His voice was as wonderful to her as she had remembered, almost tangible, she thought, like a warm hand that touched now her hair, now her face, her neck.

She ate almost nothing – the food was some kind of Italian dish she had never heard of – but she drank, emptying her wine glass each time he filled it. Even so, when it was time to go and the waiter brought her fur and she stood up and stumbled, it wasn't the wine, she knew, that shook her balance. It was him. His closeness. The smell that came off him – like taking the saddle off a horse at the end of a long day's hunting, she thought. That smell that rose up from the hot damp of a horse's back that was reassuring and intoxicating and told of hours of hard riding, the excitement of man and beast mixed with leather and linseed oil. That was Envers.

Outside, he handed her carefully into the car, his hand on her back and then her arm. By the time he had crossed over and sat in behind the steering wheel, she was terrified lest he simply drive her home. Or suggest the Embassy, the Café de Paris, any other night-time haunts where they might meet Maureen, Bertie, Honor, Chips. He didn't. Instead, he leaned over and kissed her. Did it so slowly that she had time, so much time, to move away, make a joke, turn to look out her window – any one of the many ways she had of making sure men did not kiss her. She did none of these. No one, she realised, had ever tried to kiss her with such certainty. Always, these other men had been hesitant, even a little frightened, so that there had been disjointed spaces, gaps, in which to refuse them. This time, there was nothing but the complete sureness of his slow movements. And so she stayed still, impossibly still, almost unable to bear the seconds before his mouth touched hers.

'I know a place,' he said after a few moments, as though in answer to a question. But she had asked nothing. He started the car, then took her hand, interlacing his fingers between hers, then drew both their hands to hold the steering wheel so that it was as if she too drove them where they were going. Except she didn't. She followed. She did not lead.

The 'place' he knew was a shabby hotel beside Liverpool Street train station.

'Here?' Doris asked.

'No one you know will see us here.'

No one *you* know, she noted. Not no one he knew. Maybe it didn't matter if he was seen. Of course it didn't matter. Not like it mattered to her.

She hung back in the quiet lobby while he signed the register and tipped the porter not to follow them upstairs. He took her hand again and walked her through the lobby, into a creaky lift, and out on the third floor.

'Don't be put off,' he said, opening a narrow door with a large brass key. 'It's clean.'

How many times had he done this?

That should have been a prod to send her back down in the lift and out onto the street. So should the small room with the narrow bed and pitiful headboard, orange lights of the train station leaking like rusty water in through the one window, until he pulled the flimsy curtain and blocked it. It was the worst room she had ever seen. Worse than the dormitories of Miss Potts'. But still she stayed, silent, waiting. And when he took off her fur, threw it on the bed, then moved in until he was close to her and put both his hands to her head, drawing her forward until they touched, then kissed her, she did only what he wanted her to do. And later, when he became quicker, more intense in his movements, his expressions, so too did she, matching him in an urgency and desire that she had never imagined, but that directed her as though through a scene whose lines had been written for her.

'I'm going to put you in a taxi,' he said, later. Much later. 'It wouldn't be wise to be seen dropping you home now.'

How much thought he had given to it.

'But I'll ring you up in the afternoon.'

The shabby lobby was empty and they crossed it quickly, as though keen to leave behind any clinging traces of the night before. He didn't kiss her goodbye on the street. Instead, he was brisk and distracted, patting her face once with his hand beside the taxi he found for her, before crossing the road at a slight jog, to his own car.

'Curzon Street, you say?' the driver asked, looking at her in his little mirror so that Doris was conscious of all the things that betrayed her. The hasty getting dressed, the blurred lipstick and too-quickly-pinned hair.

'No. St James's Place,' she said. Honor would not be awake, but neither would she mind being woken. The streets were grey and empty, and reflected the emptiness that Doris felt. How, she wondered, was it possible to go from full to the brim, heated with fire and energy and a golden kind of glow, to this chilly void in just a few hours? In what felt like a few minutes.

'What is it?' Honor came into the library in a rush – where Andrews, with only the tiniest expression of surprise, had shown Doris – tying the belt of her dressing gown and yawning. 'Are you ill? Is the cold worse? Do you need a doctor?'

'No. Not that. Oh, Honor . . .'

'Doris?' Honor took her in, all of her – the messed hair and crumpled evening dress. The fur that she hugged about her and the way she shook, from cold but something else too. A kind of shock that seemed to be settling in her. 'Doris, what have you done?'

'Nothing so very bad . . .' Doris said, and tried a laugh.

But it came out shaky and Honor put a hand up. 'You need a bath, and breakfast. I will ring for both. Unless there is something urgent, tell me then?'

And Doris, who had no idea what she was going to say, was grateful and said, 'Nothing urgent, darling.'

After her bath, Honor insisted Doris get into her bed, still warm from when she had left it, and have breakfast there. 'Now,' she said, settling herself heavily in beside Doris so that the mattress sagged towards her, just as Doris knew it would and wanted it to, 'tell me.'

Doris told, as much as she could. And Honor listened, quiet and sympathetic, until she was finished everything – the restaurant, the red-and-white checked tablecloths, the drive to the hotel, the orange light like rusty water, and the things that happened when Envers drew the hopeless curtain.

And Honor did exactly what Doris had hoped she would – took something unwieldy, impossible to understand, and placed walls firmly around it. 'He won't do,' she said with decision. 'You know it yourself. He isn't any of the things you say you want.'

'I know,' Doris said. 'I know . . .'

'Well, then,' Honor said. 'That's that. You will simply forget about this. And hope he isn't one of those men who talks . . . I must ask Chips about him. Chips will know.'

'You won't tell him, will you? Chips, I mean. This?' Doris pleated the silk counterpane between her fingers, running her hand, palm down, across it, fingers spread wide then closing together to gather the material into bunches so that the soft pink shine of it spread up and out from her fingers like some kind of webbing.

'Certainly not. I will think of some reason . . . Not that Chips needs a reason to tell me gossip.' She smiled fondly. 'Now, finish your tea and get some sleep. I'll look in on you in a few hours.'

'Very well. But I have to be at Curzon Street in the afternoon.'

He would telephone her. He had said he would.

Chapter Twenty-One

London, autumn 1934

'Darling,' Honor said when Doris came to the telephone, 'I have some things to tell you. Perhaps you should come round?'

'I don't know, I'm rather busy . . .' Doris said.

Honor knew Doris had been avoiding her, a little anyway, for over two weeks now, ever since the early morning when she had arrived, dishevelled and distressed in a way Honor had never seen her, to St James's Place. She had slept for some hours after Honor had left her; then, once awake, had insisted on leaving at once, refusing any lunch, although she had borrowed some of Honor's clothes to go home in.

Since then, Honor had hardly seen her, but she suspected Doris had continued to see David Envers. It's not that people were talking, not yet. Whatever they were up to, Doris and Envers had been discreet. But there was something – something new – that hovered in the air around Doris' name. A shade of a pause, the almost-weight of an inflexion. Nothing yet was known but somehow, society had intuited that there was something *to* know. Which meant it was only a matter of time. Maureen – luckily, Honor couldn't help but feel – was on a visit to Clandeboye, her husband's estate in Ireland. Otherwise she must surely have discovered what the something was. And already Chips, ever the most sensitive of social instruments, had said, 'One doesn't see so much of your friend Doris these days,' thoughtfully, and had pulled a face when Honor explained that she was still down after her cold and wasn't going about much.

'I'm sure you are,' Honor said now, 'but I so want to see you. I feel frankly neglected.' She allowed her voice to take on a hint of a whine.

'Very well, I will call this afternoon.'

'I will have Cook make those raspberry tarts you like.'

Doris, when she arrived with Mimi, looked, Honor thought, more astonishing than ever. The intense weariness of her face backlit with a powerful glow so that she was like a lamp set above them all.

Having mused on how she would approach what she had to say – would she be subtle? Slow and devious, waiting for Doris to introduce Envers' name – Honor took courage from the glow. 'What is it that you are doing with this man?' she asked conversationally.

Doris' face flickered into a quick smile. 'I wondered would you beat about all sorts of bushes for an hour,' she said. 'I'm glad, after all, that you do not. If we must have this conversation—' She made her voice enquiring.

'We must,' Honor said firmly.

'Well, then . . . I haven't really thought about it.'

'I don't believe you,' Honor said. 'You think about everything. Particularly this sort of thing. Have been thinking about it for years now – who to marry, why. You're the one who says it, not me – that you are *calculating*. And while I don't at all agree that you are' – she put a hand on Doris' hand. Doris twitched her off and bent to pick up Mimi – 'I know well that you have plans. Good plans. To do with your family and sisters. How does David Envers fit with these plans?'

'He doesn't,' Doris admitted. 'But perhaps I shall have new plans. Honor, you cannot imagine how I feel when I am with him . . .'

'I'm not sure I have to imagine,' Honor said thoughtfully. 'I have only to look at you and I see it. But what about Bertie?'

'That is a worry,' Doris admitted. 'I don't quite know. I mean, we still go about, and he is as darling as ever. Only yesterday he took me to the funniest play . . . Well, I wonder if I should begin to let him down gently . . .?' She put a hand out, palm up, and Mimi placed her front paws into it as though she would scramble off Doris' knee and into her hand. Doris raised her hand so that Mimi was stretched up on her hind legs. The little dog began to bark comically. 'Isn't she too adorable?' Doris said, kissing the dog. 'And such a fan of Bertie's.'

'Has Envers said anything to you, about the plans he might have?' Honor asked.

'No.'

'Has he said anything, at all, about marriage?'

'No.'

'Doris, this is madness, you know it is. You will destroy yourself. How much do you know about this man?'

'I know he is divorced,' Doris said, rolling her eyes. She stroked Mimi's head with one hand. 'Maureen told me.'

'Divorced for cruelty,' Honor said. 'Not the usual.'

'Yes. They say his wife – former wife – is rather a battle-axe and did her very best to make things difficult.'

It was the most animated Honor had seen her so far that day. 'People always say that about wives where there has been an unpleasant divorce,' Honor said wisely. 'Sometimes the truth is far more dull.'

'Meaning?'

'Meaning, maybe he *was* cruel.'

'Nonsense, that's just something people say. You know the way the newspapers tattle,' Doris said, but her voice caught in her throat and she bent her head further over Mimi's to hide her face. Then she bent lower again, rooting in her bag for a cigarette.

'Here.' Honor offered her the box on the table, and as Doris raised her head to take one, Honor saw something confused in her eyes where there was never confusion. She felt then as she so often felt when out hunting – the urge to turn back, to get away from the current of eager violence that pulled her along, but unable to extricate herself. Every bit of her hated pursuing Doris like this. But she had to. 'Did you know he's one of Oswald Mosley's men?' she asked. She kept her voice conversational. Light. She looked out towards the windows at the far end of the room, because to look at Doris' face would have been indecent.

'What do you mean?'

'Chips told me. Envers has been in Italy for a number of years—'

'I knew that.'

'– where he has been getting close to Mussolini. It seems he was quite the favourite with Musso.'

'But that was in Italy.' Doris tried to sound indifferent; Honor knew every tone, every inflexion of her voice. This one wasn't natural. 'People do such odd things abroad. Why, Elizabeth Ponsonby once had her hair streaked with violet . . . Now that he's home . . .'

'He's home to work with Mosley and his British Union of Fascists.' Honor pressed ahead. 'As if fascism could possibly be British . . .' she mused. 'Something to do with understanding that these are politically troubled times, and setting up a group of like-minded thinkers across Europe. Here, Italy, Germany . . . Finding common ground with these countries against socialism and Bolshevism. Chips rather approves of him, if you must know.'

Doris looked at her uncertainly. 'Even if it is true,' – it was true, they both knew it, but Honor said nothing – 'what is that to me?'

'Mosley is a most frightful thug,' Honor said. 'I cannot see what Diana see—'

'Yes, but his lot hate communists, not Jews. They are English, not German.'

'Oh, Doris.' Honor's eyes narrowed anxiously. 'I don't think it's that easy. Chips says—'

'I don't want to hear another word about what Chips says. I must go. I told you I was busy and already you have taken up a deal of my time.'

'I know I have, I'm sorry,' Honor said. 'I didn't mean to—'

'Never mind what you meant.'

After Doris was gone, Honor sat for so long that Andrews came and asked would she like the lights put on. Only then did she realise that the room had grown dark around her. Outside, the afternoon was wet and filthy, with wind that seemed to blow in every direction as though angry and vindictive but unable to make up its mind. She thought of Doris, out in that, blown, too, here and there. Even though she knew Doris must be at home in Curzon Street by now, or tucked up in the Ritz bar with . . . who? Envers? Surely not. Not so publicly. Bertie then, and that gang of giddy young people she went about with. Even so, she could not shake the image of Doris, alone somewhere dark and wet, buffeted by implacable gusts of cold wind.

A few days later, when Maureen – back in town – came to call and said slyly, 'Now tell me everything about Doris and that divine David Envers. And don't tell me there is nothing to tell because I simply won't believe it,' Honor had to blink hard to get rid of the image of Doris nipped by a vicious icy wind.

'There is nothing to tell,' she said. 'I doubt they even know one another.'

But when Maureen had gone away, she telephoned to Doris. 'Darling, in a little while, might you come and stay?'

'And why would I do that?' Doris asked, half-amused, half-cross.

'You will be company for me. Please! It will be just like Miss Potts' again. Talking after lights out, stale buns under the covers at midnight . . .'

'Why should you need company? You have a husband.'

'Yes, but I am to have an operation next week . . .'

'What kind of operation?'

'I'm not sure exactly,' Honor confessed. 'Doctor Gilliatt ordered it. My mother and Chips insisted I see him, because I have not started a baby yet.' Her voice trailed off a little. 'Gilliatt said it was needed. But I didn't ask what, exactly.'

'You are to have an operation, and you don't know what?' Doris was incredulous. 'Don't you think you should find out?'

'I'm sure they will tell me in time,' Honor said vaguely. 'In the meantime, I know only that I am to go to a nursing home, and I will be there several days, and will need to rest after that. So you see, if you come and stay when I am home, it couldn't be a better time.'

'Very well. Of course I will. And perhaps you will give me your blanket,' Doris said.

Honor laughed. 'I will if you want it.'

'It won't be for long,' Honor assured Chips later when she explained what she had done.

He was wary of Doris. Honor's relationship with Lady Iveagh, he approved of – 'That's how I would have been with my mother,' he said, 'if my mother weren't so atrocious' – and he continued to be a little frightened of Maureen, and to tolerate Oonagh. But he mistrusted those friendships that predated their marriage.

'Doris is rather grasping, don't you think?' he asked.

'I don't,' Honor said. 'She's not grasping at all, she's a dear. And she will stay only for a while.'

'I hope you will stay a jolly long time,' she said to Doris later that day, showing her the blue bedroom next-but-one to her own that was to be hers. 'In fact, once you move in, I hope you never move out.' It was the only way she could think of to keep Doris safe.

'Lovely, of course.' Doris gave the room a cursory look. Then, 'I can't believe Chips and your mother . . .'

'Oh I know.' Honor hid her face in her hands for a moment, laughing. 'And then he came to the appointment with me, and he asked such questions . . . He knew more than I did, so much more, and when the doctor asked about my monthly . . .' – even to Doris she couldn't find a more exact word – 'I could hardly remember but Chips knew, almost to a day.'

'Perhaps his family are farming people?'

'No. Shipping, he says. Oh darling, it was really rather awful . . .' And she laughed and covered her face again.

'He said there was no reason to be shy, it was all perfectly natural, and I thought I should *die* . . .'

She said nothing about Envers, and neither did Doris, but when Honor looked at her properly, she saw that she no longer had the lit-from-within glow. Now, she looked simply weary 'through and through', as Lady Iveagh might have said.

They went downstairs then and Chips joined them in the small drawing room that suddenly felt crowded with all three of them. Honor found she didn't know what to say to make it alright, but Doris, like Chips, was clever at things like that, falling instantly into the amusing, languid person she became in society. No sign then of the exhaustion that had settled over her.

She draped herself over a low divan, accepting the offer of a cocktail with a polite murmur, charcoal-coloured eyes half-closed. 'I don't know how you have the energy,' she murmured as Chips described the various people he had seen, the parties and luncheons he had attended. Every day, for him, was crowded. There were callers in the morning, then luncheon, either at home with guests or out with friends, then cocktails, dinner parties, card parties, theatre parties, balls, nightclubs. At the weekends there were visits to great houses – Longleat, Himley – for shooting, or riding, or theatricals. 'You must see upwards of a hundred people a day.'

'And that is when I'm not making friends in the Southend constituency,' he agreed, smiling broadly.

'I cannot imagine how you manage it all,' Doris said,

sliding further down on the divan so that she was nearly reclining.

'Don't you? Don't you really? I rather thought you had a fair idea how society must be played,' he said, and Honor wondered again at his astuteness. Just when she thought he was blind to everything except his own schemes and ambitions, he would come out with some observation or piece of wit that showed how closely he watched everything. Doris dipped her chin gracefully to acknowledge what he said but didn't answer. 'Are we going to have men dying of love for you all over the house, now that you have come to stay?' he said then.

'Not *dying*,' Doris said, 'perhaps languishing a little . . .' And she smiled at him, a real smile, not the feeble droop of her mouth that she so often gave, as though an actual smile were beyond her.

Andrews brought tea and they chatted about people they all knew and a speech Chips said he had to deliver to the Conservative Association, which he described as 'appallingly middle class, but important'. Then, 'I must get on. I'm due at my club.'

'I know he can be a bit pompous. But you won't fight with him, will you?' Honor asked when he had gone.

'Cross my heart and hope to die' – it was what they used to say to each other, at Miss Potts' – 'I won't.'

'Good, because he is really rather sensitive.'

'Yes, I see that. He is like a storm glass, forever taking the temperature around him, testing for air pressure and prevailing winds and what-have-you . . .'

'You don't sail much, do you?' Honor asked, amused.

'You know what I mean. If he could be hooked to a machine and the machine could produce graphs of all that is within him, I'm sure we would all be able to see the exact state of English society, politics and finance. We would have the most delicate understanding of the precise nature of everything. Why, no one would need newspapers any more, to find out what goes on in the world – or at least the bits of the world Chips cares about.'

'Really, it's a waste that you don't talk more at parties,' Honor said. 'You do say the most absurd and fascinating things.'

'Only to you,' Doris said. 'To everyone else, I am a perfect Sphynx.'

And when Honor opened her mouth to ask about Envers, she firmly switched the conversation. 'Maureen is telling everyone who will listen that Oonagh indulges her children so they are spoiled monsters. Aren't sisters simply delightful?'

Chapter Twenty-Two

How could failure be something you did to yourself? Doris wondered. So long she had looked around her for threats to her plans – threats from the outside, from those around her, even from her own mother – and yet all the time the greatest was within her. Even after Honor told her that Envers worked with Mosley, and even when she knew – as one instantly did, she thought wryly; recognising reality through every layer of reluctance – that what Honor said was true, she had continued to say yes when Envers rang her up and offered to take her out. Except of course they didn't go out. Not really. Sometimes to the same Soho restaurant with its thick red dimness, a place that Doris had begun to believe existed only in the minds of those few who went there, so completely unknown was it to the rest of her world. Often, though, they went straight to the hotel by Liverpool Street station where the sound of the trains that rumbled by was a reminder that outside the mean windows was a world where what she did could not be excused. Not by the rush of warmth and weakness that she felt when he spoke to her. Not by the way she seemed to melt to liquid when he touched her. Not by the way she touched him, driven by emotions she didn't understand and blushed to think about later when she was home again and alone.

Sometimes he collected her, standing at the bottom of the steps, almost as though he were there by chance and not for her. Often he told her to take a taxi. Always he was concerned that they not be seen. 'For your sake, darling,' he said. 'My reputation, well, it couldn't be much worse,' he laughed, 'but yours must be protected.'

'Unless . . .' she began, then stopped. How to say, *Unless you ask to marry me, and then it will be alright.* But even if she did say it – and if he did ask – how would she respond? He was not – not at all – the sort of man she had set herself to marry. There was no certainty to be found with him. No shelter in his name or reputation, for herself and her sisters. None in his person. He was intoxicating, yes, like a potent cocktail, but he wasn't, she dimly felt, terribly kind or even decent. He seemed almost to stand back and watch her, rather than stay close beside her, as Lord Bertie did. How could she ever say yes? And yet, if he were to ask, how could she say no, if saying yes meant being with him always? Waking up with him, putting a hand out and finding him there, warm beside her, or already in her arms so that she didn't even have to reach to touch him.

But he was 'one of Mosley's men', although she didn't know exactly what that might mean. However, her mother would.

What, she wrote to Esther, *do you make of Sir Oswald Mosley? I ask only because Honor's cousin, Diana, goes about with him a great deal . . .*

The answer, when it came, gave her some comfort. *I have looked around for what I can find*, Esther wrote back, *and Mosley has said that anti-Semitism forms no part of the policy of his organisation, even that anti-Semitic propaganda is forbidden. I cannot like him, or his British Union of Fascists, but I think your father is right when he says they are English, not German or Italian – and therein lies the difference.*

Doris was relieved. But she also knew that Envers' politics mattered less to her than she pretended. Less than his behaviour towards her and the way he made her feel – as though with him, she could not catch her breath or uncouple her will from his. She was like a mannequin, she thought; a doll. Empty and obliging.

So far, he had asked her nothing, except that she meet him at night, or late in the afternoon, in secret. Each time she did, she promised herself that next time, she would say no. She knew that the first time she did, he would stop asking. That was the kind of man he was. There would be no pleading, no attempt to convince her. Once she said no, he would step back, move away from her. Leave her be. And so she knew that all she needed was one moment of strength; one 'no' and the strange madness would be over.

Next time, she promised herself. *Next time I will do it.* And then he telephoned, and always she said yes.

She had seen a man shoot a horse once. In the head, out on a day's hunt. The horse had gone down badly after jumping a ditch and it became clear that she couldn't get up. Doris – all of them – had watched as the mare floundered and tried, and they had all seen the moment when the pain in her eyes had given way to terror as she realised there was no way to get off the ground beneath her. No way to scramble to her feet. That she was no longer what she had been, but a broken thing.

And Doris remembered how the man – whom she hardly knew – had sent someone for a gun. A service revolver. How he had then knelt in the mud beside the mare and taken her head onto his lap and murmured gently to her and how, when the gun arrived, he had moved his hand stealthily behind the mare's head so that she saw nothing. How he had made sure the gun was perfectly placed, crooning all the while. How someone had taken the other horses away and how they – the riders – had stood and watched silently like a guard of honour while the trigger was pulled.

She wished there was someone who could do that for her. But there wasn't. There was only herself. And she would do it, she swore. She would do it, exactly as that man had done it. With a look on his face like nothing she had ever seen. And straight afterwards he had taken a spare horse belonging to Doris' father, mounted it, and set off in the direction they had seen hounds take. Doris and the rest had gone after him and they had finished the day exactly as normal, and the terrible weight that lay over everything, the fear that had leaked from the desperate mare as she'd scrambled uselessly to get up, had remained unspoken.

But she couldn't do it. Could not pull the trigger. And so, when Honor rang and said, 'Might you come and stay?' even before she explained about an operation she must have, even while Doris was pretending she didn't much wish to, inside her a voice immediately cried out, 'Yes.'

She went to look at the blue bedroom that very afternoon – as though, she thought, it could be anything other than perfect – and knew that Honor longed to ask about Envers but she couldn't let her. Instead, Doris distracted her with conversation, even put up with Chips and his condescending airs in order that they not be alone. Because the only way, she knew, was not to speak of it. To distract herself from what she was doing, just like the man when he had taken the mare's head onto his lap and gently murmured, even while the hand with the gun moved into position. Otherwise she would not be strong enough to make the break.

After her visit to St James's, she went back to Curzon Street and waited, knowing she had only a few more days. At most a week, before she moved. Not knowing if the idea appalled her, or lay there like bright salvation. The house was emptier than usual. Mabel had decided to take tennis lessons – 'I can hardly get any better at shorthand,' she had said bitterly. 'If tennis is the thing, then I shall learn tennis!' – and was out more often. Miss Wilkes was visiting a cousin in Torquay and Mrs Benton, without her adversary, kept to her own rooms.

The telephone rang downstairs in the hallway. Doris hated that she heard it so clearly these days, as though she waited for it. Listened for the housemaid's feet on the stairs that told her it was for her, felt her heart hammering as she paused to find who it was who looked for her.

'Lord Bertram Lewis for you, miss,' the housemaid said from outside the door, having tapped loudly.

'Very well. I will come down.'

'Tom Brattney's band are playing at the Café de Paris this evening. I thought you might like to come?'

Bertie waited. Doris could almost hear the anxiousness in his breathing. Would she say yes, or no? He rang her every day at about this time, always with a plan for the evening. Something he hoped she would say yes to. And where once she had been happy that he did, now the daily conversations had become a kind of agony. Because Envers hadn't rung her up yet. And Doris didn't know if he would. Very often, he did not. But if she said yes to Tom Brattney's band now, and Envers rang in an hour . . .

She knew that if she said yes to Bertie, they would have a lovely evening. He would be kind, attentive. He would make her laugh and compliment her. They would be part of a large and merry group and the next day the newspapers would write that *Miss Doris Coates, wearing a gown by Schiaparelli, was seen on her way into* . . . And yet, if she said yes, all evening she would wonder where Envers was. Who he was with. Might he arrive with his own party to where they were? What would she do if so? What would he do? She would find herself imagining the heat of his hands on her back, her waist, and she would blush even though she stood, fully dressed, in a room full of people.

'I don't know—' she began.

'Oh say you will,' Bertie broke in. 'It's too bad if you don't, because I have to go home for a few days, to Sussex, to see my mother, and so you see if you don't come out, I shan't see you for almost a week.'

She loved how eager he was, and how little he tried to hide it. 'Very well,' she said with a laugh. 'In that case . . .'

'Jolly good. I'll come and pick you up at eight.'

She put the telephone down and was halfway back to her room when it rang again. Rather than wait for the housemaid, Doris went back downstairs herself.

'Hullo?'

'Answering telephones now, are you?' Envers. He sounded amused. 'Perhaps you would take dictation for me too, Miss Coates.'

'I told you not to call me that.'

'So you did.' He sounded not at all repentant. 'I rather wondered if you'd come out with me this evening.'

'I can't. I'm going out already, with Lord Lewis.'

'Are you indeed?' Still amused. Why couldn't he sound upset, or furious? 'Well, perhaps this afternoon, then?'

Doris longed to say no. Just no, smart and sharp, and drop the telephone back into its spindly cradle.

'I suppose I could,' she said, feeling her heart begin to thump too close to the surface. It was, she thought, like a dog that leaps up when it sees its master.

'I'll send a taxi for you.'

At the hotel, the clerk at the reception desk said, 'Mrs Aungier?' in a sneering tone.

It was the name they always used. Aungier was a boy Envers had been to school with. 'First thing that came to my head,' he had said when she'd asked why he had chosen it. 'He had a rather dashing mother. Used to come for sports day, fourth of June, and all us boys would hang around to catch glimpses of her. Aungier hated it,' he finished with satisfaction.

'Room 18. Mr Aungier is already upstairs,' the clerk said then. Doris went up in the lift, keeping her hat pulled down low and her collar turned up high although they seemed, always, to be the only people in the hotel. She knocked at number 18, trying not to smell the boiling vegetables that came from somewhere deep inside the hotel, as though it breathed it out in stinking gusts. She hated it. But only dimly. Because foremost in her was the feeling of knowing he was so near. That only a door stood between them. That within moments she would be in his arms, his hands in her hair, his mouth on hers.

'Darling.' He pulled the door open and she stepped inside.

* * *

Much later, when they had dressed and were walking back down to the lobby, Doris had a thought. 'What about Aungier?' she asked suddenly.

'What?'

'The boy from school, with the exciting mother. Where is he? Don't you worry that somehow he will discover that you use his name?'

'He died,' Envers said shortly. 'Flanders.'

'But he can't have been more than . . .'

'A month short of his nineteenth birthday.'

She was in the taxi now and he shut the door behind her, tapped the glass once with a gloved hand and turned away.

The next day Honor telephoned. 'I am so tired and mopey. I have asked that they let me home immediately. Say you will come straight away?'

'I will.'

Chapter Twenty-Three

Doris arrived at St James's Place with Mimi and a set of smartly matched luggage a few minutes after Lady Iveagh, and they found themselves in the hallway in a confusion of dogs – Bundi was there to greet them – and cases and servants.

'Let Andrews see to those valises, and come and have tea,' Honor called to them through the open door of the library. 'I'm in here, because I cannot bear to walk upstairs to the drawing room. I have been so miserable, you cannot imagine,' she said when they were settled. 'Unable to do anything except lie around and read magazines. Never was I so bored.'

'But the operation went as it should?' Doris asked. She thought Honor looked terrible – pale and bloated, with purple circles under her eyes that said she had not been sleeping.

'Impossible to say,' Lady Iveagh interjected. As usual, she stood rather than sat, back straight, beside the chimney-piece. The china cup in her hand seemed too small and delicate and Doris imagined that if she squeezed hard, the cup would shatter. 'Only time will tell if it has been successful. If Honor carries a child, it was a success. If not, it wasn't.'

'Mamma,' Honor pleaded weakly. 'Must you?'

'I must,' Lady Iveagh said firmly. 'No point shirking these things.'

'Doctor Gilliatt said there is every reason to believe it was a success. I am inclined to trust him. Chips and Mamma are not.'

'We talk about "blind faith" for a reason,' Lady Iveagh said. 'Trust is for religion, and a little, perhaps, for baking. Not for science and medicine.'

'Talk about something else,' Honor begged. 'Anything. Doris, recite the times tables or Latin verbs, anything but this . . .'

Lady Iveagh left, saying she had a meeting to attend, and Doris tucked a rug around Honor, ordered her to sit quietly, and read to her from the court pages of the *Tatler*.

It was mid-December and the days were dark again almost before they became light. The lamps at number 21 were lit early, and the fires piled high with logs, but all the same she shivered, disliking the texture of the grey day that seemed to cling to her like damp cobwebs.

Later, when Honor went up for her bath, Doris went too.

She sat on Honor's bed with the door open between them so she could hear her splashing about in the scented milky water.

'Where is Chips?' she asked after a while.

'Out. At lunch. Or perhaps tea by now or at the House. He has had an operation too, you know, appendicitis. He is more pulled down than he will admit. Or at least, he likes to complain of how tired he is, but will not refuse a single invitation. He is like a man possessed.'

'I understand, a little,' Doris said. 'I know, I think, the need that drives him on. And I know that you don't. You couldn't. You've never wanted anything that is beyond your grasp.'

'How do you know I have not? You make me sound so unromantic; someone practical and sensible, incapable of pining and yearning.'

'Which is exactly what you fear you are,' Doris said with a smile, 'and so you don't know whether to be charmed or insulted.'

'Insulted, definitely.'

'It's because nothing is beyond your grasp,' Doris explained. 'You would need to want desperately to fly, or, or . . . speak with horses, or something else equally impossible, to begin to understand what Chips and I feel about the sort of thing you take completely for granted.'

'Well . . .'

'It's alright, you needn't feel awkward. Your sublime indifference to everything we strive for is one of the things we love about you.'

'And is Envers—' Honor began.

But Doris cut her off. She couldn't. 'One of the things I strive for that is beyond my grasp?' She tried to smile. 'Yes, and no. Or rather, no and yes,' and, as Honor tried to puzzle that out, 'but don't let us talk of him. Tell me again, how is Chips?'

'I wish he would rest,' Honor said. 'He goes about far too much. I fear he will wear himself out, chasing something only he can see. And then he sulks and says that all he really wants is to be left alone.' She laughed; Doris did too. 'But he doesn't seem to be without company for longer than an hour at a time. He has these intense friendships . . .'

She paused then, and Doris said, 'What kind of friendships?'

'Ones that absorb him wholly so that he must see and talk to that person several times every day.'

'Do you think . . .?'

'No. I don't. I mean, Emerald . . . she must be 60, so it can't be that. And Prince Paul of Yugoslavia – well, it can't be that either, much as Chips raves about him. They both do, Chips and Emerald. Emerald described him as having the beauty of a tragic Apollo.'

'Good God!'

'Indeed. Revolting. And yet Chips agreed, so warmly and heartily. I think it is in him, to see the best in everyone . . .'

'Particularly everyone royal . . .'

'Yes, that is true. But it's a sign of his nature – ardent, generous.'

'As long as he isn't too generous, with himself.'

'But he is. He simply wears himself out, planning entertainments for everyone, exerting himself at their parties to make sure the evening goes with a bang. He will sap himself with his generosity.'

'That wasn't exactly what I meant.'

'No, I see that it wasn't.'

They paused, sizing up the things they might and might not say. There were, Doris realised, more now than there ever had been before. She wondered how much Honor knew of the rumours that spread around Chips like water that swirls around and about a plughole; growing in speed and intensity at the very point it disappears. Rumours of women. Of men. Of deceit. More, she wondered what she might – should – say. She remembered that party, years ago now, and the men who had made sly allusions to Chips' activities: *Who is it now? Well, Viscount Gage, of course . . . Also Isabelle Clow . . . Others? Oh yes. Many.*

At the time, she hadn't really understood – not more than that they wished to sneer and wound – and she was certain Honor hadn't either. Less, even, than Doris. But now? Well, now they both understood better. And yet, Honor said nothing, and where she didn't, Doris felt she couldn't. Almost, she thought, Honor was protected by her seeming ignorance. By knowing so little of Chips' activities, it was as though they didn't quite touch her. And that, Doris thought, was far better than the grubby smear of certainty.

'You mustn't worry,' Honor continued after a moment, so that Doris knew for sure that she would not speak; that neither of them would. 'It is all because he is in the first flush of excitement. He says he feels that now that we are married, he can do so much. More than he ever believed possible. He has such plans, Doris . . .'

'In fact, he is like a bride,' Doris said witheringly, 'flushed and rosy with the evidence of his own success.' Honor laughed but Doris said, 'I didn't mean to joke. After all, it is you who are the bride, not him.'

'Hardly. A year . . .' Honor waved the idea away. 'Anyway, once there is a family he will settle down.'

'If Doctor Gilliatt's operation has been a success.'

'Yes, if the operation has been a success.' And then, 'Come and brush my hair, darling? You do a much better job than Molly.'

Doris went to where Honor lay with her head tipped back over the high curved end of the bath, the rest of her submerged in hot clouded water. She reached for the hair-brush and began to brush through the springy weight of Honor's hair, steady and almost soothing in the familiarity of the rhythm, known since childhood. Stroke after stoke.

Honor stirred luxuriously in the milky water, releasing a cloud of rose-geranium-scented steam. 'Bliss,' she said. 'Utter bliss. I wish you could do it every night.'

'Well, now that I'm here, I might.'

Honor looked over her shoulder and flicked a spray of water with her fingertips. 'You won't. You'll be always out, having the gayest time.'

* * *

Moving into St James's Place, with Honor and Chips, meant many things for Doris. First, it meant she could send for her maid, knowing that the below-stairs household would be company for her. And this was one more certainty that Envers could be held at bay – impossible to see him now that Addie was with her. She hadn't told him that she was moving. The housemaid at Curzon Street would tell him when next he telephoned. She wondered would he try to ring her up here. But he wouldn't. She knew he wouldn't.

Addie arrived with letters from Doris' mother, and drawings done by Isabel and Marianne that Doris stood against her bedside lamp, so that they were the first thing she saw every morning, and the last thing every night.

'Those are pretty,' Honor said, coming to make sure she was settled in.

'Isabel has drawn the front of the house, "in case I forget what it looks like", and Marianne has drawn her kitten.'

Honor picked up the drawing of the house and looked at it. 'She has talent.'

'Only compared with us,' Doris said with a smile. At Miss Potts', both had hated drawing lessons. 'You better sit down, you still look ghastly.'

'I thought that was what you wanted,' Honor said, sitting on a velvet stool beside the dressing table. 'That I look excitingly pale and tragic.'

'Well, I see now that I was wrong,' Doris said vigorously. 'Doesn't suit you at all. You are far better in the pink of health.'

'What a pleasant-looking house,' Honor said then, turning again to the watercolour.

'Nothing compared with Elveden.'

'Not everything must be compared with Elveden,' Honor said. 'Here, give me those brushes and I will put them in the drawers for you.' Then, 'Remind me again why I have never been invited . . .?'

'You make it sound like a rudeness on my part,' Doris said, 'when I was trying to spare you.'

'But spare me what?'

'The dreadful dullness of Dorset country life. The peculiarities of my family, especially my mother.'

'You put up with the peculiarities of mine.'

'Not the same thing at all.'

'Isn't it? Why isn't it?'

'I've told you enough about my mother to understand . . .'

'Really, you haven't. You have told me so little. You said that she is unwell.'

'Well, not exactly an invalid. Often ill-disposed,' Doris said, conscious of how nasty her lies were getting. But it is more that she dislikes London and cannot spare the time to visit.'

'Then I will visit her.'

'Only now is not a very good time.'

'Why not?'

'There are a great many German cousins come to stay. They speak English, but together they lapse back into German.'

'And these German cousins are the same as the Jewish cousins?' Honor asked carefully.

'They are.'

'I see. But after they are gone? Then may we go?'

'I don't know that they will go . . . It seems it will be hard for them to go back to Germany, and there isn't anywhere else for them.'

'Why will it be hard for them, in Germany? Chips says there is employment for all, housing for all.'

'They had those things.'

'And now?'

'Now, they don't. Or not so as they can rely on them. The new Germany isn't for everyone.' Honor said nothing and Doris wondered again about saying more. 'How much do you read the newspapers?' she asked eventually.

'Not much, I confess,' Honor said blithely. 'Chips does, and tells me what's in them.'

'Tells you the bits he's interested in, you mean?'

'Yes, I suppose he does.'

'Well, you should read them yourself, and then you will understand better.'

'Do you mean the thing the newspapers call "the Jewish question"?' Honor asked, after a moment. 'What is the question?'

'It's not a *question*, Honor, can't you see that?'

'Then what is it?'

'They say "question" to avoid saying "problem". But problem is what they mean – and how to be rid of it. Of us.'

'Oh. I'm sure that's not . . .'

'What else? If it was a question there would be suggestions

of answers, but there aren't. Only a long silence after those words "the Jewish question", which is starting to be filled with ugly laws in Germany. They think to be Jewish is to be naturally contaminated. As if Jews cannot help being socialists, or Bolsheviks, or trouble-makers. The stain in marble, the run in silk, a blot in anything that would otherwise be pure. And as long as there are Englishmen who look to Germany for common ground against socialism, there will be many willing to accept mistrust of Jews as the entry price for inclusion. Do you really not hear how they all go on: . . . *"the Semitic thrust for self-promotion,"'* she said, imitating Chips' voice, *'"a demi-Jew"*, as though "a demi-bear".'

'I hadn't noticed.' Honor was mortified.

'Of course you hadn't. Oh I don't say that as an accusation.' Doris squeezed her hand affectionately. 'Truly, I don't. But if you listen for it, you will start to notice, for it is everywhere. I mean, it always has been, but now . . . Men are desperate and they look for change. Anything, I sometimes think, will do, as long as it is new and terribly different. More even than change, they look to blame. To make someone responsible for their lot. They blame Bolsheviks, refugees, Jews.'

'But they don't mean you.'

'They do. Even when they do not know it. Even when they see only "Doris the society beauty". They mean me. They mean all of us. And it doesn't matter that we don't even mean ourselves.' She gave a laugh that wasn't a real laugh. 'It doesn't matter that I don't think of myself as

Jewish. If it were known, they would think it for me, and that would be enough.'

'Was it always like this? You never said.'

'It is worse than it used to be.'

Chapter Twenty-Four

London, *winter 1934*

It was cosy, having Doris around, Honor thought. Just like Miss Potts', only more fun. Soon Chips forgot to keep asking when she was leaving and became used to her company – was even grateful for it in the first weeks after Honor's operation when she was tired and often peevish. Doris had her own life, plenty of it, and there were days that they barely saw each other. In the mornings she would slip into Honor's room with the breakfast tray, get into bed beside her and chatter about her evening, until Chips came in, when she would withdraw, saying, 'Better get on,' vaguely, so that even now, Chips didn't have the full measure of her. He still thought she was as she presented herself to be – hopelessly languid, rather frivolous, bent on a good marriage but with nothing much to her beyond that.

Lady Iveagh, however, now that she saw so much more of Doris, had learned her nature better. 'Not at all the doll-like creature I thought she was,' she boomed one day to Honor. 'Clever little thing, isn't she, to pull the wool like that?' And to Doris herself, a short while later, 'I see what you're about alright,' but approvingly.

Later, when Honor was able to go out again, afternoons when there were no lunches, no fittings for clothes and hats, shopping or calls to pay were spent in the drawing room. Chips would settle them there, and then go out accompanied by Bundi, on his mysterious errands. 'What does he do?' Doris asked one day. 'Only he is gone for hours, and comes home with new things nearly every day.'

'He visits his favourite antique and even junk shops. He goes to galleries and has long chats with the men who work there about paintings. He's determined Papa shall give him the money to buy a Boucher, and wants me to ask him. Seven thousand pounds, Doris, imagine! He buys trinkets – gifts for his friends, little things for me. He says it's impossible to spend less than two hundred pounds on a morning.'

'He knows that's what some men earn in a year? And they count themselves the lucky ones.'

'He does, but only in the way he knows the earth is round. Because he has been told as much, and couldn't be bothered to disbelieve it, while also not being sufficiently interested to make an effort to know if it is true.

He's joking, mostly, about the two hundred pounds. He said it to Papa, I think to encourage him to increase my share. Papa was horrified, of course. He's been well trained by Mamma to despise that kind of thing. But Chips is fascinated by the fact that I – we – get richer while not doing a single thing to make it so. He seems to feel that we neglect our money . . .'

'And you?'

'I don't really think about it. I leave that to Papa and Chips.'

'Like a litter of stable kittens.'

'Exactly! How you do make me laugh. I'm so glad you're here.'

The move, Honor thought, had worked just as she had hoped. Whatever strange miasma had swirled around Doris' name in the weeks after Envers had arrived, was gone, swiftly dissipated by the brisk energy of St James's Place, where callers came and went all day and cards of invitation were issued and delivered. Where Emerald's voice – always with a new plan or scheme – could be heard at all hours. As Honor got better and began to go about more, they picked up the habit of meeting in the drawing room for a cocktail before going out: Honor and Chips to whatever dinner they were promised to, Doris to the Ritz or Claridge's. Chips would fuss over the making of drinks – 'The mint must be fresh, Andrews' – and they would chatter about what they had done, who they had seen. Often they met again, later, either by design at a ball or party, or by chance at the Embassy, where they would greet each other as though they hadn't seen one another in weeks.

'You must save me,' Doris might say. 'I'm in the clutches of the most ghastly crew,' and she would gesture over to a group of eager, respectable young men, waiting for her return.

Or Honor would cry, 'Thank God! If I have to hear another word about what Emerald thinks of beauty, or vice, I will die. Come and cheer us all up.'

And if there was a shadow that lay across Doris in those weeks, times when she was unusually tired or distant, then they both understood not to speak of it.

'Is it very hard?' Honor asked once, coming upon Doris alone in the smallest and least used of the rooms, staring out a window at the lifeless winter garden.

'Very,' Doris said. And that was all.

Christmas that year was to be spent at Elveden, and Honor begged Doris to come with them. She still worried about her, but knew Doris would hate to hear her say it. 'We are so used to you. We cannot do without your company,' she said instead. 'It would be like being without an arm or a leg. Chips has asked especially that you come.'

'Of course I'll come,' Doris said. 'Where else do you think I would go?'

'Home?'

'Hardly! The German cousins are multiplying. No sooner does one get settled than he tries to send for all the rest of his family.'

At Elveden, Honor watched as her little sisters Patsy and Brigid fell in love with Doris. She was a bigger hit, even, than Bundi, whom they adored for his absurd size and thick golden fur. First, it was Doris' beauty and sophistication that drew them in, then her good nature and the delight with which she played any game they wanted. Together they rode out, hunted, played boules on the frozen lawn, laughing as the silver balls skidded on the icy, unyielding grass. She dressed up and acted in their plays willingly and even helped write them. From the time she came down to breakfast until the girls were sent up in the evening, they followed her about, perched on the edge of her chair, played with her bangles and generally hung on her every word. And imitated her. Everything, that Christmas, was 'frightfully clever', 'too sweet' or 'ghastly, how *can* you bear it', so that Honor heard Lord Iveagh mutter to his wife, 'I feel I am stuck at one of those terrible London parties', to which she retorted, 'Harmless enough, and I'd rather they aped Doris than any of those dreadful actresses. Imagine a couple of miniature Tallulah Bankheads?' She shuddered.

'Do you think my hair suits me like this?' Patsy asked Honor one evening when she came to her room before they went down. Now 16, Patsy was allowed dine with the adults. Honor began to smile, then stopped herself. Patsy looked so desperately serious. She had parted her hair on one side and teased it into waves, in an approximation of Doris' style. Except that Patsy, like Honor, had their father's broad face – 'just like a potato', Brigid, the youngest, had once said – and the style did not suit her at all.

'Let me,' Honor said, and began brushing bits of hair to cover Patsy's large, square forehead.

Except that when Patsy saw what she was doing she turned and grabbed the brush from her hands. 'Stop, you'll spoil it!'

Just then Doris came in and in one moment seemed to take in and understand the entire scene. 'You do look sweet,' she said to Patsy admiringly. 'I love how clever you've been at the back. Did you do it yourself?'

'I did.' Patsy was full of pride, and the agonising fear that she didn't, after all, look sweet. Standing behind her, Honor watched in the looking glass as Patsy's eyes travelled from her own face to Doris' pointed elfin features, and back again, uncertainly. And when Doris took the brush from her hands and gently began to coax a wave of hair to sweep across her forehead, just as Honor had, Patsy let her.

'You have such marvellous eyes; this way you really make the most of that. I wish I had eyes as blue as yours. They are like ice made from the bluest oceans. But all you Guinnesses have wonderful eyes.' And she smiled at Honor and Patsy together.

'It's not fair.' That was Brigid, bursting into the room, 'I don't see why Patsy can go down and I have to have supper upstairs with Miss Eustace, who makes me speak French even though all I can say is about hunting and who wants to talk about *les habitudes du renard* over supper? You are all mean, not to let me.'

'It's Mamma's rule. You know that, Brigid,' Honor said.

'Not until you are 16,' Patsy said smugly.

'But it is jolly hard,' Doris said quickly, 'and as soon as dinner is over, if they will let you come down to the drawing room, I will play Go Fish! with you.'

'You are the only one I like,' Brigid said.

At dinner they talked of the day's sport – the girls had been out riding and were to hunt the next day, but the ground was very hard. Chips, although hunting talk bored him, was mellow and affable, thanks to the Christmas presents he had received – 'a really good Watteau sketch; small, but beautifully executed' from Emerald, a pair of Regency cufflinks from Prince Paul.

Arthur had arrived that morning, from Dublin, and was disposed at first to be superior and impatient of them all. He was grown fatter and Honor thought how unfortunate that his childhood nickname – Lump, given by the groom who taught them all to ride – should have stuck. But as dinner progressed he, too, began to fall under Doris' spell. She did funny imitations of London people – Noël Coward, who's *Design for Living* had been both a scandal and success on Broadway the year before; Maureen, whose mania for practical jokes was more pronounced than ever, so that guests to her London house or Clandeboye estate never knew quite what they would encounter. Lord and Lady Iveagh looked faintly troubled at the Noël Coward impersonation, but laughed heartily at Doris' take-off of Maureen.

'That is her to a nicety!' Lady Iveagh declared.

'What about Aileen?' Lump asked. 'I stayed with her at Luttrellstown when in Dublin, and the first night I went up to bed, there was a bowl of sick in my room. Not real, of course' – he saw the look on Lord Iveagh's face – 'but jolly disgusting all the same. She is becoming just like Maureen. There was a fellow who pretended to be an American film producer who wanted to put us all in a film he was making, and the ladies were terribly excited. Only he turned out to be a kind of valet to Brinny and not a producer at all. Aileen put him up to it.'

'How extraordinary,' Lord Iveagh said. 'Why on earth—?'

'For larks,' Arthur said. 'It was rather funny, seeing their faces when they found out . . .'

'Ridiculous,' snapped Lady Iveagh. 'And Lump, you are no better than Aileen if you cannot see how foolish it is.'

There was a painful little silence then, as Arthur looked down at his plate, face flushed. Honor felt sorry for him. It had always been all too obvious that his mother found him, if not a fool, then something close, reserving her approval for her daughters, and particularly Honor.

'Tell about the sick,' Doris asked him. 'What was it, actually?'

'Porridge.' Arthur cheered up. 'Mixed with some kind of other grain. Quite artfully done.'

Honor gave Doris a grateful look, and saw that Arthur, too, was looking at her. After dinner, Brigid came downstairs and they played cards and board games in the library. In any of the games that needed pairs, Arthur was quick to team up with Doris, insisting that he didn't know how to play –

'Of course you know Old Maid, Lump,' Brigid said sharply – and that she must show him. And Doris was kind and affectionate with him, just as she was with Patsy and Brigid.

'Perhaps he would do for you?' Honor said when she went along to Doris' bedroom later that night. Doris was smearing cold cream on her face and wiping it off with a tissue. 'Viscount Elveden, one day to be the third Lord Iveagh? And a dear, kind fellow, although not always the quickest of wits.'

'Impossible,' Doris declared. 'It wouldn't be at all the thing. I never would, Honor. But if I can turn his mind from Lady Castlerosse, I will consider that my Christmas gift to Lady Iveagh.'

'Lady Castlerosse?'

'Yes. Hadn't you heard? He's been terribly *épris* for quite some time now . . . Oh Honor, you are such an innocent.'

'But she's . . .'

'Yes, married, and what of it? She has the most frightful reputation, even you know that. Which I wouldn't mind at all, only she is spiteful with it. Not at all the kind of person a nice young man like your brother should be mixed up with. She will make him unhappy and bitter. And so I will try to distract him from thoughts of her in the days that we are here, but not so much that he falls entirely in love with me.'

'How very thoughtful you are,' Honor said, laughing. 'And how confident of yourself.'

'I am, amn't I? But you mustn't worry, I know just how it should go.'

Back in her own room, Honor found Chips waiting for her, sitting in an armchair drawn close to the fire, in his dressing gown. Beside him was a tray with a decanter and a crystal glass half full of brandy. 'I assume you see what's going on,' he demanded abruptly.

'It's the day before the Christmas hunt and we need to get to bed?' She crossed to her dressing table and sat down. She began to take the pins from her hair, one by one, dropping them into a little silver box inlaid with mother of pearl.

'Don't be naïve, Honor.' He sounded far less affectionate than Doris when she had accused Honor of being 'an innocent'.

'I'm not. I don't know what you're talking about.'

'Your friend, Doris, making eyes at Arthur.'

'Oh Chips, she isn't. If anything, he's the one making eyes at her.'

'You know exactly what I mean. We can't allow it.'

'There is nothing to allow, or not allow. And anyway, why not? I think it would be delightful,' she said defiantly. She had finished with the pins and began to rub cold cream into her face as Doris had done. No sign of Molly. Chips must have sent the maid to bed, the better to quarrel with her.

'I don't.' He took a drink of brandy and placed the glass down hard onto the tray so that the decanter bounced a little and its crystal stopper rattled in the neck.

'Is it because she's the daughter of a mine owner? There are worse fortunes than hers.'

'But Guinnesses don't need money. Anyway, it's not that. The stain of vulgarity, one could bear. It's the stain of blood . . .'

'What are you talking about?'

'Now don't say you haven't worked it out,' he implored.

'Worked what out?'

'Doris' mother . . .'

'An invalid, or something.' She was deliberately vague.

'German.'

'Yes, and what of it? You love the Germans. You say so all the time. I even heard you tell Prince Charming so.'

'Germans, yes. But not all Germans are German.'

'What are you talking about?'

'Jewish Germans are not exactly German. Which is what I suspect Doris of hiding. You know she's hiding something. All that about her mother not being able for London . . . Why, it's obvious that it's Doris who won't allow her within a mile of the place. Have you ever met that woman?'

He would never have said "that woman", in that tone, about Lady Iveagh, Honor thought.

'Once, at Parents' Day at Miss Potts'.'

'And?'

'And what? A pleasant lady, affectionate and proud, though less in awe of her daughter than Doris' father . . .' Honor laughed, remembering the look of bewildered pride on Mr Coates' face as he watched Doris racking up medal after medal in the various sports they played. 'Her English is good but stiff, and I could see why Doris did not wish to burden her with society and balls and parties. Which

I am perfectly certain is what it is, for all that Doris pretends that she doesn't want her mother with her.'

'You are determined to see the best in her.'

'Of course I am. She is my dearest friend. But you seem determined to see the worst.'

'Not the worst – just the truth.'

'You are being ridiculous. In any case, Doris has already said she has no interest in Lump except to flatter him a little and take his mind off Lady Castlerosse. I'm sure you can see the value in *that*? He is altogether too young for Doris, and not at all her type.'

'I don't believe she has a type, beyond a title.' He sniggered.

'How cruel you are. And whyever should it matter if her mother is Jewish or German or both? No one cares about such things, not anymore.' Even as she spoke, she remembered what Doris had said – how, more and more, people did care about such things. But she would not believe it, she told herself. Certainly she would not say it to Chips.

'That's where you're wrong, Honor.'

'You are not to go about saying such things.'

'Don't worry, I won't breathe a word. For your sake.'

'And yours,' she said ironically.

But he chose to misconstrue. 'Not a word,' he promised enthusiastically. 'No one will find out. No one will think to look as I have done.'

'Because they have no interest,' she muttered. Then, loud enough for him to hear, 'On this, at least, you and Doris are as one. Please, leave it alone, Chips.' And when he did not answer, again, 'Chips, please. Leave it alone.'

Chapter Twenty-Five

The next morning, instead of breakfasting in his
room, as he usually did, Chips went down early.
It infuriated Lord Iveagh that he didn't go downstairs as most men did, and Honor had many times tried
to persuade him that, while staying with her parents, he
adopt their habits.

'But I cannot stand conversation in the mornings,' he
had insisted.

'No one can stand conversation in the mornings,' she
had agreed. 'And no one would think of such a thing. You
may take a plate and a newspaper and you will not be
expected to talk.' But he'd refused.

This morning, however, he arrived, looking a little puffy
around the eyes. Honor had breakfasted already, but sat

with a piece of toast thinly covered with marmalade to keep Doris company.

'We'll make an Englishman of you yet,' Lord Iveagh said with approval, looking up.

Chips made a non-committal sound and took a plate to the sideboard, where he peered gloomily under domed silver dish lids at the devilled kidneys and kippers, before spooning out a small amount of kedgeree.

'You'll never get through the day on that,' Lord Iveagh said as Chips sat beside him and took the cup of coffee Mason, the butler, handed him.

'That rather depends on what the day holds,' Chips said.

'Hunting,' said Arthur. 'We're off straight after breakfast. Isn't that right, Doris?'

'She said she'd ride with us,' Patsy said immediately, 'didn't you, Doris darling? And we have to stay close to Roberts.'

Roberts was the groom, charged with bringing Brigid and Patsy home after a couple of hours' hunting. A full day was considered too much for them.

'But how dull,' Arthur said. 'Doris will hate that.' He looked across to where Doris sat demolishing a plate of devilled kidneys and sausages enthusiastically.

'Lump, don't spoil things,' Brigid begged. She looked as if she might cry.

'Don't werret, Brigid,' Doris said. 'I can ride with you at first, and when Roberts takes you back, I will have plenty of time to follow more closely then.'

'Werret? What is "werret"?' Arthur asked, in high delight.

'It's what they say in Dorset,' Doris said with a grin, 'for worry.'

'Don't werret,' Arthur repeated. 'How charming. But maybe you will be tired, after the morning, and want to go back with Roberts and the girls?'

'Never,' Doris asserted. 'I will be the last on the field.'

'I will ride with you, Arthur,' Chips said then. 'It will be a pleasure to have your company.'

Honor was so surprised, she bit down hard on a piece of toast-and-marmalade and caught the edge of her cheek so that she winced.

'But you never hunt,' she blurted out.

'Rarely, not never,' Chips corrected, looking beadily at her, 'and today I feel a wish to. Arthur, will you stay close by me? It's been a while since I've been out.'

'Of course,' Arthur agreed politely. Reluctantly, Honor thought. Then, 'Honor, will you come?' he asked, hoping, she was sure, that the duty of looking after Chips might then fall to her.

'No.' She thought of how much she disliked hunting. The silent terror, and the shame of that terror, as they crashed through fields and down ditches; the impersonal cruelty of the hounds, who were not like dogs in those final moments but like devils. 'I promised Mamma I would go on an errand with her. In fact, I must go and change.'

As she left the breakfast room, she heard Lord Iveagh say again, in quiet satisfaction, 'We'll make an Englishman of you yet.' Chips, head bent over the newspaper, did not reply. She wished her father were right – that Chips had finally understood the correct way to behave. But she feared propriety was not what had got him out of bed that morning.

That afternoon they came back, mud-splattered, weary and able to talk only of the hunt. Once they had had baths and had rested, they gathered in the library for tea. Chips pulled a chair close up to Arthur and asked him questions about his studies at Cambridge, made comparisons with 'my day' and generally prevented him joining in with the game that Doris had got up with the younger girls. Honor saw Arthur look longingly at the fun going on beside the fire, while Chips moved on to ask him about his plans for the future, and when Doris put down her teacup and said she would 'rather fancy something stronger', Arthur leapt instantly to his feet. But Chips beat him to it.

'Allow me,' he said. 'I'll ring for the tray. And Arthur, you might be a sport and see have I left my copy of Mr Huxley's *Brave New World* upstairs in my room? I'd ask old Mason, only I know he'll take forever.'

'Couldn't you go, and I'll take charge of drinks?' Arthur asked, but Chips was breezy and adamant: 'Not at all, dear boy.'

So Arthur went reluctantly upstairs, and by the time he came back down with the book, furious, saying, 'It was in the library this whole time,' Chips had positioned himself beside Doris, with Brigid squeezed close to her on the other side, and was reading aloud from *Five Children and It* so that there was nothing for Arthur to do except obey when Lady Iveagh said, 'Come and sit here, Arthur, and tell me what you plan to do with yourself during vac this summer. We will be in Italy, and I rather thought you might come with us.'

For the remainder of their visit, another three days, Chips did everything he could to make sure Arthur and Doris were never in one another's company for long. He did it gravely and joylessly but carefully, as though a great duty had been assumed and faithfully discharged. Indeed, he seemed surprised that no acknowledgement of his sacrifice was made by Lady Iveagh.

'I have quite given up my holiday to this,' he said peevishly on their last night, coming to Honor's room late.

'No one asked you to, and I very much wish you hadn't,' Honor said. She was sitting up in bed reading, wearing a violet quilted bed jacket.

'You do look thoroughly adorable,' Chips said, coming closer to the bed. 'I know you like to keep to our separate rooms while at Elveden, but perhaps tonight . . .'

'No, Chips, I am about to go to sleep. It's very late. Perhaps if you hadn't spent such hours playing billiards with Arthur . . .'

'I thought it wise,' Chips said pompously.

'Well, no one else agrees with you. Mamma wondered what could you both be doing, taking such ages.'

She spoke irritably and wasn't surprised when he stepped back and said stiffly, 'I did what I thought right.'

'I know you did. Now I must go to sleep; will you turn off that light?' There was something in his face she had not noticed before, she thought, something calculating and not terribly kind. Was it new, or had it always been there and she had been blind?

If Doris had noticed anything, she gave no sign of it, continuing to be jolly and friendly to all so that when they left in the motorcar the next morning – Honor seated in the middle, with Chips and Doris on either side of her – they all, even Lord Iveagh, begged her to come back soon and for longer.

But from that time, Honor saw an edge between the two of them, her husband and her friend. Faint, but sharp.

Chapter Twenty-Six

It wasn't that she minded him doing it, Doris thought, watching Chips turn himself inside out to anticipate and sully Arthur's attempts to be close to her. It was the way he did it. The way he made it so insultingly obvious.

She had never thought of Lump in that way. And that, she reflected, was what made it all so painful. He was a viscount, yes, but also childish, somewhat spoilt, and most of all Honor's brother. All those things meant that he simply never had a place in any of her plans. Rather, she felt sorry for him. He had come home feeling grand and grown-up and even important, and within just a few hours had been squeezed back down into the size and shape the household expected of him. It was exactly what happened to Doris when she went back to Dorset – except that the shape she was forced into was the capable, energetic form she had held as a child in that house. Lump, squashed by his mother and overlooked by his father, had been made again into an awkward, diffident youth. She saw it in his face, heard it in his voice, together with the bewildered resentment he must feel that this could happen to one who was now, in the larger worlds of London society, listened to and even admired.

And so she made a small fuss of him, teasing him gently. Just enough to cheer him and make him feel, again, a good fellow. And now Chips had made her intentions ugly and mortifying.

She told herself that it spoke of him, the contents of his mind and the consciousness of his motivations, far more than it did of her. And she knew she was right – that if Chips saw deceit and duplicity, calculation and shamelessness, it was because his own eyes put those things there. But even so, she felt a hot wave of humiliation when she realised the speed with which Chips began to police them, making, always, a third if they proposed a game of cards or a walk or ride.

'You hate hunting.' She had tackled him after breakfast.

'I dislike all forms of hunting alright,' he agreed.

'So, why come?'

'Horseback is a good way to see the countryside. To take the lie of the land.' And he raised a mocking eyebrow.

'You'll never keep up,' she said. And indeed he hadn't. Within the first ten minutes, he'd fallen to the rear with the old folks while Doris, on one of Lord Iveagh's better horses, had been the triumph of the meet.

'Anyone who wasn't in love with you before is now,' Honor told her when Doris came in to chat with her in her bath, before dinner. 'The MFH says any minute you aren't on a horse is wasted.'

'How kind.' Doris smiled mechanically. 'How did Chips enjoy himself?'

'Not much.'

'Good.'

But Honor pretended to misunderstand her. 'I suppose he forgot how he dislikes it,' she said. 'One does. It's a useful reminder, to go out every once in a while and remember all over again what it's like: the sitting around waiting for hounds to find, rain trickling down the back of one's neck; then the crazed dashes across fields, the mad scrambles up steep banks, the mud. And then, worst of all, the impossibly long hack home when all one can think about is one's bath and tea . . . I don't know how you bear it, darling.'

Had she really not noticed? Doris wondered. Or could she not bring herself to acknowledge what was in front of them?

She walked back to her room through the dark hallways – Lady Iveagh was strict about lamps being turned off – trying to untangle the various threads of misery within her. Chips was a new one to add to the mass, so that now it was like a cat's cradle of painful things snarled up within. She had known that putting herself beyond David Envers' reach would be hard, but even so she was shocked at the almost physical wound that seemed inflicted.

The way she found it hard, at times, to stand fully upright because of the empty space within her. Although she had not seen him in weeks, she thought so often of his voice, his smell, the touch of his hands, that really, it was easier to count the few moments when she didn't think of these things. She looked forward to being alone, the better to replay their moments together in her mind, or invent new and larger possibilities for the two of them – scenes in which he said what she wanted him to say; in which she acted with the energy and conviction that disappeared when she was actually with him. And then, knowing how dangerous the narcotic of her own imagination was becoming, she forced her mind away from him and how much she wanted him, so that it seemed as though all day and even in her sleep she played a game of tug with herself that was exhausting.

Coming to Elveden had been a relief because here, at least, she knew she would not see Envers, and so she was free of the constant watching over her shoulder, tensed always against his possible appearance. These days had soothed her – the delightful company of the girls, their confiding flattery, even the shy admiration of Lump. She had found that she missed Bertie. Missed how he made her laugh, missed the easy way he made her feel cared for. Mostly, she missed the person she was when she was with him – someone open, sunny, direct. Not someone who snuck around and dissembled, or who felt herself incomplete; half a person. Being with the children and Lump had restored her to herself, just as Bertie always did.

And then Chips had taken all that was wholesome and good, and extinguished it. And in doing so, had added a bitter nugget to her store of unhappiness.

Back in London, they all carried on as though the visit to Elveden had been nothing out of the ordinary – a pleasant way to spend Christmas, a few days of country pursuits – and perhaps in Honor's mind it was indeed just that. But Doris knew that something had changed between her and Chips, and she knew he knew it too.

The warmth of his personality, turned up to its fullest for others, was turned down for her, like one of the oil lamps at Elveden that must be dimmed. When he looked at her it was quickly, impatiently, his eyes flickering from her face and onwards, to something that compelled him more. Or it had been. Now, she noticed that he paused more in his observation of her. But it was a watchful, considering kind of pause, rather than a fond one.

Some weeks after Christmas, when London was made tight and hard with frost so that the buildings seemed to contract a little, stand taller and thinner in the freezing air, Doris came home, late, alone, from a nightclub. Dropped by a merry group of her friends, all squeezed into a taxi cab, she let herself in to number 21 with her key. The house was in darkness, the servants long gone to bed. She had insisted that no one wait up for her, including her maid. In the hallway she took off her evening coat and threw it onto a chair. Someone would hang it up in the morning. She kicked off her shoes and was about to start up the stairs in her stocking feet when the door behind her opened. It was Chips, wrapped in an elaborately patterned silk dressing gown.

'I thought I heard something,' he said, walking towards her. 'Come and join me for a nightcap?' He put his hand on her arm, where she felt it hot through the silk of her evening dress, and looked directly at her. His brown eyes were warm and shiny, like toffee, and ever so slightly crossed. It was the squinting look he got when he had drunk too much. He increased the pressure on her arm. 'You can tell me all about your evening.' He drew her into the library, before she could think of any reason why he should not.

'Where's Honor?'

'Gone up. Asleep.'

He moved closer to her, and Doris held herself perfectly still. As though somehow, by doing so he might not notice her. For once, she didn't know what to do – which way to go. To move back, away from him, or forward, past him? She was used to men making passes at her. It happened often, but almost never that she didn't expect it, and feel able to manage it. Never, as now, when she was alone except for her friend, his wife, asleep upstairs. Her heart beat too high in her chest, almost at the base of her throat so that she could feel it thick and full and choking her, closing her voice so that she couldn't say anything.

He must have been sitting in darkness, for all the lamps were off and only the lazy flickering of the fire cast any light. Bundi was curled up on the rug in front of it, breathing deeply. Doris looked for a book, or one of his diaries, to show what he had been doing – something that she might ask about: *Are you enjoying that book? How do you find so much to write about?* Anything that would provide conversation and a diversion from the intense and charged silence. Words that would break that silence up and rearrange it into something more usual, something that she could manage. But there was nothing.

He leaned a little closer to her and she smelt the brandy on his breath. How long had he been sitting there? Had he been waiting? She had never been this close to him. He smelt of cologne and hair cream and lavender water, and something else too. It was, she thought, the way metal smells when it has been heated too much – a candlestick where the candle has burned too far down and the brass or silver heated to an angry scorching point.

He moved closer again, so that his mouth was barely an inch from hers. And she felt then for the first time that under those impeccably cut suits, the veneer of charm and chatter and silly obsessions, his scented hair oil and mani-cured hands, he was after all as fully male as any bull or stallion. She thought of all the rumours that swirled around him, and wondered at how much she had allowed herself to be fooled by the charming and carefully civilised surface.

'Where are you coming from?'

'The Café de Paris.'

'You do look delicious,' he said. He made it sound like an insult. 'Hot and rumpled, as if you've just been in bed.'

'Dancing,' Doris said firmly.

'Hmmm.'

He breathed in sharply, as though sniffing at her. He was so close now that the thump of her heart was the only thing between them, but she didn't know what he wanted. To kiss her? To sink his square white teeth into her? Either, she thought, was possible. And what, then, would she do? Call out? It was his house. Anyone who heard and came would be his servant.

'Please don't pretend to an inexperience I know isn't yours,' he said in a low voice, almost crooning.

'I pretend to nothing,' she said. 'You, on the other hand . . .'

'I what?'

'Well, you certainly pretend, if even half of what one hears is true.'

'*Half of what one hears* . . .' He mocked her. 'What a little prude you are, really. A teasing little prude. Do I pretend?' He looked thoughtfully at her. 'Perhaps. But you needn't think I will be called to account by you.'

Now his hand was on her arm, gripping it. And just when Doris had begun to realise that she had no plan for this, just when Chips' mouth was all but on hers so that his breath was already wet on her face and she was frozen still in one spot, Mimi, who must have heard her come in, came trotting into the library. Pleased to see her mistress, she veered too close to Bundi and startled him awake. Bundi leaped up, teeth bared in a snarl. Mimi yelped in fright, then turned to face Bundi, growling comically.

It was enough. It was everything.

'Mimi! Come here,' Doris called sharply, stepping back and away from Chips and making great play of calling the dog, who still growled.

'Down, Bundi!' Chips said, and Bundi went to him and pushed against his legs so that Chips had to move back and away to avoid falling.

Once he was no longer in her orbit, Doris found she could move. 'I'm going up,' she said firmly, Mimi in her arms. 'Goodnight.'

Part Two

1935

Chapter Twenty-Seven

London, January 1935

In late January, Honor discovered she was pregnant.

'Or rather, Chips has discovered it,' she said, coming into Doris' room and dragging the curtains open. 'I mean, thinks he has discovered it. Nothing is certain yet.'

'Must you?' Doris muttered sleepily from her bed, turning away and pulling the flowered silk bedspread over her head.

'Yes, I must. Now, pay attention.'

Doris sat up. 'Tea first,' she said.

'Very well.' Honor poured a cup of lukewarm tea – the maid had brought the tray up hours earlier – and handed it to her.

Doris' hand was shaking slightly. She smelt stale, of cigarettes, sleep and sweat. 'Go on,' she said, when she had drunk the tea and held out the empty cup for another. She dragged the counterpane high up around her so only her bare shoulders were exposed to the dull morning light, the rest of her cocooned in ruched flowery silk.

'Chips tells me I am nine days late.'

'I see.' Doris pushed her hair back, out of her eyes. Through it was threaded the headband of silver beads she had worn the night before so that the tousled curls were like a spider's web heavy with drops of shining dew upon them. 'How gruesomely specific.'

'Isn't it? And in front of the maid too . . . But he's right. I hadn't noticed, but I counted back and he's right. It's still far too early to be sure. So we have told no one. Only you.'

'Is that why he's been watching you as though you might explode into a fountain of gold or diamonds?'

'He's jolly pleased. Says he hopes it's a boy, but that he doesn't much care so long as it is bonny, and what else could *his* child be?'

'*His* child?' Doris asked, mouth twisting into an ironic smile.

'Yes. His.'

'And how do you feel?'

'Rather as if I had said yes to something without really thinking about it,' Honor said. 'You know, one of those Friday-to-Mondays that seem like a good idea when one accepts, and then the day comes to pack and travel down, and one simply can't think why one ever agreed to go . . .'

She didn't say how many times, already, she had replayed

her disgust at the child in the Paddington Street tenement, how intensely she had wanted not to hold him, so that she'd had to force herself not to let him drop from her stiff arms. The way that memory followed her, like the toad that hopped after the princess in the fairy story, spoiling much of what she did.

'But that's not all I feel,' she said hurriedly then, seeing Doris' face. 'Relieved too. I mean, I hope he is right and there is a child. But it's so early yet . . . I told Mamma and she was shocked that Chips should talk about such things so soon.' She paused and took a piece of toast from Doris' tray and nibbled a blackened corner, then made a face and put it back. 'She says anything can still happen.'

'Yes,' Doris said. 'But Chips is not one to wait. He's a counter of chickens well before they hatch.'

'Oh yes, he schemes and plots for the future the way a farmer might think over his fields, planning what to grow where, dreaming of the day his crops will stand tall and proud in the summer sun.' Honor laughed. 'Sometimes I think he enjoys the contemplation more even than the realisation. Once he gets something, he straight away looks for something else.'

'So what now?' Doris, ever practical, asked.

'I will see Doctor Gilliatt, but not just yet. For now, Chips says I must simply rest.'

Although, Honor thought later, Chips' interest in her meant that rest was hardly possible. He followed her about the house, coming upon her wherever she was and asking questions – how did she feel, did she want anything – and making plans. 'Paul, if it's a boy – for Paul of Yugoslavia – Gwendolen if a girl, for your mother?' He seemed not to notice that Honor said little, contenting herself with ums and ahs instead of actual answers.

In fact, she felt an itch to escape him. On the one hand, she enjoyed being so much the object of his attention – as she hadn't been since before they married – but his intensity alarmed her. His plans were so fully formed, so thorough – who the child could marry, where he or she would be schooled, what they must say to the nanny who had care of him or her – that Honor was frightened by them. It was the detail of the plans that alarmed her, because she had no corresponding detail. The idea was a hazy one still, for her, entirely without solid form. They didn't even know for sure she was to have a baby – how could he be talking of names, of attributes: 'As long as she is nothing like my mother, I will not mind if it is a girl.' She couldn't make similar plans, or even show a proper interest in his, not while she still interrogated her body silently for proof.

'You must continue to rest,' he said that afternoon, settling a rug around her that she did not want. But then a short time later Emerald was announced and he did not deny her, nor did he suggest that he would take her out.

'You must both absolutely come for lunch tomorrow,' Emerald declared, entering already halfway through a sentence, and setting down a large crocodile-skin handbag beside a rolled copy of her newspaper on the table by the door. Honor could see where she had made notes by hand in the margins. 'A late lunch. Come for two o'clock.'

'I'm not sure . . .' Honor began.

But Chips held up a hand. 'Why must we?' he asked with a smile.

'I have Mr and Mrs Ernest Simpson coming. It's time you met her properly. And I have promised to introduce *her* to the people who matter.'

Honor stifled a giggle as she watched Chips sit a little straighter and throw his shoulders back at that. 'Now that she is someone "who matters" too?' she asked, smiling.

'Well, but is she?' Chips wanted to know. 'Can we be sure?'

'I think we can,' Emerald assured him seriously. 'At first, I thought not. Strictly palate cleanser, I thought, the bridge from Lady Furness to someone new. I had ideas in mind for that someone new, but now . . . The prince brought her and Mr Simpson – a friendly bear of a man – to dinner yesterday evening. They simply dropped by, unannounced . . .' She paused, to let the full glory of this sink in. 'Then he took us to the Embassy Club for supper. He drank Vichy water all night – he is started on a new diet, you know – and talked like a prophet. As indeed I told him.' She looked brightly around, that they might admire her skill. 'But much as he talked to all of us, it was her he watched. Her he danced with. Her whose opinions he listened to. Even though her opinions were not at all well formed . . . No, it's clear to me that this is serious enough that you must now meet her. And so, lunch tomorrow. Now I must go. No, no time for tea.' And she reached for her bag and newspaper.

Honor started to say that she was not going about just then – even though she knew how eagerly Emerald would seize on this – but Chips' voice was loud over hers.

'Of course we will. You may depend upon it,' he said warmly.

And, when Emerald had gone, he took Honor's hand in his and said, 'It's only lunch, darling. You will be able for it. And after all, we aren't completely certain of the baby yet.'

How fast he changed, she thought, when it suited him.

'Whereas Emerald is clearly certain of Mrs Simpson,' he continued. 'I wonder what she will be like.'

'Like Freda Dudley Ward I assume,' Honor said, 'tiny and darting, rude and indifferent to everyone, and revolt-ingly obsequious to the prince.' She felt tired and cross. 'I think I will rest now, if you want to leave me,' she said, and when Chips said he would stay very quietly by her she snapped, 'No thank you, I prefer to be on my own,' so that once he had gone she felt miserable and sorry and her rest wasn't pleasant at all.

But Mrs Simpson was not tiny, darting, rude and indif-ferent. Or at least not all those things and not at once. Arriving at Emerald's the next day, Honor, despite the fatigue that dragged at her, was curious to see this woman. They were early – Honor had insisted – because she wanted to see who came in first, Mrs Simpson or the prince; or would they arrive together? Emerald wasn't down yet and Chips, cross at being unfashionable, picked up a magazine and buried himself in it. Which meant that Honor was free to wander about the drawing room that was papered in a lavish russet metallic wallpaper against which the firelight flicked so that the room appeared like the inside of a burnished copper box. It was crammed with paintings and *objets*, full like a curiosity shop and oppressive in the clamour the various pieces of china, silver, carved wood and canvas set up, to be looked at and commented on.

She walked over to the large windows that looked onto the street. It was empty, except for a long black motorcar. She watched it draw to a slow halt in front of number 7. Out of it stepped a small, neat woman with smooth hair tucked under a chic little hat. Mrs Simpson. So she was early too. And alone, Honor saw. She looked up and down the street, then crossed the pavement in three quick steps to the front door. Honor went out into the hallway and stood half in shadow, looking over the banisters as Emerald's butler went to open the door.

From where she stood, Honor had a clear view down. She watched Mrs Simpson walk in, remove her coat and hand it, with her hat and gloves, to the butler. Her movements were quick and competent, little rushing forays at buttons and hat pins executed with economy, all yielding the desired result without fuss or delay. She said something in a low voice – Honor couldn't hear it – the butler nodded, and within less than a minute she was ready to walk up the stairs.

Her self-possession was considerable. She drew it around herself like something tangible: a fur or opera cloak. Honor saw that she didn't stop to check her reflection in the looking glass that hung above a slender table at the bottom of the stairs. Beyond a cursory pat of her dark hair, she did nothing about her appearance at all. And she didn't need to, Honor thought. She was impeccable. More smartly dressed than anyone Honor had seen, beating even Doris and cousin Aileen. Nothing was showy or flamboyant – a flapper she was not – and she wore only black with touches of white, but everything very modish and carefully precise.

She started up the marble stairs behind the butler, and Honor slipped back into the drawing room. Chips, still engrossed in his magazine, had noticed nothing, and Honor felt pleased that she had been first to see this woman they had been bid come and meet. It felt like a silent victory. She arranged herself by the fire and waited.

Emerald came down in a rush then, and said to Chips with a sly grin, 'Our guest of honour has arrived; look lively.'

Mrs Simpson stepped in discreetly, almost meekly, Honor thought, and paused in the doorway that they might get a look at her.

'How do you do?' Her voice was well-modulated, with the American in it subdued. She was tiny, and old, Honor thought, seeing her close to. A middle-aged lady with brown skin wrinkled from too much sun. She had good teeth – square, white, even and neatly spaced – and there was something reassuring about her impeccable grooming. Not a hair strayed from place, not a seam that wasn't perfectly straight, the powder with which she had dusted her face even and smooth. So groomed was she that the large mole on her chin, just below her bottom lip, seemed all the more outrageous. Like a quite different Mrs Simpson trying to erupt from beneath all that clean-pressed freshness.

'Delightful to see you again so soon,' Emerald said, sweeping forward and shaking her hand.

'Wonderful of you to invite me,' Mrs Simpson said.

'Allow me to introduce . . .' Emerald then began an introduction that was so long – encompassing Honor's parents, Chips' writing career, their wedding – that at the end of it Honor, squirming at having to stand silent for so long while this woman observed her, could think of nothing to say except to blurt out, 'Is your husband here, Mrs Simpson?'

'Call me Wallis. No. Ernest is unable to get away today.'

She spoke with gravity, as though this Ernest were engaged in something delicate and wonderfully important. He was 'in shipping', Honor knew, so what could possibly be so important?

'Your family are in brewing?' Mrs Simpson asked.

Honor stiffened. What a thing to say. She opened her mouth to reply . . . what? She didn't know, but Chips was quicker. And more diplomatic, she thought.

'The Guinnesses have many interests,' he said urbanely, 'and there are a great many of them.'

'Have you found anywhere yet?' Emerald asked then. She spoke to Chips, but with a quick and reassuring look at Honor. 'The Channons have been looking for a place in the country, somewhere within the constituency of Southend where Chips will stand at the next general election in place of Lady Iveagh,' she explained to Mrs Simpson, who nodded politely, without much interest.

'We looked over The Lawns at Southchurch,' Chips said. 'Any good?'

'I fear not,' he said regretfully.

Honor remembered him musing as they drove away from that impressive property – 'A fine house. If we had only, say, two thousand pounds per annum I think we should be happy living quietly there. But with our wealth, I fear it is not grand enough.' She had started to laugh, then turned it into a small cough when he'd looked beadily around at her.

'I'm sure you'll find somewhere,' Mrs Simpson said reassuringly.

Quite why she needed to reassure them, Honor couldn't imagine. Certainly she was nothing like Freda Dudley Ward. She was polite. Goodness, how she was polite. Almost deferential. In a low, modulated voice she asked pleasant questions that were dull but correct – had they enjoyed Christmas, did they shoot, had Honor been to America, did Chips miss Chicago – at which he shuddered and said, 'Not only do I not miss it, I would move heaven and earth never to see the place again' – until the room filled with the rest of Emerald's guests and Mrs Simpson was taken away to meet others.

'Well?' That was Oonagh, coming to join them the very minute Mrs Simpson was led away. She had a martini glass in each hand. She drained one, set it down carefully on a marble-topped table, and took a sip from the other. She was as ethereally beautiful as ever, Honor thought – more so even since the birth of her daughter, Tessa, three years before – but she looked tired. There were violet shadows under the pale blue eyes and her once-golden hair was coloured a more subdued brown. She had been in Ireland for almost a year and was back in London 'to settle things with Philip'.

That meant a divorce, Honor knew. Chips had been furious at the news. 'First Diana leaves your cousin Bryan for that fellow Mosley . . . I can *quite* see what she sees in him,' he had said with a flash of his white teeth that seemed rather lascivious, Honor thought uneasily, 'but must she be so histrionic? What is wrong with a discreet affair? And now Oonagh and Philip. Between them, they will drag the Guinness name through too much mud.'

'What did you make of our new lady-in-waiting?' Oonagh continued.

'Hard to know what exactly all that quiet deference is a front for . . .' Honor mused.

'Indeed,' Oonagh agreed. 'Actual deference? Or arrogance disguised?'

'But definitely a front?' Honor asked.

'Oh definitely,' Oonagh said with a laugh. She lit a cigarette and blew out two streams of smoke through her nostrils, like a blue-and-silver dragon. 'Did you see the pearls?'

'Mmm . . . Even Mamma's are quite cast in the shade.'

'And the dress? Aileen has one just like it. Straight from Paris. Givenchy.'

'Marvellous clothes alright, and so slim.' Honor sounded wistful.

'She doesn't eat,' Oonagh said. 'That's something else they have in common. She has all sorts of new American notions about diet, which he simply adores. Can't get anyone here to take him seriously, with his funny ideas about food, but she has all the same ideas. I heard them one night talking about how fatal bread is, for hours.'

'Isn't she clever,' Honor marvelled.

'But is she?' Oonagh wanted to know. 'Or just . . .' She gestured, unable to describe what she meant. 'Chips, do tell. As a fellow countryman, you must have a better understanding than we do?'

'I don't know what you mean,' Chips said, looking from one to the other. 'She seems rather a little nut of a woman to me; polite and discreet. That mole, though . . .' He waved his hands in the air for a moment, as though to ward something off. He was horrified by imperfections generally, but particularly of the skin.

'Emerald is showing her off as though she were the winning cake at a church fête,' Honor said, watching their progress. 'She must have noticed the pearls too.'

'She smiles so much and almost never shows her teeth,' Oonagh said thoughtfully, looking over to where Wallis was shaking hands with Duff Cooper. 'What do you think that means?'

'Why must it mean something?' Chips demanded.

'Don't be dull, Chips, please,' Oonagh begged.

Mrs Simpson – 'call me Wallis' – continued on her path

– polite, pleasant, discreetly charming right through lunch, and then, just when Honor was ready to be thoroughly bored by her, the prince arrived, and a different Mrs Simpson emerged.

'Oh sir!' she said, before every remark. 'As though,' Oonagh whispered, leaning in to envelop Honor in a heavy cloud of scent, 'she is playing a part in some Vaudeville theatrical.'

And yet, beneath the show of meekness, she ordered him to and fro – 'Do please fetch me a drink, darling'; 'Stop fidgeting with your tie'; 'Put that down, you smoke too much' – always as though she didn't care if he obeyed or not. But he did. Every time. And when she wasn't giving him things to do, he waited, hovering by her, for the next instruction. She was like someone who has tamed a wild animal or a savage dog, some creature that might still turn on everyone else, and cannot stop showing her dominion over it. The man who has the Minotaur on a chain. Except that she was a woman, and the thing she had on a chain was the future King of England.

Honor looked at her with new respect. And at Emerald with sympathy. It was a lunch party that showed no signs of ending. The prince arrived so very late, and then refused to eat anything, or drink anything except his Vichy water, of which Emerald had ordered dozens of bottles, so that the afternoon hovered at the point where it should have broken up, and then, instead of departing, the guests moved seamlessly on to cocktails and jazz records on the gramophone. No one seemed disposed to leave. Mrs Simpson, who drank only whiskey and soda water – 'just a splash' – became especially animated, chattering loudly to the group that had formed around her. With the prince attentively by her side, surrounded by his cronies, she looked quite different to the 'little nut of a woman' who had arrived.

Now, she was speeded up, like a cinema reel that has been put on wrong, thought Honor with a giggle. Speeded up, but also slowed down, like a foxtrot: quick, quick, quick-quick-slow . . . Because just when you thought she was in perpetual motion, whirling through the evening, with a cigarette holder, a glass, a powder compact in hand, a song, a laugh, a joke on her lips, so that you wondered how she could take anything in at all, you would look up and meet her eyes. Those slow brown eyes, the centre of the storm, that soaked it all up and stored it somewhere.

'Isn't she something?' It was the prince, at Honor's side.

Honor looked around, for who he must be talking to – he never spoke to her; sometimes Honor thought he couldn't see her; as though his royal birth had given him the gift of other people's invisibility. But there was no one else close by. It must be her. Maybe he would have spoken to anyone, so strong was his need to talk about this woman he had fallen in love with.

'Everything, with Wallis, is a fire sale,' he said admiringly, leaning thin and elegant against the copper-coloured wall. 'I saw one once, you know, in Germany. A rush of energy around one spot, a coming-and-going with intent and purpose. That's Wallis.'

Honor agreed – what else was she to do? – but he paid no attention to her, because Wallis had gestured for him, and he leaped forward. The man Honor had seen in the Embassy nightclub barely a year before – that petulant, arrogant man – was gone. In his place this eager adolescent.

'It's rather sweet, isn't it?' Oonagh said, coming back to join her once the prince was safely gone. She slurred her words a little. Looking down, Honor saw that the hem of her silvery dress was torn.

'Is it?'

'Why, yes. Romantic,' Oonagh said vaguely. She might have been talking about a novel she hadn't bothered to read. 'Love. You know.'

'But she already has a husband.'

'Two, apparently.' Oonagh gave a wicked grin. 'Hard not to approve, though, when she is so very good for divorced ladies.'

Honor tried to look disapproving – Lady Iveagh was very clear that divorce was a thing to be avoided – but it was impossible with Oonagh. 'How *is* Philip?' she asked.

'So happy with Valsie that he is ready to agree to anything I want. I must say, it is *mortifying* to have him so eager to let me go.'

'But you are equally eager to be gone?'

'Yes, but that's not really the point, is it?' She pulled a face, pouting a little.

'And Dom?' Honor asked. Dominick, Lord Oranmore and Browne, was the man Oonagh planned to marry, as soon as the divorce from Philip came through.

'Simply heaven,' Oonagh said triumphantly. 'Have you seen Maureen recently?'

'They came to dinner a while ago, her and Duff.'

'And?' Oonagh asked, wobbling a little on her high heels.

'Hard to say.' Honor was thoughtful. 'Does her constant rowing with Duff mean she's unhappy? Or simply being Maureen? Chips adores her and thinks her tremendous fun—'

'Which she is, when she isn't simply lacerating one . . . but I know what you mean. The rowing. What started as a game does rather seem to have become a habit. How was Duff?'

'He looked tired. And,' – Honor lowered her voice and leaned in – 'he drank an entire bottle of crème de menthe. At the dinner table.'

It wasn't really done to mention such a thing, she knew, but it had been rather odd, the way Duff had slid the thick green liquid into himself steadily and stealthily. She had found herself watching him, trying to catch a glimpse of the darkly handsome young man she had once been rather in love with, and finding only a distant resemblance; as though this were an older, coarser relative. It had made her feel sad.

'Oh Duff – drinks like an absolute fish, and it never seems to do him a bit of harm,' Oonagh said airily. She teetered a little and leaned against a small octagonal table inlaid with dark and light wood. It didn't look very solid, and Honor put a hand out to steady her.

'Don't *fuss*,' Oonagh said irritably.

'Anyway,' Honor continued when she seemed anchored again, 'Maureen is furious about Diana and Mosley, and takes great pleasure in telling me how *démodée* Diana now is – "a divorced woman in love with a man whose wife died oh-so-*conveniently*, and still he won't marry her". I think "tarnished" was the word she used, with glee.'

'I'm sure she says the very same about me,' Oonagh said. Then, so swiftly that Honor was confused for a moment, 'How are you finding it all?'

'Finding what?'

'Marriage. The great purpose.'

'Delightful,' Honor said, looking across the room to where Chips was deep in conversation with Mrs Simpson. As she looked, he took a cigarette from the gold and sapphire case Honor had given him for Christmas – the man in Cartier's had said it was for a woman, but Honor had known Chips would adore its rather wistful elegance – put two cigarettes into his mouth, lit them, then handed one to Mrs Simpson, who fitted it to her ivory holder and took a deep drag, releasing a cloud of smoke along with a laugh at whatever it was Chips was saying to her. 'It's delightful,' she said again. But Oonagh was no longer listening. She had turned away and was fidgeting with one of Emerald's curios, a tiny Chinese dragon-dog in blue china.

'Why does she have so many things?' she asked in disapproval, looking around the crowded rooms.

'She likes things, same as she likes people. Lots of them. New people, old people. She collects them.'

'And then sorts them out and ruthlessly discards those who are no good to her.'

'True. But think how good she is to those she keeps.'

'She'll certainly be keeping Call-me-Wallis,' Oonagh said, nudging Honor to look over to where Mrs Simpson was now dancing, waving her cigarette holder in time to 'Anything Goes'.

'We're all going to have to run a little faster,' Honor said gloomily. 'She's going to double the pace, I know it, and I can barely keep up as it is.'

Chapter Twenty-Eight

'Gilliatt says two-to-one you are indeed having a baby,' Chips said gleefully the next day, coming back into Honor's little upstairs sitting room after showing the doctor out. He rubbed his hands eagerly, as though he would create fire from the sticks of his satisfaction.

'You'd think he'd tell me,' Honor said peevishly. She was tired after the interminable lunch party and the doctor's visit had embarrassed her, as it always did – his practised hands, as though she were fruit, to be felt for bruises or blemishes.

'You are to avoid rich and acidic food, but you may have – of all things! – a glass of Guinness.' He laughed. 'Even Gilliatt says it will be good for you.' He laughed again, at his own wit in referencing the advertising campaign that had proved so successful, though also rather humiliating, as Lady Iveagh and Honor had confessed to one another.

'I hate the stuff,' Honor said.

'Let me read to you,' he said then. 'The latest copy of the *Sketch* has just arrived.'

'I'd rather a book, and I can read to myself,' Honor said. Then, relenting, 'But you can sit beside me, and if there's anything *terribly* good in the *Sketch*, you can tell me.'

They sat companionably, although not in silence. Every few minutes Chips had something to tell her – to his mind, the *Sketch* was positively bursting with 'terribly good' snippets of news: 'Kitty Brownlow dined at the Café de Paris wearing Chanel . . .' – so that by the time Doris put her head around the door, he had read the whole thing cover to cover, told her half of it, and was clearly bored.

'Am I terribly *de trop*?' Doris asked.

'Not at all. Come.' And Honor sat up straighter. 'Darling, pull up that chair for Doris.'

'Have mine.' He stood up. 'I was just leaving. I have errands to run.' And he kissed the top of Honor's head and – with relief, she suspected – was gone.

For a moment Honor thought about how little Chips and Doris were now in the same room with one another, ever since Christmas at Elveden, then pushed it from her mind.

'So, what was she like? Doris asked immediately. She didn't need to say who.

'Rather plain, very chic, not at all what I expected.'

'A pal?'

'Goodness no. Ancient really. I don't see it lasting. I mean, what's the point?' Honor sounded irritable, she knew. But something about the prince, so boyish suddenly, so eager, dangling after his mistress, both of them so old . . . It had been, she thought, undignified.

'Must there be a point? I mean, other than love.'

'I would have thought so.'

'You don't believe in that kind of love, do you?' Doris asked thoughtfully.

'Perhaps not . . .' In fact, Honor didn't, and was a little sorry that she didn't. Because she had, once. Only it had proved as illusory as Lady Iveagh had promised – or threatened. Up close, love within marriage had turned out to be . . . *pleasant*, she thought. Rather nice, friendly, commendable, but not the divine displacement of all things that she had once secretly hoped for. 'You know, when I read Chips' diaries – oh I know I shouldn't, but he does leave them around, almost as if he hopes one will –'

'I'm sure he does,' Doris said with a grin.

'– so much of what he writes is scandalous. The love affairs of our friends, desperate acts of seduction and intrigue. People climbing in and out of bedroom windows . . .' She laughed. 'It all reads like a novel, not real life at all. I think he must make most of it up, because I never notice any of it.'

'You know people do do those things?' Doris said, giving Honor a curious look.

'Well, but do they?'

Honor was silent then. She thought about the way she had felt, reading Chips' lurid accounts of these things that must happen – if they happened at all – under her nose as much as his, only she never seemed to see them. She had felt . . . cheated was the word that came to her mind. Only she didn't understand – cheated of what? Certainly she didn't wish for the trouble and upset that seemed always to rebound from these love affairs. And yet. She discovered a strange wistfulness in herself. There was a part of her that remembered how she had felt about Chips in the very early days of their marriage. Those first nights, the two of them together in the dark and quiet of her bedroom; before she knew much more about him than that he was wonderful company and a charming companion. Before she had understood that those nights were to be frequent but dutiful, and had forced herself to mute her own response to match his, because to be abandoned where he was contained was too mortifying. Before she had watched him scheme so hard for things that weren't his to have, meddle in business that was not his to order.

It's not that she wanted to have secret meetings and painful separations, she thought, but there was a part of her that wanted to know how it must feel, to be driven like that. 'Do you believe in that kind of love?' she asked.

'Perhaps.' Doris was silent then so that Honor almost asked her what she meant – who she meant. Then, 'I must,' Doris continued, more cheerfully, 'otherwise it's not likely that I will find the right person to marry. Unless he can fall, in that desperate way the Romantics go on about, no suitable man is going to take a chance on me.'

'Darling, don't talk like that. I hate when you do.'

'It's the truth, though. I am what the Americans call 'a hard sell'. Doris laughed, with no bitterness. 'I have plenty of money, but I'm not rich enough to be irresistible. Not rich enough to offset the inconvenience of background. I'm in the balance, always – money, no family—'

'You do have family.'

'None worth speaking of. None whom will be an advantage. Some who are a distinct disadvantage. Everyone gets to weigh me up. To ask themselves, is she worth it? To pick over what they know of me with exacting parsimony and make a decision, in my favour or against. And so far, usually against.'

'Is there no one?' Honor asked sympathetically. Then, 'Give me that.' She gestured for the jar of La-rola hand cream that Doris was unscrewing. Doris put down the lid and passed over the jar. Honor scooped out a dollop of the thick white cream. 'Hand.' Doris meekly held out one hand, dropping the other into her lap. Honor took the proffered hand in both of hers and started to slowly rub the cream in, massaging the length of the fingers and across the back of the hand where delicate blueish veins stood out against the white skin. A scent of orange blossom rose up.

'Well . . . perhaps someone . . .' Doris said.

'Not Envers?' Honor asked gently.

'Goodness, no.'

The hand that Honor held stiffened suddenly and twitched, as though Doris would pull it back. But Honor held firm and continued to massage gently. They never talked about Envers, and mostly Honor didn't know what to ask. She could see that Doris, when she first came to St James's Place, had been less than her usual self, almost as though she moved and talked around an absence that could not be mentioned – like a dinner guest who has not turned up so that the table must be reset swiftly to hide the gap, cutlery and crystal shuffled up to disguise it, Honor thought. But recently, she had seemed more robust.

'Go on then,' she said. 'Lord Lewis? You used to go about rather a lot with him . . .'

'And might again,' Doris said with a smile. 'Nothing yet, but I'll tell you if there's anything to tell.'

Honor turned the hand over and continued to massage. Compared with her own, Doris' hands were tiny. 'Other hand,' she said, and Doris obligingly swapped. 'There will be,' she said loyally. 'I'm sure of it.'

But perhaps there wasn't anything, because in the weeks that followed, as Honor went out less, Doris made sure to tell her all manner of detail about her own nights out – 'almost as good as being there!' Honor said – but nothing about Lord Lewis. Honor thought of asking Chips – he, too, was as sociable as ever, even without her, and could surely be expected to hear any interesting whispers that gathered. But she didn't. Since Christmas at Elveden, even though he was as courteous as ever, seemed to derive the same fun, even pride, in Doris' popularity, her charm and languid beauty, Honor now understood that there was a sliver of coldness in the way he looked over her – a gaze that calculated her actions, and their possible effect on him. That he was not all kindness towards her. And so Honor said nothing and waited.

At first Chips announced grandly that he would go nowhere but would stay by her side. Then he found a thousand invitations he couldn't possibly refuse, and for those cold early spring months was out every night and much of every day. But Honor was glad.

When he was home, his constant agitation was too much for her. The baby – there was no doubt, now, that there was a baby – slowed her, dragging at her insides, taking what strength she had. Listening to Chips' endless musings on where they had been invited, what one had said and another done and what might be drawn from these facts, became too much for her.

How could he possibly care so much, she wondered, but indulgently, because she liked to see him poring over his plans, gloating at a new friend or when a coveted invitation was delivered. He seemed to keep, in his head, a chart of the whole of London society, so that he could tell at a glance where everyone belonged, and what events might shift them up or down, forwards or backwards in the confined space of battle.

'We really must move into a bigger house so we can entertain properly.' He cast a look around. 'Have you thought more about Belgrave Square?'

After more than a year of considering and rejecting alternate properties, Chips had settled on number 5 Belgrave Square as their future home, 'the only really *good* square left in London,' as he said. Number 5 was next door to the Duke and Duchess of Kent, and that, too, weighed in its favour. 'Why, the prince will have to walk past us every time he wishes to see his brother.' He rubbed his hands at the thought.

'If you wish,' she said. She had no desire to move, certainly no desire for the exertion that would be required. But it meant so much to him. And, truth was, it had become more exhausting to refuse Chips than to acquiesce. 'Make an offer, by all means.'

'We will need to redecorate,' he said thoughtfully. 'Nearly the whole house must be modernised. It will take many months. And a great deal of money.' He looked sideways at her.

'Perhaps you had better talk to Papa.'

He took up her hand and kissed it enthusiastically. 'Best of wives!' he said. 'I will see about it immediately.' And, calling to Bundi, he left her. The dog, at the sound of Chips' voice, leaped off the sofa, where he had been dozing, knocked Honor's book to the ground and ran to the door.

Honor, with a sigh, bent to pick it up.

Chapter Twenty-Nine

At first, the morning after that strange encounter with Chips, Doris thought she must leave St James's Place, for how could she stay? She ordered the maid to pack her things. But when she went to tell Honor, still turning over what excuse she might give, she found her so lethargic and ill that she said nothing. *I will wait a day or so*, she told herself, *until she is better*. And then, when Honor told her of the pregnancy, saying impulsively, 'How glad I am that you are here, for I have never felt worse,' Doris knew that she must stay.

By then, Chips had apologised, stiffly. He accosted her after breakfast. Not the next morning – he kept to his room very late that day – but the morning after. 'I fear I was a trifle uncivilised the other night,' he began. 'You mustn't—'

'Mustn't what?' Doris asked. 'Tell Honor?'

'Make too much of it,' Chips said, staring at her, his handsome face very still. Doris found her heart starting to thump again. 'What, even, would you tell?' he continued. 'That you and I had a short, late-night conversation, about what I can scarce remember? Not much to tell, is there?' He stepped forward and Doris very quickly stepped back and to the side, away from him.

'There are other things I could tell,' she said.

'But you won't,' he said smoothly. 'I know you won't. Because to tell would only wound her. And after all, what is there to tell? Nothing. Nothing at all.' He looked beadily at her and Doris knew – knew that he knew – she would never say anything.

She told herself it was an apology, but could only believe it for as long as she didn't remember the smell of scorched metal and the hot, wet rasp of his breath on her face. And for all that they were civil, the two of them, thereafter, something was changed between them, and could not be changed back.

The day after she learned of Honor's pregnancy, feeling strangely fragile and low-spirited, Doris telephoned to Bertie. 'Are you busy?' she asked.

'Not if there's a chance of seeing you,' he said. 'Why don't I come and take you for a drive?'

'I should like that.'

He picked her up and they drove as far as Richmond with the top of the car up and a rug tucked firmly around Doris' knees. He had brought a thermos of coffee

– 'In case you get cold' – and Doris was touched, again, by the care he took of her. They sang along with the radio and Bertie told her funny stories from his evening. 'Elizabeth Ponsonby has a *job*, at a nightclub in Staines.'

'They have nightclubs in Staines?'

'Apparently. She says they have hired her for her address book, saying she knows everyone who is anyone in London, and that therefore we must all be sure to go to the Blue Cat, as this place is called, because otherwise it will be "too shame-making" for her. So Baby said, "Not half as shame-making as when we all turn up!"' He laughed happily.

'Well, I shan't go,' Doris said. 'And I hope you won't either. It sounds to me as though you are spending too much time doing giddy things with those very silly people.'

'If you won't go, I won't either,' he promised, delighted at this proof of her concern.

They walked along the river, where it meandered through parks and green places, and though it was cold, Doris thought how pleasant it was to be out of London. Away from the roar of traffic, the endless scurrying of people, all hurrying home or to do their shopping, always eager – even frantic – to be done and out of the chill spring fog. Bundled in layers and smelling of coal fires and damp clothing. She breathed deeply, relishing the rich scent of earth and leaves, then gave a gurgle of laughter.

'What is it?' Bertie asked at once.

'Nothing. Only I wonder if I am turning into my mother.'

'Tell me about your mother.' As always, he seized the chance to know more, to create something deeper between them than the shared familiarity of nights out and daytime strolls.

'Really, there is nothing to tell.' Doris made herself sound vague and bored. 'Mothers are all rather alike, are they not?'

'Mine is splendid. I'm sure yours is too.' It was, Doris thought, unusual and rather sweet to hear a young man talk so enthusiastically of his mother.

'Splendid? Perhaps,' she said. 'But,' – firmly – 'an invalid who does not come to London.'

'Nor does Lady Lewis. Not much, in any case. See how much they have in common already?'

'Is that an otter?' she asked, pointing to something moving in the murky water, in order to change the subject. But his company was so cheerful that later, as they drove back into London with the day darkening rapidly around them, pierced here and there by lights going on in windows as they reached the suburbs of the city, she said, over the friendly roar of the engine, 'Come back to St James's Place and have tea with me. You can meet Honor.'

'Isn't she frightfully starchy?'

'Not a bit. Although some foolish people say it.'

'Well, I will not be a foolish person,' he said stoutly.

'Of course you will not.' She gave him an affectionate push that made him blush.

At St James's Place, Honor said she was not a bit too tired to come down to tea, and even thanked Bertie warmly for coming. 'I have been so dull here all day. It's jolly decent of you to keep me company.' She handed him a plate of tiny sandwiches, saying with a laugh, 'You must eat them all, for then Cook will think my appetite is returned, and will stop concocting "special dishes" to tempt me.'

'Nothing easier,' Bertie promised, taking five.

'And you must carry on taking Doris out so that she isn't dragged down by my being indisposed,' Honor said then, looking from one to the other like, Doris thought with a laugh, someone playing pairs, who thinks they have spotted the match for a card no one else has found.

'Happy to oblige,' Bertie said, blushing again. 'Always happy to oblige.'

Doris made him tell the story about Elizabeth's nightclub, which he did, and then another story about Maureen dressing as a slatternly maid and answering the door to her guests with so much crude impertinence that some of the gentlemen were thoroughly discomfited, even though – 'especially because!' – they knew it was Maureen all along.

He was so funny, and he and Honor got along so well, that Doris didn't even mind too much when Chips joined them and began to quiz Bertie on his estate (how large?), his family (had he brothers? sisters?) and his plans. On these last, Bertie was vague, saying he would 'have to see', and looked at Doris as he said it.

Afterwards, when he had gone, and Chips had gone out too, Honor leaned back in her seat and said contentedly, 'What a very nice young man.'

Chapter Thirty

Honor found her excessive tiredness passing. Doctor Gilliatt reassured her that all was going 'as it should', and so she didn't immediately say no when Chips, tracking her to the drawing room one afternoon, suggested a Friday-to-Monday at Belton House, the pretty Lincolnshire home of Perry Brownlow's ancestors, where they had been invited to shoot.

'You never shoot, so why are we going?' she wanted to know.

'Perry has invited us, and I think it would be rude not to.'

'But he knows you don't shoot. Who else is going to be there?'

'Emerald.'

'Of course.'

Honor didn't say it, but she was a little sick, these days, of Emerald. Of the way she placed her hand on Chips' arm and demanded – and got – all his attention. Of her constant presence in their lives, always arranging and planning. Mostly, of the way Chips was when he was with her: planning and arranging too, oblivious to everything except the careful calculation of their joint schemes. At such times, he was not her husband, but a man engaged in matters that had little to do with her. And in that guise, he served to highlight the lack of such pressing matters in her own life. Within their marriage, purpose and determination were all his, and she had nothing with which to match them. It was, she thought, galling.

'Duff Cooper and Diana. The Cavendishes. Your cousin Maureen. Mrs Simpson.'

'But not Mr Simpson?'

'No. He has business elsewhere.'

'And the prince?'

'He might look in for a night or two.'

'I see. Well, no wonder you want us to go. I am to be a sort of chaperone.'

'We are all chaperones,' he said grandly.

'What is it you call yourselves these days? The New Court?'

'Hush, Honor, someone might hear you and not understand the spirit in which it is meant.'

'Who will overhear me here, only Doris.' She looked around the drawing room which, for all Andrews' efforts, still carried a faint residue of the night before. All those people with their glasses and decanters, their cigarettes and the weight of their scent. Even though the room had been thoroughly aired, polished and dusted, she still thought she could detect a faint cloying remnant. The echo of a shriek of laughter among the cushions on the sofa, a whiff of Emerald's iron determination stirring the curtains.

Doris sat with her feet drawn up in a corner of the far divan. She flicked through a magazine, ignoring the conversation. 'I'm not listening,' she said, turning a page. 'Trust me, I couldn't be less interested.'

'No, you have other fish to fry, don't you?' Chips said nastily.

'I do.'

'I'll come if Doris can come too.'

'And I'll come if Lord Lewis is invited,' Doris said.

'Oh very well. I will see what Kitty says.'

'I'm sure she'll say exactly what Perry wants her to say. And *he* will say exactly what Emerald wants him to say.'

'How mean-spirited you are at times,' Chips said, casting a look at Doris which meant that he believed her to be responsible for his wife's irritability.

'Not mean-spirited really,' Honor said, relenting, 'only pregnant. You have no idea how tired and cross it makes one.'

'My dearest!' At once he was sorry. 'You will say if it's too much for you, won't you?' And when Honor assured him that she would, he kissed her and left.

'I think you just did,' Doris said then, putting down the magazine and sitting upright.

'Did what?'

'Say that it's too much for you. In your own way. Why don't you just say you won't go?'

'Oh I don't mind going. I don't feel as bad as all that. And how can I say no, when he is so excited? Anyway, if it's a chance to get you and Bertie together . . .'

'You are kind. I do think we've gone as far as we can in nightclubs and parks and taxis . . . Time to see what a few days under the one roof will do. But why doesn't Chips shoot?' Doris laughed. 'All that plotting and intriguing might suffer if he was away from the telephone or out of contact with Emerald for longer than an hour.' Downstairs, they heard Chips on the telephone, querulous: '. . . she says she can't . . .'

'You know he rings her up the minute he has finished breakfast?' Honor said. 'They truly seem to think that the future of the country rests in their hands.'

'It's a harmless enough affectation. Stops them getting into any worse mischief.'

'Yes, but the way they go on . . . As though this affair with Mrs Simpson were a matter of state and that everyone – the government, the opposition – has missed its significance; that only they understand what's at stake here.'

'You are tired and cross,' Doris said, amused.

'I don't mean to be, only they do go on . . .'

Chips came back. 'The Brownlows would be delighted to see you, Doris. And Kitty had already invited your Lord Lewis, along with some other entertaining young people.'

'*Entertaining young people*,' Doris mocked. 'Are you the

Dowager Princess of Ruritania? Anyway, he's not *my* Lord Lewis. Not yet.'

'*Not yet*,' Chips mimicked her softly. Then, before she could retaliate, 'We'll motor down in the morning.'

'I'd better tell Molly to pack,' Honor said.

'I'll do it,' Doris said. 'You rest. There's nothing in the newspaper anyway except an account of some ghastly ball at the Grosvenor House hotel, which sounds a dead bore.'

'We were at that ball,' Chips said, aggrieved.

'Well, then you know exactly how much of a bore it was.'

He gave her a furious look and, as she was on her way out the door, a caution: 'Not a word about this party, mind. No one must know. Honor, I know you are the soul of discretion, but Doris, you are not to utter a word.'

'A word to whom?'

He said he knew the raffish sort she went about with, and emphasised again the vital importance that nothing be leaked to the press 'who are bloodsucking bloodhounds'.

'Such a lot of blood . . .' Doris complained. 'But "vital importance"; got it.'

The drive to Lincolnshire got off to a bad start. They left London later than Chips wanted, because Doris was 'infernally slow' in coming down. This he said to Bundi, sitting on the bottom step in the hallway, rubbing the dog's giant golden head. It was how Chips often dealt with fractious situations – by placing the dog between them and himself. 'What's taking her so long?' he asked, tugging gently at Bundi's ears. Honor, sitting on a spindly chair beside the hall table with her hat on and handbag on her knees, fought back the urge to laugh. 'Don't we wish that when people said nine they meant nine and not twenty-past, Bundi darling?' Chips crooned. 'Yes we do, we do.'

'By *people*, do you mean me?' Doris asked cheerfully. The noise of her heels, which had been muffled by the stair carpet, was suddenly sharp on the blue-veined marble of the hall floor. 'I'm so sorry, darlings. I know I'm being monstrous.'

'You should come in earlier if you can't get up in the morning,' Chips said. 'I told you the car was ordered for nine.'

'Oh it wasn't that I couldn't get up. I'm not tired a bit. Only I couldn't decide what evening gowns to bring, and then when I did decide, they were different to the ones I chose yesterday so the maid had to pack more jewels to go with them. So you see, it was all vitally important.'

'Don't,' Honor whispered to Chips, who was about to say something cutting. 'It is vitally important to her. You're not the only one with schemes.'

They set off, Chips and Honor by the windows, with Doris in the middle and the dogs between them.

'Strange how they have grown to dislike one another, isn't it?' Honor said, as they turned out of St James's Place, looking from the big golden hound to the tiny dachshund. Recently, the dogs had been irritable with one another, snarling and snapping if either came too close. 'I don't believe they did at first.'

'Bundi's jealous,' Doris said. 'He's not as wise as Mimi, and he knows it.'

That annoyed Chips, who loved Bundi in a way that was not, Honor thought, quite reasonable, so that he turned quite away from them both and looked out the window.

They reached the outskirts of London and, as the city dwindled around them to just a smattering of grey houses separated out by more and more green fields, Honor began to relax. Surely now, no longer hemmed in by buildings, the sky pressing its smoke-filled weight down upon them, Chips would cheer up. But they rounded a corner a little too sharply, so that she had to put a hand out to the seat in front to stop herself lurching sideways, and the car disturbed a magpie, which flew violently up in front of them, a light froth of black and white feathers rising into the sky. The chauffeur sounded the horn in irritation, which made a fat piebald horse in a field raise its head and shy away from the fence close to the road.

'Oh really, it's too much!' Chips said.

'What's the matter?' Doris asked.

'Bad luck,' Honor explained. 'A magpie is bad enough, but a piebald . . .' She tried to get the laugh out of her voice.

Doris didn't bother. 'I shouldn't point out the black cat sitting on the doorstep then, should I?' she said. 'Joking, darling. I should tell you that, in Dorset, piebalds are considered best of all. They call them "coloured ponies" and they prize them above other animals.'

But Chips wasn't to be mollified. He muttered something about 'typical of Dorset . . .' and turned his shoulder to look out the window.

He cheered up when he saw the glorious limestone façade of Belton House, as elegantly symmetrical as though carved from a single block of golden stone. 'Such a *complete* example of a typical English country house,' he said in approval, as they turned in through the heavy wrought iron gates and up the driveway towards the house that glowed rosy in the afternoon light. It was small, certainly by the standards of Elveden, but pretty; rows of neat rectangular windows lined up one above the other, its two identical wings linked by a broad and capable front. Everything in proportion, everything in place. 'Built all at once,' Chips continued. 'The perfect realisation of a singular vision, rather than bits and pieces added here and there over centuries.'

'He means to criticise Elveden,' Honor said with a laugh. 'That was begun in the seventeen-hundreds, and added to by almost everyone who has owned it since, most significantly the maharaja, and most recently Papa.'

'I would never criticise Elveden,' Chips said, on a pious breath.

They arrived at the same time as Duff and Diana. 'Did you have a dreadful journey?' Diana called to them, stepping down from a large maroon-coloured motor. 'Ours was simply dreadful. Poor Duff cannot bear to be away from the telephone. He thinks the government may fall at any moment, and that he must be there to catch it.' She smiled and patted his arm affectionately and Honor wondered again that such a beautiful woman could love such an ugly man. But she mustn't think that, she reminded herself, because then maybe people would think the same sort of thing about her and Chips.

Kitty came out to greet them. She stood silently, staring at the ground and scuffing the gravel slightly with one foot as they stretched and let the dogs run about for a moment. She wore a plain cardigan and tweed skirt, with a row of fat silvery pearls around her neck. 'You made it,' she said eventually. She sounded disappointed and Honor wondered how much she had wanted to have them all. As ever, the disparity between the enormousness of her wide-apart grey eyes and the tiny pursed nothing of her mouth took Honor by surprise. 'Like an insect,' was how Doris described her. 'Goggling at one with those ferocious eyes.'

'I've put you and Chips in the yellow room,' Kitty continued, 'and Doris, you are beside them in the Chinese bedroom. I'm sure you'll want to go and change.'

'There is no end to the benefits of being under your wing,' Doris whispered, as they went up. 'Normally, I get somewhere pokey with a window that rattles, rather close to the servant quarters.'

'I'm sure you don't,' Honor said.

'Oh but I do. Only not this time.' She squeezed Honor's arm. 'I'll call for you when I'm ready to go down.'

'Do, you'll be much longer than I will. I'll read while I wait for you.' They had stayed in the same room the last time, she and Chips – there wasn't space enough for separate rooms at Belton – so that the Yellow Room, really, more gold, she thought, was familiar. A canopied bed that had seen better days, its yellow silk damask curtains faded and mothy in parts, took up almost the whole of the centre of the room, but the windows, with their deep recessed seats, had views out over the back, where the obsessively tended formality of the front gave way to something looser, wilder, gently ragged around the edges. She opened one of the windows as high as the sash would go and leaned out. It was such bliss, she thought, being out of London. Breathing air that felt like none had breathed it before, rather than the permanently stale breath of the city, passed from mouth to mouth like a whisper.

'Darling, you'll freeze us,' Chips complained, coming in. 'Now, I've been talking to Kitty. It seems the prince won't arrive until tomorrow. He has laid a false trail, by going to Fort Belvedere tonight, and will stay there, but plans to arrive quietly tomorrow by mid-afternoon. Meantime, Kitty – rather clever I thought – has invited a whole lot of neighbours for this afternoon. Probably dreadful' – this said with satisfaction – 'but they will help with the subterfuge.'

'Such a fertile mind,' Honor said.

He ignored the sarcasm. 'Let me tell you who else will be here . . .' and he started to run through names and plans of action, until Doris tapped at the door.

'Shall we?' she said. She looked particularly beautiful, Honor thought, in an afternoon dress of grey silk with gathered front and full sleeves and a white fur around her neck. Honor, in flowing lilac, was conscious that she looked thoroughly matronly.

'Mink?' she asked.

'Fox. I know these houses . . . vast, chilly drawing rooms, and only the old getting anywhere near the fire. Only your lot, born to that kind of cold, can withstand it. Little me, brought up in a merchant's cosy little house, doesn't stand a chance.'

Honor laughed. She picked up her bag, ready to go down, but Chips interrupted.

'Doris, perhaps you should be briefed too,' he said importantly.

Doris shook her head. 'I couldn't possibly,' she said with a laugh. 'Because I know I shan't listen to a word, even though I *long* to.'

He tried again. 'The prince will arrive . . .'

But again Doris interrupted. 'Darling, I truly cannot make myself pay attention!'

And with that he had to be content.

Arriving downstairs, they made their way to the drawing room. Conscious that so many things made her feel ill now, Honor decided she would hover on the fringes for a bit. She chose a secluded spot far from the fire – which smoked – beside a book-lined alcove. The room was very large, although not as big as the marble hall at Elveden, with walls upholstered in silk that was as pink as a cat's tongue, white plasterwork and a great deal of gilt furniture to break it up. This had been dragged about rather carelessly, which told Honor she was late down and that the others had been here all afternoon. It was a larger party than she had expected. There were the country neighbours

– carefully dowdy, watchfully self-conscious – whom Chips and his friends studiously ignored after the first hullos. They were, Honor saw, the kinds of country neighbours who wanted to be ignored, that they might the better make spiteful comments to each other about 'London types'.

There was also a group of younger people, good-looking boys and girls in crisp clothes and giddy spirits, Bertie among them. 'I say, there you are,' he called out, as soon as he saw Doris, detaching himself from the group and coming forward to take hold of her hands in his. The rest welcomed Doris with a cheer and the offer of 'Pull up a pew, do.' That, clearly, was where she belonged, while Honor, the very same age, just as clearly now belonged to Emerald and Diana and Perry Brownlow and other, older people. She looked wistfully at Doris' lot. They were playing some kind of game with paper and straws, and laughing a lot.

In contrast, Chips' friends were gathered in a tight, almost defensive knot around Emerald in a far corner of the room – very much the court in exile, Honor thought. They leaned close in to one another and spoke in low, rumbly voices. Emerald looked more birdlike than ever, wearing a great number of feathers in her hair, separated out by rich jewels, and nodding her head so that the plumage quivered and bobbed.

'She'd better be careful no one shoots her,' Doris murmured, passing by with Mimi in her arms. Honor laughed and nearly spilled her drink.

'We will be fewer tomorrow,' Kitty said, coming to join her. She had changed into a deep red dress that clashed with the walls. 'When the prince arrives. He prefers not to meet so many people.' She looked gloomily around at the neighbours.

'Are you certain he'll come?' The prince was famous for wrangling invitations – to shoot, to hunt, a trip on her uncle Walter's yacht – and then chucking at the last minute, because something better came along, or he no longer fancied the exertion.

'Oh yes. Certain.'

At that moment Mrs Simpson entered the room. She stood in the doorway, wearing a plain black dress with white satin gloves to her elbows and a great number of diamonds. Her hair was parted severely in the middle, as always, and twisted into two knots, almost like horns, on either side of her head. Honor immediately felt unbearably frumpy. Mrs Simpson always had that effect on her. The concentrated nature of her elegance was too intense, too unrelenting. She seemed never to have an off-day, a dubious choice or an uncertainty. It was as if she had made a pact with her own sense of style – that she would honour it above all else, tend to it first in any situation where duty was divided. Maybe she had learned that, Honor thought meanly, over the years. She was, after all, old.

'She wore pyjamas all afternoon,' Kitty murmured. 'Silk, and beautifully striped in black and white. But pyjamas! I'd better fetch her a drink. She won't take cocktails. Only whiskey and soda.'

It must be hard, Honor thought, for Kitty. Women like her were raised and trained to see off interlopers like

Mrs Simpson. To freeze them out with callous efficiency, massing the weight of generations of impossible tradition behind them to show the door to newcomers. And now, here she was, having to make the woman welcome in her house; indeed, turn the house inside out. No one else would be offered whiskey and soda, that was for sure.

Kitty moved off and Honor watched as the room re-arranged itself around Mrs Simpson. She stood for the longest time in the doorway, allowing this very thing to happen.

The country neighbours clearly had no idea who she was and, after scanning the plainness of her attire and hearing the American uplift to her accent, turned their backs firmly on her and returned to discussing the terrible weather and where they had found at yesterday's hunt.

The younger set – Doris' lot – stared at her, then whispered quietly among themselves, and stared again. Then they turned back to their games. They made no move to approach or speak with her. That was left to Emerald and Perry Brownlow, who both leaped to their feet. Emerald stayed where she was, feathers nodding invitingly, while Perry moved forward to take Mrs Simpson's arm and lead her to a seat that Duff Cooper pulled up for her. A decanter of whiskey and soda syphon were placed close by on a side table and there were earnest consultations around how much whiskey, exactly, compared with soda water, to put in her drink.

'A splash,' she was saying, 'just a ripple really.' Chips handed her a heavy, savagely cut crystal glass and said, 'Try this.'

'Perfect.' Mrs Simpson smiled tightly at him.

'Now you're here, we can start to liven things up a little,' Chips said then, in a way that Honor found ingratiating.

'Perhaps some music? For a start,' Mrs Simpson responded gayly.

So someone produced a gramophone and put on a record. Ethel Waters sang about a heatwave, crisp and joyous. The country neighbours looked as though they had been sprayed with ice-cold water. 'Before dinner?' one said in tones of horror. Kitty went to smooth things over with them, murmuring something placating about 'London ways'. She signalled desperately to Honor, who went to her.

'Allow me to introduce Lady Honor Channon. Formerly Guinness.'

'I know your mother,' one of them said, 'Lady Iveagh.' She looked relieved, and began to talk about the Conservative committee she was a member of, and how that intersected with the works of Lady Iveagh. Honor, conscious of her bridging role, nodded a great deal and made sympathetic noises.

The country neighbours went away then, and the gramophone was turned up. Emerald stood and moved closer to the fire, to the large dusty sofas vacated by the neighbours. A court returned, Honor thought, watching how the others arranged themselves around her. More drinks were poured and there was some dancing. Maureen arrived and stood for a moment, taking it all in, then moved swiftly to where Honor sat alone.

'I told myself it couldn't be all that bad, spending a few days under the same roof as her,' she said loudly, 'but now I see that I was wrong.'

'Hush,' Honor said with a smile. 'You will draw all sorts of fire. They have quite decided to champion her.'

'They?' Maureen demanded. 'You mean your husband and Emerald.'

'Yes.'

'But of course.' Maureen rolled her eyes.

'You look wonderful,' Honor said quickly, before Maureen could say anything else. 'And that was a charming photograph in the *Tatler* last week.' It was indeed charming. Maureen, wearing magnificent heavy diamond-and-emerald earrings, a ruffled satin dress that showed her bare shoulders, with little Caroline, now four, on one side of her and baby Perdita, just seven months, on the other. 'Caroline is a darling. Such a sweet smile.'

'What you can't see is Duff, off to the side of the photo,' Maureen said. 'Madly making faces and doing funny voices for Caroline. He is the only one she will ever smile at.' She sounded peeved. 'Every time she sees me, it is as if someone had pinched her.'

'Where is Duff?' Honor asked, looking around.

'Not here. Gone to Clandeboye. To see the children. He is positively soppy about them.'

'And you? Are you not soppy?' She was honestly curious, still trying to understand what it would mean when, in a few months, she, too, would be a mother.

'Certainly not. It does them no good to fuss.'

The butler announced dinner then, but Wallis cried, 'Can't we delay? Surely no one is hungry?'

'Not a bit,' came many voices, dutifully.

With difficulty was Mrs Simpson persuaded to move into the dining room, where Honor saw that she had been seated beside Chips, too far for Honor to hear what they were saying, but the expression of close attentiveness he wore told her everything she needed to know.

The food was plain and hearty, 'the best kind of country house food', Honor imagined Chips saying, but would have been better after a day's shooting rather than a day in the car and a long afternoon in a drawing room. It was too much and no one seemed terribly hungry. Kitty did her best to draw the disparate groups together but the young people, bunched at the end of the table, were indifferent to the intentions of their elders, and insufficiently deferential. Honor caught Doris' eye and saw that she was happy. The violet shadows under her eyes were as dark as ever, the set of her shoulders just a shade off completely exhausted, but her eyes sparkled and she paid close attention to what Bertie, beside her, said. His pink-complexioned face glowed with pleasure, while light from the large lamp on the sideboard behind him shone through the tips of his sticking-out ears, turning them rosy. She thought again how amiable he was, and how thoroughly infatuated with Doris. He looked up then, and she caught his eye and smiled.

When dinner was finished, Kitty stood up and Mrs Simpson immediately said, 'Tell me you aren't going to do that dreadful thing you English do, where the men sit over the port for hours while we ladies languish in the drawing room?'

Honor, startled, thought how much bolder she had become.

'Of course not,' Kitty said, with a glance at her husband, who stood immediately.

'Let's go and listen to some music in the library, shall we?' he said.

'And just when it seemed we might have a little time without you all,' Maureen said loudly, to no one in particular.

'Hush,' Honor heard Kitty say to her, 'for it is bad enough already.'

As soon as she reasonably could, Honor went up to bed. Her room was freezing, just as Chips had threatened, and she cursed the generous impulse that had made her tell Molly, her maid, not to wait up. Molly could have gone to the kitchens and got her a hot water bottle. Even a hot drink. She changed quickly into her nightgown then rushed into bed and dragged the covers close around her. But it was no use. She was too cold to sleep. She thought of going down and getting Bundi and bringing him upstairs with her. His shaggy golden warmth would have been such a comfort. But he was undoubtedly lying at Chips' feet and would be hard to persuade away.

After a while she heard the door to Doris' room open and close. She wondered how long Chips would be. Hours, because Mrs Simpson hated going to bed. 'I like to see the sun rise so that I know it will,' Honor had once heard her say. 'Then I can go to bed knowing the world is in safe hands 'til I get up again.' She had laughed immoderately and no one had seemed surprised that she saw herself as overseeing the continuation of the world.

Honor got up and, pulling the counterpane around her, went out into the corridor, which was in darkness except for a small lamp at the far end. From somewhere downstairs she heard a distant shriek. She hauled the counterpane higher over her shoulders – it was heavy – and wrapped it tighter. She opened the door to Doris' room. Doris was in bed already – she often slept in her make-up, Honor had noticed. It never seemed to do a bit of harm to her complexion.

'Doris,' she hissed.

The figure in the bed moved. 'Honor?' Doris sat up.

'Yes. Are you asleep?'

'Obviously not. Are you?' Ironically.

'Oh, Doris, it's so cold. Come and share my bed with me, will you?

'Get in here.' Doris twitched the blanket.

'I can't, Chips will wonder where on earth I am and raise the house. Come back to mine, please. I'm going to die of cold in that room otherwise.'

'Oh very well.' Doris got up and threw an ivory silk dressing gown on over her pyjamas. 'Only go quickly before we both freeze.'

Back in her own bed, Honor arranged the counterpane over both of them. 'I can't believe you brought me another blanket,' Doris said sleepily and turned onto her side, Mimi tucked into the crook of her arm.

Honor laughed, and, warm at last in the hollow beside Doris, fell asleep. When Chips blundered in some hours later she woke long enough to tell him, 'You'll have to go next door.'

'But the servants . . .' he said, wrestling with his necktie.

'Never mind the servants.'

'Perhaps I could get in with you both,' he said then. 'It is very cold.'

'Go to bed, darling.'

Chapter Thirty-One

Honor woke early and, leaving Doris sleeping, went next door to get Chips up. The room was dark and close and smelled of the night before: of what they had eaten for dinner, of the cigarettes and cigars smoked, of brandies and cocktails and jazz music. Her stomach lurched and she went to pull up a window, tucking the curtains back into their ties so the fresh cold air could sweep in.

'Must you,' Chips grumbled. Bundi lay sprawled out beside him, and Honor thought of all that thick golden fur shedding onto the crisp linen sheets. One must tip one of the maids to change the bed before poor Doris had to spend the night there.

'Darling, you know you must go down to breakfast. They will think you terribly odd if you do not.' Worse than 'terribly odd', she knew they would think he was degenerate in some unspecific way.

'Go away,' he said sleepily. 'I am not ready to get up. Wallis had us up 'til dawn.'

'Yes, I know what time you came to bed.'

'She was being terribly funny.'

'I'm sure. But you must get up, I can already hear them getting ready for the shoot.'

That was true. The stirrings inside the house – doors opening, trays rattling, voices calling gayly to one another across bathrooms and dressing rooms – were matched now by the activity outside. She looked out. Here and there in the morning mist were beaters in their moss-and-stone-coloured clothes, dogs frantic with excitement, Perry in close consultation with the gamekeeper. She leaned forward and breathed deeper of the morning air. It reminded her of Elveden, where the shooting was legendary. Shoot mornings were always different to other mornings, and even though Honor didn't go out with them, there was a sense of energy and bustle to the house that she enjoyed. The feeling that across those many rooms, a unity of purpose held them all and propelled them forward at pace, until finally guests were spat forth onto the gravel, men ready to fan out and take up their ground, women following far enough behind that they might chatter and laugh together without disturbing the birds, before they all met for a picnic lunch.

'Come along, everyone else will be up already,' she insisted. 'You don't want to be left behind.'

That galvanised him, and he sat up. 'The English mania for early mornings,' he said on a yawn. He looked so handsome; tousled hair and puffy eyes, but already alert and ready for whatever came next.

Breakfast was like Miss Potts', Honor thought, watching the distribution of plates, food, cups, the clatter and chatter as food was served and quickly eaten. This was a fuelling rather than a leisurely meal; a fortifying for the day ahead.

The many smells – bacon, kippers, kedgeree – made her feel sick, so she retreated to a corner of the drawing room – not yesterday's riot of pink, but a smaller room, panelled in dark wood with mossy green wallpaper – with a copy of *The Times*. After a while, Chips came in with Emerald and Duff.

'. . . not up yet,' Emerald was saying. 'Americans never can take the pace of these country house parties. *New* Americans, that is.' She spoke with satisfaction, as one who had had time to alter the course of their upbringing.

'Sit here and I'll ring for coffee,' Chips said invitingly.

'Stop sabotaging, Chips. We're here to shoot.' That was Duff.

'I only thought . . .'

'There you are.' It was Perry, bustling in, looking harassed. 'We must set off. Dogs are ready. Come along now.' And he shepherded Duff and Chips out.

Honor thought with a laugh of all the ways that people like Perry – like all of them, really – hid their feelings by appealing to dogs, to servants, to 'people'. *Mustn't let people down. Mustn't keep the servants up. Mustn't keep the dogs waiting*, when usually what they meant was they themselves wanted, or didn't want, something.

'You're down early,' Emerald said, spying Honor and coming to sit beside her.

'Hard to sleep with all that row going on outside,' Honor said. 'You?'

'I am always up at this time,' Emerald said energetically. 'May I?' she indicated the *Times* that Honor had put down on the arm of her chair.

'Of course.' In fact, Honor had barely started on an article about refugees from Germany, something she wanted to quiz Doris about. She was trying, as Doris had said she should, to read the newspapers more, rather than rely always on Chips. The article she had begun said that Lord Marley had asked in the Lords about the new refugees coming from somewhere called the Saar region, many of them Jewish, and if they were to become under the responsibility of something called the High Commissioner for Refugees. She hadn't read much further, and understood very little, but she had immediately thought of Doris and her relatives. She would read it all later, she had decided, and then she would know what to ask her friend.

But Emerald picked up the paper, and buried herself in it, turning pages slowly, reading, it seemed, every word on every page. Sometimes she made noises – of approval, of dissent; once she said, 'The very idea!' – but otherwise was silent and absorbed. Honor looked out the window. The mist had lifted a little, like a net curtain pulled sloppily aside, and she watched the men walk off: first the beaters, then the guns, dogs milling wildly in between. Bundi was with them and she felt a moment of misgiving. He was hardly trained as a gun dog, and had, she thought, quite the wrong temperament: affectionate, enthusiastic, but undisciplined. Chips, she saw, trailed a little behind the others. She could see by the set of his shoulders how much he expected to be bored.

Sun drifted feebly through the window, subdued by the ragged curtain of mist but strong enough to bring a little warmth. The fire was lit and the room cosy. Cosier, she was sure, than anywhere else in the house at that hour. It was always hard to pass the days at these Friday-to-Mondays. One's hostess never really seemed to have a plan for those who didn't shoot, or hunt, and unless it was summer and one could stroll about the grounds, there was little else. Honor had long since got used to picking a warm spot, gathering plenty to read, and simply curling up out of sight.

Beside her, Emerald finished the newspaper, folded it neatly and said, 'I must go and write some letters.' She tucked the newspaper under her arm, and before Honor could remember to ask her to leave it, had taken it upstairs with her.

The morning passed slowly. Honor declined the offer to go with the other women and have a picnic lunch with the shooting party. 'But what will I do with you?' Kitty wailed when Honor told her she didn't feel up to coming out. 'You must have company.'

'I must not,' Honor assured her. 'I don't want it a bit. I will sit quietly where I am and be perfectly happy.'

'Lunch on a tray?' Kitty asked sympathetically.

'Exactly.'

Because of her solitary lunch, and because Mrs Simpson kept to her room until late, Honor was the only person around when she finally surfaced.

'So here you are,' she said brightly, putting her head around the door. 'May I come in?'

'Of course,' Honor said, heart sinking. Being alone was one thing – perfectly pleasant – but if they were to get stuck talking, it could be hours before anyone came back to break them up.

'I thought I was on the *Mary Celeste*,' Wallis said, settling herself in the chair vacated by Emerald. She pronounced it *Maree Celeste*. 'I went to bed and the house was full of people. I woke up and there wasn't a soul to be seen, just a stone-cold cup of tea beside my bed. It's a good thing I don't eat breakfast.'

'What, never?' Honor asked. She thought of Lady Iveagh: *A good start to the day is so very important . . .*

'Never.' Wallis shook her head adamantly.

'You don't shoot?' Honor asked then, because she couldn't think of anything else.

'I do not. Golf, I do not mind, but shooting I consider a dead bore.' Her hair was perfect as ever – parted abruptly in the centre, coiled into smooth ropes on either side – and she wore a tweed suit in soft brown check that was so beautifully cut, Honor couldn't stop herself.

'Where did you get that heavenly tweed?'

'I had it made,' Wallis said. She leaned back and stretched out her slim legs, crossing them at the ankle.

'The prince's tailor. I favour a masculine style and cut, and so we deal very well together. Nothing can be worse than tweed that bags' – Honor thought of her own skirt, and how much it bagged no matter what she did, and resolved that she would not be the first to stand up – 'I said to Sholte, "You must do whatever is necessary to ensure the fit", and do you know what he said?' She turned to look at Honor, head tilted at an angle so that she was like a smooth brown bird – something bright and inquisitive, Honor thought; a little starling or sparrow.

'No. What?'

'He said, "It's not what *I* do, madame, it's what you do. If you put on any weight, even a pound, it will destroy the cut." So I assured him he need not worry.' She laughed, head thrown right back so that her throat presented itself brown and slender to the ceiling. 'Why, I would as soon paint my face purple as start gaining weight in that sloppy way some women do.'

'I'm to have a baby,' Honor said in a rush, lest Wallis think her like those *some women*. 'In September.'

'Charming,' Wallis said, without interest. 'I say, how can one get a drink around here? I haven't seen a soul since I came down. I suppose when Perry and Kitty go out, the servants take the chance to slack off a little.' She smirked.

Honor nearly winced. It was the kind of thing Chips might say. 'Ring the bell,' Honor said. 'Someone will come. But I'm sure you have things to do. I'll let you get on.'

'Lord, please don't,' Wallis said. 'You English are always "getting on".' She laughed again. 'You seem happy only if you have a great deal to do. But I daresay the things you do don't need doing at all.'

Honor thought of Emerald, upstairs writing letters. To whom? About what? Keeping her many fires tended, Honor supposed. Adding a branch here, poking a blaze there, dampening down somewhere else. Did those things 'need doing'? Perhaps not.

'Now I,' Wallis continued, 'I like to have nothing at all to do. That way I may do whatever I like.'

'And what do you like?' Honor asked, genuinely curious.

'I like to have fun,' Wallis said. 'I love to have fun. And speaking of fun, here's sir now.' There was the sound of wheels on gravel outside. Wallis jumped to her feet, quick and vigorous. 'Now we shall be more lively.'

She left the room and Honor watched through the window as she came out the front door and ran lightly down the broad stone steps, passing the Brownlows' butler, who looked pained, halfway down.

The prince drove a long cream two-seater, so low that it almost scraped the ground. Beside him in the front seat was a man Honor didn't recognise, and behind them a wire-haired terrier. He stopped the car so abruptly that it spat gravel from the wheels; he thrust open his door and jumped out in time to greet Wallis as she reached him. Honor watched as he put both his arms around her waist, then squeezed her and nearly lifted her off her feet. The two of them laughed and the terrier barked. The other man got out of the car slowly and stood, looking around. Having held Wallis for a long time, his arms tight around her, her face turned up to his, the prince took hold of her hand. From the back of his tiny car, now the centre of activity as two footmen went back and forth, carefully lifting out a great quantity of monogrammed travelling cases and bringing them to the front door, the prince caught up a small black box with a leather strap. From it protruded a metal handle. His portable gramophone.

With the gramophone strap in one hand, Wallis' held tight in the other and the terrier at his heels, he came up the front steps and into the hall. Honor, terrified that they would both come to the drawing room where she sat, wondered should she risk trying to get away before they came in. But she need not have worried. She heard them pass the drawing room door, chatting together, and go straight upstairs. She tried to feel shocked – she was, in fact, a little shocked; it was the middle of the day, the butler must certainly have seen them – but mostly what she felt was a funny kind of envy. In the early days of her marriage, she, too, might have run through the front door and cried, 'Here's Chips.' But it was so long since she had felt like that, so long since she had greeted the arrival of her husband with anything like Wallis' excitement. And no one had ever looked at her the way the prince had looked down into Wallis' little brown face.

She looked out the window. The other man was only just starting up the front steps. As she watched, he turned his head suddenly towards the window where she stood. She ducked behind the heavy curtain then went to sit down again, hoping the servants would not show him in to where she was.

They didn't, and after a moment she heard a door slam in the upper reaches of the house, and then the sounds of Duke Ellington's 'Sweet Jazz O' Mine' drifted down the broad staircase. Curiously, even though the house was now busier, Honor felt more lonely than she had before.

Chapter Thirty-Two

News of the prince's arrival must have travelled urgently, because less than an hour later, Honor, still in the same spot by the window, now deep in a dusty copy of *Middlemarch*, heard voices and the hoarse barking of dogs. She looked out. The light was starting to fade and bleach colour from the air so that those who walked towards the house did so in silhouette with the last of the drooping sun behind them. At the front were Doris and Lord Lewis, close together. As Honor watched, she stumbled slightly on an uneven patch of grass, and he put a hand out to steady her. Behind them came Maureen, in a cloud of cigarette smoke, then Chips with Bundi by his side. He was holding the dog's collar tightly so that he had to stoop somewhat. On the other side of Chips, Duff Cooper stalked rather than walked, keeping pace with Chips' longer strides in a way that struck Honor as unhappy.

At the back came the beaters, dogs twisting and boiling at their feet, dead birds draped over their shoulders like feathered question marks slumped the wrong way; things that would never now be answered.

The party divided at the front steps, the beaters carrying on around the back of the house to the stables while the guests straggled up and into the hallway.

'You must be terribly tired,' Honor heard Lord Lewis say as they came in.

'Perhaps a little . . .' Doris murmured, which made Honor smile, knowing well that Doris could have walked hours longer and barely noticed.

She stood to join them and came into the hall in time to hear Duff say furiously '. . . told not to bring that dog. He is undisciplined.' For all that the hall was full of people, taking off coats, unwinding scarves, changing shoes, there was a pocket of space around Chips and Duff.

'Our Bundi has disgraced himself,' Chips said, looking up from where he still held the dog's collar, to meet the question in Honor's raised eyebrows.

'He is undisciplined,' Duff said again. 'Should never have been allowed out.'

'What did he do?' Honor asked.

'Darling Bundi,' Chips said, 'he was rather overeager . . .'

'Mimi was an absolute angel, weren't you, darling?' Doris said loudly from a chair by the front door, kissing the top of her dachshund's head and giving Chips a mischievous sidelong look. He ignored her.

'An absolute disgrace,' Duff spat out. 'Blundered along the lines, knocking the other dogs off their scent, careering wildly around with any bird he found so that it was impossible to tell who shot what.' He was, Honor saw, biting at his bottom lip so that his moustache twitched violently. 'That dog has no idea how to behave. Unruly, ignorant and spoiled.' He looked at Chips as he spoke, placing his words precisely into the air between them.

'Naughty fellow,' Chips said, leaning down to Bundi, who leaped up and licked his face. The dog's thick fur was damp, made darker by the wet so that he was no longer golden but a sodden brown. 'From here on, I shall call you Blundi.' And he laughed.

Duff looked as if he would explode and Honor, knowing that Chips would never be able to understand just how much it mattered that Bundi had caused confusion among the gun dogs, hastened to say, 'I'm terribly sorry. How horrid for you all. I will see that Bundi is sent to the stables immediately.'

'But he never sleeps outdoors,' Chips said, looking up sharply.

'The stables are hardly outdoors,' Honor said reasonably. 'I daresay Kitty's horses eat better and sleep more soundly than many people.' She thought suddenly of how true that was; of the Paddington Street tenements: the rancid smell of the over-crowded flat, the way the wind stole in through the cracks and around the edges of the ill-fitting windows. She shook her head slightly, to clear the image.

'Bundi sleeps with me,' Chips said, standing straight and planting his legs further apart. 'He always has and I am not about to banish him now.'

'Not banish . . .' Honor tried, but Chips snapped his fingers and moved briskly through the hall and towards the stairs, dog at his heels. He passed them all out and was halfway up before Honor could think of what else to say, and then it was too late. She couldn't shout up at her husband's retreating back.

'Tea in the large drawing room,' Kitty said loudly and firmly then, unbuttoning a long grey coat and handing it to a footman. 'Go along now.' She made a shooing motion with her hands at those still standing in the hallway so that they began to straggle further into the house. Then, quietly to Honor, 'Where is our Prince Charming?'

'Upstairs.'

'Wallis?'

'Also.'

'I see.'

Doris, who had stayed behind in the hall to change her shoes, looked up then and murmured, 'You can't be doing much of a job as chaperone,' so that Honor had to stifle a spurt of laughter.

'I believe David Envers is with him,' Kitty said then crossly. That must be the man she hadn't recognised, Honor thought. She watched Doris whip up her head towards Kitty as though jerked on a string, then bend over her shoes again. Did her hands tremble a little as she untied the laces of her walking shoes?

'Although he did not say he would be accompanied and the servants have put him in quite the wrong room . . .' She walked off, saying, 'I must see to it . . .' irritably. Honor knew that when she saw the prince she would say only what a delight it was to have him bring a friend.

She turned back to Doris, but Doris shook her head – whether to clear it or to signal 'no', Honor didn't know – 'I'm going up,' she said. Honor watched her run up the stairs, then followed slowly once Doris was out of sight.

In their room she found Chips drying Bundi. He was on his knees with the dog before the fireplace, rubbing vigorously with a large cream-coloured towel. 'Why did you say that?' he asked, looking up at her. His face was red, whether with exertion or irritation she couldn't tell.

'Darling,' Honor said, sitting down on the end of the bed, 'you must see that Bundi needs to be punished.'

'Never.'

'But Duff was so angry.'

'And what of it?'

'Bundi behaved frightfully.'

'Because he took a few dead birds? When there were so many that it was like a battlefield out there. Waterloo after Napoleon.' He laughed, enjoying his own joke. 'They must have shot a thousand.'

Honor's stomach lurched at that, as though she felt inside her the heavy slump of bodies as they lost their feathered buoyancy and plunged towards the ground.

'It's not a question of how many, you know that,' she said. 'It's knowing who shot what, and letting the dogs go about their work as they have been trained to do. You have no idea the work that goes into training these dogs . . .'

'He makes too much of it,' Chips said. 'Anyway, I don't suppose it's about the birds at all. It never is, with Duff,' he added darkly. Then 'How was your day?'

'Tiring, though I did nothing at all.' She leaned sideways against the bed post so that above her, the gold silk canopy swayed slightly. She wished he would come and put his arm around her, sit beside her so that she could lay her head on his shoulder, or just rest against him and feel, in his warm solidity, the silent comfort of his affection. But instead he looked sharply up at her, still holding the towel around Bundi so that the dog peered out as though from a cape.

'Is it the baby? Perhaps you need to rest more. I can have Kitty send up a tray.' His concern was intense, but focused not on her so much as on one part of her.

'No. No more trays. I am perfectly fine. Just . . . you know . . .'

'Dull,' he supplied, with relief. 'Of course you are. A day all alone without company. Anyone would be dull. I don't know why Doris didn't stay with you, rather than coming out and distracting that Lewis fellow.' He sounded peeved.

'She's not a companion, darling,' Honor said. 'A friend, free to come and go . . .'

'Well, she would have done better to have stayed behind,' he said. She was about to ask what he meant, but he brightened a little. 'You'll see, now that the prince has arrived, this evening will be the best of fun.'

It was just what Wallis had said: that the prince's coming would bring fun. Honor wondered why they said such things. It didn't seem to her that the prince was ever very entertaining. He sought fun, that was true, demanded that it take place around him, but himself, he was too petulant, too dissatisfied, always looking peevishly about him for something better. Maybe now that he had Wallis he would be different.

'David Envers has come with him,' she said.

'Has he indeed?' Chips said eagerly. 'Why didn't you say so?'

'I am saying so.'

'Interesting . . . I wonder what this means . . . One of Mosley's men . . .'

She could see he had to almost restrain himself, so eager was he to be gone, to find Emerald and sift through the meaning of the new arrival. She thought of what she might say to detain him, keep him with her, but she could think of nothing. Nothing that would work. Except more complaints about her pregnancy, and that would only make him fuss and insist she stay, alone, upstairs. Would he stay with her, were she to ask? she wondered. But she knew he would not. He would agree to, instantly, of course he would. And then he would drift away, almost without noticing – 'There is just one thing I must attend to . . .' He would promise his own quick return. And he would not come back. She would be left alone, knowing that wherever he was, he was barely aware of her absence.

'I'll leave you to change and see you downstairs,' he said then, and, stopping briefly to kiss the top of her head absently, he went out, Bundi with him.

Chapter Thirty-Three

'Might I have a word?' Chips asked firmly, coming right into Doris' room and shutting the door behind him, so that she didn't have much choice in the matter.

'Of course. Pull up a pew. Well, there isn't one,' – Doris sat, unmoving, in the only chair – 'but you can have the powder stool. Cigarette?'

'I'm not here for a cosy cig and a gossip,' Chips said, sitting on the delicately carved stool that was much too low for him, and planting his legs solidly on either side of it. Of course he had no idea how absurd he looked.

'I thought you were always *everywhere* for a cosy cig and a gossip.' She turned a page of the book she had been leafing through.

'I say this because I think you don't realise it,' he said heavily, 'and so it falls to me to point it out.'

'Point what out?'

'The way you behave reflects on Honor, you know.'

'Reflects on *you*, you mean.' She gripped the covers of the book tightly, to hide that her hand trembled slightly.

'Honor,' he said firmly.

Doris said nothing, so he continued. 'After all, she is the only reason you are invited here. And so, I do think you might be more . . .'

'More what?'

'More of a team player.'

'You mean because I laughed at you and Bundi? Anyone would. That great oaf of a dog, blundering through the line of beaters, like a ball through a pile of pine cones. And you, behind him, trying to call him back when we all know he is hopelessly ill-trained. You were told not to bring him, and you insisted, and so you jolly well deserve all the jeering you get.' Doris laughed, or pretended to. She knew that any mention of Bundi's manners was a sore spot, and sure enough, Chips' face tightened into a haughty mask.

'This has nothing to do with Bundi. I mean because you spent the day distracting Lord Lewis,' he said. 'Having little private giggles with him when you should have made an effort to be charming to all. That's why you're here.'

'I thought I was here as Honor's little charity case.'

'You know what I mean. You have a great deal of charm, Doris' – was he trying to flatter her now? she wondered.

The idea made her feel rage like a needle point – 'but you need to use that charm *broadly*.' He swung an arm up and out to show what he meant, and wobbled on the little stool. 'To make sure the whole visit goes with a bang, and not just your little schemes.'

'So you are the only one allowed to scheme?'

He ignored that. 'For your hostess's sake. There are *duties* in society, you know.'

'How fun you make everything sound . . .'

'Don't pretend to be silly, Doris, for I know you are not. I say nothing you don't already know. Consider this a friendly warning.'

'And what happens after the friendly warning? An unfriendly one? Something worse?'

'I'm doing my best for you,' he said. Then, 'Oh and by the way, I hear David Envers has arrived.' He looked at her, a little too long.

'I hear the same,' she said with a shrug.

'Well, I must go down, they will be looking for me.' He sounded disappointed.

'Of course, nothing may happen until Chips is there,' she muttered when he had left. Did he realise how insulting he was? Probably not but that meant only that he didn't care enough to bother to. If she had been Emerald, or Kitty, especially if she had been Wallis, he would have measured out every word and calculated its weight and intonation, exactly as though he were baking a most complicated cake, so as to achieve his precise aim. Because it was her, he didn't bother, just blurted out his advice that was nothing of the sort, only an effort to make her useful to him. What he wanted was a tame creature who would be charming on his command, as though she were a particularly fine horse or clever dog that he could show off.

She felt smaller than she had before he came into her room. Physically diminished, as though, were she to stand up, she would no longer fill the dress she had chosen to put on, but would be shrunken within its seams. As if he had taken some of her. Knowing that David Envers was in the same house, perhaps just a few rooms away, disturbed her in a way that was physical. She felt as though everything she had believed of the house, its occupants, her place there, was suddenly different. Even the colours were different, she thought – less rich, less assured. There was a spiky, tremulous quality now to everything she looked at.

She got up and walked to the window. Outside, the lawn was mostly swallowed up in shadow, the crisp green overlaid by a fine mesh of grey. As she looked, Wallis and the prince came onto the broad stone terrace beneath her. Both held glasses, and after them came a footman with a tray carrying a cocktail shaker, a cigarette case and a silver bucket of ice. Doris opened the window a crack. They had the gramophone set up in the room behind them, turned to its fullest volume, and the double glass-paned doors open so that music drifted out to follow them.

Wallis said something to the prince, then laughed gayly. He caught one of her hands in his, then took the other hand, and pulled her close into him. They danced a few steps, pressed tightly together, then she broke away from him and took a cigarette from the case on the tray. She held it up to the prince to light, which he rushed forward to do. Smoke trailing from her hand, blurring into the charcoal evening air so that Doris could smell it but not see it, Wallis stepped down onto the lawn and began to walk about, little forays from one side to the other as she bent to examine a lavender bush, then a stone urn filled with some yellow flower.

She wore a slim-fitting black evening dress with touches of white at the neck, sleeves and waist. Her usual colours. Down there, moving about the lawn with quick, bold steps, she reminded Doris of something. Finally, as she watched Wallis kick idly at a croquet ball someone had left behind, Doris got it: a magpie. Cocky and strident, strutting almost; the impeccable black and white dress and watchful little face.

Doris laughed to herself and shut the window, closing the curtains and turning on the bedside lamp. She finished pinning her hair – the maid had done her best, but Doris was cleverer – and went down to where the party had assembled in the same pink drawing room as the night before. There were no neighbours this time, just the self-conscious intimacy of the small group chosen to stay on. And David Envers. He stood alone by the fireplace, flicking cigarette ash into the heap of burning logs. He looked up as she came in but made no movement. Doris couldn't remember how well she was meant to know him.

She joined the group around Bertie, who made room for her on the lumpy sofa and began telling everyone just how wonderful she had been at the shoot. 'Walked for miles,' he said proudly. 'Not any kind of bother to her. I'd say she could have walked all day. Well, she almost did walk all day.' He laughed.

'We were there, Bertie,' one of the other young men said patiently. 'We saw, just as you did.' But he said it kindly, looking from Doris to Bertie with a smile.

'I must get a drink,' Doris said. She was agitated by Envers' nearness. Trying to understand what it meant that he was there. That he stood alone by the fireplace and made no effort to speak to anyone. The room hummed with people now, like a summer meadow, Doris thought; brightly coloured creatures moving around, chatting, with the gramophone playing quietly behind them, so there was a steady rising-and-falling of sound. And yet no one approached him except Kitty, with a drink, and even she did not stay.

'Let me.' Bertie began to stir.

'No, stay.' She put a hand on his arm and got up swiftly herself. The prince and Wallis hadn't yet come in, so it was easy to find a quiet moment with Chips beside the drinks tray, where he was once again overseeing the mixing of cocktails.

'Have you thought about what I said?' he asked, paring a lemon with a knife as thin and sharp as a razor.

'I've thought about little else,' she promised him. 'I say, have you noticed something about Wallis?'

'What?' He was eager, she could tell, for what she had discovered, in case it could be useful to him.

'She's rather like a magpie.' He said nothing, so she continued. 'Always in black and white, so sleek, but with a garish sheen to her if you look in the right light . . . I wonder you don't consider her bad luck?'

He looked startled and the thin knife slipped a little, very nearly slicing the fingers that held the now half-peeled lemon.

'Careful,' Doris said. 'Watch what you're about.'

Before dinner was announced Doris went upstairs again, saying she needed a hair pin, but really to get away for a minute. To be on her own so she could force herself to breathe properly. To squash air deep into herself, forcing it below the tight band that seemed to wrap around her chest. She was light-headed, as though she had been playing that game of breathing fast – panting, really – so as to induce a faint, which she and Honor had practised at Miss Potts' to get out of lessons sometimes. Honor had always found the game easy, fainting almost as soon as she began to pant, whereas Doris had never been a fainter, had had to try harder for longer, and even then became dizzy rather than falling to the floor.

Now, she saw the same tiny black spots dancing in front of her eyes. Except that this time, she didn't want them there. In her room, she opened the window as high as it would go, and stuck her head far out and breathed in deep gulps of damp evening air that smelled of leaves and earth and simple, lovely things.

As she came back down the stairs, she saw Envers leave the large drawing room that was at the far end of the hallway. He shut the door carefully behind him and walked towards the staircase, but he didn't look up. Doris slowed her descent, watching him. The hallway was dim and the sounds from the drawing room were muffled as though by a blanket. She dawdled so that she came around the end of the stairs and encountered him just before he reached them.

'There you are,' he said, stopping.

Doris trod the last two steps, and thought she would continue to walk past him, but she didn't. She paused, and that was fatal because once she was close, close enough to smell the tang of cologne and saddle sweat that she associated with him, she could not make herself walk away from him.

'Come in here for a moment. I want to talk to you.' He opened a door behind him. A small library of some kind. Doris followed him in, silent still. She felt hopelessly young and uncertain.

'Did you know I would be here?' she asked when they were inside and the door shut again. His answer mattered, but she didn't know which she wanted him to say: *Yes, I knew, that's why I'm here*; *No, I had no idea* . . .

'I knew. But I chose to come anyway. I have business to attend to . . .'

'What business?' Was she his business?

'A chance to talk to our prince discreetly.'

Of course. The sun around which they all turned, faster than ever now that the old king was rumoured to be sicker than he would let on.

'About what?'

'Mosley needs to know where the future king's heart lies. Rather, he knows, is sure of it, but wishes to see if the prince will be bold and a leader, or weak and a follower. If he will give in to Duff Cooper and Churchill, who talk loudly, and wrongly, of where our allies are.'

Doris sighed. Did they really care, these men who fussed about world affairs, or simply pretend to?

'But now that we are here, both of us . . .' Envers continued.

He put his hand on her arm and she felt the nearness of him and wondered for a moment that two men – Envers and Chips – could stand so close to her and the effect could be so different. And yet, was it really? Her heart hammered in the exact same way, so that she could not speak and could scarcely breathe, and the longing she felt to lean forward and into his arms was no stronger than the urge she had felt to be away from Chips. She wanted to move, but couldn't and so she was there when he put his other hand out and took hold of her and pulled her to him. And she stayed there even as he pressed his mouth on hers, and when he moved her backwards she allowed him, until she was pressed up against the wall behind the door with his weight on her, pinning her where anyone who came in might see them.

He was swift and almost brutal and she matched him in those things, pushing hard just as he did, and in very little time they were done.

Later, as she walked the dim hallway back towards the drawing room, she found that her legs shook, as though

she had been in an accident. A car crash, or had fallen off
her horse when out hunting. Inside the drawing room, she
saw that Bertie watched the door for her.

'There you are.' He hurried over. 'I thought perhaps you
were tired after all, or had a headache, you were gone so
long. I quite worried about you.' He smiled down at her.

'You mustn't worry about me,' Doris said. 'I am quite
alright.' But her voice wobbled.

'You have changed your dress,' Bertie said.

'The other was too warm.'

'You look even more beautiful.' He smiled enthusiastically at her and she had to put a hand firmly to her throat
to stop herself from crying.

Kitty and Honor came over, and dispatched Bertie to
change the record on the gramophone. Once he had gone,
Doris could not stop herself from asking, 'I did not know
you had asked that man, Envers.' She felt Honor twitch
beside her.

'Oh I didn't ask him,' Kitty said. 'He simply arrived.'

'You do not know him, then?'

'I knew his wife quite well.'

'Knew?'

'Yes, no one knows her much anymore. She doesn't
come to London, you see.'

'She was rather mean about the divorce, I believe.' Doris
tried to sound simply gossipy, not interested. 'Refused to
grant him adultery?'

'I'm not sure adultery was the problem . . .' Kitty leaned
in closer, dropping her voice. Doris saw that, on the other

side of the room, Envers had returned and was talking to Chips by the cocktail tray. 'No, I rather think the cruelty was real,' Kitty continued thoughtfully. 'I don't know so very much, but she did get frightfully thin and lost great clumps of hair. Like a fox with the mange – just tufts left on her head, here and there, not enough to make anything of,' she said vaguely, hands hovering in the air in front of her. 'She was rather beautiful, before all that. Before they married.'

'What kind of cruelty?' That was Honor, sharply.

'She said it was intolerable, the way he ran her life for her, chose her friends, made her appointments, wanted an account of exactly where she was every day, with whom and for how long. She said if 20 minutes couldn't be accounted for, he would accuse her of all sorts of things. Even while he was getting up to goodness knows what with half of London . . . So no, the adultery wasn't so much the thing . . . I said I'd simply love if Perry would bother himself at all about my affairs,' Kitty laughed, 'but she said I didn't know what I spoke of. She became something of a bore, if you must know. I was glad when she moved away. Now, I must ring the gong for dinner or we'll never eat and the servants will be simply furious.'

Doris watched her go, conscious of Honor close beside her, and the things Honor wanted to say – she could feel them, brimming inside her, but refused to turn to her.

She wondered what she would have done if she had known this earlier, before she met Envers at the bottom of the staircase. Would she have behaved quite differently, sweeping past him and on into the light and crowd of the drawing room? Perhaps. Perhaps not, she thought with a shiver.

Chapter Thirty-Four

At dinner, the prince sat beside Wallis, his chair pulled close in to hers so that they were the point at which the table snagged, Honor thought, watching them. He refused all food, waving servants loftily away, but ate small bites from her plate that she cut for him. Sometimes they whispered together, exchanging private jokes at which they giggled. This had the effect of making other conversations feel stilted, as though the rest of them were actors on a stage, valiantly performing, only to find the audience they looked to had lost interest in their play.

Duff Cooper and Emerald discussed the situation in Germany – Emerald talked at some length about the refugee commission Honor had wanted to read up on – and Chips interjected comments about the smartness and efficiency of Hitler's men, how he was a barrier to Bolshevism, and it was time England understood where their opportunity lay – to be part of what was new and bold and brilliant, alongside Germany. An ally. A partner. A force for change in the world and a serious opposition to the evil of socialism. The prince, turning his attention from Wallis for one moment, agreed enthusiastically. 'It's what I say,' he said in tones of approval. 'A barrier to Bolshevism.'

'The real enemy,' Envers agreed quickly. 'Something of which Mosley is keenly aware. And not just aware. Anyone can be that' – he held up a finger – 'but actively working to defeat.'

The prince nodded at him. 'Very good,' he said. 'Very good.'

As though, Honor thought, someone had put a dish of something delicious in front of him.

When the prince had turned back to Wallis, Duff leaned over to Chips, quiet but angry: 'Your views are vile, and worse, ill-informed. You are like that dog of yours.'

'My views at least have influential support,' Chips said.

'It is not a bonny baby competition,' Duff said.

'Who thinks as you do? Only that old soak Churchill, and Glamour Boy Eden. Everyone who matters is of my mind on this. You heard Envers, and our prince.'

'Yes, I did,' Duff said. 'And it gives me no pleasure to say he is wrong. You are all wrong. You look at Germany and you see order, change, shows of strength. You ignore the disorder that roils beneath that. You ignore the evidence that Hitler is greedy for land and power. You choose to see discipline and the seductive pageantry of display, and you are blind to the grasping reach behind that and how much he is willing to destroy.'

He might have said more, but Emerald put a hand on his arm. 'Hush,' she said, 'not now.'

Afterwards, there really was a play – or rather, an amateurish entertainment got up by some of Doris' lot. They put up a makeshift stage in the drawing room, arranged themselves into tableaux wearing a series of daring costumes, and sang the songs of Mr Coward, but with new words of their own devising. These words were about people they all knew, some of whom were present.

'The cheek,' Maureen muttered in delight, as a girl with cropped blonde hair sang something about 'the making of a marchioness called *Maureen* . . .' and rolled her eyes towards where Maureen sat beside Honor.

'The original words were much cleverer,' Honor whispered back. 'I wonder they felt the need to change them . . .'

None of it was terribly funny, and they weren't very well rehearsed, so that the time dragged. Honor saw that Chips – on the other side of the room to her, in an armchair pulled up beside Diana Cooper – was tapping his foot, while Emerald, on his other side, was openly reading something she held in her lap.

Just when Honor felt she could stand it no longer, Doris came on. She had a solo and walked onto the makeshift stage dressed as a young boy in a kind of Dick Whittington outfit, in a very short tunic, tights and a floppy hat.

'Well, isn't she the best boy,' Maureen said with a sly grin.

To the tune of 'Let's Do It', Doris sang, clear and true, what sounded like nonsense to Honor, but had all the younger set falling around laughing. Every once in a while Honor caught a name – Ida Rubinstein, her uncle Walter Guinness – but she couldn't understand the allusions. Chips, clearly, did. Now, he paid attention. She watched as he threw his head back and laughed heartily. Beside him, Envers watched the makeshift stage, and Doris on it, with intense concentration; an angler who watches the surface of the water.

When she got to the bit where she should have sung about Ernest Hemingway, she substituted 'Ernest Simpson could-just-do it', with a stagey wink at Wallis and the prince. At that, Maureen sat forward with an eager smirk. 'I say,' she said. 'Well, I *say* . . .'

Everyone looked, while pretending not to, towards the small sofa where Wallis and the prince sat side by side. There was a pointy silence, and then Wallis laughed heartily. She raised her martini glass in a kind of salute to Doris, still on the stage, and said, 'How wonderfully wicked you young people are.' Beside her, the prince smiled too.

Perhaps this was the fun she enjoyed so much, Honor thought. Looking across the room, she saw that Chips was furious, Envers impossible to read.

'What were you thinking?' she whispered to Doris a little later.

'Daring, wasn't it?' Doris said. She had changed into a plum-coloured evening dress that clung and draped but was at least more decent than the tunic. 'I'm sure I shouldn't, but they are so absurd, the pair of them, with their matching tweeds and their ridiculous baby names.' She laughed, but something that wasn't mirthful glittered in her eyes. Maybe she had been more frightened than she wanted to let on. 'You know that she kicks him under the table in a kind of code? Hard, if he should stop what's he's saying; softly, if he should go on. What do you think of that?'

'It seems an uncertain kind of system,' Honor said with a laugh. 'So difficult to tell what was hard, what was soft.'

'How can that man ever be king?' Doris asked.

'Well, but he will, and so perhaps you shouldn't make fun . . . Chips thinks—'

'Yes, I thought Chips would enjoy my little show alright,' Doris said. She turned from Honor and looked to where Chips was whispering with Emerald. There was a curious, listening kind of expression on her face, Honor thought, like someone who has thrown a stone into a well and waits to hear it land.

'Did you write it?'

'I did.' Doris sounded proud. 'I wrote it before dinner, in my room.'

'And you only went up for an hour,' Honor marvelled. 'What a mind you have. But please, don't be foolish, darling.'

Somehow, there never seemed a moment when Honor could excuse herself. After the play, Wallis insisted she would make a new kind of cocktail, and Chips rushed to help her. Honor saw that in between the fiddling about with olives and lemon peel, he had his little paper twists with him. He tipped some of the powder from them into the jug. Wallis gave him a knowing smile and stirred vigorously at the powder with a slim cocktail stick. They poured, sloppily, and handed drinks out to all. Honor took hers to avoid a scene, and took a tiny sip from it. Some kind of a martini, she decided, but with a dash of something orange-y.

'Here.' She handed the glass to Maureen, who had drained hers in one gulp.

'Don't mind if I do,' Maureen said. 'Your husband really does make a divine bartender. He has quite missed his calling.'

'Don't be catty, darling. He makes a divine husband too.'

'Nearly as good as he does a courtier?' She nudged Honor then and inclined her head towards where Chips was laughing loudly at something the prince had said. 'Still angling for a title? I suppose it's all he's missing now. Pity they're not so easily come by as all that. Not the good ones, anyway.' And she smirked, secure in the grandeur of her own trappings.

Honor settled into a quiet corner where no one, she hoped, would try to talk to her. The drinks had done their work, injecting gaiety into the evening of a kind that was loud and frantic and unfocused. Pockets of people here and there shouted happily at each other. So much laughter, no one listening. The gramophone was turned up and some of the younger people danced. Honor watched Wallis and the prince, deciding that they were curious together. She whirled about the room, constantly in motion, as though she was afraid that, once she stopped, she would never start again. She was quick and gay and full of laughter. He, meanwhile, followed her around, physically if he could, reaching out to touch her often, his hand on her arm, his hand on her hand. He asked for her handkerchief to dab at something on his top lip, then folded it small and put it into his own breast pocket. And if he couldn't be beside her, he followed her with his eyes. Because she moved so much, it was obvious: his head turned every time she changed direction. It was like a dance, Honor thought. Or maybe a chase.

'Everyone loves him and nobody loves him,' Envers said, coming to stand beside her. 'Adored and ignored.'

She wondered why he spoke to her. Did it have to do with Doris? She decided to try to be civil. 'Do you know him well?'

'Does anyone?' It seemed he would stop at that. Then, 'His efforts are towards concealment, not candidness, I would have thought.'

'Certainly there is something furtive about him, for all that he plays at being open and sunny,' she mused. The knots in the prince's forehead bunched more tightly than ever, his lips pressed one against the other in case he let something out – a scream, thought Honor, looking at the darting eyes in his handsome face. A cry for help. But then, Mrs Simpson was his cry for help. A woman so impossible that she couldn't be anything else.

'Furtive, and indecisive,' Envers agreed. 'Except on one topic.'

They both looked at Wallis then.

'Chips, darling, another round!' she demanded, as they watched, and Honor saw Chips leap forward to begin gathering lemons and ice.

'I think I'll go up,' Honor said quietly, to no one in particular.

Chapter Thirty-Five

London, summer 1935

The summer, Honor thought, was like something wicked out of a fairy tale: day after day of heat like treacle, thick and slow and cloying. Never a breeze, no hint of rain, and nights so chokingly airless that sometimes Honor rang for Molly and asked her to run a bath of cold water, that she might simply lie and remember what it was like to not wish to slide out of your own skin.

London was deserted. Her parents were in Scotland for a month – Lady Iveagh wrote every second day, giving minute accounts of everything they did, and asking questions of Honor – how was she; what did Doctor Gilliatt say – that Honor scarcely knew how to answer. She was tired, and heavy, and the idea of more than three months before her baby was born was unbearable. But she couldn't write that to her mother and so she wrote, *I am well. Chips too.*

That wasn't the truth, but what else could she say? *Chips is on edge? Giddy with near-success and driven hard by opportunities he thinks lie within his grasp, and what he must do to get them. He sleeps little, either because he is out or because he is up, at his desk half the night, writing. But I don't know what it is that he writes. He talks of research he must do, the peace and quiet he needs in order to work on a new book, but he fills his days, as ever, with people and plans and parties.*

He complains of indigestion, of exhaustion, of his liver, but when I try to suggest he go to bed earlier, follow a simple diet, he scoffs at me and says I do not understand the world and the way he must be in it. He drives up and down to Southend, canvassing. He complains of those he meets – how bourgeois they are; how uninteresting – and yet he exhausts himself trying to charm them . . .

She was conscious, too, that with Lady Iveagh absent from London, she had neglected most of her charitable duties. She could hardly force herself to make her way to Paddington Street, in the summer heat, where the stink of rotting vegetables was overlaid, now, with something that came up from the drains under the street, breathing out a putrid breath.

She went once, to visit the same family, with a basket packed full by Mrs Murphy, the cook, and tried to pretend she was Lady Iveagh, sweeping in and through, like a brisk wind that reaches every corner but does not linger. But it was impossible, and instead she felt that the thick ill-smelling air, fed by piles of rubbish and old clothes, had caught at her like tar and held her fast. The stairs up to the mean flat were more scuffed than ever and had holes where the wood was worn right through so that she wondered would the entire staircase simply fall away, leaving those on the upper floors trapped.

She knocked hard on the door of the flat and a voice called out, 'Our ma's not in,' from behind it.

'I have brought some things,' Honor said loudly. 'May I enter?'

The girl who opened the door was as Honor remembered, except thinner and taller, with a pale face. She had lost the angry, capable energy of childhood and was apathetic, seeming hardly aware that Honor was there as she stepped to one side to let her pass. By her side was a small boy. Was he the baby? Honor wondered. She tried to count, but the years slid from her grasp.

'I hope you are well,' Honor said brightly, feeling how ridiculous the words were. Without her mother to lend the visit purpose, she felt only the awkwardness of her intrusion.

'You can leave them there.' The girl pointed to the table by the window. No longer covered by heaps of clothes to be mended, it had a layer of newspaper laid across it, on which was a scant pile of potato peelings that were limp and blackened and curled at the edges.

Once she had put the basket down and unpacked it, Honor had no idea what to do. The girl, uninterested, had returned to a magazine she was reading. Honor caught sight of photos of film stars as she flicked. She paused at a photo of Jean Harlow in a froth of ostrich feathers and sequins. The same photo Doris had pointed out to Honor a month or so ago, saying, 'Doesn't she look absurd? Like a bird in its grubby nest. Especially when we know how dusty ostrich feathers get.' She had laughed. Now, as Honor looked, the girl reached out a finger and gently, reverentially, traced it down the page.

The boy sat on the floor at her feet. He wore a pair of shorts and a man's shirt cut down to fit him. He had a battered toy car in one hand and an empty sardine tin in the other, and he bashed the two together, making 'vrooming' noises; two cars crashing into one another. He looked up at Honor and silently offered one of the 'cars' – the sardine tin – to her. Honor thought of sitting down on the floor beside him, and playing this game. How easy it would be. She need only play for ten minutes, half an hour. But she couldn't. It wasn't her size, or the dirt of the floor, although it was filthy – it was that she couldn't bear to take up common cause with him, even for a minute, even for a child's game, in case she began to feel the truth of his life. As long as she stayed in motion, and did not settle, this need be no more than a swift visit, a duty discharged.

'I must get on,' she said. 'Please tell your mother I will call again.'

Neither of the children said anything but the girl watched over the top of her magazine as Honor walked from the room.

She didn't call again. When Chips didn't demand her company, she was content to lie for hours on the sofa, reading. Doris was away in Dorset, Oonagh was in Ireland, Maureen at Clandeboye: *We murder grouse and occasionally one another*, she wrote.

Then it was July and her wedding anniversary. 'Two years,' Chips said, coming to her room early. 'Two wonderful years.' He bent to stroke her head. 'And you are lovelier and sweeter than ever.' He sat heavily on the bed beside her, then swung his legs up until he lay on top of the counterpane, resting against the headboard. It was, she reflected, the first time he had been in her bed in many months. In fact, since he had first suspected the pregnancy.

He had ordered sweet pastries for breakfast, which he knew she loved, and when they had eaten they exchanged gifts – a sapphire and diamond clip brooch for her, a watch for him. Leaning back, Chips crossed his arms behind his head and began to muse, delighted, on all that had happened in the two years.

'It feels as though we are moving in a different world,' he said. 'No longer the short-stay social world of *le tout monde*, where balls and parties must be attended simply because they are given and one is invited. No, now we have purpose. A place well beyond merely affable guests. We have,' he said grandly, '*intent.*'

Honor wondered at the 'we'. He couldn't possibly believe that she was part of this purpose, this intent?

'Soon,' he continued, 'we will move into Belgrave Square, Channon House' – this was what he had taken to calling it, even though Honor squirmed every time – 'and the next, even more magnificent chapter of our lives will begin. A family,' – he looked warmly at the round lump that rose up beneath the peach silk counterpane but did not touch it – 'dear friends.'

She knew he thought of the prince, of his brother the Duke of Kent, who would be next door to them.

'Perhaps a title. Emerald hopes for Master of the Horse, or even Lord Chamberlain, for Perry Brownlow. What, then, may I hope for?' He put his arms behind his head, elbows so wide that she had to move a little to get out of their way.

She knew he wanted a cosy discussion of the glories he was fit for – the honours that would surely be bestowed upon him, what exactly these might be, and why it was that he deserved them, but she wasn't in the mood. 'It is your mother's birthday in five days,' she said instead. 'I have sent a gift from both of us.'

'That poor abandoned, peculiar woman,' he said, sighing heavily.

'Yes, abandoned. By you.'

'She infuriates me. She infuriates everyone. I never knew anyone so without friends. But it is no surprise. She is unattractive and irrational.'

'You speak as though you hate her.'

'I don't hate her. Or at least,' he corrected himself, 'not any more. I did love her once, and then, as a teenager I hated her.' How specific he was. 'But now I do not. Not for years. Now, I feel almost nothing, perhaps some small sympathy.

Almost the same dull contempt I feel for my father.' He smiled, as though this were a victory.

'How can you say such a thing?'

'I say it because it's the truth. My only fear is that our child will be like its grandparents. Like my parents,' he emphasised.

'You cannot hate your mother, Chips. You simply cannot.'

'You know nothing of it. Thanks to me, you have never had to meet her. Not everyone can be lucky enough to have Lady Iveagh as a mother.'

'No. Indeed. But all the same, I cannot imagine how someone could hate their mother.'

'Many people hate their mothers. Look at your cousins, Maureen and Oonagh, and how they are with Cloé.'

'They don't hate her. Not exactly.'

'As good as. I'll tell you what, though: Doris, whatever she says, does not.'

'How do you know?'

'I know. I know the signs. She doesn't display them.'

She wondered. Chips was far better at people than she was – at understanding them, interpreting them. 'Well, I'm glad of it. It is unnatural, to hate your mother.'

Perhaps because she went nowhere, saw almost no one, in the days that followed, the conversation stayed in Honor's head. *Many people hate their mothers*. What if her baby, like Chips, hated its mother? He had said, *My only fear is that our child will be like its grandparents*. Her fear was that their child would be like its father – with a cruel eye and cold intent. She had lived too closely and too long with Chips by then not to understand that beneath his warmth and beauty was a constant chilly appraisal. Mostly this was turned upon himself and his own endeavours – the getting of those things he wanted. Sometimes, though, he could turn it outwards. As he had with Doris and Lump at Christmas at Elveden. And then, well, the force of it was something surprising.

In the long clammy nights when she couldn't sleep, she turned the idea this way and that, wondering at it. At what it might mean. She saw a boy with Chips' face, turned away from her even as she called him. Another time, it was she who shrank from him, because in her dream that was more like a delirium, he smelt like the boy in the Paddington Street tenement. He repulsed her and she pitied him, with a pity that was close to disgust.

I will have a daughter, she told herself. And they would be just as she and her mother were together – content and purposeful. A daughter, she could understand. Would know how to be with her so that they were the good in one another's lives. A daughter who would fill the space that had appeared in her marriage; at first a sliver, now grown wider, in which she still saw with secret sorrow all that she had once hoped for and had learned to put aside.

Chapter Thirty-Six

'I've never been so far from London,' Mabel said, looking out at the patchwork of yellow and green fields bordered by dusty trees. The lack of rain was obvious out here – the countryside was subdued by it; made threadbare but somehow more vast because there wasn't the usual lush fullness of growth. They were on the second Dorset train, the little old engine that chugged from Bournemouth to Wareham, where Mr Coates' motorcar would be waiting for them. 'I didn't know the countryside was so big.' She sounded respectful, and cast a sideways glance at Doris. 'I'm glad you asked me to come.'

'I couldn't leave you all alone in London. Not in that heat. You would have burned right up. Didn't I tell you it would be cool in Dorset?'

'You did, and it is.' Mabel reached up and pulled the little window down further, letting in the clear, sweet-smelling air.

Doris had found her in Curzon Street, where she had gone to pick up her mail a week or so earlier. There had been nothing essential – a periodical she subscribed to and had forgotten to cancel, two cards of invitation from hostesses who didn't know her, or London society, well enough to realise she had moved – and the house had been almost completely empty. Mrs Benton was away for the summer, and the servants had been given leave, all except the housemaid who let Doris in. She had been about to depart when Mabel came home, coming wearily up the steps and in through the front door, and all but collapsing in the cool dark of the hallway.

'I thought I should die on the bus,' she gasped. 'It was like an infernal machine such as Mr Heath Robinson might design.'

'Hullo, Mabel,' Doris said. 'You do look hot.'

'Don't "hullo, Mabel" me,' the girl replied, fanning herself with a piece of paper she pulled from her purse. 'Not when you no longer live in this house and don't have to suffer the kind of summer rations Mrs Benton leaves. In fact, it's since you're gone that she's started leaving the house empty of anyone except that silly maid. Weeks at a time, not a soul only me and her, and no more provision made for me than if I were a mouse. She'd never have dared when you were here.'

'I have much to answer for,' Doris said with a smile.

'You do.' Mabel sighed. 'Oh, Doris, you can't imagine how dreadful. Meat paste for tea, day after day. And the tea so weak it's like liquorice water.'

'Perhaps you'd better come to Dorset with me,' Doris said, looking at Mabel, who was pale under the damp red of her cheeks, with purple circles under her eyes. 'Have you holidays you can take?'

'I do,' Mabel said. 'Only I wasn't going to because of having nothing to do only go home, and I don't fancy that. It's as hot in Hampshire as it is here.'

'Well, then, Dorset it is,' Doris replied. 'I'll write to my mother.' And she had, sending a letter that evening, written from the cool of her bedroom at St James's Place, where the servants had had the shutters carefully closed all afternoon, and where the large window was now open to catch the evening breeze so the curtains stirred gently, while outside in the back garden wood pigeons made complacent throaty sounds. *I will be bringing a friend . . .*, she wrote.

'Is this really your house?' Mabel asked as the motorcar brought them along the last stretch of driveway. She looked with respect at the big square house that wore ivy twined around it like a light scarf. Her eyes were wide, and Doris wondered had she herself looked like that the first time Honor had taken her to Elveden.

'Yes, and it is nothing grand at all so you mustn't think it is. It has hardly any rooms that are any use, and more dogs in it than people.'

'No wonder Mrs Benton gave you the best of everything.' Doris had known her mother would assume the friend was Honor, and sure enough, 'Shall I call you Mrs Channon, or Honor?' Esther asked, in her usual direct way, as soon as Doris and Mabel had got down from the motorcar.

'You may call her whichever you please,' Doris said with a laugh, 'but her name is actually Mabel Suggs.'

'From the boarding house?'

How quick her mother was. It was months – many of them – since Doris had written anything about Mabel. 'Yes, although Mrs Benton would rather you call it an hotel.' She and Mabel exchanged a grin.

'You are very welcome.' Her mother moved forward to shake Mabel's hand.

Behind them, running up the driveway, came the children, who had, as usual, been watching for the car. 'You are mean not to stop,' Isabel called.

'You are too many and too big to all pile in the motorcar any more,' Doris said, throwing open her arms so that the children ran into them. 'Especially when you have such a quantity of dogs at your heels. Now come and say how do you do nicely to my friend Mabel.'

'I have a rabbit now too,' Marianne said.

Dinner was early so the children could join, and once they were all seated, including Tante Hannah, newly arrived from Germany, the table was crowded. Over dinner, Doris' parents asked Mabel a great many questions, which she answered as best she could, explaining willingly her grasp of shorthand and the best way to file accounts, stumbling over any questions about politics and the make-up of the government. The children chattered about their pets and projects, so that Doris didn't have to talk much; could watch the way her parents were and try to understand was there more harmony between them than the last visit home. She decided that yes, there was, and yet, there was something off all the same. Something that lay beneath the noisy, merry surface that wasn't either of those things.

Her aunt, she saw, got up and down from the table many times, going to the kitchen to talk to the cook, removing soup plates and bringing in the pudding, even though there were, as usual, two parlourmaids to do the serving. She seemed, Doris thought, agitated, uttering half-sentences in German and English – 'I will see if I can find . . .'; 'I said there must be cream with this' – almost as though talking to herself, but aloud. She was quite unlike the serious, quiet person Doris had met in Berlin – now unfocused. Sometimes Esther said, 'Leave it, Hannah, the maid will see to it,' and even, 'Please, sit,' but she spoke in English rather than German, and Hannah either didn't understand – which was impossible, because her English was good – or pretended not to hear. In any case she didn't answer.

Afterwards, Hannah did not linger with the family in the drawing room but went immediately to her room, saying she had things to attend to. Once the children had been sent, protesting, to the nursery and Mabel had gone up, Doris drew her chair closer to her mother and asked, 'What is wrong with Tante Hannah? She was like a clock-work toy at dinner, up and down so many times, I quite thought she had been over-wound.'

Her mother sighed and cast a quick look at Doris' father,

sitting just beyond them in a pool of greenish light from the lamp on the table beside him. 'It has been very difficult,' she said.

'Very,' Doris' father agreed.

'What has?' Doris looked from one to the other.

'We could not get Hannah into the country without an offer of employment. The Home Office would not allow her in otherwise,' her father said.

'And so I have had to say that she would be our house-keeper,' her mother continued. 'But now, she insists that she must do the job I have said she is here for.' Her voice wobbled. 'Even though that was the excuse, not the intention. I do not want her to behave as a housekeeper in my house. But you've seen how she is now – forever jumping up from the table to fetch things.'

'Dreadful,' Doris agreed with feeling.

'I understand that she is humiliated. But this? It is not necessary. Because of it, I am humiliated too. That my sister should call me Mrs Coates . . .' Her voice broke.

'Is there no other way?' Doris asked. 'I see in the news-papers that there are committees for refugees . . . relief funds . . . I thought that must mean there is a way for them to be welcomed?'

'Everything they do in Mr Baldwin's government is designed to keep people out,' her mother said bitterly. 'Although they will never say as much. They talk of prudence. Of disposing carefully, or ensuring there is not competition for English workers, but what they mean is to keep people away.'

'How did Otto and Aron get in?'

'I was able to say they have skills that cannot be found here,' her father said, edging his chair closer to them. 'But even so, their papers are temporary and they are expected to teach what they know to my men, so that their skills will no longer be unique. Once that happens, I do not know . . .' He spread his hands out in front of him, fingers wide. It was a gesture of uncertainty unusual in him.

'And my cousins?' Doris asked. 'Hannah's sons?' She thought of those four serious young men with their solemn views on life and art.

'They are studying in Belgium, but already they have had to change what they study. There is no room, here, for more doctors, they say, and so they must study what will be accepted and not what they wish.'

'Eventually they, too, will try to come here,' Doris' father said, 'and I do not know how I will manage.' He said it wearily, but without the edge that had been in his voice when Doris was last home, and with a warm look at Esther, so that Doris knew they were again united, and had found a common enemy in government rather than bickering with one another. That, at least, was something.

Chapter Thirty-Seven

In the second week of August when Chips suggested they go and stay at Bailiffscourt, her uncle Walter's house near Littlehampton, at first Honor said she was too tired, and didn't want to be away from Doctor Gilliatt, but Chips persevered. 'We will be only a few hours from London. We can't stay here, the city is empty . . .'

'Hardly *empty*,' she tried, but he ignored her.

'. . . and it is no good for your spirits to be where you have no companionship,' he continued.

'But what about Belgrave Square? There is so much there to do.'

There were by then 23 men working daily on the house. Mostly, as far as Honor could see, tearing down what had been there before. Chips had told her the cost for everything would be forty thousand pounds; 'but we can afford it'. Honor knew well that would not weigh with Lady Iveagh, who would be shocked – deeply shocked – at the extravagance.

'Very true, but I can leave instructions,' he said now. 'In any case, the weather is intolerable.'

That was certainly true. Each morning, Honor woke, her skin already damp with sweat, and spent the day moving from room to room, ahead of the sun. In the morning, the drawing room at the front of the house was dark and almost cool, so she went there. Later, as the sun crept around, inching its blistering fingers towards her, she moved to the back of the house, to the library or small sitting room, where she used to write letters when she had the energy. Almost, she looked forward to the move to Belgrave Square, a house so large that there were deep interior rooms that scarcely saw the sun at all. How she longed for them now – their echoey coolness – even though at first sight she had said, 'So dark, and impossible to heat. And what could anyone want with so many rooms?'

'At Bailiffscourt there will be sea breezes and clean country air,' Chips continued. 'Your uncle Walter, Lady Moyne; perhaps some of their amusing friends. I believe Diana's sons, little Desmond and Jonathan, are there too, as Diana is off with Mosley, and he does not care to have them with him.'

'Very well,' Honor said then, 'let's go to Bailiffscourt.' It was the words *sea breezes and clean country air* that did it – already the day pressed her down with a damp and heavy hand, as though she were a dog to be disciplined, she thought – but also, she wanted to see these little boys; were they still beautiful? Would their beauty still impress Chips, as it had when Jonathan was page boy at their wedding? And what might that mean for their own child, if he or she were not beautiful? Especially where the gifts of beauty were so clearly divided, lying all with Chips and none with her?

They motored down in easy stages, Bundi beside them, panting extravagantly in the heat. They stopped to picnic at the side of the road, and again for Honor to put her swollen feet into a stream of cold water, arriving at Bailiffscourt as the afternoon light clotted thick to evening, the day's harsh brightness softening to a deep and easy gold.

'It is like an entire medieval village,' Chips said in admiration as they drove past clusters of buildings – guest houses, a chapel, thatched cottages and thick-walled outhouses – before approaching the main house. 'Impossible to believe that it is brand new. He has succeeded in making it look exactly as though it has been here forever.'

At first, Honor knew, he had thought Lord Moyne's scheme silly – 'Why, when you can have the newest and latest designs,' he had asked, honestly bewildered – but now, looking at the clever flow of buildings and trees, the subdued undulations of the carefully worn stone – he was enchanted.

'Welcome.' Walter came out to the front lawn to meet them. On one shoulder, arms clasped tight around his neck, was a tiny monkey with thick black-and-white fur and huge round eyes. Chips gave it a wary look. With him were Desmond and Jonathan, dressed in shorts and white shirts, their hair bleached almost silver by the sun. Behind them, the house sat low and long, secluded behind a screen of trees that shook their leaves in a light breeze. Burned-looking wisteria climbed over the mustard-coloured stone, and the mullioned windows with their many diamond-shaped panes of glass were set deep into their stone arches. It looked dark and cool and Honor longed to go straight in and lie down.

'How do you do,' the boys said politely.

Honor held out a hand and they shook it, first one, then the other. She cast around for something to say. 'Have you been having the same frightful weather as we have?' she asked eventually.

They looked at her, confused. 'It's been very sunny,' Jonathan said. Desmond, nearly four, said nothing. 'Can we play with him?' Jonathan asked then, of Bundi.

'Of course. He is as gentle as a lamb, for all that he looks like a lion,' Chips said. 'Let me show you the exact spot he loves to be scratched – here, behind the ears – and now that you know that, he will be your slave.'

Honor, who felt as though she had been stitched into her skin, so tired and swollen was she, wondered at his energy, his gift with children of saying the right thing, and in the right way. Within a minute, he was on the grass in a heap with Bundi and the boys, all laughing merrily. The monkey, watching from the safety of Uncle Walter's shoulder, twitched its long tail up and further out of the way, reminding Honor of Mrs Simpson.

'Shall we go inside?' Walter said, offering his arm.

'Please.'

The house was just as she had hoped. The thick walls, low ceilings and deep windows stood firm against the sun, holding it at bay. Honor sank gratefully into an armchair, where she half-dozed while Chips and Walter spoke of politics. There had been what Walter called 'atrocities' in Germany, about which he seemed greatly exercised. 'There will be an end to it at last,' he said, stroking the monkey, which sat quietly on his knee. 'Now we can all see – here, as well as in Germany – what these National Socialists really are. Why, *The Times* this very morning carried the text of a leaflet distributed throughout Berlin. See here.' He pulled a copy of the newspaper from behind his chair and unfolded it. '*The Jew violates your child, ravishes your wife* . . . there's more of that rot . . . *spoils your culture, infects your race* . . . What vile nonsense.' He sounded angry.

Honor thought of Doris: . . . *the stain in marble, the run in silk, a blot in anything that would otherwise be pure*. So she had been correct. And what Honor had hoped was exaggerated, was nothing so easy.

'But now that it is so thoroughly out in the open – not to mention the attacks on Jewish property and people – we will see a natural revulsion,' Walter continued. The monkey now held his thumb in both its little hands, like a child clinging to an adult, Honor thought.

'I'm afraid you are not right,' Chips said, leaning back. 'The press might make a fuss, but do not mistake the matter – there will be no natural revulsion. No active revulsion, at least. The violence and window smashings, the allegations and outrages' – he sounded bored – 'they are not close enough, they do not mean enough, to stir action beyond idle outcry.'

'That cannot be so. I think you are wrong,' Walter said.

'Certainly the outcry against these outrages will not be louder than what we are already hearing over refugees entering Britain,' Chips said. He sounded self-consciously shrewd. 'As long as the flow of refugees remains, that will be the primary concern of most people – how to stop them taking jobs from our own working men.'

'The stopping seems to be effective,' Walter said wryly. 'I have heard of Jewish doctors and dentists working as chauffeurs, middle-class women taking jobs as domestics.'

'You cannot blame people,' Chips said, shifting comfortably about in his chair. 'Why should they look to help others when it is already so hard to help themselves?'

Honor realised how she hated when he spoke like that – as if he were King Solomon in charge of a dispute, consciously weighing one side and then the other. It was, she thought, the pomposity, the arrogance of his own certainty, more even than what he said, that grated upon her. Perhaps it was the heat making her irritable, she thought.

'You must admit,' he continued, 'the idea of welcoming in those who have been rejected by another civilised nation . . . well,' – he gave a laugh – 'hardly the most appealing, is it?'

There was silence then and Honor tried to think of some way to say to Chips that he sounded cruel, but could not.

'So you are for Germany still, despite everything?' Walter asked at last.

Chips shrugged easily. 'I am. Perhaps it is in response to my mother's excessive love of all things French when I was a child.'

And perhaps you are too quick to blame your mother for everything, Honor thought, but again, she did not speak.

'That's hardly an answer,' Walter said. 'You would do well to think more on it.'

'I am not the only one,' Chips said. 'The prince himself made a speech advocating friendship with Germany, to the British Legion, only a month ago.'

'I know he did,' Walter said grimly. 'And he would do well to think more too. Or talk less.'

Lady Moyne came in then, so Honor sat up and opened her eyes fully. Her aunt wore pale grey trousers and a tiny blue bow in her hair and looked both austere and girlish. The pronounced angle of her jaw was sharp, as ever. 'Get that beast out of here,' she said sharply. 'I have said not at meals.' The monkey, as though it understood, leaped back to Walter's shoulder in one nervous fluid movement and clasped its tiny arms around his neck again.

'Off you go,' Walter said gently, unpeeling the skinny hands and handing the monkey to a housemaid. 'Give him some water and a little fruit, but only a little, mind.'

Others began to trickle in. First the boys, accompanied now by a tutor, then a dancing instructor, a fiddle teacher, two nurses, a secretary. Each was introduced solemnly to Honor and Chips. 'You have a busy household,' Honor said.

'It's the boys,' said Lady Moyne. 'They do come with so many trappings. You'll see.' She laughed. 'Now, tell me about the house – Belgrave Square – I believe London can talk of little else . . .'

Honor was unsure where to begin – the expense? The blue-and-silver dining room? The 23 men? – and was relieved when Chips, having overheard, swivelled around in his chair.

'It will be magnificent,' he said. 'A place for entertaining in a way that no one does anymore. All the great houses have dwindled. Why, we were at dinner at the Cavendishes' recently, and really you would have sworn they intended a casual supper, not a dinner at all . . .' Where he had been comfortable and genial in talking about Germany and the atrocities committed there, now he was cross.

'And who will you entertain, that the setting must be so lavish?' Lady Moyne asked mischievously.

'Our friends,' Chips said grandly.

Honor laughed and he frowned at her. She knew exactly what he meant – these people he was so pleased to call 'friends' were as carefully chosen as though they had been paintings or tapestries for a collection. He didn't mean Doris, or Oonagh, or even Maureen, the casual friends of their daily lives. Nor did he mean, any longer, the Duff Coopers, now that *he* was so belligerently anti-Germany.

He meant the New Court – the prince, Emerald, Mrs Simpson, the Brownlows – and on outwards: Mussolini's ambassador Grandi, Herr von Ribbentrop, himself busily courting Mrs Simpson and being courted by Emerald in turn – so that all of Europe might soon be ordered and arranged from the blue-and-silver dining room.

'Your *friends*?' Lady Moyne said. 'How charming.'

On the last full day, Maureen arrived with her children. 'I didn't intend to bring them,' she said, 'but various things happened and then it seemed I must.' She exhaled lazily, a plume of cigarette smoke drifting slowly through the still air. The weather had become hotter again and more still, and even the garden at Bailiffscourt was no longer the reliable refuge it had been, but blanketed thick and airless.

'How sweet that they can play with their cousins,' Honor said. 'Caroline is only a few months older then Desmond. I'm sure they must be great friends.'

'Hardly,' Maureen said. 'Caroline doesn't care for anyone, except Duff, a little. I haven't seen her smile since we left Clandeboye. It's like lugging a cross-faced doll about with one.'

Honor looked over at where Caroline sat on a plaid rug under the chestnut tree. She had in front of her a toy horse on wheels but she paid it no attention. Rather, she stared solemnly about with large blue eyes set wide on either side of her face. Her mouth was folded very tightly as though to stop herself crying.

'She looks like she has seen a ghost,' Honor said.

'She always looks like that.'

The day got hotter and the children were taken inside for a nap. Maureen and Chips gossiped endlessly. They seemed to have an inexhaustible supply of scandalous stories. For every person either of them mentioned, the other had a tale – 'did you hear that he . . .'; 'I know for a fact that she . . .' They even gossiped about Cousin Bryan: 'I hear he is to marry Betty Nelson,' Maureen said, 'and now says that divorcing Diana is the best thing he ever did, but I remember how he looked when she left him; quite as though he was a hollow man with nothing left inside him . . .' – so that Honor kept looking over her shoulder warily in case her uncle or aunt should come close enough to hear what was said of their son.

She felt sick. There was no wind to blow away their words, or bring reminders of other, more pleasant things, so that the stories built and built around her, each one more lustful and scandalous than the last. It was, she thought, like going to a butcher's counter and seeing the many cuts and joints on display, glistening wetly; all those many pieces of flesh, sundered one from another, laid out and disposed of differently – a chop, a leg, a shoulder – but all from the same source. It was the same now, she thought – lust, greed, envy attributed here and there to this friend and that – all part of the same frail human origin.

When Lord and Lady Moyne came to join them, arriving from the house in plain view across the lawn so there was plenty of time for Maureen to drop what she had been saying about Cousin Bryan, Honor was relieved.

'Shall we have tea here? Lady Moyne asked. 'Or inside?'

'Here,' Maureen said. 'For it is too hot to move.'

Chips disagreed. 'Inside,' he said. 'It is far too hot to sit out.' He was sweating a little, Honor saw, dabbing at his top lip with a folded handkerchief. They went inside and the darkened interior was a relief after the hot glare of the day.

'Now, tell me about your plans for Southend once you are elected,' Walter said to Chips, who began elaborating on what he hoped to do and say in the Commons.

'What is that sound?' Honor asked, properly conscious at last of a dull pounding somewhere in the distance that had been going on for, she thought, quite some time without her really noticing. As she listened, it grew stronger. Now the windows rattled in their frames, shuddering with the pressure of the booming and causing the glass panes to jitter.

'Guns,' Walter said.

'So many? But what are they shooting?' Honor asked. Those were not the guns of grouse- or pheasant-shooting – in any case it wasn't yet the season – but a deeper, heavier sound.

'It is gun practice.'

'Practice for what?'

'For war.'

'Surely it is not come to that?' She was honestly surprised. There had been vague talk, but for so long now that she had decided it would never be more than vague – that men just liked to talk of war, it made them feel important. 'No one wants another war,' she said. It was something she had heard, repeated again and again, in the last year. 'Not so soon after the last.' That, too, had been said in her hearing. She had paid little attention. The last war, she had been nine when it ended, her brother Lump, six. Her father had been a captain in the Royal Naval Reserve, it's true, but on a drill ship stationed in London. None of it had been real to her, although the fact of it had been, for years, a kind of painted scene placed behind so much else – talked of, though not directly; referenced but always obliquely; remembered in the strange pockets of emptiness at balls, where men seemed to be old, or young, but rarely in between; in the looks on old men's faces when they talked of France. It had been a horror from a nightmare, never seen properly, only half-glimpsed. Yet even so, she knew enough to feel afraid.

'The talks in Paris have broken down,' Walter said gently. 'Lord Eden is back. His mission has failed and cabinet will meet tomorrow.'

'I must ring up Emerald,' Chips said busily. He went at once to telephone and stayed so long that Honor saw her aunt twitch and consult her watch several times. At Elveden, Lady Iveagh would have been exactly the same, counting, to the ha'pence what the call would cost and wondering would a letter not have been just as good. Finally, he came back. 'Emerald has been seeing members of the government all day,' he said, rubbing his hands. 'By the time we are back tomorrow, she will know precisely what's to happen.'

'The government will want to sound out public opinion,' Walter said. Clearly, he knew already. 'Then there will be an attempt to ask the League of Nations to enforce embargoes against Italy. That will fail but it will not be our fault when it does. And it will, at worst, buy time.'

'A great deal of time, I hope,' Chips said. 'At least until I am too old to go.'

'How old must that be?' Maureen asked.

'Forty-one,' Walter said.

'They will hardly delay five years,' Maureen said, doing the sums.

'Not five, three,' Chips said. 'For I am 38 now.'

'Are you indeed?' Maureen stared at him so long that he dropped his eyes and stirred his tea. She burst out laughing. 'Funny how we get to the truth of it at last, when to be older is suddenly an advantage.'

'I am not a coward, Maureen,' Chips said. 'I will fight if I must, but I would be far more useful in a government department. At the front, in the trenches, well, I do not see it.'

'I do not see it either, darling,' Maureen said, leaning back in her chair and waving her cigarette around. She made it sound like an insult. Perhaps it was an insult.

From outside came the sound of the children playing. And behind that, the guns went on, deep and loud, an ominous rumble that, on a day like that, Honor thought, could easily have been mistaken for thunder.

Chapter Thirty-Eight

Dorset, summer 1935

Doris found Mabel an easy companion. She asked for nothing, was content to do whatever Doris did, or to sit and read in the drawing room. In particular she liked to read periodicals, and couldn't believe the great number to which Doris' parents subscribed. 'I could learn everything I want to know by sitting here reading,' she said.

'Except I won't allow it. It is far too nice outdoors.'

'Yes, I never knew the summer could be so pleasant,' Mabel said. 'In London hot weather is always a trial, but out here, it is something quite different.'

They swam in the river every day and lay around to dry in the sun, taking picnic lunches. In the afternoons when it grew cooler, they played tennis or croquet. Isabel and Marianne came with them everywhere, and Maxim came and went, depending on what else was happened about the house. Mabel refused to get on a horse – 'Such beasts!' – and was shy with the children – 'They talk an awful lot, don't they? And so many questions' – but enjoyed talking to Esther, and even more to Hannah when she could be made to slow down and take the time.

'I can practise with her,' Mabel said. 'You never said you had German cousins, Doris.' She sounded admiring, envious, rather than showing the polite disinterest or amused incredulity Doris was used to.

'Practise what?' Doris asked lazily. 'And why must you be always learning?'

'Because I don't have a big grey house in the country and a father who owns a mine,' Mabel said tartly. 'I must earn my own living. And I've been advised to learn German.'

'By who?'

'One of the senior men at my course. The nicest of them. He said to never mind tennis, or Flora Elmsworth's father who works in a bank. That if I want to get on, learning German is the most useful thing I can do.'

'Did he say why?'

'No.'

'And you didn't ask?'

'No. But I went out and bought a book and have already learned a little, and now I can begin to learn more. Hannah is jolly decent about teaching me.' She sounded more excited than by anything yet, except the food ordered by Esther and put before them at dinner every day: 'I never knew ham could taste like this. Oh, what price Mrs Benton's meat paste now!'

But for all that Mabel was an easy and willing companion, Doris found she missed Honor. Missed their conversations, and the way Honor always knew what she meant even when she didn't feel the need to say so. The way they seemed together facing the world; one, rather than two. Honor's marriage had changed much less between them than Doris had once feared. She wondered what might happen when the baby was born. Nothing, she decided. Nothing much. She missed Honor's affectionate ways, the way she liked Doris to stroke her hair, her hands, and the gentle feeling it gave Doris to do so.

After the first few days, when she gloated over the distance that lay between her and David Envers, counting each mile with relief, she woke one morning to the realisation that it was not so easy to put him from her thoughts, as it was to put miles between them. She still spoke constantly to him, or so it seemed; replaying conversations in her head, inventing new ones, exchanges that could never be, in which he told her he loved her, needed her. It was, she thought, as though he had stained her somehow, coloured her with a dye that ran through every layer and could not be washed out. She wished she could take out that part of her head that must always be thinking of him, chasing him, searching for him. Reach into her own skull and simply lift it clear of the rest of her, and place it in a glass jar and close the lid tight so that she could keep it locked away but still see it. Because even though she hated the hours she gave to him in silent imaginary exchanges, still she marvelled that such a thing could have happened to her. Was it love, or obsession? Did it matter? She hadn't seen him since that disturbing night at the Brownlows', although he had written to her once, suggesting she telephone him. She hadn't. But neither had she thrown away the letter. Meanwhile, when she had said goodbye to Bertie, the night before leaving London, he had said, 'I say, there's something I'd like to ask you when you get back,' blushing to the tips of his ears, so that Doris knew just what it was that he wanted to ask.

'In time,' she had said to him. 'In time.' But what did she mean by that? she wondered. Would she allow him – encourage him – to ask what he wanted: marriage, she was sure, or was that vile and unsporting when she didn't feel in thrall to him the way she did to Envers? It was an impossible question, and so she didn't even try to answer it.

She took to rising early, while the mornings were fresh, before the gathering heat turned them stale, and walking with her mother to the farm gate to collect milk for breakfast. 'Why do you not send one of the maids?' she asked on the first morning.

'I like doing it,' her mother replied. 'There are tasks one should do oneself, and others that can be left.'

'How does one tell the difference?'

'By choosing the one you prefer,' her mother said with a smile. 'It's not so complicated.'

'Mabel has been advised by a chap at her school to learn German,' Doris said.

'How interesting. I wonder what that means. That we are to be allies with Germany?'

'Or not.'

Mabel left after her two weeks, and Doris stayed on until almost the end of August. 'I am sleepy and fat,' she said to her mother with a laugh. 'I do less and less each day. It's time I went back to London.'

'You are better by far than when you arrived. Then, you were like a carpet worn down, trodden over by too many dusty feet. Now, you are yourself again.'

She arrived back to London while Honor and Chips were away, so that the house at St James's Place was half shut-up, with Holland covers over the furniture in the larger rooms. 'Leave it,' she said to Andrews. 'I shan't need any of these rooms.' She liked the holiday feeling of the house at half-mast, the way it was so quiet that any traffic from the street outside became of consequence; the way the birdsong from the back garden could be heard in every room now because there was no longer the sound of the gramophone. She found that, left to herself, she loved quiet far more than she had ever supposed. When the telephone rang late on the afternoon of her arrival, she heard it from her bedroom.

Andrews came and knocked. 'A Mr Envers for you, miss.'

'How did you know I was back?' Doris asked, taking the heavy receiver warily.

'I didn't. I ring every day at this time, in case you might be. Will you come out with me this evening?'

His voice shot through her like alcohol, leaving a sudden dizzy lurch behind it. This was the moment, she thought. This was the 'no' that could be made to stick. She had never said it. She had moved, and escaped, and put distance between them, made it impossible for him to reach her. But she had never yet said no; the no that would drive him away for good. And so he still pursued her. She had spent the summer readying herself to do this very thing – growing stronger on her mother's food, her mother's direct and energetic ways, on the fresh Dorset air, all so she could put an end to this. She opened her mouth. And her words came out wrong.

'Yes, alright,' she said. 'I will. But you mustn't pick me up.'

Andrews, she knew, would talk. He would ask Honor something innocuous-seeming that wasn't innocuous at all – *I wonder did Miss Coates leave anything in Mr Envers' car the other evening? A pair of gloves was handed in at the kitchen door . . .*

'I'll take a taxi and meet you,' she said.

And she didn't, after all, ring up Bertie to tell him she was home. *I will wait a few days*, she told herself. *What's a few more days?*

Chapter Thirty-Nine

London, autumn 1935

The tap at her bedroom door roused Honor from a deep lethargy. She hoped it wasn't Chips. She had no energy for his energy.

'Well, how do you feel?' Doris put her head around the door. 'Shall I come in, or are mysterious things happening?'

'Nothing at all is happening. Do, please come in.' The maid had already been and the room was bright – curtains tied back to let in a thin gleam of morning sun. 'Sometimes, I fear nothing ever will happen. Only I will get larger and larger, and one day I will burst and disappear, and that will be an end to it.'

'But in the meantime,' Doris said, pulling a chair up beside the bed and sitting with her feet tucked under her, 'we may as well make ourselves comfortable.' She wore a velvet dressing gown in deep blue, the skirt of which she draped around herself to cover her knees.

'I suppose we may,' Honor said, laughing. 'Almost, I wish they wouldn't give a date. The expectation is too much. Already Chips has been watching me like a dog watches one eat when it hopes for scraps' – she turned her head eagerly from one side to the other and back again, in imitation – 'for weeks now. You should have seen when it came to the 13th of September, which fell on a Friday. He was in such fear that the baby would be born that he sat up 'til midnight, alone, to make sure it wasn't so. Only when the clock passed the hour did he go to bed, but not before coming in and telling me in a loud whisper, *It's alright, darling*, as though I, too, had been lying awake in dread. Whereas really, I couldn't care at all for his superstitions, and was only lying awake in discomfort.' She shifted as she spoke. 'Today, he will be thoroughly unbearable. You'll see. He'll be along any moment now.'

And indeed, there was Chips' robust rap at the door and his head appeared. 'It will not be today,' he announced, 'it will be tomorrow, I am sure of it,' then beamed at them both.

'Such a relief,' Doris murmured.

Honor caught her breath on a laugh, then frowned at her to be quiet. 'I am certain you are right,' she said. 'I feel nothing out of the ordinary at all. In any case, Nanny Burns is here – she has delivered simply hundreds of babies, and two of royal birth,' she explained to Doris with a grin, 'so all will be well. What will you do today, darling?' she asked Chips.

'I must go to Southend – I am to speak at St Margaret's Hall. Mr Baldwin will call a general election any day, that is for sure, and I must be prepared. Italy and Mussolini have turned down the League of Nations' offer for peaceful settlement, and so there will be war.' He looked significantly at them. 'But where, and with whom? We do not know.'

'Yes,' Doris said, 'I, too, read *The Times* yesterday.'

Chips ignored her. 'I will be back tonight. And Doris, you can ring me up if you need to. But you won't.'

'How fortunate that he can tell exactly what will happen,' Doris said solemnly, once the door had closed.

Honor burst out laughing. 'You mustn't,' she said. 'He is so happy. It would be wrong to tease him. His schemes are coming along beautifully; the prince, far from tiring, is more in thrall to Mrs Simpson every day. Chips' life is very nearly complete, you know. Belgrave Square is all but finished – in another month or so we will move in. His baby is all but born.'

'Which is exactly where men usually stand immediately before they fall into an abyss,' Doris said wisely.

'Not Chips,' Honor said. 'He's simply not the type.'

'Tell me about Belgrave Square. It is all anyone can talk of. They say the dining room is to cost more than seven thousand pounds.'

'I wish gossips would not put that sum about,' Honor said crossly. 'It can't be true, and I'm sure makes many people simply hate us.'

'It is Chips who puts it about,' Doris said. 'He has told so many people "in confidence" that half of London has it direct from him, on pain that they tell no one else.' She laughed.

'Well, I wish he wouldn't. If my parents hear, they will be horrified. Chips wants me to ask Papa for money to buy yet another painting. But if Papa knows what he is spending elsewhere, I fear he will not be sympathetic to claims of poverty.' She wrinkled her nose anxiously. 'I do hate that I am to ask him. There is never the right moment, for he and Mamma simply never discuss money at all. Unless it is Mamma telling how she has saved a shilling by concocting her own cold remedy rather than send to the chemist.' She laughed. 'What they will make of Belgrave Square, well, I hardly dare think . . .'

'They will have a grandchild to take their minds off all that,' Doris said. 'Any moment now, it seems.'

Honor shifted again, moving to slide further down. Doris took a pillow out from behind Honor's head, shook it and replaced it at a better angle. 'There.' She settled back into her chair and hugged her knees in. Her bare toes stuck out from the end of the blue velvet dressing gown, the nails varnished a gleaming pearly pink.

'You will come with us, won't you?' Honor asked. She had not yet asked Doris this, but it had been much on her mind. They had all been about so much over the summer – Chips and Honor to Elveden after Bailiffscourt; Doris had been to her family in Dorset, on visits to friends around the country – that they had scarcely seen one another.

'Perhaps it is time you started your family life on your own,' Doris said. 'This may be a natural time to break. After all, it was only ever a visit.'

'But it has been such fun.' She did not mean fun, Honor realised, as she said it. She meant that knowing Doris was close by had been reassuring. Familiar. A comfort. What had begun as an effort to get her friend away from David Envers, away from the scandal she was making for herself, had grown into something more. She was the person most reliably to make Honor laugh, take her mind off things that perplexed or bothered her; the person to put the pieces of her world to rights when they became disordered. Vital, as Chips was not, to that sense of who she was that Honor tried so hard to tend, knowing always how fragile it was, how easily swallowed by others if she didn't take care to mind it.

'You know what a relief it is to me, to have you here?' she said.

'Yes, because you are forever saying it.' Doris smiled at her.

'I say it, but I'm not sure you listen. I fear you sometimes think that it is I who have much to give . . .'

'You do have much to give.'

'Yes. But so do you. And I don't ever think that there is more on my side than on yours. I know there is not.'

'You're very serious suddenly. Is something the matter?'

'Not a thing. Only I have wanted to say that for a while, and now I have said it. So there.'

'So there indeed,' Doris said. 'But really, you did not have to. I knew it. One always does know what one means to someone,' she said thoughtfully. 'Now, let me brush your hair for you.' She took the brush from the dressing table – it was heavy, backed with silver on which cherubs' faces had been picked out, all curving silver smiles – and began running it through Honor's thick hair. 'You have hair the colour of tea,' Doris said. 'A milky brown. Very nice.'

'Mouse,' Honor said, 'and you know it.' But she stayed very still, allowing Doris to keep brushing.

'You're like a cat,' Doris said.

'Only with you. When Molly does it, I simply hate it. And Mamma brushes too fast so she pulls. You do it just right.'

All too soon Doris stopped. 'There, you are like a show pony,' she said. 'Gleaming and glossy.'

Honor looked at herself in the hand mirror. Her hair was the same springy mass as ever. 'Liar. But thank you.' Still looking straight ahead into the mirror, she reached behind her head and took hold of Doris' hand, the one with the hair brush, and squeezed it. Doris, in the act of putting the brush back on the dressing table, halted and looked up. Their eyes met in the mirror. 'I don't know what I would do without you.' Honor thought how affectionate Doris' hands felt, how intimate, as though Doris knew that it was Honor she touched, and was glad that it was. Unlike Chips, who might have been a doctor or one of his antique dealers, so practised and impersonal was he.

'You'd do very well and you know it,' Doris said, squeezing back briefly.

'There will be even more space for you at Belgrave Square,'

Honor continued after a moment. 'It has so many rooms. Not even Chips can use them all. You know he will have an entire room only for his diaries?' Doris said nothing, only looked at her with half a smile so that after a moment Honor said, 'Ah, you have other plans?'

'I may. I hope to.'

'I see. Lord Lewis?'

'Mmm.'

There was something in the way Doris made the noise, or perhaps more in the way she didn't look at Honor while she did so, that made Honor pause. 'Is there someone else?'

'No,' Doris said. 'Who else would there be?'

But she still didn't look quite at Honor, more past, almost through, her. And Honor thought suddenly of the hours when Doris was missing – saying she was shopping, but coming home with nothing new, because 'there was nothing pretty' – and the few times Honor had asked idly, 'Who were you talking to?' when Doris was telephoning, to be told, after a second's pause, 'Mabel.'

'So you will not move with us, because of these plans? Even if I asked, oh even if I begged you? Perhaps you would come to Belgrave Square temporarily? While your plans fall into place?'

'Better not. It's time you and Chips kept house alone. Well, alone except for an army of servants.' She grinned. 'And I – I am happy to return to Mrs Benton. For a little while anyway.'

'And then?'

'We shall see. It rather depends.'

There was something in the way Doris talked – or rather, in the vagueness with which she talked – that made Honor wary, caused her to say, 'I believe Mosley is becoming more of a nuisance,' as though changing the subject when really she was not.

'In what way?'

'Well, now that the British Union of Fascists has become so very unrespectable – even Lord Rothermere declines to be associated with them – he is become more ugly in his views.'

'How odd to hear you say such things.'

'You're the one who told me to listen, to start to notice. And so I have. And this is what I find. There is more talk of "the Jewish question". And it comes from Mosley. Or,' she corrected herself, 'Chips says it comes from an Irishman, William Joyce, but from Envers too. And Mosley is finding he must listen. Because he believes it will win him supporters. For all Diana says he is the most popular man in England, it simply isn't true. The people have not flocked to him as he hoped, and so he chases them, with this talk of the Jewish question.'

'How do you know?'

'Chips has explained some of it, and I have read the newspapers, just as you told me to. There's lots I can't recall – horrid words Mosley now uses – but I promise you, I am right about this.'

'But my mother said Mosley is not concerning himself with anti-Semitism; that he concentrates on promising jobs, houses, and the defeat of socialism.'

'And maybe she was right when she said it, but it isn't so now. He has not any more the support he once did, and in order to restore that, he is chasing those who feel violently anti-Jewish. He sees a return to popularity of the BUF by playing this tune, and so he plays it. And Envers not only plays but composes it.'

'In any case that is nothing to me.'

'Of course not.' Then, 'Bertie seems terribly fond.'

'Oh he is.' Doris cheered up. 'Positively bombards me with ideas of where to go, entertainments to attend, things he'd like to buy for me.'

Andrews tapped discreetly at the door then to say that Lady Brownlow had called. 'Ask her to come up,' Honor said, 'for I will not come down. And send fresh tea. Doris, help me sit up a little. Pass me that bed jacket.'

Kitty came in wearing a tiny hat perched to the side of her head and trimmed with a jaunty feather. She looked dashing and vivid so that Honor felt more than ever that she herself had sprawled beyond the limits of her own confines; that her edges blurred into obscurity so that she was fuzzy and indistinct. 'Are you telling secrets?' Kitty asked, pausing in the doorway and blinking her enormous eyes rapidly. 'If so, you may continue.' She waved a hand grandly. 'After all, I have been designated entirely *safe*.' She laughed and came fully in. Doris switched to sitting at the end of Honor's bed and Kitty sank into the chair she had vacated. Andrews followed behind with a tray of scones with jam and cream, and the silver teapot.

'Kitty and Perry were royal chaperones,' Honor explained. 'Two weeks with the prince and Mrs Simpson at a villa in the south of France.

'He does nothing – nothing! – without her say-so,' Kitty said. 'Eats nothing, drinks nothing, won't go anywhere or meet anyone unless she has agreed it.'

'How strange it is,' Doris mused. 'One wonders what . . .'

'What indeed,' Kitty agreed.

'I think she must be terribly good at . . . you know . . .' Honor blushed, unable to continue.

'In the bedroom?' Doris shot her a mischievous look.

'Yes. At least, that's what they say.'

'They do.' Kitty nodded wisely.

'Although I don't in the slightest know what that might mean,' Honor confessed.

The other two laughed so hard then that Kitty spilt her tea and Doris rang for someone to clean it up.

Chapter Forty

Lying to Honor about Envers – or at least, not lying exactly, Doris thought, but not telling, either – made her feel sickened and guilty. She had taken up with him exactly as they had been before, only now she did it from Honor's house, and lied directly to her: 'I must see Mabel,' she would say, to account for an afternoon's disappearance. 'I promised Mrs Benton I would look into Curzon Street,' if she was late for dinner. It was because of that that she said she would not move to Belgrave Square when the time came. The lies were too much. But also, somewhere, she felt that matters could not continue as they were. Change must come, and if she couldn't force it, at least she could offer not to resist it. She would not allow herself to drift onwards in Honor's wake, she decided. She must seize the moment of upheaval, and harness it.

Otherwise, she thought with a shiver, she might well find herself slowly becoming the very thing she disliked Chips assuming she was – a companion, an upper-house servant, though never one described in those terms: *I don't know what I would do without Doris, who always knows where everything is . . .* She shuddered as she imagined Honor speaking those words or words like them. How often had she come across such creatures – paid in all but name, pointlessly flattered to disguise the transaction at the heart of the friendship – and secretly despised the cowardice that had led them to accept those roles. She would not be that. And yet that was what she risked by succumbing to the seductive inertia, the failure of will, that Envers brought upon her.

How, she wondered, had her life become so untidy? So without direction? Where were the clear plans and sense of purpose that had carried her all the way from Miss Potts'?

Now that Honor was so preoccupied, only Bertie seemed able to lift Doris out of the dreamlike state in which she existed, doing what Envers wanted of her even as she told herself she would not. And even Bertie seemed to understand that she was not fully herself.

'Are you quite well?' he asked one day, as they rode around Rotten Row in Hyde Park, Doris on a bay mare with a docked tail. He had – as he so often did – planned the day carefully. Riding, then lunch at the Mirabelle.

'I am. Although perhaps a little tired.' She really was, she realised. She who was never tired. 'Anyway, what about you?' she asked. 'From what I can tell, you burn the candle at all ends these days.' She knew he was drinking too much, spending too much time in company with Baby, Elizabeth, Maureen; at the Café de Paris and the Embassy.

'Only because I hope to see you,' he said.

'But you know that until after the baby comes, I must be home with Honor.' She felt the lie twist inside her. 'And going about so much isn't any good for you. You mustn't be allowed to become one of those idle men who hang about London ballrooms.'

'Never!' he promised.

'At least you don't have a novel you are working on, like poor Sebastian Wright.' She laughed. 'And therefore, you will be alright.'

'Dreadful idea,' he agreed. Then, 'I say, I wish you could meet my mother. Perhaps you would come on a visit to Sussex? She does not come to London much since my father died. She does not go anywhere much.' He sounded thoughtful. 'I feel rather terrible that I am not more with her, you know. I am her only child. But she is frightfully decent, and insists that I not ever stay too long.'

'Someday, I should be happy to meet her,' Doris said cautiously.

'And then she will see how absolutely delightful you are, and that will be that.'

'Or she will meet me and not see . . . And that will

be that.' Doris laughed. She knew what such a meeting might mean. She also knew – Maureen had been quick to tell her – that gossip had it that Lady Lewis was not at all pleased at the idea of her, and she couldn't bear the thought of Bertie having a row with his mother, whom he clearly adored, when she, Doris, had no real idea yet of what she hoped from him, beyond the friendship that was so pleasant to her. She had never, yet, allowed him to say what he sometimes hinted at, heading him off each time he strayed close. Until she understood herself better – what she wanted, intended – she couldn't.

'Impossible,' he said gallantly. Then, seriously, 'She is old-fashioned and even strict, but has been always so kind to me; patient and affectionate.'

As any mother should be, Doris wanted to say. But didn't. She sensed that any breath of criticism of his mother would upset him. 'Come, let's canter. There is no one about and I feel certain this mare can go better than she would have me believe.'

If only she could feel for Bertie some of what she felt for Envers, Doris thought. Not everything – there was too much discomfort in her feelings for Envers, too many ways in which she questioned his character, his behaviour. But some of that intensity of emotion, the squirming need to be close to him, to feel his skin against hers. Was it ever possible, she wondered, to feel a combination of affection and excitement? Or must one always choose? She wished she could ask Honor, but she suspected Honor knew no more of the matter than she did.

She continued to meet Envers. Not often, but still too much. They no longer went to the hotel beside Liverpool Street station. Doris had refused to go back, refused to be Mrs Aungier anymore. And so they went to a different hotel, which was almost identical – the same sad smells and furtive shadows, the same worn curtains and thin bedspreads – where they checked in as Mr and Mrs Spain, because that was the first name that came to Doris when Envers said, in an undertone, as they stood together before the register, watched by a bored clerk, 'Very well, you choose.'

'Why Spain?' he asked her, upstairs in a room that looked out, not at the train station but at the backs of a row of tall grey houses and yet somehow seemed to have ghostly rumbles that ran through it, exactly as the last room had.

'I heard my father talk a great deal about Spain when last I was home. He said there was trouble there between landowners and workers. He was concerned that the trouble would grow and spread. It stayed in my mind.' She shrugged. 'It means nothing.' Was that why she chose it? she wondered. Because it meant trouble? Or because it meant nothing? Like this thing with Envers that was also nothing, only a sequence of moments that led each to the next, but without forming a pattern.

On one visit, after Envers had poured a splash of whiskey from his flask into a tooth mug and handed it to her, Doris found herself unusually inclined to talk. Maybe it was the fact that it was afternoon, rather than late at night.

'What do you do?' she asked. 'I mean, when you aren't doing this.' They lay propped against the headboard of the bed, the dusty pink bedspread pulled up against the draught that came from the ill-fitting windows. There was a fat round stain on her bit of it, bleach of some kind, that had faded the pink to a dull cream in a spot the size of a sixpence.

'This and that.'

'This and that what, though? And where? Or are you like Chips, walking a beat between antique shops and art dealers, as though your job were to spend money?'

He laughed, as she knew he would. 'If you must know . . .'

'I must.'

'I'm rather busy meeting people these days.'

'What people?'

'People who care about the future of this country, as I do.'

'And what form does their caring take?'

'Understanding that Europe is about to change, and that there are friends, allies, we must make for when that happens.'

He looked at her as he spoke. Again she had the thought that his eyes were the very same colour as hers, and the disconcerting feeling that came with that. Not as though she looked into a mirror, she thought, but more as though there were parts of him that only she could see. That maybe existed only in her imagination. The thought made her laugh.

'What?' He looked at her.

'Nothing.' He lit a cigarette and passed it to her, then another for himself. 'So, these "friends" and "allies",' she said. 'German?'

'Yes. And Italy now that Musso has smartened them up somewhat.'

'I see.'

'They see the importance of new ways that break with the old.'

'Don't they have rather, well, strong views about who is to be included in the new way?'

'What if they do?' He was impatient now. 'Surely that's rather the point of new ways? You don't just take all the old lot with you.'

'Who would you leave behind?'

'Socialists, trade unionists, degenerates, defectives.' He spoke briskly, as though telling off something learned by rote.

'Jews?'

'If they are socialists and degenerates.'

Honor had been right. Of course she had.

'Not that I care much about all that,' he continued, 'but it matters an awful lot to some of those we wish to be our friends, and so . . .' He shrugged, his bare shoulders rising up white and freckled from the pink bedspread.

'A sprat to catch a mackerel?' It was an expression she'd heard her father use. Mostly, he meant some small expend-iture – on machines or men – that would bring large gain.

'Precisely.' Envers breathed out a jet of smoke and shifted himself more comfortably against the headrest.

'I must get on.' She pulled away from him, out from under the arm that had lain across her shoulders, and began to dress. She pulled on stockings, underthings, conscious for the first time of the alien nature of his nearness. She felt embarrassed by him watching her as she never had before and dressed hurriedly. He finished his cigarette and ground it out in the soap dish he had taken from the chipped sink. He dressed fast and waited while she pulled on her shoes. Together they walked in silence to the lift and down to the lobby. She wondered would he speak again, or simply put her in a taxi and wave her off. She saw him check the heavy gold watch he wore on his wrist, then lift his arm to hail a taxi from the rank opposite.

'I have got a ticket for you to attend a meeting,' he said suddenly.

'With you?' she asked. 'Isn't that . . .?'

'It is a public meeting, and anyone might attend. There is no reason why you should not go if you choose. It's in Stratford, so you're unlikely to meet anyone you know. We will not be seated together. I agree that would be unwise. But I will meet you afterwards.'

'What is the meeting? I warn you, I have little interest in charitable works. It's Honor you need for that. Better still, Lady Iveagh.' She knew it was nothing of the sort.

'It is organised by the British Union of Fascists. Mosley will address the troubles in Spain, which are indeed considerable, just as your father warned. I think you will find his views interesting.'

Why, she wondered, would he think such a thing?

What had she ever said that suggested she would find Mosley's views interesting? And yet, she realised, she did want to go, and listen, and hear for herself exactly what it was this man had to say. 'Very well.'

Two days later she took a taxi to Stratford, arriving as a stream of people – men and women – walked through the glass-panelled doors of the shabby town hall. A group of policemen stood at the edge of the pavement, with another group of young men in plain black shirts with shiny black leather belts standing close to the doors. They reminded her of the men in Berlin who wore the National Socialist uniform; the same intensity and self-conscious air of discipline. A small crowd had gathered at the outer corners of the hall and were jeering the men and women going in. She heard shouts of 'We want Mosley!' followed, with much laughter, by 'Dead or alive!'

As Doris moved towards the doors, the man ahead of her was roughly stopped by two policemen, who said something to him she didn't hear.

'This is a public meeting,' the man said loudly. 'Why should I have to show a ticket? Why may I not walk right in, as I would with any other public meeting?' He looked around at the crowd, who began to agree with him: '*It's a public meeting, anyone should be allowed in what wants to go.*' To Doris' surprise, the policeman who had first barred the man's way called to one of the black-shirted men, a steward of some kind, and deferred to him: 'Is he alright?'

'He'll have to stand at the rear,' the steward called back. 'All the seats are reserved for ticket-holders.'

'Reserved!' the man spluttered. 'In a public meeting . . .' The policemen released him and he went in ahead of Doris, still loudly demanding why anyone needed a ticket to a public meeting. Doris, having shown her ticket, was escorted inside to a seat four rows from the front by a different black-shirted steward, who saluted smartly as she went past him. She looked behind her to see was there someone else to occasion the stiff hand gesture. There wasn't.

The room was almost full and indeed every seat was taken. Around Doris, there were more men than women, but not by much, and most seemed to be smartly dressed. She had chosen a discreetly tailored grey suit with a rather drab long coat, and she kept her hat on and veil down. Not that any of the faces were familiar. She looked around for Envers and spotted him in the front row beside a man who scribbled into a notebook and must, Doris assumed, be a newspaper reporter. On Envers' other side, a woman with pale hair and a silver fur around her neck sat straight-backed and facing forwards. As Doris watched, Envers leaned in and said something to her. She inclined her head to listen but made no reply.

Beyond the seats, another row of black-shirted men who stood with legs planted firmly apart and arms behind their backs, staring out at the crowd. On the other side of them, a platform had been built out of wooden pallets. Against the back and on either side swayed large banners, crimson red with the white circle and blue lightning bolt running through it that Mosley had chosen to represent his party. Doris had always thought it silly and childish, owing more to the funnies that appeared weekly in the *Daily Mirror*, but now, when it was repeated large across so much of the town hall, she saw it was overbearing.

She remembered what Chips had said of Mosley – that his cruel brilliance was yoked to the cause of destruction – and how admiringly he had said it. Alas not, she thought, looking impatiently at her wristwatch, yoked to the cause of timeliness. He was late. She wished Envers was close enough that she could whisper the joke to him. The crowd around her was restive; talking loudly, even some singing. There was a smell of sweat and excitement, like the bullocks' pen at a country market. And then, a roar. Around her, men and women leaped to their feet, fists raised aloft, and Mosley came striding onto the stage, which shook slightly beneath his feet. Doris could see where the edges of the pallets didn't quite meet and scratched against each other. Envers remained seated, as did the silver-haired woman beside him. The man with the notebook started to scribble furiously.

After the first few minutes, Doris found that she watched, rather than listened. Mosley's words washed over her – they seemed so much the same; waves of cant about '. . . the mass inertia of socialism . . .'; '. . . the principles of patriotism and progress . . .'; '. . . poverty in an age of plenty . . .', each accompanied by loud cheers – leaving her free to consider what she saw. His gestures were carefully rehearsed to appear spontaneous, she decided, and choreographed to signal power. There was the hand that rose and fell in time with the rhythm of his sentences, up and down in a sort of threshing motion, while his stance stayed solid, rooted, even as he swayed back and forth on the balls of his feet.

And then, as Doris decided she had seen enough, the momentum began to alter. Signalled first by a change in the pitch of Mosley's voice, then the rapidity of the arm – more, now, like a piston than a pendulum – the tone of what he said changed. No longer vague and enticing, now he was specific. Coarsely so. 'The Jews more than any other single force in this country are carrying on a violent propaganda against us,' he declared. 'The Jews attack us, deride us, provoke us.' He began to shout words that Doris had never heard before, the words, she supposed, Honor had been reaching for when they had talked just days earlier, when Doris had refused to believe her. But she knew the tone in which they were shouted. It was the tone in which such things were always said: a jeer beneath the violence.

The crowd was more agitated now, a sea of ugly approval. She turned in her seat and a man two rows back caught her attention. Thin and blond, his hair rather too long, he was familiar. It was Elizabeth Ponsonby's friend, Sebastian Wright. The one who had told the joke: *Spectacles, testicles, wallet and watch*. Doris looked and saw his beautiful face distorted, mouth open as he yelled approval at Mosley's words, arms pumping up and down in imitation of the man onstage. He wasn't telling jokes anymore.

From the back then came scattered heckles. Cries of

'Mosley out!' and 'Liar!' from one spot. Doris saw a group of black-shirted stewards move smartly past her and down towards the back of the hall. She turned to watch. Two of them plunged into the very last row and took hold of a man. They dragged him to the aisle where the rest waited, and all began to punch and kick him. They continued to hit him even after he had put his arms around his head and curled into an agonised ball. All the while, on stage Mosley kept speaking, voice rising and falling in that rehearsed way, hand still moving up and down as though sketching the bright future he promised. He made no reference to the violence taking place in front of him, nor did anyone in that crowded room pay much attention except a girl sitting beside where the man had been. She began to scream, or so it seemed. The noise was impossible to make out in that hall of shouts and cheers. But her mouth was open wide and the empty seat beside her yawned.

As though the girl's silent scream had released her, Doris found herself able to move. She got up hurriedly and made her way along the row, bumping the legs of those still seated, sidestepping the ones who were on their feet shouting. At the end, she looked back to where Envers sat. He still watched the stage. But the woman beside him with the pale hair and silver mink turned, as though her head were attached to a thread in Doris' hands, and stared at her with large light eyes. Diana Mitford. Once married to Honor's cousin Bryan, now defiantly Mosley's mistress. She stared curiously at Doris. Doris put her head down and rushed out, past the spot where the man had been. He was gone but where he had been there was a thin smear of blood.

Chapter Forty-One

The day that Chips had marked in his diary came and went with no sign of the baby. Another week went by with still nothing. 'It is like the entire pregnancy again, all squeezed up into a few days,' Honor complained to Doris. 'Waiting and getting larger and more tired, and more waiting, and nothing, ever, actually happening!' Her parents were constantly in the house, unwilling to go back to Elveden, and she had a cold – 'all that walking about in the park that Doctor Gilliatt says I must do'. Every day the telephone rang constantly, and each time Chips would answer and say, 'Nothing yet, but you are good to call,' so that she knew they telephoned for news of her. And instead of feeling interesting and sought-after, she felt humiliated. As though she were somehow behaving badly; sulking or teasing. Not following through with something she had sworn to do. She felt everyone must be as fed up of her as she was of herself.

When Andrews announced Diana Mitford, she was inclined to ask that he say she was indisposed. But it was too late. Diana, rather than wait downstairs, had simply followed Andrews up, and put her head around the door.

'I haven't come to enquire,' she said brightly.

'Well, in that case . . .' Honor managed a laugh. 'Come in. Andrews, send . . . not tea, for I cannot bear more tea. Lemonade?'

'Delicious,' Diana assured her. She sat and observed Honor for a moment out of those pale blue eyes with their pinprick pupils. *Trust Diana to have more blue than anyone else*, Maureen had said crossly when they had first met her, all those years ago when she was a shy 16-year-old, and cousin Bryan so hopelessly in love that he married her against everyone's wishes. Now, grown up, a mother of two, divorced and the scandalous mistress of a highly public man, she was more beautiful than ever; as though, Honor thought, someone had lit a fire within a temple so that it glowed creamy and warm through translucent marble. And yet, as always, there was a chip of ice in Diana's gaze that repelled her. It had been there in the shy 16-year-old, and was still there now.

'So,' Honor said when the lemonade had arrived, and a plate of tiny cakes, 'if not to enquire, why?'

'I rather thought I saw someone the other night, and I wanted to find out was I right.'

'Who?'

'Your little friend Doris, the one who lives here and goes about simply *everywhere* . . .' Diana opened her large blue eyes even wider.

'As you say, she is very popular. You may well have seen her.' Honor was bored. 'And what of it?'

'Oh not at a party,' Diana said. 'At a meeting. Stratford Town Hall.'

'Doesn't sound much like Doris,' Honor said. 'Not her kind of thing at all. Whose meeting?'

'One of ours,' Diana said. 'Mosley. Rallying the faithful. And very faithful they were too. Simply packed,' she said smugly. 'You cannot imagine how they adore him.'

'No,' Honor said dryly, 'I cannot.' She thought about what Diana had said. What it meant. And she made a swift decision.

'Most certainly it was not Doris,' she said carefully. 'However, while we are chatting so delightfully,' – she paused and Diana gave a tiny wry smile – 'I have something to ask of you. I want you to ask Mosley to send that man David Envers away.' Dimly, she felt that perhaps for the sake of politics and the matters of the world, she shouldn't ask. But she didn't understand those things. Couldn't play them out – as Diana seemed able to – weighing the different possibilities and what each might lead to. What she did understand was that Doris must be got away from Envers.

'Why should I?' Diana looked blankly at her.

'Because you owe my family something.'

'Because of Bryan? Even though he is so happy now with Betty Nelson?'

'No, because of the way we treated you, even after the way you treated Bryan. Don't tell me that Uncle Walter hasn't simply poured money your way.'

'Very well. You Guinnesses have been fair, I will grant you that. So, you are certain it was not Doris?' she asked with a laugh.

'Absolutely certain.'

'And are you going to tell me why you are so anxious to be rid of David Envers, a man you scarcely know?'

'No.'

'I see.' Again Diana looked at her. Then, 'As it happens, we do need a man in Italy again. Musso isn't reliable; if not watched, he goes off on terrible tangents . . .' She tittered. 'Very well, I'll do it. But don't ask anything else of me.'

'Nothing,' Honor promised. 'Just this.' Envers gone must mean something for Doris. Then, 'Has it been worth it?' she couldn't help but ask.

'Has what?'

'Divorce. Disgrace. All of it. For love.'

'Oh yes. And is still worth it. Every day.' Diana stretched languorously. 'Every night.' She smiled, and Honor found herself blushing. This was why she disliked Diana's company. The way she always seemed to be teasing in a way that was suggestive, even when she talked about something perfectly ordinary like clothes or . . . *cushions*, Honor thought crossly. Diana laughed as though she knew exactly what Honor was thinking. 'You must get on?' she enquired, raising her thin, arched eyebrows.

'I must, as a matter of fact.'

'I'll see myself out,' Diana said. 'I cannot understand how you Guinnesses continue to employ so many servants. You cannot believe the freedom of a house without.'

Sixteen days after first expected, with no encouragement – if one didn't count the enormous brandy-and-hot-water Chips made her drink before bed, 'to cheer you and help you to sleep' – early on the morning of October ninth, still hours before dawn, Honor woke suddenly to pain that she knew was real, at last. Then, she waited quite happily, knowing that it was begun, only calling Nanny Burns when what she felt became deep and sharp.

Even so, it was slow. Gilliatt came and warned her that nothing would happen quickly. Chips came in and out, to check on her and bring her news. Around mid-morning he put his head around the door and said, 'Princess Marina has had a boy. In the early hours of the morning and in great haste. They say ten minutes, but that can't be.' Honor, immediately, felt her own hopelessness in comparison with the Duchess of Kent. 'I suppose this means no more boys,' Chips said gloomily, going away again.

But it didn't mean no more boys, and at last, after long hours in which she dozed and groaned, then existed somewhere that was neither awake nor asleep, only lying wrapped around her pain, the real pain began and Honor wondered how she hadn't understood that what she had felt earlier was not pain at all, just a sketch of it. Gilliatt came back and induced twilight sleep and she fell into nothingness so black and deep that when she woke it was as though she fought her way, slowly, up from under something heavy and thick. Her head ached terribly and she was sore in a new way.

'You were magnificent.' Chips was there, beside her bed. When she opened her eyes, it was to meet his. She wondered how long he had been there, watching her. Her hair felt matted and the clamminess of her skin told her she had sweated, and the sweat had dried on her. She twitched her nose a little at her own rank smell. 'You *are* magnificent.' He took her hand in his and kissed it. He let it go and she had not strength to keep it up so that it fell like a dead thing between them onto the counterpane. 'Dearest.' His eyes were wet with tears. 'A boy. Paul.'

Chapter Forty-Two

A boy. Paul.

A mother. Her.

Honor could not get used to the idea. She hugged it to her like a secret, a small kernel of joy. When she woke in the morning, it was to that new thought – she was a mother; she had a baby – and each day, again, she would find the glowing part inside herself that was hot and bright, and marvel at it. And yet, she kept that glow mostly secret, because if she were honest, as she could not be with anyone – even Doris – she didn't know what exactly it meant to be Paul's mother.

Had she wanted to spend her time with her son, really, she thought, she should have been his nanny. Because then, she would have been all day with him, and not forced to follow a strict pattern that was not of her making.

From the earliest days it was Nanny Burns who took charge, swaddling Paul, who was a solid, hefty baby like a lusty Jesus from a Renaissance painting, and carrying him to and from Honor's bedroom. He would be brought in, howling, to be fed, then taken away again to be put down in his cot or taken out in his pram. Nanny Burns was strict about fresh air and what she called 'routine'.

'Babies must learn,' she'd said, when Chips had suggested that 'perhaps the little chap doesn't wish to go out?' one particularly windy day, when Paul cried mightily on being put into his pram. 'I myself don't,' he had continued. 'I can quite see why he wouldn't.'

'Babies need fresh air,' Nanny Burns had responded, pulling the pram hood up and fixing it securely so that Paul's face was barely visible, red and crumpled, in the gloom between his knitted blanket and the shadow of the hood. And off he was sent, with the nurserymaid whose job it was to wheel him across to Hyde Park – not Green Park, although it was closer, because Nanny Burns considered it 'common'. Honor could hear his angry howls all the way up the street. The sound set off a fluttering in her that was like something in her chest that struggled to get out and she had to work to catch her breath.

So strict was the routine that within a couple of days, Honor realised that her body understood it perfectly. She would be ready for her baby's arrival minutes before he appeared and in those moments, with Paul at her breast after Nanny Burns had discreetly withdrawn, when they were alone together for at least half an hour – sometimes longer if she could persuade Nanny that he had fallen asleep halfway into the feed and needed more – she would stare at his tiny, perfect face, his strands of fairish hair and wide-apart blue eyes that were already darkening like his father's. She would let the hot brightness within her rise up and flood her entire body, that was made whole by the child in her arms. She would gaze at Paul, while he gazed at her, and in his eyes she saw a completed circle and the world as it might have been. As she hoped it would now be: deep and true and complete.

And then Nanny Burns would appear at her side and say, 'Time for baby's nap,' and take her child, no matter how he struggled, and Honor's time would be over and she would feel, again, not a whole person but a half of one; less. But only for a few hours, she told herself. Then he would be brought to her again.

Nights were best because the house was quiet and dark and it felt as though there was nothing in it except the two of them. Then, it was easier to persuade Nanny that he had fallen asleep and must be fed for longer. Once, he was left with her for many hours. Honor suspected Nanny Burns must have fallen asleep herself, to allow such a thing. Tired though Honor was, she had found joy in staying awake, watching the flutter of Paul's eyelids, the way the eyes behind them moved and twitched under the delicate skin while he slept.

She felt such pride in the part she and her body played. It no longer felt as though she were too large, too solid, too ungainly. This, she knew, was what all that heft and weight were for, this very thing. The carrying and birthing and feeding of this child. 'He is ten pounds today,' she would say to Chips, and then smile and blush as he congratulated her.

'You are welcome any time in the nursery,' Nanny told her. Which made Honor understand that she was not. And within a few weeks she realised that saying she was welcome did not mean that Paul was there, or that she would get to see him even if he was. There were many mysterious things that needed to be done with him and that could not be interrupted. There was bath time, at which she was allowed to assist, although always there was the unspoken feeling that she couldn't possibly attempt it herself. But there was also something called 'tummy time' which involved Paul lying on his front and which he seemed to hate. That, too, could not be interrupted, and Honor could not bear to be present, because the cries disturbed her so. There was 'play time', involving a rattle shaped like a rabbit's head shaken to and fro in front of his face, and a string of coloured beads. Other times, he would be in his cot, asleep, and must be left alone.

When, after six weeks, Nanny Burns decided it was time Paul be given a bottle, Honor's place in his life slipped further again. 'You may come to the nursery and watch him being fed,' she was told. What they didn't tell her, or not properly, was how intensely her own body would resent the sight of her child sucking at a rubber teat in the nanny's arms. The way her body would ready itself for her baby, prepare to settle into the rhythm of their time together, the flow of life from her to him, and how much that would hurt when it found it was not wanted. She bound her breasts with thick cloth, to soak up what was leaked, and suffered Nanny Burns to press them – to expel the milk that curdled within them and relieve, a little, the intense discomfort that built up. The nurse's confident hands were so unlike the frantic, grateful grasp of Honor's baby that she flinched from their firm grip.

'It's the same with the herd at Elveden when we wean the calves,' her mother said bluntly, sitting with her knees planted far apart on the chair beside Honor's bed. 'They feel great pain in their udders' – Honor twitched at the word – 'for a few days, and low most terribly. And then it is over. As it will be for you too. After all, you have duties to resume, and you cannot take them up again as long as you are bound to the nursing of a baby.'

And Lady Iveagh was right – it was over, although not in a very few days – but Honor found she missed even the pain. 'It was terribly uncomfortable, but at least I felt there was a thread, a line between me and him,' she tried to explain to Doris, who nodded, but probably politely. Was this, Honor wondered, why Maureen had turned away from Caroline? The pain that came with wanting what could not be – so that perhaps no longer wanting it was the easiest course?

The only person who seemed to understand any of it was Chips. His pride and passion for Paul were like hers, only louder. 'He is the most beautiful child I have ever seen. More beautiful even than his namesake. He is the strongest, the best-natured,' he would declare. 'The joy I feel, to come upon a pram in the park, and know that when I approach it, it will be my child inside!' He even liked to hold Paul – which many fathers, Honor knew, did not – and would stare, enraptured, into the tiny face that turned so quizzingly up to his own.

'I cannot believe how much my life has changed in the space of a few short weeks,' he said quietly to Honor one night in the nursery. They had taken the habit of dining in Honor's room, then going there together at ten o'clock and watching the evening feed. It was so still in the nursery, curtains drawn and just one carefully shaded lamp. Nanny Burns in a rocking chair, moving gently back and forth with Paul in her arms, the glass feeding bottle firmly tilted at an angle. 'I am now a father, and an MP.' He had been elected by Southend, with 'over 65 per cent of the vote', as he said repeatedly. 'I am utterly content.'

But would it, Honor wondered, be enough for him? A child, a place in the Commons. Would he now dampen down some of his other ambitions? Perhaps, she thought, they might live more quietly. Perhaps they could be there, in the quiet nursery, every night at ten o'clock with only the rhythmic sound of Paul's contented sucking to break the harmony of their silence. She felt new hope that now, at last, the secret heart of marriage that had constantly eluded her, twisting always out of reach, would be revealed to her. They would be content and contained, a little knot of three.

But the fever of a new government, a new cabinet, new possibilities – Duff Cooper was appointed Secretary for War, something Chips, exhilarated, described as 'enchanting' – were too much, and soon Chips, instead of plotting with her how they might find more time to spend in the nursery, said instead, 'It is time we have a dinner party. This may be the last we give at number 21 for I plan absolutely to move to Belgrave Square in the new year. We will keep it small – ten or so.' And when Honor tried to say it was too soon, he said, 'Princess Marina is already out and about this last week.'

And so a month and a half after Paul's birth, Honor put on an oyster-coloured satin evening dress and her rubies, and welcomed her cousin Maureen, Diana and Duff Cooper, the Cavendishes, Emerald and others.

'Motherhood suits you,' Emerald said, scanning Honor's face and form with her bright quick eyes, 'as pregnancy did not. You did not glow through that, but you glow now.' And then she saw Duff Cooper and went to quickly greet him. 'Almighty Mars,' she cried out, 'you walk among us.'

The food was too rich, Honor thought, the wines too abundant. Chips was noticeably drunk. She wondered had he been at his powders again. The conversation was too heady; giddy and fast and brilliant, animated by the certainty that there was nothing, now, they could not do. They had always been like that, Honor knew, but now she saw that they were more so, and she was less. Her interest in the world they wished to create, and their positions within it, which was already slight, had waned entirely, while theirs was double what it had been. The common ground that had been between them was less. Far less.

That night Honor did not make her way to the nursery for ten o'clock. Nor the next night when the Brownlows came to call, nor the next when she dined with Chips at the House of Commons. And then, as though the invitations – the 'summonses', as she thought of them – had been waiting patiently for some bell to ring and let them loose, she found that there were again dinners, parties, lunches, the opera, shooting, shopping. So many that the hours they demanded were too few. Soon, to be in the quiet of the nursery was rare, and by the time Christmas came, she felt that her son knew her less.

That was when she began to resent Chips.

His pride in Paul was so easy. He felt no need, no ache to be with him, no guilt that he was not, only enjoyed the times that he was. Honor, meanwhile, felt sick at all the hours she was not with her son, so that, more and more, the simple peace she had felt with him was gone. When she did see him, he seemed not to know her. If he cried while she held him, she hastened to return him to Nanny and felt that she must herself be to blame; that she had held him wrong or too tightly. More and more, she remembered Chips and his talk of hatred for his mother. Was this, perhaps, how it had begun?

Yet when she tried to talk to Chips of what she felt, he could not, or would not, understand her. 'You are not at all like my poor half-mad mother,' he said. 'Why should Paul hate you? You are magnificent, the best wife a man could have.' He patted her hand in a way that she supposed he thought was reassuring.

'I am talking of being a mother,' Honor said. 'Not a wife.'

'It is the same thing,' Chips said confidently. 'You think far too much of it. There is no reason at all for Paul to hate you. The very idea!'

And of course he was right, Honor realised. Paul did not hate her. She wasn't there enough for him to hate. He was the same smiling, cheerful, pretty baby as ever he had been. Only his pretty cheerfulness now was impersonal. It was for all the world – the nanny, Chips, Doris, Lady Iveagh, callers – just as much as it was for her. There would be other babies, she hoped, and when there were, she would find some way not to have Nanny Burns.

Chapter Forty-Three

After the Stratford meeting, Doris didn't telephone to Envers. Not the day after, nor the day after that. She knew that he would not ring her, and indeed he did not. It was not that she had made any decision. Only that she could not bring herself to telephone, because she did not know what she could say.

Where she had been fascinated, held in thrall as surely as though he had a hand upon her even when she was not in his company, now she was sickened too. Those words of Mosley's still rang through her with the intense thrumming of a tuning fork: *The Jews attack us, deride us, provoke us.* Provoke what? she thought. Hatred? Surely. Violence? Possibly. Who had written those words? Was it Mosley? Or the shadow men behind him: the Irishman Honor had spoken of, William Joyce? Envers? And if so, what did he mean by it? Was it indeed hatred that inspired him, as it seemed when Mosley spoke? Or was it expediency – the creating of common ground with allies, as Envers had described it to her? And which, she wondered, would be worse? She had no answers, but what she did have was a feeling of disgust now when she thought of Envers. And even though the disgust lived alongside the desire that was still there, she knew she could nurture one, and starve the other. As long as she did not see him. As long as he did not come near her.

And so she did not telephone, and relied upon the certainty that he would not telephone her.

In any case, she consoled herself, there was no time. Once baby Paul arrived, there was suddenly much more to keep her occupied. Who would have thought that one tiny baby, with his very own nanny and nurserymaid as well as two parents, could make such an amount of work? And yet he did. Mostly, the work was to sit with Honor, who seemed strangely displaced by becoming a mother: tired, fretful, unable to settle. She paced around the house, waiting for Paul to be brought to her, or went to stand awkwardly in the nursey, waiting for Nanny to let her in. She reminded Doris of a kitchen cat, standing mewing pitifully at the back door.

'Why do you not just march in and pick up baby Paul?' Doris asked her.

'I cannot. Nanny would not permit it.'

'Nanny is employed by you, you do remember that?' Doris pointed out wryly.

'Yes, but it's not the same as a servant. Although, I would not march into Andrews' pantry and take something, either. You know I would not. It would be, well, ill-bred, to do such a thing. And Nanny is different again. The nursery is her domain. She will not stand for otherwise.'

'And so you must ask permission to see your own son?'

'You make it sound so strange,' Honor complained. 'But yes, if you must put it like that.'

Doris couldn't persuade her to take time with her son, and so instead she made sure to be where Honor could spend time with her. It was easy to ignore the cards of invitation, to evade the hostesses who sought her presence. In any case, she found she had no real inclination for parties.

Lord Bertie telephoned several times to St James's Place and sent around flowers, a basket of fruit, a pretty silver rattle. These were gifts ostensibly for Honor and baby Paul, but each card contained a message just for Doris – 'I wonder might I call and see you?'; 'Perhaps you would meet me for a walk?'; 'May I telephone you?'

And then, early one morning, when she left St James's Place to walk briskly to Harrods, she found David Envers falling into step beside her as she rounded the corner into St James's Street.

'What are you doing here?' she blurted out.

'I hoped to run into you.' He fitted his pace perfectly to hers, matching her stride with his, in a way that made her remember suddenly, blushingly, how much they were a physical match for one another. 'Come and have coffee with me?'

'Very well. But I haven't much time.' It wasn't true, she

had all the time she wanted, but she couldn't bear to let him know that. They found a Corner House open, and almost empty. The girl who brought their coffee was very young, and looked admiringly at Doris, dressed in a neat navy suit.

'Sugar?' Envers asked her, when he had poured first coffee, then a splash of cream, into it.

'No.' How little they knew of one another, Doris thought. 'Aren't you worried that we will be seen?' she asked, stirring with a small silver teaspoon.

'No. Not now.' And Doris didn't know did he mean because it was daytime, and so their being seen would not have the same significance, or was it because it no longer mattered if they were seen or not. 'I am to go away,' he said then. 'Back to Italy.'

'I see.' She had no time to understand if the lurch she felt was upset or relief.

'Yes. Mosley has asked me. It seems Musso can't, after all, be left without supervision for very long.' He sounded amused.

'And yet you still choose him as an ally?' Doris asked.

'Yes.' He shrugged. 'What is one to do? He has chosen the same side and so we must deal together.'

'Even though you clearly despise him?'

He shrugged again.

'You know, you could choose a different side.'

'Why would I do that?' He sounded impatient. 'No, I am not here to talk politics. I came to ask you something. Something I did not intend to ask . . .'

'What is it?' Her heart beat unpleasantly fast. Not the gay, breathless fast that came from dancing or riding hard, but a rapid thump like an alarm. He took a cigarette case from his pocket, took out a cigarette and tapped the end several times against the yellow metal of the case, then put it in his mouth and lit it. Only then did he offer one to her. 'No, thank you.' She waved the offer away. She realised she was gripping the edge of the table too hard, and forced herself to let go.

'I rather thought I'd ask you to marry me.' He blew a stream of smoke out of the side of his mouth.

'Why would you do that?' she blurted out.

'Odd, isn't it?'

He smiled at her and the lurching feeling got worse.

'I certainly didn't expect it. But I find I miss your company. I want you with me.'

'You hardly know me.'

'I know enough.' He smiled again, a slower smile, that made her blush.

'But what about . . .' She didn't know what she was going to say. There were so many things . . . *What about the life I wanted? What about Bertie? What about what Honor will say?*

But Envers had his own interpretation. 'I am a divorced man,' he said, grinding out his cigarette onto the saucer in front of him. 'It doesn't much matter who I marry now . . .'

By which she understood that he didn't think she was his equal. But also, that he had no idea of her background.

Her family. Clearly, he had made no enquiries, as Chips had. It was, she supposed, a small point in his favour.

'We could be married quickly, here, and then set out for Italy together. We would go to Rome, and then later, perhaps, on to Germany. I know you speak German' – he looked at her then, and she wondered did he know after all, would he ask – 'but I wouldn't expect you to involve yourself much in politics. In fact, I'd rather you didn't.'

He reached over and took her hand, the one she had released from the table edge, and held it in both of his. She felt the way a moth must when it is picked up in human hands – the searing heat, and how the touch must burn its delicate wings and feet. She went to pull her hand away, but he held it tighter. 'I find Diana altogether too meddling, and Mosley too indulgent of her. You will not need to be anything like her.'

She saw that he was offering her a cage – and that he knew it. A cage where she could look out and be observed, but could not leave. And even so, she found she wanted to say yes. Wanted to step inside and watch as he closed and locked the door. Within that cage, the question of who she was would be answered. No longer would there be rumours, half-sneers. She would be Doris Envers and all questions would end there. That was some of it – after all, where better to hide an awkward truth than in the shadow of a man who lived to dispel it? – but mostly, it was because he would be there with her; sometimes, anyway. He would come and go, as she could not, but the times he was there might be enough. She shook her head. How had she become someone who considered such a thing, even for a moment?

She forced herself to look properly at him, to see beyond the dazzle of his charm. Had his eyes always been so close together? she wondered. Funny that she had never noticed. She looked, and she saw a man, handsome, well made, but with an air of thin disappointment. How much more than he was had she allowed him to be. More, by far, than his slightly weary frame could support. It wasn't his fault. He was many things – indifferent, cynical – but he hadn't lied to her or deceived her. She'd done that all by herself.

'I cannot marry you,' she said. And the words came out as though she had rehearsed them – clipped, precise, considered.

'I thought you might say that,' he said. The smile he gave was thin. She could still see the faint outline of the greater stature she had given him.

She got up. She knew she needed to get away quickly before he said something that would change her mind. He said nothing. Did not try to stop her. He sat and watched her leave. The coffee shop had filled up in the time they had been talking, and Doris bumped against tables as she went, heard two women with shopping bags tutting in her wake. At the doorway, she stopped and looked back. He had lit another cigarette and was leaning back in his seat, smoke gathering in a cloud about his head.

That afternoon, she rang up Bertie and asked would he meet her for a walk. He said yes instantly, as she knew he would, and that he would call for her within the hour.

'Where to?' he asked once he had settled her into the seat of his car and handed her a rug for her knees because the day was cold. 'We can go as far as you like.'

'Hyde Park?'

'Hardly worth the drive.' But he said it cheerily, then asked a great many questions about baby Paul, quite as though he were interested in babies, although Doris didn't see how he could be.

In Hyde Park they walked briskly, their breath coming in thick white clouds. The afternoon was losing itself, swallowed up in fog that threatened to grow thick, so that Doris knew Bertie would soon insist on bringing her home out of it.

She took a deep breath. Even though she had decided on this – decided it that morning after her meeting with Envers – it was hard to begin. But easier, she told herself, now that his face was indistinct beside her, with only the warmth of his shoulder next to hers to reassure her that he was indeed there. 'You once said you had something you wanted to ask me,' she said, breaking the silence that had fallen between them.

He turned quickly towards her. 'I did. I do.'

'Well, if you still wish to ask, I will listen.' She tried to laugh but it came out wrong.

He was silent, so that she wondered had he changed his mind, and was about to change the subject and suggest he drive her home, when he blurted out, 'I say, Doris, you will marry me, won't you?'

'I will,' she said, and looked up at him with a smile.

'Will you really? How I hoped you would!' He leaned in to kiss her and Doris braced herself not to compare the way that felt with the way she felt when Envers touched her. But to her relief, she found she had no instinct to do so. Being kissed by Bertie was different entirely. It was warm and friendly and certain, quite unlike the giddy lurching that Envers' mouth on hers brought. Bertie didn't kiss her for very long, pulling back to demand, 'Do you really mean it?'

'I do. I think it will be very nice, to be married to you.' And she did, she realised. It was an idea that filled her with a glow that was warm and bright like a fire on a damp foggy afternoon. A feeling to lean back into, knowing it was solid and good and reliable. She sighed, then laughed and stepped forward into his arms again.

'I will go to Sussex and see my mother,' Bertie said when at last he let her go. 'I have things to see to on the estate anyway, so I will be gone some time. But when I come back, it will be with her so that she might meet you.'

And Doris understood that his mother's approval was necessary to him, and that he was young enough, enthusiastic enough, to believe that a simple matter.

Part Three

1936

Chapter Forty-Four

London, January 1936

The early days of the new year were unsettled, Honor thought. Variable and hesitant, as though uncertain what to do with themselves. Change was coming – the move to Belgrave Square loomed, and King George was dying. They all knew that, and it was as though the seasons felt it as keenly as his subjects did.

Why should it matter so much? Honor wondered. After all, men died. And yet it did. Or perhaps she read too much into it. Too much from her own life – the questions she still asked herself around her place and purpose, that she had thought becoming a mother would answer; that becoming a mother might have answered, if she knew better how to do it – was beginning to bleed into a greater sense of change. The ground under her felt slanted and uneven. As though it would pitch her forward.

This was to be expected, she told herself firmly. Once they were settled in the new house, once the transition of kings was complete, everything would calm down.

Partly, she knew, it was Chips who unsettled her. Although he had anticipated and worked for what came next, he was, she realised, suddenly frightened. He took to coming to her bedroom late at night and getting in beside her, but as though he looked for comfort, rather than anything more. Sometimes he was still there the next morning but she suspected he did not sleep much. And if she turned to him in the night, he turned away. Shifting his body so that there was a shoulder, a hip, an empty trough between them always.

'I dreamed the old king died,' he said portentously one morning mid-way through January, coming upon her and Doris in the hallway. They were on their way out to look at an exhibition of paintings.

'Well, he has been very ill for the last weeks,' Doris said, drawing on her gloves. 'I think, when he does go at last, you need not blame yourself.' Her mouth twitched as she spoke, but she managed not to smile.

'How insensitive you are,' Chips complained. 'I suppose I should not be surprised.'

'Why, because I am not American?' Doris asked. 'Only English, and therefore I cannot expect to understand the importance of this? *England, wasted on the English* . . .' she finished, misquoting George Bernard Shaw with a laugh.

'Not English either,' Chips said tetchily. 'Or not completely English.' There was a chilly little pause then, which Honor rushed to fill.

'Let us telephone to Duff before we go and see is there news,' she said.

There was news – the king was worse – and so they did not go out but waited in case there was more. They chose the library because it was sunny at that hour. Chips began to reminisce in a way that was, Honor thought, excessively maudlin. He talked of the king's tobacco-streaked beard with affection, of the pleasure to be got from hearing his chesty laugh. And yet, she could see, he was excited too. When he spoke of the Prince of Wales, and what would now befall him any day – to become king – it was with a gentle but heavy sympathy. 'My heart goes out to him,' he said, sighing rather. 'To lose a father, and gain such a weight of duty, all at once, and when he has always said how little he wishes the task that must be his.' But he could hardly hide his fevered speculations. 'Shall we be in his set?' he mused. 'Honor, you had a cocktail with him only the other day. How did you find him?'

'As ever. Perhaps a little more highly strung even than is usual with him. Talking fretfully, looking around, ever, for her.' In fact, at Emerald's she had found him to be painfully thin, his face drawn so that his eyes sank deeper than usual into his weathered cheeks. From a distance, he still looked a young, jaunty man, but close to, the lines etched about his mouth told a different story. And even though he mostly ignored her, as usual, she had found herself pitying him. It was a feeling she felt far more now, since Paul's birth, and for all sorts of people. As though her heart had been opened by her child, but now could not distinguish between him and all the many others who seemed unhappy and in need of something, so that sympathy seemed to pour from her. It was a most uncomfortable feeling.

Lady Iveagh had proposed she return to her charitable works, suggesting a visit to Paddington Street. Honor had refused. She found she could not bear the idea. She remembered Doris, so many years ago now: *Honestly, Honor, how can you? Already, I know I shall find it almost impossible to get them out of my mind. To forget those dreadful faces. Do they not haunt you?* Finally, she thought she understood. Since Paul, the idea of charity that was impersonal, almost indifferent, was no longer possible.

'How will they arrange themselves,' Chips mused, 'when he is king? I wonder. I imagine *she* will move from that dreary flat she and Ernest have taken in Marble Arch. But will Ernest move with her, for respectability, or will she move alone? Perhaps she will have a discreet apartment within the palace? But no, that would not be tolerated . . .'

'I can't imagine they give it as much thought as you do,' Doris said tartly.

He swung from certainty of the king's demise – 'I have said it all autumn, that he will soon die', so that Honor wanted to scream at him that kings do not die for the saying and speculating of others – to hope that 'he might, after all, rally yet . . .' And there did not seem anything much to do except wait.

'One wouldn't want to be seen looking at paintings now . . .' Doris said in the afternoon, 'but perhaps a brisk walk would not considered too disrespectful? If one wore a very *sombre* hat . . .'

On the evening of the third day, over the wireless came the announcement they waited for: '*The king's life is moving peacefully to its close.*'

They dined quietly, the three of them, and Honor waited impatiently for the servants to clear so she could go up to the nursery.

'I will wait up,' Chips said. 'Until there is more news.'

'There may not be more news,' Honor said. 'You would do better to go to bed.'

'I will stay up,' he insisted.

'A vigil?' Doris asked.

'If you wish to call it so, yes.' He was full of the dignity of the occasion, refusing to let Doris needle him. Much later, when Honor was nearly asleep, Chips came in to say that the king had died.

'Would you like to get in?' Honor asked, sitting up and pushing her hair out of her eyes. He did, laying himself heavily on his back beside her so that the mattress shifted and everything seemed to slide towards him. Honor lay back down and pressed closer to his solid warmth. She moved closer again, fitting herself into the length of his side, and put an arm across him. In the dark she turned her face in towards his, lifting her chin that he might kiss her. He did not. And after a moment he turned away onto his other side, and then sat up. 'I think I will be alone with my thoughts,' he said, and Honor didn't know was it the occasion, the solemnity of it, that had sent him from her, or was it she herself who could not draw him close.

'Very well,' she said. She hoped that he could hear – and hoped too that he could not hear – the humiliation in her voice.

The next morning they walked in the park, in their mourning clothes, surrounded by so many others in black so that they were like a giant flock of crows. They nodded silently to anyone they knew, and Chips stared coldly at the few stragglers who were not dressed as they should have been.

He talked so much of how sad he was, how monumental the occasion, that Honor wanted only to be away from him, away from all the solemn people and their hushed voices.

She went to the nursery, where Paul was lying on his back, staring up at an arrangement of brightly coloured wooden birds above him that were suspended from two crossed pieces of wood so that they swayed and dipped with the stirrings of the air. He waved his hands up towards them, seeming entranced by their movement, far more so than by her presence, she thought.

She sat there for an hour, until she could no longer ignore Nanny's polite impatience to have her nursery to herself, then went slowly downstairs.

'There you are, darling,' Chips greeted her, coming out of the library. 'We dine at home tonight. Emerald will join us, and Duff and Diana. He has been with the Privy Council at St James's Palace, to witness the king's oath. Edward VIII.' He dwelt on the words as though tasting a very old and expensive claret, rinsing them around his mouth, allowing himself to absorb their full-blooded headiness.

Dinner was intimate – they were six, including Doris – and gossipy. 'The question is whether he will take on his father's entourage, or keep his own?' Emerald said, as soon as the first course was cleared. There was no need for her to say who she meant by 'he'. 'Duff, what do you think?' Duff made some non-committal response, so Emerald took the conversation back from him, faintly reproachful, as though she had given him something precious to hold, and he had dropped it. 'I am certain – and I am certain I am right' – she nodded her head brightly at them – 'that he will keep his own. He has too much to lose, now, to be surrounded by old men who do not understand him. He will not pursue the same round of Ascot, Windsor, Balmoral. He has so many new ideas. But, more importantly,' – she leaned forward, conspiratorially – 'there is Wallis. He cannot permit anything to separate them, even momentarily. Where he goes, she must go. And she will not always be welcome. We know this,' – she held up a finger – 'because even in his own family, she is not welcome. His brothers will not meet her, nor their wives.'

'Odd,' Chips said, 'when you think that Wallis is the very best chance the little York children have of succeeding . . .'

'Hush,' said Duff reprovingly. 'Too much.'

'And what of her in all this?' Honor asked, to cover the moment.

'Has hardly been seen these last days. She is constantly with the king, consoling him,' Emerald said.

'What for, exactly?' Doris asked pleasantly. 'The loss of a parent he didn't love? Or finally putting away his idle existence and taking on the job he's known was his from birth?'

'Doris!' Chips was scandalised, as much, Honor thought, that Doris dared to speak so boldly, as at what she had said. Which was, indeed, no more than any of them had said already. Except when they – Chips, Emerald – said it, it was done solemnly, in lowered voices.

But Duff, who was disposed to admire Doris, said, 'Nonsense, Chips, you know she's perfectly right.'

Emerald came back then to the new king's entourage: 'He will have new men, I am sure of it,' she mused. 'Men who have been loyal. To him and to her. Perry Brownlow, Lord Londonderry. You, Chips.'

'I do not look for it,' Chips said modestly. Doris and Diana both laughed at that, and Honor had to fold back a smile. They talked of Italy, Mussolini's war in Abyssinia, and on, around Europe, speculating, plotting, scheming as they went. Honor listened quietly. Partly because they knew so much more than she did so that she did not wish to speak and show her ignorance – Doris, she noticed, had plenty to say and seemed to be well-informed, especially on Germany – but also because, where once she had been excited at the sense of vitality these people brought to what they did – the feeling that came from being with them that she was at the heart of things – now, she was merely bored. The days when she had cared, as they did, and largely in imitation of them, were remote from her. She wondered how much longer she could pretend to any amount of interest. And what would happen to her and Chips when she no longer could.

'Shall you introduce that adorable baby to his namesake?' Emerald asked, when they were done disposing of the nations of the earth.

'To Prince Paul?' Chips asked, leaning back to light a cigarette. 'Yes, I expect so. He will arrive for the funeral. And I will see him when there is time.'

'Why *is* baby Paul called after him?' Doris asked, eyes opened wide in innocent enquiry. Opposite her, Diana tittered.

'He is my oldest friend,' Chips said stiffly. 'Although not of course old.'

'Perhaps not *exactly* a friend, either . . .' Doris said, then cast an apologetic look at Honor.

There was a queer little pause that Honor cast around desperately to fill. She would not let that pause grow and become something real. Quickly, she asked, 'How many monarchs have travelled for the funeral?' and watched Doris leap to respond.

'There are six kings and many more princes dining at the palace tonight,' she said. 'I wonder how they will arrange the seating. Chips, what do you think?'

Honor smiled at her, and the moment was gone before it could become anything.

Then came the funeral, which they observed from the windows of St James's Palace – Honor saw that even as the new king walked behind the body of his father, he looked up as he passed where they were, eyes scanning the windows for Mrs Simpson.

Three days later, Doris moved back to Curzon Street – 'for now,' as she said, 'just for now' – and Chips and Honor moved to Belgrave Square. 'You'll be in time to watch the visiting royals pop in and out of next door,' Doris said cheerily. 'No wonder you have brought the move forward. Another few days and they would be gone.'

'Don't be absurd,' Chips said. 'This was always the week.' And then, in the disarming way he had of suddenly poking fun at himself, with a grin – 'I confess we dropped by our house on the afternoon of the funeral, and were in time to see the royal family drawing up on their return from Windsor.'

Chapter Forty-Five

London, summer 1936

The house move was strangely tiring, Honor thought, although really, all they did was walk from St James's Place to Belgrave Square, a pleasant walk of some 20 minutes. She hoped that a new house would shake them into a new way of being with one another. It was the only reason she looked forward to the move. She was terrified of her parents inspecting Belgrave Square and starting to understand the cost of it. Unhappy, too, at the jealous gossip it would generate. But if she and Chips could find a new closeness, if his new happiness could be brought to embrace her, and their marriage, then she could bear all that.

When they arrived, the servants were already there and the work of moving complete so that all their furniture and objects, her clothes and jewels, even the silver-backed hair brush she had used that morning, were all in place. 'It is like slipping into a perfectly tailored new coat,' Chips said with satisfaction as they went through to the morning room. He made her a slight bow – 'Welcome, Mrs Channon.'

But it wasn't. The sounds of the house were different, the echoes more abundant and even all their things – and all the new things Chips had been buying, steadily, for a year now – were not enough to fill the place. Honor could not find her bearings in those many rooms, and could not imagine using more than a handful of them: her bedroom and dressing room, the small study off the bedroom where she might sit in the mornings and write letters; the nursery, and downstairs, the morning room and drawing room. The dining room, that glory in blue-and-silver that Chips so loved – she had found him stroking the panelling more than once, his sensitive fingers lovingly tracing the elaborate curves – oppressed her. She felt herself swallowed up in its ostentatious preening, and the endless reflections of her face in all those mirrors was a constant trial. Only someone supremely confident of their own beauty could have designed it, she thought.

The move did not change them as Honor had hoped it would. Still he did not come to her at night, and she found she could no longer suggest it. The way he looked at her – pleased, but faintly preoccupied – was no different to the way he looked at the white silk curtains he'd had copied from Clandon Park that hung in the first-floor drawing room. As though, she thought, she were a task completed to his satisfaction, and now belonged, not to the future he strove for, but to a past on which he depended, but no longer much considered.

'Perhaps I should do the starvation cure, like Diana?' she said one morning, as he read the newspaper in her little study while she answered her correspondence. Instead of regaining her energy in the months after Paul's birth, she felt more pulled down than ever.

'Do not, I beg you' – he looked up – 'for it makes her terribly bad-tempered. In any case, what does it matter with you?'

'You mean what does it matter what I look like?' She was offended.

'Not that, or not exactly,' he said smoothly. 'You are like your mother – both as magnificently unvarying as a stately ship. What you wear, how you do your hair, whether you are thin or fat, it does not matter at all.'

'You think I am fat,' Honor said. She was fat. She knew it. After Paul, she had lost some of the weight that pregnancy had brought her, but not enough. Her clothes did not fit. Even her shoes felt tight. But she did not think Chips had noticed. Or, that he would be cruel enough to say it.

'You look wonderful,' he said, but vaguely. 'I know no one who can wear rubies like you.'

'Perhaps it's a tonic you need?' Doris said later that day when she came to call. She looked at Honor with her head slightly tilted, squinting her large eyes with concern.

'Perhaps. Although I don't know what a tonic could do. I don't feel unwell.'

'No, perhaps not. But you say you are tired, and I hear that you are despondent.'

'A little, it's true. Although there is no reason for it.'

'Does one need a reason?' Doris asked, wry, but also serious.

'One does,' Honor said firmly.

'Well, then give yourself a reason. I'm sure there are many to choose from.'

Honor opened her mouth to ask what Doris meant, what these 'many' reasons might be, but decided not to. After all, Doris was right and she knew it. Naming any of it would not make it better. Not when she had still no words to describe the vague eddies of feeling that ran through her, murky and formless, like a stream swollen after spring rains.

'I am perfectly alright,' she insisted. 'Only I fear that I look very heavy and dowdy. Certainly I feel as though brackish water runs in my veins, rather than blood. Something slow and muddy.' She laughed, to show she joked, but it must not have been a very convincing laugh because Doris gave her a considering look.

'You know that before you married, you thought yourself "well enough"? And now, you think yourself deficient in looks, and feel apologetic for it.'

'Did I?' Honor asked vaguely. 'I don't remember.'

'Well, you did. And that is even though you look better than you ever did.'

'Emerald said the same. But I do not feel it.'

'Can you not take it a little easier?'

'No,' Honor sighed. 'There is, apparently, a great deal to be done to ensure the king's happiness. So much, that Chips says we will not go to Italy this summer. That we cannot spare the time.'

'Meaning he cannot spare the time.'

'I suppose so. And what of Bertie?' Honor asked then.

'Still in Sussex with his mother. I fear I am a harder case to make even than I thought.' Doris spoke lightly, but Honor could hear the strain in her voice.

Since the move to Belgrave Square, the pace of their lives had intensified. Days passed in a blur of too many people, invitations, changes of clothes and endless letters of thanks and acceptance. Chips was more often drunk, and she, too, was drinking more than agreed with her. Every morning now she woke to a dull, flat feeling in her head that took until lunchtime to shift. It was a combination of too much wine and champagne, too much rich food, cigarette smoke that clung to her hair and clothes so that her bedroom was clogged with it, and Molly had taken to spraying lavender water on her hair between wash-and-sets, to drive away the stale odour that hung about it. Her walks were less brisk, and when she played with baby Paul in the mornings now she had less energy for his determination to chew or poke or scrabble at every single thing in his path, and often called Nanny Burns to take him earlier than she needed, saying she had to change for lunch and would see the child in the afternoon. Except that when the afternoon came, if she was at home, she found she preferred to rest quietly on the divan in the corner of her study, hidden away with a rug draped over her, rather than venture upstairs to the nursery and yield herself to the energetic insistences of her child.

'You are moping,' her mother said frankly one evening in the motorcar, as they returned from an assembly of women who had pledged themselves to end the malnutrition that was, they said, sapping the nation's health, giving rise to cases of rickets and anaemia in children, weak chests, stunted height and soft bones. Like Doris, her mother was quick to spot that Honor wasn't well. Except she, of course, looked for the cure in activity, not in doctors and tonics.

'Not moping, exactly,' Honor protested from her corner of the car. 'Just a little tired.'

'Moping,' Lady Iveagh insisted, sitting upright with one gloved hand resting on the back of the chauffeur's seat, so that Honor felt herself slouching in comparison. 'I see it, you know it. My question is what you plan to do about it.'

'I haven't quite worked that out yet,' Honor admitted. 'I have not been sleeping.'

'Why not?' Of course Lady Iveagh would seek instantly for a cause; something wrong to be put right.

'I don't know. I go to bed, so exhausted I can barely sit while Molly brushes my hair, and then I fall into bed and am wide awake as though there were needles behind my eyes to prod them open.'

'Warm milk,' Lady Iveagh said. 'Have the maid bring you up some before you retire.' She spoke with utter conviction – as one who had never yet encountered a problem that could not be solved.

Honor nodded, even though she knew well that neither warm milk, nor chamomile, nor lavender spray would have any effect. There were drops that Chips took, something strong and evil-smelling, that she resorted to sometimes. They did the trick – she slept – but heavily, sodden, so that she woke in the mornings unsure of where she was and disturbed by the feeling that something terrible had happened while she was unconscious. The thin grey exhaustion of insomnia was better than that vicious disorientation.

'Another baby? Paul is seven months. It wouldn't be unusual.'

'No. Not yet.' She couldn't say more. Didn't know how to.

'Very well,' her mother said placidly, 'that is not unusual either.'

But what bit of it, Honor wondered, was not unusual? Was it usual, or not, that her husband never came to her bedroom? But remembering that Lady Iveagh had left many years between babies cheered her, and being cheered gave her back some energy.

'Darling, could you not think of doing something, when the stories of hunger are so bad?' she asked Chips when she got home, thinking of the assembly she had been to and the frightening things that had been said, about children almost unable to see or stand, the effects of starvation destroying their eyes, their bones.

'There is a debate on malnutrition coming before the House,' he said.

'So you could lend your voice to that?' she asked, enthusiastic suddenly. Perhaps she could help him, she thought. Read and study and talk to people and find information that would be useful to him.

'It's a Labour proposal,' he explained patiently, as though to a child.

'But you could support it?'

'No, darling, I could not. I must be very careful where I place my allegiance. I must be particular and strategic. One cannot simply scatter influence here, there and everywhere. It's more delicate than that, you may trust me on it.'

Honor forced herself not to say that she had grown up with both a father and a mother in politics, one in each House, so that she knew very well the delicate nature.

'But this one does not seem complicated,' she said. 'If you could see the children in Paddington Street . . . even in summer they cannot seem to get warm but shiver constantly. There is a boy, a few years older than Paul' – she did not remind him that she had spoken of this child before – 'and yet he is barely the size of him.' It was, she thought, so simple. So straightforward. Help was needed, and it was his to give. She could do small things – bring food, sit on committees, help one or two families – but he, a man and an MP, could do so much more.

But 'It is a delicate matter' is all he would say, albeit thoughtfully, rubbing his hands together. And in the days that followed, as she listened to his accounts of his time at the House, she sought any mention of the debate or his part in it. But there was nothing.

Her parents both separately confessed that they were surprised – they did not say disappointed, but she felt it – at the way he looked outward for his political efforts – towards Germany, and the business of brokering friendship there, rather than inwards, to the people in need of assistance around him.

'His ideas are unsound,' Lord Iveagh rang her up to say. 'Un-English.'

Honor tried to say to her father what she believed – that he was not unsound so much as politically naïve, impressed by Hitler's confidence and sense of himself, by Mussolini's aura of exaltation, by Ribbentrop's impeccable tailoring. That it was the discipline and devotion of the men around them that moved him, rather than their ideals or policies. The Nazi glorification of youth and beauty over age resonated with him.

'Then he shouldn't be in politics,' her father retorted. And that was unanswerable.

In the summer heat London emptied but they stayed. 'We cannot leave,' Chips insisted. 'Not now. Not when His Majesty has need of us.' How he loved the sound of the words, Honor thought. And then, somewhere in between the balls and parties, the dressing up in satin and rubies, the agonising over invitations – what to refuse, what to accept – the tone of the New Court changed.

First, in June, came their own dinner party in honour of the king – 'the summit of all we have worked for', Chips, greedily ebullient, called it in the days preceding – and it was the next day, as they took tea in the afternoon with Emerald and Kitty Brownlow, all of them tired from too much champagne, but too eager to dissect the party to wait longer, that Honor first heard the word 'morganatic'.

'What is "morganatic"?' she asked.

'A marriage where there is a great disparity of rank,' Emerald explained. 'And where the usual succession and inheritance rights are given up. In this case, Wallis would not be entitled to anything in the estate that is entailed, and if there were to be children, they would not form part of the succession.'

'Children?' Honor blurted out. 'Surely that is not likely?'

'Not at all,' Emerald agreed with a sly smile. 'But one mustn't be seen to assume . . .'

'In any case, he won't hear of it,' Kitty said. 'He says it would be to insult and humiliate her.'

They talked of the continuation of the current discreet arrangement. Then, 'There is another possibility . . .' That was Emerald. And she meant the finding of a complicit bride.

They drew closer together, as if by prior agreement, to discuss. Names were mentioned, and dismissed, until Chips, with a sideways look at Honor, said, 'Lady Patricia . . .' and let the name hang there between them all in the dim and dusty afternoon air.

'Patsy?' Honor was astonished. 'But she's just . . .'

'Eighteen,' Chips agreed. 'Not now, but in a year, a little more . . .' He looked directly at her then, eyebrows working hard to both reassure and encourage.

'Absolutely not,' Honor said, sickened at the very idea. She thought of the king's thin, striving face, Mrs Simpson's taut mask, and Patsy's sweet dimples. 'Never.'

He looked disappointed, but Emerald, who had paused in her conversation, bright eyes resting on Honor's face for as long as it took her to answer, immediately moved to propose someone else.

In the weeks after that talk, it became clear that the 'discreet arrangement' couldn't continue, or not exactly as it had. Too many people now were loud in their insistences that a scandal known to 'half of London' couldn't possibly be kept hidden any longer. The rumblings that had been distant, sly muttering by unimportant folk who couldn't be expected to understand, were now close and finding champions. As yet, the country – 'the people', as Chips called them – knew nothing. 'But can we rely on that?' Chips asked, the 'we' the most pronounced part of his question.

Even then, the New Court believed in themselves. In their ability to work this all out, to make sure that nothing stood in the way of the king's happiness and their own advancement. They had ideas and solutions for every possibility. Except the one the king landed on.

When he first began to talk of marriage – full marriage, without compromise – Chips thought he was joking.

Even after he had said it many times, Chips and Emerald continued to propose alternatives. But Honor, meeting him at the Kents', saw immediately what they couldn't see – that he didn't want compromises and solutions. He wanted an end, a breach, a final torching of all behind him. They couldn't see that he would take all their clever plans and throw them over with abandon. Nor could they see that Wallis was now terrified, jumpier than ever but animated by fear, not the frenzy of fun she had first brought with her. And, like a scalded cat, she didn't know which way to leap.

'I have had letters,' she confided to Honor over tea at the Ritz. They were tucked away in a private room, but even so, Wallis darted alarmed looks over her shoulder every time the door opened. 'Anonymous letters, threatening me.'

'With what?'

'Disgrace, exposure. Worse,' she said. She lit a cigarette and her hand shook. Her nails were varnished a deep blood red and that, combined with the white cigarette that trembled between them, made Honor think suddenly of a candy cane. A singularly inappropriate image, she thought, biting back a laugh. Wallis' hair was as smooth and shiny as ever – the deep glow of a conker in autumn – drawn back sleek on either side of her head. She wore a black dress tightly belted at the waist and a double row of fat pearls that glistened like globules of rendered fat around her neck. 'They aren't signed, but the handwriting is educated, and they are addressed to me. At my apartment. Some are even addressed to my husband.' It was the first time, in Honor's hearing, that she had ever referred to Ernest as her husband, rather than simply by name.

'What does he say? About it all,' she asked tentatively, thinking of that large, silent man.

'Very little.'

'And yet you live together, side by side still?'

'Yes. What of it?' Wallis snapped.

Is that what marriage always was? Honor wondered. Men and women living alongside but separate? Wrapped in an autonomy they could not blur? The idea did not cheer her. She thought then of her own parents. That was not how they were. Somehow, they had taken their distinct forms and run them together into a whole. So it was possible, she thought. Possible, but not simple.

'What will you do?'

'I don't know.' It came out as a whine. 'As I see it, I have two choices, neither of them good. I tell His Majesty, and he is angry and orders investigations and punishment. Or I say nothing, and the letters keep coming. Either way, I am hated.'

'So which will you choose?'

'I need to think.' She put a hand to her forehead. A less tightly disciplined woman might have ruffled her hair, Honor thought, but not Wallis. 'I cannot think like this. I have found a little hotel by the seaside, and I shall go there secretly for a few days. I will be alone and I will think.' For a woman who was never alone, who seemed to exist for company and fun, it seemed, Honor thought, rather sad. But just as she was feeling sympathetic, Wallis, looking beadily at her, said, 'You better not tell anyone where I'm gone. I shall know it was you.'

And all over again, Honor wondered why Chips persisted in saying she was a polite, discreet woman.

Chapter Forty-Six

London, winter 1936

The mutterings grew, and the scandal with them; swelling like a fire that has caught on and cannot be contained. 'Time is against us,' Chips said, agonised. 'Every day this is unresolved, there is a loss of respect for the Crown.'

'I'm sure the Crown will weather it,' Honor replied, irritated as always by the proprietorial way he spoke of the English monarchy.

To Honor's surprise, Doris was enthusiastic about the king's plans. 'Only for my own ends,' she clarified cheerfully. 'After all, if he can marry Mrs Simpson, surely I can marry some half-decent chap with enough energy in him to take up the example?'

'Such as Lord Lewis?'

'Such, exactly, as Lord Lewis,' Doris agreed.

'And . . . how goes it?'

'It goes, at last. He is back now, and soon his mother will come to London. She who never comes to London. I will go to Dorset, to talk to my father. But I think it must come good. Especially if the king will lead the way in impossible love-matches. It might become the thing.'

'You seem more in favour than Wallis herself,' Honor said, as they walked about Belgrave Square park, in and out of the froth of trees that blurred the edges and across the neat square of close-cropped green that was the centre. 'She doesn't seem at all sure. It's as though the creature she thought she had tamed turned out to have some of the wild left in it after all.'

'Not what she bargained for,' Doris said wisely.

'Surely it's exactly everything she bargained for?'

'Not like this. It is too much. *He* is too much. Imagine if the sun were to suddenly burn with desire for us? And seek us out wherever we went so that there was no shade, no escape, no merciful cool and dark? Imagine love that is not love, but demand? So singular that it becomes obsession?' She sounded, Honor thought, both wondering and sad. There was silence between them. And then, with a gurgle of laughter, 'I've heard *he* follows Ernest – Mr Simpson – about their apartment, even into the bathroom while he shaves, badgering him to agree to a divorce.'

'So unrestful,' Honor complained. 'Well, she won't be the

first woman to be trapped into a marriage she didn't want, but surely she is the most complicit in her own misfortune?'

'You really think it will be a marriage, then?'

'I don't see how it can be,' Honor admitted. 'But neither do I see how it cannot.'

'And what about you?' Doris asked then, glancing sideways at her friend.

'The same.'

'Meaning?'

'I still don't sleep. Or not much. And not only because we are out so often. Even the nights we spend quietly at home, I don't sleep either.'

It was easier, she thought, to talk only of the tiredness, the wakefulness that made her night-times a series of watchful grey hours. Because it was true. But it wasn't everything. They went out more, not only because Chips asked it, but also because she no longer cared for their quiet evenings at home together. Easier to be out and gay than to be home and have press in upon her the things she did not wish to think about. His relentless manipulations of people and politics irritated her. His cheerful indifference to her, except in the matter of what she wore, the diamonds or rubies she put on, sickened her. Her own inability to be the mother she had wanted to be made her most unhappy of all.

Paul was a year now, just over, and as fair and smiling as ever. He made devoted slaves of everyone who came to the house, played happily with whatever little friends Nanny, an even greater snob than Chips, decided were suitable, and still he showed no preference for her, his mother. No sense that she was unique among all in his affections, so that she began to forget what it had been to sit alone with him in the long quiet nights, to watch his delicate eyelids and rounded cheeks as he fed and slept, to smell the warm smell of him that was half herself and completely intoxicating.

She listened to Chips describe the boy's future – the prep school he would go to when he was seven, then Eton when he was 13. If there was indeed a war, he must be sent to America, although not to Chips' family, he said. And continued to say it even when Honor, sick at the very thought, said, 'He will be perfectly fine at Elveden – there is no need to send him so far from us.'

'He must be safe,' Chips insisted. 'And America will be more safe than here. I will see if the Astors will take him.' He sounded excited, and Honor knew he was thinking of the link this would be between the two great families – to entrust their most sacred possession, and the bond it would create. More than ever, she hoped there would not be a war.

After school, Oxford, Chips mused, perhaps the Navy. And as he spoke, Honor realised that her time with her child was already wasting. She saw herself, awkward, as her mother had been with Lump when he was home from boarding school, asking him stiff questions about a life she had no knowledge of; Lump's half-answers, full of words they didn't understand – 'beaks', 'furk' – and the gulf that had gradually grown up between them all, so that when he began to write and say he would go to this or that fellow's house for the hols, it was with relief that Lady Iveagh had agreed.

Honor saw all this, and found she could do nothing about it. The thing she missed was right there in front of her, and yet she couldn't grasp it, could only watch helpless as it was taken from her. The distance between herself and her son steadily stretched out and increased until it was worn gossamer-thin.

Chapter Forty-Seven

'Please, do not disturb Mrs Channon,' Doris said. She had called to Belgrave Square early and instead of going up, told Andrews that she would wait in the morning room for Honor. In fact it was Chips she wanted to see, but she had no intention of telling him that.

As she waited, she looked about her, curious about this house that she had almost come to live in. The grandeur was comical, she thought. Every inch had been quizzed and planned and plumped, and nowhere could she see evidence of Honor, only Chips. He was present in each lavish flourish and ornate finish. Truly, this was his monument to himself.

She contrasted it with the heavy, dark silence of Curzon Street, asking herself had she made a mistake in not choosing to come here, and decided with an inward laugh that she had not. For all that Mrs Benton filled her house with mismatched furniture and odd reminders of her husband's years in India, there was space to breathe and reflect there that Doris could not find in Belgrave Square, a place eager to be seen, be noticed, so that everything in it seemed to press forward for her approval. Probably, she thought, it was a house formed in the image of its owner.

She had gone back to Mrs Benton's with a curdled feeling of defeat, seeing it as a place to bide discreetly until she could present herself to society as the fiancée of Lord Bertie Lewis – something she hoped might happen soon – but she had found, back in her rooms there, an unexpected contentment.

Cups of tea in the afternoon with Mabel when she was home, a chance to find out how her studies were coming along; the gentle, almost idle exchanges between them that were soothing because they amounted to so little. Many of the conversations were forgotten almost as soon as uttered, but they were sweet for all that. These were not veiled discussions of Doris' future, oblique questions about how she spent her time or what direction her heart lay, as happened with Honor, whose concern for Doris was so great she could barely hide it, nor keep it from lurking beneath everything they spoke of. With Mabel, there were chats about German verbs, about knitting, the quaint things said by Mrs Benton and Miss Wilkes in the nightly dinner wars – Doris had discovered that the only point on which these two gentle ladies agreed was that the king and Mrs Simpson together *would not do*. She must, Doris thought, tell Chips. Perhaps that would show him how little appetite ordinary people had for the affair so dear to his heart.

She heard him then in the hallway and went to meet him, trying to give the impression of paths crossing by chance.

'What luck,' she said. 'I have something to ask you.'

'Anything.' He was in a good mood. Partly, she suspected, because she no longer lived under his roof. 'The library?'

'Yes, alright.' And, when they were settled, 'You see, I have just come from Dorset—'

'So I believe. You want me to fill you in on what's been happening here?'

'No. I want to ask you something else. My mother's family – they have come from Germany. I suppose they are refugees, although that word doesn't seem to suit them very well. They are . . . Well, they aren't what I thought refugees would be.' She recalled her aunt, still with the simmering resentment that led her to adopt the position of housekeeper, although no one wanted it of her; her uncles, brimming with energy and the desire to be busy and useful – Otto with his suggestions for the factory, Aron convinced he could improve the transport of stone. 'In any case, what I mean is that they are not the only ones who wish to get away. There are more, and they would like to come to England, but it is harder for them because they don't have family. Or offers of jobs. And my father cannot take in everyone. Although he would if he could.'

'And what have I to do with this?'

'I thought, now that you are an MP, you could ask a

question in the Commons, or maybe throw your weight' – she smiled at him, to indicate the considerableness of his weight – 'behind Lord Marley and his efforts to find settlement for the refugees.'

'You want me to intercede for your relatives?'

'No. My relatives are the lucky ones. I ask if you would intercede for the others, those who have to leave Germany but don't have family to go to.'

'But they don't have to leave Germany. They choose to.'

'They say there is no real choice.' She tried to be patient as she explained, as her mother had explained to her, that since the passing of new laws, those with Jewish blood could no longer be citizens of Germany and had no political rights. 'So you see, they cannot stay. It isn't safe for them. You know of the street violence, the breaking of windows and beatings? I know you know, because I have heard you discuss it.' She tried, hard, to keep the note of irritation out of her voice. She forced a smile. 'They must leave. But where are they to go? Many are going to Belgium, because it is nearby and they have connections there. But my mother thinks Belgium is too close, and they will not be safe there for long. That they should come here, even though the upheaval is so much more for them. But here they find it hard to get work, skilled work. Instead, they are domestics and labourers, if they are anything at all. And so, I thought, now that you have so much influence' – again she smiled, trying to charm him, appeal to him as a friend, the husband of her friend, a man – 'and now that you know these things, that you might help.'

'But I do not know these things.'

'I have just told you . . .' She was confused.

'Ah, you have told me.' He wagged his finger at her, condescending. 'But what, really, do I know?'

'You think I have invented this?'

'I don't say that, but perhaps you have been fooled.' He nodded once, wisely. 'People who wish to leave a place that no longer suits them are inclined to say anything that might be required to get them in somewhere else.'

'You think my mother's family have lied to us? But the laws are there, on paper, for all to see.'

'Laws can be made as a . . . a precaution.' He beamed and made an expansive gesture with his hand, a throwing wide of one arm as though encompassing all that might, and might not, be. 'Not acted upon, you understand, but passed, ready, in case they are needed.'

'Like asking your cook to make an extra dish in case your dinner guests are more numerous than expected?'

'Exactly.' He beamed at her.

'Do you actually believe that? Even when you know – the papers are full of it – that these laws are already being acted on?'

'What I am saying is that you see only the needs of your own family. Not the larger picture.'

'And what is the larger picture?'

'This country's relationship with Germany. Friendship with Germany is what's best for England. And what must be pursued. It's a question of politics.'

'And of course you yourself look only at the larger picture?' she asked.

'I do.'

'Not the smaller, meaner picture whereby your appreciation for this new Germany of Hitler's is one of the little bonds you have established with His Majesty, and something you will cling to?'

He stayed still and silent for a long time then, staring at her, and his face wasn't handsome at all. It was cold and pale as though someone had set it in plaster of paris. 'Perhaps you are busy at something else,' he said at last. 'Perhaps you have a different plan that you are working for. If so, I can tell you now, it won't come off.'

'What different plan?'

'That in your eagerness to make yourself respectable, to marry well, you wish to engineer a change in public opinion that would see affection and sympathy for your race. And you wish me to be the instrument of this doing.'

'Can you honestly believe that?'

'It's only natural. One could hardly blame you. But your narrow desire to marry well cannot be let influence the progress of a nation. And so, my answer to you, after all consideration, is no.'

'Your answer was already no, before I even began to speak. I see that now.'

Doris said nothing to Honor. At first she wanted to, indeed, tried. When she and Honor were alone in the nursey with Paul that afternoon, she started to find her way into the conversation. 'I spoke with Chips this morning . . .' she began.

'Let me guess, he told you his plans for another dinner?'

Honor held a silver rattle just out of Paul's reach so that he stretched and reached for it with his fat little hands, laughing as the sunlight caught the silver and threw dancing patches of light onto his face.

'No, not that. We talked about politics . . .'

'Then it was, yet again, the comfortable margin by which he was elected?' Honor laughed and put the rattle into Paul's hands.

'I asked what he intends to do in the Commons . . .'

'Did he tell you that he has as yet no idea? No, I am sure he did not. But it's true, you know. I have asked him too.' Honor looked up, sweeping her hair behind one ear where it had fallen in front of her face. She sounded concerned. 'He makes all the right sorts of noises, but I can tell he doesn't have any sense of the place yet. But my mother tells me that is very usual. She says it can take ages before a new MP finds their feet and begins to understand how it all works. She has offered to help him, using all her experience, but he says no, he knows what he is doing. He doesn't, at all,' she said, smiling, 'but is determined to seem as though he does.' And then, before Doris could say any more, 'Oh look! See the way darling Paul tries to fit the whole rattle into his mouth? Is he not the most angelic?'

And Doris agreed that he was, the most, and no longer tried to tell Honor what had happened. What, she thought, was the point? She could see how Honor sought content-ment, or at least peace, within her marriage, and how hard that already was. She, Doris, would not do anything to make it harder. She would stay silent, she resolved, and simply pretend not to see the awkwardness that must now exist between her and Chips. And if she pretended well enough, Honor, who was far from observant, would never notice. Chips, she was certain, would say nothing.

But there was no awkwardness. Or at least, none that he seemed conscious of. They met that evening, over dinner, and Chips, instead of avoiding her, or seeming strained in her company, was exactly as ever: pressing her to another cocktail, sharing some morsel of news he had learned in one of his shopping expeditions; exactly as though their conversation had never happened. At first, she decided that he must be a better actor than she had ever imagined, and almost admired him for it, but as the evening wore on and still no sign of strain showed, she realised that, for him, the conversation had been nothing. She might as well have asked could she borrow the motorcar for an hour and be told that alas, no, he needed it. Her request had been no more important to him than that. Turning her down, humiliating her, had meant nothing to him.

Chapter Forty-Eight

Honor fidgeted with the chain strap of her tiny evening bag, marvelling at its absurdity. What, even, could she fit into such a bag? A lipstick? A pen? And why would she need either? She sighed and tried to give her attention to Lady Bessborough, now talking about the impossibility of finding servants. How many times had Honor heard that conversation in the last years? And always, she thought, from those who were known to be unpleasant to work for. Did they not think servants talked, same as everyone else? From listening to Molly, and observing the exact lift of Andrews' eyebrows, Honor could have told half the people in that overcrowded room just how they were regarded by those who staffed their houses.

'. . . isn't as if I were asking so very much . . .' Lady Bessborough complained.

'Who's that?' Honor interrupted. 'Talking to Chips?'

Lady Bessborough put on a pair of spectacles. 'No idea. She doesn't look terribly interesting. The worst of it is . . .' and Lady Bessborough went back to talking of her domestic difficulties.

Honor watched Chips, and the woman with him. She was a surprising sort of woman for him to be talking to, even at a party as dull as this. Small, plainly dressed. Honor was sure she had not seen her before. Certainly she wasn't one of the New Court. And yet Chips was not, that she could see, moving smartly away from her the way he usually did with people he felt were unimportant. As Honor watched, he took a small step closer to the woman so they were almost touching, just the two of them alone in a corner.

How sick she was of these parties. And they had their own the next day. Another dinner for the king, which Chips had fussed and gloated over, 'as though it were a prize laying hen that might be sickly', Honor had said to Doris. She had thought that quite a funny remark, but Doris had merely smiled and said, 'Ah yes, Chips . . .'

She looked around the room. Nothing, she supposed, was so very different – the same rooms, the same crowd, the same drinks on trays and music drifting from a gramophone. And yet something about it was different. It was, she thought, like seeing photos in the newspaper of a party she had attended – the smudged black-and-white rendering of that which had been gay and bright. Except that now, it was the original that seemed grainy, without definition or colour.

'Will you excuse me?' she said to Lady Bessborough. She walked over to Chips and the small woman. Chips stepped back a little as she approached. Because he had seen her, Honor thought. The small woman did not. She was in full conversational flow as Honor arrived.

'. . . I cannot thank you enough,' she said, nodding emphatically at Chips. 'You've been most instructive. Most *useful.*' She nodded again.

'Who was that?' Honor asked when she was gone.

'Lady Lewis.'

'Who . . .? Oh, Bertie's mamma?'

'Yes.'

'Why was she talking to you? And thanking you? Chips . . . what have you done?'

'Nothing.' He waved a hand airily. And he walked off, leaving Honor standing alone in that corner.

In the taxi on the way home she tried again. 'Darling, that woman, Lady Lewis . . .' She put a hand out to touch his arm. But Chips, who was staring out the window, shook her hand off. He turned then towards her and she saw, by the orange street lights they slid in and out of, that his eyes had that squinting look they get when he had drunk too much.

'We need to talk about *placement* for tomorrow's dinner,' he said, slurring faintly on the ends of his words. 'We can't put Duff beside . . . well, beside anyone, at this point. His views are simply too much.'

* * *

The next afternoon, Honor had finished the flowers and was listening to Kitty crow about the fact that Perry was now Lord-in-waiting and how she 'barely saw him any more' because he was so caught up in the king's life, when the telephone rang. It was Doris. 'I can't come to dinner tonight,' she said.

'Goodness, why not? You will throw out the placement, and Chips will be in misery.' Already Honor was running through alternatives and planning the exact tone of voice one would use for a late invitation, but one with the monarch.

'I'm sorry, but I can't, Honor. I cannot face it.'

'Why, what is it?' Honor was suddenly concerned. 'What has happened?'

'Oh nothing much.' She tried to laugh. 'Only Bertie's mother – Lady Lewis – has decided, after all, that she does not wish to meet me. And has insisted Bertie accompany her back home to Sussex.'

'But darling, that is not nothing. It is everything.'

'Not *everything*, Honor, we mustn't exaggerate. But it is . . . I don't know . . . upsetting all the same.'

'Maybe he will be back soon.'

'He won't. She'll see to that. Really, I shouldn't mind as much as I do. We were not in love, not really, although he is a dear fellow and I am certain we could have been happy.'

'But what happened?' Honor's heart sank.

'I don't exactly know. She arrived in London only two days ago. Last night she went to a party, and this morning she no longer wishes to meet me.'

'What party?' Her stomach knotted horribly. 'What party?' she said again.

'I'm not sure. Does it matter?'

'I will talk to her. I will tell her she must at least meet you, and then she will see.'

'It's too late. You cannot. And even if you could, I couldn't bear the humiliation. No. It is over. Half of London knows it. Knew it almost before I did. I will be alright, Honor, but I am not alright just yet, and so I cannot come tonight.'

There was no time to talk to Chips before their guests arrived, but as she watched him fussing about with Dresden china, last-minute menu changes, the setting up of a film projector for the king's entertainment, Honor, holding the knowledge that he had done something small and mean, found that she saw him, not with the eyes of every day that hardly registered him, but as though she had not seen him in the three years since their marriage. And she saw how different he was. His face was heavier, with paunches under his eyes and a waxiness that spoke of late nights and rich food and too much drink. He looked tired, and she thought that he would wear himself through with his ambitions, if something did not happen soon – the title he craved, some measure of the success he felt he deserved – so that he could relax. More than tired, he looked frantic.

They sat down to dinner and Honor wondered was she the only one who felt, not excitement, but sameness. The same people, the same sort of food, a weary similarity with so many other evenings.

'There were hunger marchers in the Commons today,' Chips said. 'From Lancashire and south Wales. A thoroughly gloomy-looking lot.'

'You'd be gloomy too if you walked from Lancaster on an empty stomach,' Duff said.

'Ah, but I watched them get into taxis outside the House, and I wondered whether they hadn't in fact hitched a ride all the way, and not walked at all.' Chips laughed and looked encouragingly around him for more laughter.

Honor tried to remember his kindnesses over the years – to her parents, her sisters, to a stray dog or two, but found the memories were hard to hold. Perhaps they had not been very strong to begin with.

The king nodded vigorously at what Chips said, and began to talk fretfully of his two-day visit to the 'distressed areas' of Wales, and how depressing he had found it. 'Glad to be back,' he said, rubbing his thin hands and looking around at the candlelight glinting off crystal and silver. Looking especially at Wallis and the fat rubies that sat around her neck. He talked then of the contrast with all he had seen in Berlin that summer, the energy and sense of purpose, as against the hopelessness of Wales.

The party broke up early and the king left, then sent his car back for Wallis. Once they were gone, the stragglers drew close and began pawing at their conversation again – how to do this or that, in order to get him what he wanted.

'Why do they keep talking about it?' Honor asked Duff quietly. 'It seems the king has made up his mind, and has chosen to do what they cannot help with. If he marries Mrs Simpson, all their scheming is at an end.'

'They have forgotten they have no power,' Duff said. 'Happens all the time. Too easy to forget that talk, for all its brilliance, is just that: talk. Not action.'

It was surprising to hear Duff speak so openly against these friends of his, but then, she thought, he had moved far from them, once the nations of Europe began to shuffle towards and away from one another in readiness for war.

The other surprising thing was Emerald asking for Doris. 'I like that girl. Why is she not here?' she demanded, coming to where Honor sat with Duff, who nodded his agreement. Honor told them a little, a very little, of why Doris had not come, leaving out Chips' role. 'I must see what I can do for her,' Emerald said.

'She is proud and could not stand to be patronised,' Honor said.

'I should hope not,' Emerald said. 'It is not patronage I have in mind.'

'Well?' Chips asked, when their house was empty again. 'A success, I think,' he continued, before she could say anything. 'Yes. Very definitely a success. A brilliant and beautiful evening. And now, to bed. We will talk it all through in the morning.' He sounded like a child anticipating a day out. He came forward to kiss her goodnight and Honor, who had decided she would not ask him about Doris until the next day, found suddenly that she was not at all sleepy, and that rather than lie awake fidgeting over what, exactly, Chips had done, wanted to know whatever was to be known now.

'What did you say about Doris?' she asked. 'She says her chances with Lord Lewis are spoiled. That his mother will not meet her. You spoke to Lady Lewis last night. What did you say?'

'She asked me about her,' he said petulantly. 'Sank her claws into me last night. You saw.'

'I saw you talking to her. I did not see her "sink her claws", as you say.'

'She demanded I tell her: *What do you know of this Doris?*'

'What did you tell her?'

'I cannot even remember,' he said, carefully vague. 'That her mother is an invalid?'

'That her mother is German?'

'She knew that.'

'That her mother is Jewish?'

'It may have come up . . .'

Honor was silent then. She was not surprised. She had already worked out what it was that Chips must have said. She was silent with the realisation that this one thing – this piece of unnecessary, almost indifferent cruelty – would now be the drop that stained everything else she knew of her husband. Would spread and spread like mould until it covered all that he had ever done or would do.

'I think I will go up,' he said, edging away.

'Just because Germany is closer than Chicago, you think it fair to deny others the chance you yourself have had,' she said at last.

'What do you mean?'

'You know well what I mean.'

'But it was not malicious.' He seemed genuinely perplexed. 'I would want to know. And so I told her. Because she wanted to know. But don't worry,' – he reached to pat her hand, reassuringly – 'she won't say a word, I've made sure of that. She will be completely silent about Doris' family. There will be no *unfortunate* association.'

Honor snatched her hand away. 'You think I care? For that? What you did was cruel. You spoiled Doris' chances, and for no reason. Have you really forgotten what it was like for you, before we were married?'

'What do you mean?'

'Don't tell me you weren't jumpy and anxious and striving; like a cat that is unsure of a warm spot by the fire.'

'I don't know what you're talking about.'

Maybe it was that – the lie – that finally turned her from him. But maybe it wasn't and she was only trying to be grand in claiming it. Perhaps it was the accumulation of all the things – a life she had come to hate so that almost she welcomed the idea of a war that would at least interrupt the endless round of lunch and dinner; the distance between herself and her son that had first torn at her, and now did not tear enough; the acceptance that there would be no more children for her and Chips, no chance to be a mother in a different way; the impossibility of finding anything useful to do with her time and now this piece of meanness – but she knew then that she would never see him in the old way again. The time when she tried to make things right between them was at an end. But it would change far less than she would once have expected. Now, she knew that to live within a marriage that was a husk was not only possible, but common. Others did it.

'When we were in Germany, many people told me what a coup it was for the Iveaghs to have me in the family,' he said stiffly. 'I know that is not the common theme here in England. But there are those who think it.' He drew himself up then, and stared down at her.

'Are there indeed?'

The next morning, Honor rang up Doris. Her husband had done something bad, but she hoped that he might yet be persuaded to do something good. 'You should ask Chips for help,' she said. 'He would, you know. And he can be jolly clever about such things.'

'I see why you might think that. Indeed he is. Where it suits him. But I did . . . Ask for help, that is. Not with this, something else.'

'And?' Honor asked eagerly.

'He refused.'

'Refused? He can't have understood.'

'He understood perfectly.'

'But what was it you asked?'

Doris explained.

'He said no?'

'He said I tried' – she imitated Chips – 'to "engineer a change in public opinion that would see affection and sympathy for your race". And that I wished him to be the instrument of the doing.'

And to that Honor found she had nothing she could say. She knew she would see less of Doris for a time. That Doris would no longer come to Belgrave Square. And she was sorry for it. More than ever, Honor felt, she was alone now, with Chips, with Emerald, Mrs Simpson, the king.

Two weeks later, Wallis called to the house unannounced as Honor was about to go out with Lady Iveagh. 'I must use your powder room,' she said, coming in directly behind Andrews. 'Someone spat at me. Outside Claridge's.' She was agitated; her bony hands trembled as Honor took her bag and gloves and brought her upstairs.

'They hate me,' Wallis whispered. Her voice trembled too.

'Not hate,' Honor said. 'Just . . .'

'The letters continue to come. They say I am a bitch. And worse. They are never signed. I have asked that the postman no longer deliver them, but he says he must. So the hate comes right in through my front door and is brought to my bedroom with my morning coffee.'

'Let me find you something to change into,' Honor said soothingly.

'There isn't a thing of yours that will fit me,' Wallis snapped.

That evening over dinner, Honor told Chips of Wallis' visit.

'Things cannot go on like this,' he said gloomily. 'But I cannot see how they can possibly change.'

*   *   *

A week later, they sat in the drawing room after dinner. For once, they were alone. Chips huddled close to the wireless as though it were a fire. Through the shiny grille the man who had talked so fretfully of Wales and its depression in their dining room just a few weeks before sounded, Honor thought, different. Lighter. '*A few hours ago I discharged my last duty as king and emperor . . .*' His voice drifted to them through the small square mesh. '*I have found it impossible to carry the heavy burden of responsibility and to discharge my duties as king as I would wish to do without the help and support of the woman I love,*' the voice continued. Chips was crying openly now. Tears chasing one another down his cheeks. When the king had finished speaking, Chips stood and drew the curtains of number 5 as though the house were in mourning.

The next afternoon he came back from the House very early. 'Perry Brownlow tells me he was roundly ignored at the club,' he said. 'Shunned, outright.' His voice was stripped of the bustling bonhomie that usually rounded it out like a plum soaked in brandy.

The day after, Honor, shopping in Harrods, overheard Emerald telling a woman in the shoe department that she had never met Mrs Simpson.

Chapter Forty-Nine

Doris' farewell to Bertie was, in the end, less sad than she expected. 'Meet me at Rotten Row,' she said. 'At least we can ride out.' That way there would be horses to manage, walkers to watch for. Better, she thought, than the two of them alone somewhere together without the camouflage of interruption.

'It is for the best,' she insisted, when they had cleared the last straggle of nursemaids with prams and found an open patch of ground.

'How can you say that?'

'I say it because it is true.' She reached a hand out towards him, across the gap between their two horses. After a moment he took it in his and squeezed it, before their horses forced him to let go.

'You know that for myself I do not care. Wouldn't care if you were a . . . a . . . centaur.'

She laughed. 'I believe that.'

'You almost are a centaur,' he said admiringly as her horse shied and Doris moved easily in her saddle. 'But I cannot go against my mother,' he continued. It was almost a question, and she knew that he worried that she would try to persuade him to.

'Of course you cannot,' she said, and saw his face flush with relief.

'I have tried. I have told her everything about you. All the wonderful things that you are. But she is old' – she heard what it cost him to say even that much – 'and has some notions that are even older . . .'

'Bertie, darling, no more, I beg you. I would never allow you to go against your mother. And neither will I allow you to force yourself to explain her.'

'Thank you.' Then, 'I say, you won't go and marry some other chap? I know I have no right to ask that. But I couldn't bear it.'

'I think I may not be terribly suited for marriage after all.'

'But what, then, will you do?'

'There are other things.' She laughed. 'Rather a lot of other things. I just never thought about them before.' It was true, she realised. Her mother had been right, back in the Berlin coffee house. It wasn't worthy, the life she had set out for herself. How had her mother known? And when, she wondered with a smile, had she become so much like her?

The thought – rather than dismaying her, as once it would have – was strangely encouraging.

'And for you, too, there are things,' she continued. 'Promise you will not be foolish. That you will not waste your life in idleness. Look at Elizabeth Ponsonby. She is like a cautionary tale, drifting through parties and nights out. Pay attention.' She tapped him smartly on the arm. 'You do not wish to go that way.'

'You sound as though you intend to tell me what to do an awful lot,' he said.

'Well, perhaps I do. For someone must. And you are a very dear fellow. I worry that you will be quite dissolute and hopeless if you carry on as you are. Your mother may not approve of me, but she will approve of that far less, I promise you. Now, if you can bring your horse alongside, I will let you kiss me once, and we will promise to be friends.'

'I don't wish to be friends,' he said sulkily. But he did as she said and once his horse was standing side by side with her own, Doris leaned forward in her saddle and kissed him.

'Thank you,' she said.

'For what?' He was astonished. 'I have done nothing. Certainly nothing that I set out to do.'

'You've done more than you know. You have been a good friend to me.'

'I hoped to be more than that.'

'We must get back before it starts to rain.' He was unhappy, but he would heal. He was too young, too sunny of disposition, too sweet-natured not to.

As they rode back, through leaves that had fallen, dried and drifted into piles along the path so that the horses sent up the odd scatterings, like the shavings from a box of cigars, she wondered at her own good humour. Had she always known, somewhere, that it could not be? Certainly, since the afternoon when he had talked of his mother – how good she was to him, how much he cared for her – she had felt uneasy. And now her fears had been realised, and instead of being cast down, she was strangely buoyant.

She knew that after this, it was unlikely that she would get another chance at a good marriage. Not now that she had failed so spectacularly. Half of London knew Lady Lewis had come to meet her, and left before doing so. It wouldn't be easy to rally from that. And yet she cared far less than she would have expected. Not now when the world seemed to be in a state of agitation – the king gone and a new king in his place; strikes, hunger marches, rumblings of war. Not when all that agitation promised something new for everyone. Within the certainty of turmoil Doris felt something so unfamiliar that it took her time to understand that it was freedom of a kind she hadn't known. Not the old, anticipated freedom – a husband, a name, a reputation that would allow her do as she pleased – but something headier altogether that she didn't yet understand because it contained none of those things. But was maybe stronger, more intoxicating, for it.

At the stables, when they had returned their horses, he said, 'May I walk you home?'

'No need,' she said briskly. Better to be done, she decided.

'Will I see you again?'

'Of course you will. In fact I'm sure you will be heartily sick of me before long. And now, I must make a phone-call.' From Curzon Street she telephoned to Belgrave Square.

'Miss Coates.' Andrews recognised her voice. 'I'll see is madame in.'

'Thank you, Andrews, but it's actually Mr Channon I want.'

'Doris, what is it? I am just on my way out.' Chips sounded peeved.

'Don't worry. I won't keep you. I just wanted to give you a message.'

'What is it?'

'I told you she was bad luck.'

'What?'

'Wallis. I told you she was bad luck. She was a single magpie all along, only you never saw it.'

'Sometimes I think you are quite mad.' But there was something almost fearful in his voice, and in the way he too quickly replaced the receiver, that she enjoyed.

Chapter Fifty

A week from the abdication they motored to Elveden for Christmas. Honor waited to see would the sight of it rouse Chips' spirits, this tangible proof of what he was. 'Doesn't Elveden look splendid?' she asked, leaning forward in the motorcar. Bundi twitched and raised his shaggy head to stare at her, then dropped to his paws again.

'Splendid,' he agreed, but indifferently.

'Lord and Lady Iveagh will not be at tea,' Mason, the butler, informed them gravely. 'They are engaged and will join you when they can.'

'Thank you, Mason.' Honor supressed a sigh. Without her parents – and with Paul already in the nursery where Nanny Burns would be presiding over his tea – she knew there was nothing to stop Chips ruminating, again, on his woes. For a moment, she longed to be upstairs, a dish of crumpets by the fire and her child on her knee. Away from Chips and his melancholy. Perhaps if she distracted him . . . 'Father must be in the new laboratory,' she said brightly. 'He hopes they will have real advancements in the new year.' But Chips ignored that. He looked gloomily around. The comfort and luxury of Elveden brought him no joy that year. The fires, heaped high with apple and oak logs, blazing in the deep fireplaces, the thick rugs and smooth glow of polished wood, the careful arrangement of furniture so that it both emphasised and reduced the size of the great room – these were as nothing. Brigid or Patsy had placed brightly coloured Christmas ornaments on the chimney-piece, pine cones and acorns painted with silver and tied with red ribbon – but even that failed to cheer him.

'I feel I have let you down,' he said heavily.

'How so?'

'Everything I promised to achieve was for both of us. And for our children. I said we would lead London society. And now, it is all in ruins.'

'How dramatic you are.'

'How else should I be? When we came so close.'

'You. You came so close.'

'I did it for both of us,' he repeated.

'But you never asked me did I want it. And anyway, why must you insist that all is in ruins? You are not the only one this concerns.' His histrionics had begun to irritate her. That was always, now, how it was with them.

First, she felt sorry for his dejection. Sorry that he should blame himself so completely. And then, like a small, hot needle working its way under her skin, came the irritation that he should make everything – even this, the abdication of a king, the confusion of a country – about himself.

'No,' he agreed, 'but we are each single beings in our own eyes. What is perfectly bearable in another – Perry Brownlow, for example – is too painful in oneself.' He said it wryly, and Honor laughed. He could still, even now, sometimes make her laugh, when he switched from one of his moods of self-pity or anxious striving to the mocking self-awareness that lurked beneath his snobbery to redeem it.

Later, when Paul was brought down before his bath, she watched as Chips took the child onto his knee and read him a story from his picture book. He did funny voices for the characters – a mole and a rat – and even though Paul couldn't possibly have understood any of it, he watched, mesmerised, as his father turned pages and pointed things out. In those moments, when Chips was entirely concentrated upon another – his mercurial, fascinating personality focused in one, outward direction – she remembered, so clearly, what had first drawn her.

Once tea was cleared, her parents appeared. Honor wondered had they waited deliberately in order not to be required to sit down, and thus be trapped in conversation.

'How was the journey?' Lady Iveagh asked now, letting go of her husband's arm and refusing the offer of a seat beside Honor on the sofa. She stayed standing, shoulder resting against the chimneypiece. Beside her was a small heap of the painted fir cones, winking silver and scarlet.

'Easy. We scarce saw another car on the road.' Honor answered for them both.

'Well, now that you're here, I would welcome your thoughts on a speech I promised to give on Boxing Day. To the Mothers' Union of Southend,' said Lady Iveagh.

'Of course. Shall we go up now?'

'Don't see why it must be Boxing Day,' Lord Iveagh said. 'Now that you are no longer MP' – he cast a look at Chips – 'surely you are allowed a day off?'

'I have a day off,' Lady Iveagh said. 'I have today. Tomorrow too.'

'Tomorrow is Christmas Day,' Lord Iveagh said. 'Hardly counts.'

'No post for three days,' Chips said gloomily. 'No newspapers either.'

'What are you hoping for?'

'News.'

He still couldn't understand that it was over, Honor thought.

'Where are the girls?' she asked. Not that her sisters were girls anymore. Patsy was 18 and would have her coming-out next year, Brigid was 16; young women, both.

'Out riding. Arthur and Elizabeth arrive shortly.' Arthur was married almost six months. It was to be their first Christmas at Elveden.

After dinner, her parents retired early, as they always did in the country. Honor asked Chips if he would like to take a late turn around the grounds. 'A spot of air before bed?' Usually, he liked to do this, admiring the broad bulk of Elveden with all its solid regularity of form and lit-up windows splayed against the night sky.

'No, thank you,' he said now. 'Lump and I will play at billiards.' And Honor bit back the desire to tell him that spending the night drinking brandy with her brother would not do him any good at all.

'Very well,' she said. 'I will say goodnight.'

'I might look in later,' he said.

'It's been a long day.'

'Then I won't look in,' he said bitterly, and she knew he would drink more now, because she had refused him, indifferent to the many times he had refused her.

How had they got here? she wondered, as she got into bed between the heavy linen sheets and arranged herself under the lumpy weight of the feather eiderdown. Around her, the house settled itself for the night, sighing a little and creaking, as though it breathed out and relaxed its vigilance. How had any of them got here?

Chapter Fifty-One

A week later, a hard frost covered the ground, draining colour from the landscape and from the air. It was like looking at a photograph, Honor thought, staring out at the shades of white and grey and black that made up the broad flat parkland around Elveden. She held the heavy tasselled edge of the garnet-coloured curtain in her hand, and kept the weight of the velvet between herself and the icy air that came in breaths off the frozen windowpanes. The bedroom fire was already lit – Honor had heard the maid while it was still dark gently laying logs and kindling – but the room was not warm.

'Not a white Christmas, but certainly a silvery one,' she called through the door that led from her room to Chips' dressing room. She could hear him moving about but there was no answer.

'Honor!' Her mother's voice through the door. 'Shall we go to matins?'

'Yes. Give me ten minutes,' Honor called back. 'Will you come?' she asked Chips.

'No. I'll go later. Will you tell Mason to bring up the wireless?'

Outside, Honor fell into step beside her mother. Behind them walked the servants at a careful distance of a yard and a half. The air was crisp as the bite of an apple and their feet made scrunching sounds as they walked across the frosty grit.

Afterwards, they shook hands with the rector and, one by one, with the servants. Behind them the bells pealed with the joyful solemnity they kept only for Christmas Day. On the way back to the house they walked more slowly. The morning was empty now, pleasantly so, to be filled any way they wished, until it was time to dress and go downstairs for the late Christmas lunch that meant the servants could finish early and go to their own celebrations. Paul would join them, sitting at table in his wooden high-chair, with Nanny Burns hovering silently close by to whisk him away as soon as he got bored. There would be the usual dull-but-inevitable visits from neighbours, then, in the evening, games of chequers by the fire, Lady Iveagh reading aloud from Dickens. Honor set her shoulders back and revelled in the easy familiarity of it all. Even the neighbours were her father's responsibility, not hers.

They were part of Elveden life, not part of hers. Chips would hate it, she knew, considering it time wasted, but that, too, no longer seemed her concern.

Lady Iveagh matched her swifter steps to Honor's and they were companionable in their silence. 'I'm sure Chips will be more cheerful today,' Honor said after a while. 'It was Archbishop Lang's speech that did it. You will have heard how he denounced the former king's set, all Chips' friends, saying their ways of life were alien to the best instincts and traditions of the country. Coming just when Chips had determined to become intensely loyal to King George and Queen Elizabeth . . .' She laughed. 'It upset him terribly.'

'You spend altogether too much time thinking about that man,' her mother replied. 'And he spends altogether too much time thinking about himself.'

'You liked him once.'

'I still like him.' Lady Iveagh's face softened. 'He is charming company. Always knows everything. I barely need to read a single one of the society papers anymore. Chips knows what's going to be in them before they know themselves. But recently he is different. *Agitated*.' She sounded displeased. Lady Iveagh didn't like people to change. That wasn't the deal she made with them. 'And so are you,' she said, faintly accusing, to Honor. 'How are you sleeping?'

'A little better, not much.' And then, before her mother could say anything, 'I have tried the warm milk, Mamma. It does nothing. And I have tried hot baths, lavender, possets, everything else you are about to say.'

'Then it is something of the mind, not the body, that ails you.'

'I suppose it must be.'

'You know that a marriage is not a surrendering,' Lady Iveagh said thoughtfully. 'I have tried to say this to you before – that you must have your own interests.'

'You have,' Honor said dully. 'I do try.'

'I don't just mean interests in the way of something to occupy your time. I mean an independence of mind within your marriage. Matters for which you care deeply that are not fixed around your domestic life. These may not be charities and committees – as they are for me – but there must be something.'

'What kind of something?'

'The truth is,' her mother said, conspiratorially, 'it doesn't much matter. If politics and committees aren't to your liking, and I see they are not, it could be collecting snuff-boxes, or breeding horses; anything at all. The point is not *what*, so much as it is *why*. To open up your gaze upon the world, rather than close and narrow it. No woman can or should be complete within her home. So you see, you must find something, and find it quickly.'

It was, Honor thought, the most surprising thing her mother had ever said. How much she must worry about Honor to say it.

At the house, Lord Iveagh was waiting by the front door with the dogs, Bundi among them like, Honor thought, a lion among lambs. Her parents favoured smaller dogs. 'I thought we'd take a turn about,' he said. 'I want to look in at the farm before lunch.' He disliked the nothing hours before lunch, Honor knew.

'I'll come with you,' Lady Iveagh said instantly. 'Only let me change my coat.'

'Honor?'

'Better not. I must see what Chips is up to.'

'Haven't seen him,' Lord Iveagh said gruffly. 'Hasn't come down yet.' That, Honor thought, could only be bad. He must be brooding somewhere by a fire. Mason would know. Chips would have sent him hither and thither, to bring drinks, a rug, to stoke up the fire or find the source of a draught. He would, even now, Honor felt certain, be fiddling with the wireless and flicking restlessly through the pages of whatever newspapers he had found, considering the abdication from every angle, wondering what it meant in all its manifestations. Wondering what could still be salvaged and how.

She found him in the hall outside their bedroom. He was dressed and carried a heavy jacket over one arm. Honor braced herself – for his disappointment, for the petulance that would have grown hard on him by now.

'There you are,' he cried. 'I wondered where you'd got to. Was it a very long sermon, poor dear?' He put an arm around her and drew her close to him, trying to kiss her cheek, except that she moved her head and his mouth landed, wet, on the side of her head close to the temple. 'I have news. The Duchess of Kent has had her baby. A girl. Princess Alexandra.' He dwelt affectionately on the name. 'Emerald rang up to tell me.' The pouchy disappointment of his face was gone; once more it was smoothed and pulled upwards by the animation of his excitement. 'I thought, when we get back to London, we might have a small party . . .' He would already have considered the single year that lay between their Paul and the little Princess Alexandra, the friendship between the families, the way Guinness wealth was steadily increasing. All these things would have been reflected on, turned about rapidly in his fertile mind, new hopes to set against those that had been dashed.

'Who do we have for lunch?' he asked then. 'I wonder would Lady Iveagh object if I was to go to the kitchens and talk to Cook about a gravy I have in mind for the goose?'

Honor began to laugh. 'You are rather astonishing, you know.' Already the irrepressible opportunism of his nature was reasserting itself. Soon she heard him on the phone to Emerald, plotting how they might yet make something of all this, rejoicing in the fact that the palace hadn't turned on them as it had on poor Perry Brownlow, congratulating themselves on having always taken time – even when caught up in the jazz-scented whirl of Mrs Simpson and the prince – to be charming to Bertie, now King George VI, and Elizabeth. 'She is too slothful to be a good queen,' Chips said. 'But that, and the casual disloyalty of her nature, will be useful.'

Because it was Christmas, the long dining room table was decorated, the thickly starched white damask of the table-cloth contrasted with the crisp green of the ivy and holly leaves that were wreathed around silver candlesticks and twisted along the centre of the table. Here and there, the seductive red of berries beckoned from within the shiny green, and Honor thought of all the fairy tales she had known as a child, and how the colour red – in apples, shoes, the fruits of winter – brought, always, death of some kind. Death to the wicked, but death to the good too. Mrs Simpson, she thought then – small and polished and glistening, with her shiny dark hair and shiny red lips – was rather like a berry herself.

Her sisters came down early to admire it, and be admired. Both had new dresses and Honor watched them as they turned this way and that to show off to one another. Patsy had adopted a grown-up, almost fond way of behaving towards Brigid that infuriated the younger girl. 'You are not so very much older than me,' she snapped, when Patsy tried to tell her something about dinners in London. 'I don't need lessons from you.' But they were too happy and excited to quarrel properly, and a moment later, Honor saw them bent busily over a new backgammon set someone had given Brigid. She thought again how she would have liked to have had a sister close in age, and gave thanks for Doris.

Chips came down then. Honor wondered had he heard Mason arriving with the tray. He went to pour himself a glass of champagne punch, but Honor stopped him. 'Wait for Mamma,' she said.

'Of course.' But he stayed by the tray and Honor saw that he discreetly dashed a large measure of brandy into a glass and tossed it back. The girls were laughing now, as Patsy tried to remember the words of a song, something about 'pennies from Heaven', and Brigid put her off by singing a different song entirely. 'Brigid is very pretty,' Chips said thoughtfully, watching them. 'Marvellous bone structure. We must see what we can do.'

'Leave it alone, Chips,' Honor said wearily, as she had said once before. He hadn't listened then. She wondered would he have learned anything that would allow him to listen now.

Lord and Lady Iveagh came down then, followed almost immediately by Arthur and his new wife, Elizabeth, and then the neighbours who had been invited for lunch. They were a dull but respectable family who lived a half hour drive away, with one daughter aged between Patsy and Brigid so that she was theirs to entertain – or not, Honor thought with a grin, seeing the friendly way her sisters patronised the girl, whose name was Ammalie.

For all Lord Iveagh's efforts, the talk at lunch was of little other than the abdication. The girls were fascinated by what they called 'the darling romance' of it all. 'He must be very much in love,' Patsy said, eyes round in wonder. She said it solemnly. Honor wondered had she ever been as naïve, as yearning as that. She knew she had not.

'He should be very much occupied with duty,' Lord Iveagh said reprovingly. The girls ignored him, except for Ammalie, who nodded approval.

'I've heard she leads him by the . . . nose,' Arthur said with a snicker. He was fatter again, Honor saw. 'They say

she has certain . . .' he paused lasciviously '. . . *unusual*
talents . . .' Elizabeth wriggled uneasily in her seat but said
nothing.

'That's quite enough, Arthur,' Lady Iveagh cut in. 'You
are not at your club now.' Elizabeth blushed.

'So what is the king now?' Brigid asked. There was a
pause. The answer to that question said much. Too much.

'He is the Duke of Windsor,' said Patsy, who, when not
speaking of love, had a pleasingly literal mind.

'Yes, but there's never been a duke of Windsor before,'
Brigid persisted. Brigid was an avid reader of *Debrett's*.
'And he's still a former king. There's never been one of
those either. So does that mean he's still king, a bit?'

'There can only be one king,' Lord Iveagh said heavily.
'And that is now King George VI.' The neighbours signalled
their agreement with mournful smiles.

'The once and future king,' Chips murmured.

'Arthur,' Lady Iveagh said firmly. Lump looked up. But
she didn't mean him. 'That is King Arthur. The once and
future king is what Merlin calls him in the stories. *We*
have one king, and we have a new duke.'

'And the new duke will soon have a new wife,' Patsy
said, looking across at Brigid with a smirk. Brigid made a
swooning face in response, so that Lady Iveagh, casting a
look at the neighbours, who were not smiling now, drew
her brows together across her beaky nose and said, 'Do not
be silly, girls. That's enough now.'

Honor, watching her sisters roll their eyes secretly at one
another, smiled to herself. She envied them, standing in the

doorway of adulthood, like children at a party peering in, fascinated by everything they saw. With eyes only for the shine, the gloss, the sparkle; knowing nothing of the strain and tedium that lay beneath it all.

'Shall you study more?' she asked Patsy, who had finished school.

'Not I!' Patsy said. 'I don't see any purpose to it. After all, what did the study of economics do for you? No, I shall be too busy, by far.'

'With parties and balls?'

Honor tried to keep her voice neutral, but Patsy seemed to detect something in it, for she snapped, 'Precisely. Just as you were.'

'I didn't mean . . .'

But Patsy had stopped listening to her. 'Ammalie,' she demanded, 'you agree with me, I'm sure? Why spend time with lessons and all that boring waste, when there are parties, and dancing, and *nightclubs*.'

'Not nightclubs,' Lady Iveagh said firmly.

'What I want to know,' Brigid said, returning to the matter that preoccupied her, 'is why, when he is so much in love with her that he has given up everything, you cannot see how romantic it all is.'

'It is not a question of romance.' Lord Iveagh sounded revolted. 'He has let people down. Let the country down. That is the matter here.'

'It is,' Chips said heavily. 'He has.' Most of all, Honor knew, he felt the former king had let him down. How typical of her husband to see only his own travails, just as he had only seen his own ambitions. It was his great strength, and his great weakness.

'I used to know *her* well before she married, when she was simply Elizabeth Bowes-Lyon. We spent summers in Scotland,' Lady Iveagh said.

'Did you indeed?' Chips said eagerly.

Almost as soon as dinner was over, he came to Honor in the drawing room. His inability to sit still in the dining room while the decanter went around was another irritant to Lord Iveagh. 'I think a dinner when we return to London,' he said, pouring a generous splash of brandy.

'With Emerald and the Brownlows?' Honor asked sweetly.

'Not them,' Chips said firmly. 'Your parents. And I think the Plunkets. They are known to be great friends to Queen Elizabeth.' The words took root in his mouth and she heard how he savoured them. 'Too soon to invite her personally, I think, but let us begin to lay the groundwork.' His eyes shone with possibility.

'No dinners,' Honor said.

'What do you mean? You feel lunch would be better? Perhaps you are right.'

'No dinners. No entertainments. I am no longer minded to plan them.'

'I will plan them,' – he reached out and pressed her hand absently – 'you need only attend.' And he smiled, the full dazzle of his charm upon her.

'No. I will not attend either. If you must entertain, do not expect me to be there.'

'But where will you be?'

'I do not yet know.' She didn't, she realised; only knew that somehow, she would discover. 'But somewhere. I will be busy.'

'At what?' he said querulously. 'Perhaps I can be of help?'

'No, Chips.'

Epilogue

London, spring 1937

There was something echo-y about Belgrave Square, Honor thought. As though it were still empty, despite the heaps of paintings, furnishings, antique *bibelots* and curiosities Chips had filled it with. Her refusal to carry on entertaining his friends, to fuel his ambition with parties and soirees, had meant a dwindling of callers. No longer was this the centre of feverish reachings. And even though there were still many – too many, she thought – who came through the doors of number 5, more and more there were days like this one when no one called at all. When Chips went out, to do what, Honor did not know, the house seemed to slump around itself, aware perhaps that it need not maintain itself for her.

Paul was at Elveden with Nanny Burns. He was there more often these days, and Chips still talked of sending him to America. Honor had first protested, then resigned herself to the certainty that her son would spend less and less time with her, in the same house as her, even in the same country as her. When they were together, she had so little now to say to him. Her understanding of the pattern of his days was scant. How much this hurt her, she told no one.

She walked through the silent rooms, catching her reflection in the many looking glasses and mirrored panes Chips had so gleefully installed. Everywhere she went, her reflection was thrown back at her, coaxing, gloating, teasing. And each time she turned to confront herself square on, she saw the same thing: a large woman of advancing age, with a squint and a decisive chin.

On the piano in the drawing room was the photo of her taken by Cecil Beaton in the first months of their marriage. Honor usually avoided it, for the memory of his visit was not a kind one. But now she stopped and looked, and instead of seeing all the ways Beaton had distracted from her, forcing her into the background of her own portrait, as she usually did, she saw instead the decisiveness of her chin; the firm, even stubborn thrust that he had tried to disguise with well-placed light and shade and how it couldn't, in the end, be disguised. And she tilted her actual chin in imitation, and walked on.

Around her, the faint echo of laughter, the lingering reminder of expensive scent, the ghostly glitter of candlelight on crystal. She thought of all the dinners, all the suppers, the parties, lunches and cocktails, here and at St James's Place. The intriguing and scheming, the self-satisfied plotting and certainty that the real voices in the country were theirs, the belief that the hands that shaped the direction of the nation yielded to their touch made her laugh again. What rot it all was.

'Miss Coates,' Andrews announced, opening the door to the drawing room.

'I can't stay, darling,' Doris said coming in, heels landing, smart and decisive, on the marble tiles of the hallway. 'But I wanted you to be the first to know. Actually, you are the only one to know. Not a word, mind.'

'A word about what?'

'Only guess!'

'You are to be married?'

'Certainly not.' Doris' eyes danced. 'I'll tell you now, but first, where is Chips?'

'Out.'

'Shopping?'

'Perhaps.' Honor shrugged. 'Probably.'

'I see.' Doris gave her a shrewd look. 'Well, good. I hoped he would not be here . . . I've got a job.'

'A job?'

'With the Foreign Office. I speak German, quite like a native, they say. Turns out I'm rather bright.'

'That doesn't surprise me.'

'Well, it surprised me.'

'So tell me . . .'

'It started with Emerald, who has turned out to be a decent sort. She rang me up and insisted I take tea with her, although I did not at all want to. She quizzed me a very great deal, and then said she wanted me to meet some people, so there was more tea, but this time in a quiet grey building that I may not tell you more about. Duff Cooper was there, and some other men. They made me do whole heaps of tests, and seemed rather chuffed with the results.'

'Which were?'

'That I am suitable for a particularly delicate kind of business.'

'So you won't be getting married?' Honor said, amused.

'Not for now. Wars do rather shake things up though, so perhaps something will come of that someday . . .' Then, 'I say,' Doris said suspiciously, 'why don't you seem more surprised?'

'I am surprised.'

'No, you're not. Not nearly enough.' Doris looked at her for a moment, then began to laugh.

'What?'

'It was you, wasn't it?'

'What was me?'

'I don't know, exactly – though I mean to make you tell me – but somehow this was you. Admit!'

'It wasn't me,' Honor said, shaking her head, 'it was you. Very much you. All I did was answer Emerald's questions about you. She rang me, after that dinner for the king – I mean the Duke of Windsor.' She stopped, confused for a moment. 'Well, the king as he was then.

You know, the one you chucked at the last minute. Emerald rang me up the next day and asked a great many questions about you, which I answered. It's certainly the most interesting conversation I've had with her.' Honor laughed. 'Then she asked me to be truthful, did I think you were suited to a project that needed guts and brains both, and I said none better. But that's it. I swear I know nothing more. So now you must tell me: what have they in mind for you?'

'I am to have a part to play in the coming war.'

'Will there be war?'

'Oh yes, no doubt about that. Or not among the chaps in the Foreign Office. Already there is war in Spain. They say it's a matter of when, not if. That sooner or later Herr Hitler will run out of rope, and then . . .' She made a smashing motion, bringing the sharp side of one hand like a blade down onto the outstretched palm of the other. 'I leave for Germany in a few days.'

'Germany? I didn't know that! Is it safe? I thought being Jewish meant leaving Germany these days?'

'Yes, but almost no one knows that of me. And I am to have a cover story. I go as a reporter, a friendly pair of eyes, keen to look on all the wonders Hitler has performed, and report back to a sympathetic British people. I even have a secretary. Mabel, who will type up my reports in a very clever sort of code we have developed.'

'Mabel from Mrs Benton's?'

'The very one. She has been learning German. In fact, she has been spending rather a lot of time in Dorset, with the German cousins. And she and I have studied together, at Curzon Street. She turns out to be rather a pal.'

'So, you are a spy?'

'Certainly not!' Doris opened her big black eyes as wide as they would go and looked innocently at Honor. 'I'm an honoured guest. After all, I am a friend of Herr Channon, himself such a friend to the German people. As such, I will be welcome everywhere.' She grinned.

Honor started to laugh, and found she couldn't stop. She laughed and laughed, and Doris sat and smiled at her laughing, until at last Honor drew breath, threw her shoulders back and said, 'Well, this is the best yet.'

'Isn't it? So fitting. This is Chips making amends for doing me a thoroughly ill turn.'

'Lady Lewis? I wondered would you find out about that . . .'

'There were any number of people eager to tell me. But it doesn't matter. If it hadn't been him, it would have been someone else. In a way, I'm glad it was him. At least those who wish me harm are contained to a small, known group.'

They were both silent then.

'Thanks to Chips,' Doris continued, 'news of my Jewish family did not travel. He was so terrified of the association, and what it might do to him, that he stopped it in its tracks. And now, the mantle of his approval sits over me as I go to work for the very people he dislikes. It is the very best. He *has* done me a good turn. Only think how angry he would be if he knew.'

'He won't hear it from me.'

'My cover, as they call it, is simply perfect. Why, I even attended a meeting of the British Union of Fascists . . .' Here Doris shot a look at Honor, adding, 'Yes, I know that you know. I know because Diana saw me, even though I tried to hide. And I know she called to you the next day. Andrews told me. And I suspect Envers' move to Italy had something to do with that visit. You needn't tell me anything.' She reached out and squeezed Honor's hand. 'Only know that I am grateful. It seems that through everything, you have been there, working in the background to help me.'

'As you have been for me,' Honor said. They stood like that for a moment, hands clasped together. Then Doris gently disentangled.

'Aren't you scared?'

'Yes,' Doris said, 'but more scared of doing nothing. Of having nothing to do.'

'What about Mimi?'

'My mother will take her. She says as long as she doesn't fight with Marianne's cat, all will be well. My mother arrives in London in a few days. I hope you will dine with us? Lady Iveagh too? She says it's time she met you.'

'It is, and I'd love to. Mamma will too.'

Then, 'Will Chips be there?' Doris asked. 'Not that I mind. Only I'd like to know, if he is to meet my mother.'

'Probably he will not. You know,' Honor said, almost conversationally, 'he never has said he loves me.'

'Never?'

'No. He says how much he loves his dog, his life; everything I have done for him. But not me. Not *love*. Like, affection, respect – yes, those – but not love. I feel one should have love. In a marriage.'

'Certainly one should have love. You should have love.'

Doris left then, and Honor sat alone in the smallest of the drawing rooms. War was coming. Already it rumbled, noisy as the wheels of a heavy cart across a shallow wooden bridge in the background of all their lives. War changed everything, Doris had said.

Honor had always looked upon her life as a gradual unfolding along a known path – marriage, children, seasons in London, winters in the country, good works, comfortable dinners, old age. Recently, those certainties had receded from her, with nothing to put in their place. Now, suddenly, she saw something else shimmering out there. A break in the path. A new path. She couldn't see where exactly it was or anything much about it, but she knew it was there. And if it was there, it might be followed.

Afterword

While writing *The Guinness Girls: A Hint of Scandal*, which is set in the 1930s, I found that I very much wanted to stick with this troubled decade for at least one more book. By then I had also become very intrigued by the life of Honor Guinness. Writing about Honor allowed me to stay within the 30s, as a great deal happened in her life during this time, including marriage and motherhood, two things that always interest me.

Also in the 1930s was huge social and political upheaval. The Great Crash of 1929 was followed by the Great Depression, and there was serious poverty – accompanied by malnutrition, and diseases such as rickets and scurvy – and unemployment.

Agitatated by lack of opportunity, ordinary people

looked towards political extremes – chiefly fascism and socialism. Through the 1930s there were marches, meetings, demonstrations, often violent clashes between protestors and police, as well as between different political factions.

This is the backdrop to the stories of Honor Guinness and Doris Coates in *The Other Guinness Girl*.

So, what's 'real' and what's not?

The 'true' bit – Honor was the eldest daughter of Rupert Guinness, Lord Iveagh. She was, therefore 'grander' than her cousins Aileen, Maureen and Oonagh, with a title to prove it. She was also, from what I can tell, a more serious person. Definitely better educated – she spent time studying at the London School of Economics. Honor was far less a fixture of the gossip columns of the time and she didn't inhabit the same giddy circles as the three Glorious Guinness Girls.

That in itself is intriguing. Because Honor was married to perhaps the most comprehensive and notorious chronicler of the times – Henry 'Chips' Channon. His diaries, first published in rather curtailed form in 1967 – recently re-issued in all their candid glory (and brilliantly edited by Simon Heffer) – are a hilarious and detailed guide to the doings of the British aristocracy throughout the 1930s (and beyond).

What was interesting to me is how enigmatic his own wife is throughout these diaries. He writes exhaustively about everyone he meets, everything he does, and yet Honor is intriguingly vaguely sketched. He records what they do together, but he doesn't reflect on her character and personality the way he does about even casual acquaintances.

Some things sprung out at me. Chips writes – often! – of how much he loves his dog, Bundi, his life, many of his friends, but not so much of his love for Honor. Here's an entry from March 1935 that is quite typical: 'I am happy, rich and flourishing and very much to be envied, with a lovely, sympathetic wife . . . a dog I love . . . and perhaps soon a son.'

Then there are intriguing mentions of Honor being so abstracted or absorbed in a book that she doesn't answer him when he speaks. And maybe she was. Or, maybe, she was fed up with his constant scheming and intriguing?

The couple married in 1933, and by 1937, the marriage seems to be effectively over. Chips writes that marital relations have ceased – 'after three years, eight months, two weeks' – and shortly after, that Honor is having an affair. He himself had affairs during the marriage, and was attracted to men and women. He also writes that she is cold towards Paul, their son, and has 'no deep love for him or for anyone else on earth.' When they finally divorced, in 1945, Chips got custody of Paul, and Honor didn't contest it. There are of course various interpretations of this, and in this book, I have given one possible explanation for Honor's lack of maternal affection. One that seems convincing to me.

Chips' enthusiasm for Nazi Germany was dampened by the war, but before that, it was considerable. He repeatedly writes admiringly of Mussolini, Hitler and the Nazis, and was a supporter of Neville Chamberlain and an eager appeaser.

As for whether Honor shared his enthusiasm – it's hard to say. But given that after she divorced Channon, she married Frantisek Svejdar, a Czech pilot – apparently the true love of her life – who came to Britain to join the RAF and fight the Nazis after Czechoslovakia fell to the Nazi onslaught, I think it's reasonable to guess that she did not.

Honor and Frantisek later moved to Ireland, and lived at Phibblestown in North Dublin. She died in 1976. Those I know who knew her then remember her as someone direct, energetic and often funny.

Doris – my favourite person in the book – is an invented character. I wanted someone who could reflect the awfulness of anti-Semitism in a way that would feel personal to the reader – not an abstract, but a reality.

David Envers is also invented by me, heavily influenced by what I read about some of the men who hung around with Oswald Mosley, founder of the British Union of Fascists.

A word about anti-Semitism in this book. It is a shameful truth that far too many of the British aristocracy were shockingly anti-Semitic at this time. Their prejudice was casual, ingrained, unreflecting, and finally poisonous.

Some of the dialogue spoken by Chips in this book is an example of that – frankly, the words I have given him are a muted version of what appears in his diaries when he writes about Jewish people he knows.

To be fair to him, as Britain grew closer to war with Germany, and the persecution of Jewish people became better known, he did halt his horrible talk. In that way, I think he is quite typical of the social trajectory of the time.

There is often a certain amnesia around Britain's attitude to Jewish refugees in the 1930s. The truth is, the immigration policy was designed to keep them out. By the time war began, in 1940, some 70,000 European Jews – fleeing the consequences of Nazi aggression – had been admitted to Britain; about half a million more had been denied.

It is also true – as I have it in the book – that Oswald Mosley's BUF did not start out anti-Semitic. In fact, in January 1933 Mosely made a statement to the *Jewish Chronicle* that 'anti-Semitism forms no part of the policy of this Organisation, and anti-Semitic propaganda is forbidden'.

That began to change around 1934, when the popularity of the BUF waned dramatically – due in large part to the violence and thugishness of their rallies. Faced with a loss of support, Mosley cast around for something to appeal to voters – and, led by William Joyce, 'Lord Haw Haw' – he found anti-Semitism, which became more and more a feature of his speeches.

My own interest in the plight of Jewish refugees goes back to the house I grew up in in Brussels, Belgium. It was on a street called Albert Jonnart, named for a man whose house was three doors from ours. He was a Belgian lawyer and a member of the Resistance, who hid a German Jewish boy, Ralph – the son of a friend – in the top floor of his house from 1943–4, when the Gestapo arrived very early one morning to search the house. Ralph got out in time, and scrambled across the neighbouring rooftops to escape. Our house was one of those that he crossed – I know exactly how he did it, because we used to walk along those same rooftops. There were enough balconies and flat roofs to get all the way to the end of the street.

Ralph made it out, and was then hidden by a friend of Albert Jonnart's in the museum of the Parc Cinquantenaire, where I spent an awful lot of my childhood. Jonnart himself was arrested, and went to prison, where he continued his resistance work. He was later transferred to a work camp, and died there aged 54. An American journalist, Katherine Marsh, has written a very good book based on this story: *Nowhere Boy*.

I still think about Albert Jonnart – and the difference between those who help, and those who don't.

Acknowledgements

First, I want to thank the readers who have been so enthusiastic about the Guinness Girls. It is in great part because of you that I decided to write a third in the series. Thank you for the wonderful response.

My thanks also to the people who are such a big part of making my books happen. First, foremost, my editor, Ciara Doorley, who is brilliant, supportive and smart; the perfect person to work with. Ivan Mulcahy, friend, agent and advisor. Breda Purdue and everyone in Hachette Ireland – particularly Joanna Smyth – for their help with getting the book out into the world and looking so fine. Aonghus Meaney for a careful and sensitive edit, Tess Tattersall for the impeccable proofreading, and Ami Smithson for the gorgeous cover design.

To my friends – you know who you are. I cannot do without you. You know that, I think, given how little I manage to do without your help!

Last – never least – my family. David, as always. Another book for you, because of you. My three wonderful children who are the greatest joy I know. My mother and siblings. I never get over my luck at having you to make me laugh, cheer me on, and tell me when I'm being an idiot.

Bibliography

In writing this book, I am indebted to the work of many others, including

Henry 'Chips' Channon – *The Diaries 1918–38*, edited by Simon Heffer

Louise London – *Whitehall and the Jews*, 1933–1948

Andrew Morton – *Wallis in Love*

Marion Crawford – *The Little Princesses*

Joe Joyce – *The Guinnesses*

Frederic Mullally – *The Silver Salver: The Story of the Guinness Family*

Michele Guinness – *The Guinness Spirit*

Jonathan Guinness & Caroline Guinness – *The House of Mitford*

Claud Cockburn – *The Devil's Decade*
Paul Howard – *I Read the News Today, Oh Boy*
Bryan Guinness – *Diary Not Kept: Essays in Recollection*
Andrew Barrow – *Gossip 1920–1970*
Robert O'Byrne – *Luggala Days: The Story of a Guinness House*
D.J. Taylor – *Bright Young People*
Nancy Schoenberger – *Dangerous Muse: The Life of Caroline Blackwood*

And the wonderful novels of the 1930s, particularly those by Patrick Hamilton, Stella Gibbons, Virginia Woolf, Aldous Huxley, George Orwell, Evelyn Waugh, Daphne Du Maurier and Agatha Christie.